Southern Discomfort

One Black Man and One White Man
Change Segregation

H. Dwight Kelsey

Southern Discomfort
One Black Man and One White Man Change Segregation

H. Dwight Kelsey

Although a work of fiction, several characters depicted in this novel are based on actual persons known to the author. Any perceived slight to these individuals is unintentional. Words and actions attributed to the characters have been chosen to advance themes of the story and not to demean, disrespect, laud or champion any of these persons. Like personalities in a great number of novels, flaws as well as exemplary human traits can manifest through innate character, persons of influence, occurring events, new found knowledge and/or a reexamination of self.

Paperback Edition: ISBN-13: 978-0-9992217-0-9
Kindle Edition: ISBN 13: 978-0-9992217-1-6

Library of Congress Control Number: 2017950060

Published by KrazyLegs Press

Printed in the USA

DEDICATION

Marion Spinks is a true friend and inspiration to me as an author. She has provided advice and encouragement throughout the entire process of writing this novel. Her recent passing is a great loss to me personally and to her family and friends as well.

ACKNOWLEDGMENTS

The Palos Verdes Library writers group has given invaluable advice on each chapter of this book with special thanks to Jeff Guenther, Dolores Davis, Laura Hines-Jurgens and Tom Mooney. Vietnam veterans, Jim Yokotake, U.S. Army, Pete Pettler, JAG officer and Ed Schleicher, U.S. Marines offered stories of their death defying experiences in Southeast Asia.

A very special thanks to Jack Finley. Champion of the civil rights battles of the 1960's and stalwart for the cause of peace throughout his adult life, he has been an inspiration providing his insider information as an active member of the Southern Christian Leadership Conference concerning those heady days of social conflict.

Expert instruction on use of an oxyacetylene torch was provided by Art Coe.

For sage advice on improving the telling of this story, I want to thank Dotti Arcovitch, Sherral Morford and Eva Ward. Lynette Cornwell provided her copy-editing expertise. And, a special note of gratitude to Betsy Lowry, my indomitable and talented sister for her work designing the cover, aided by the effervescent Stephanie Nguyen. And, for dredging me out of a suffocating vat of computer ignorance, I owe a debt of gratitude to my loving wife, Ruth who is not always understanding of my stubbornness to remain stuck in the mindset of the previous century

CHAPTER 1

'Lord, help us to understand that in the midst of this unbearable sorrow over the death of one of your faithful servants, your way of peace and brotherhood will guide us to a better place on this earth. A place that will have both black folk and white folk living in harmony and love for one another. I ask this in Jesus' name. Amen.'

Reverend Jeremiah Jones completes the funeral service for Billy Walker with those words. He looks down from the pulpit over his congregation in the small wood framed house of worship that bonds them together. An intense feeling of grief permeates the air as that faithful gathering fears what terrible things the future might bring for themselves and those they hold dear.

The choir erupts into a heartfelt rendition of an old negro spiritual, 'I Want to Go Home' to close the service.

'Dere's no rain to wet you,
O yes, I want to go home,
Der's no sun to burn you,
O yes, I want to go home,
O, push along believers,
O yes, I want to go home,
Dere's no hard trials,
O yes. I want to go home,
Dere's no whips a-crackin',
O yes, I want to go home,
My brudder's on the wayside,
O yes, I want to go home,

Where's der no stormy weather,
O yes, I want to go home,
Dere's no tribulation,
O,yes, I want to go home.'

Sobbing and moaning from the sea of black faces in black clothing fill the church with a release of emotions accompanying the voices of the choir. The family of Billy Walker occupies the front pews. They cry and sway with the music while the rest of the mourners join in unison with the Walkers, all except one person. James Walker, a ten-year old cousin to the victim sits frozen, staring straight ahead in a state of shock.

As the choir completes its singing, the congregation slowly and wearily shuffle their way toward the exit from the church and into the bright afternoon light. Reverend Jones works his way through the people gathered outside, then offers his condolences to the family along with the others. Lastly, he approaches little James.

'James, I know your cousin Billy was close to you. And it must have been terrible for you to find his dead body. I want you to come and talk to me about it. Meet me tomorrow here at the church around 4 p.m. after you finish your chores. Will you do that?'

There's a long pause. James continues to stare into space avoiding eye contact with the preacher. Finally, after the minister places a comforting hand on the boy's shoulder, he responds.

'Awright, sir. Ah suspect Ah can come, but Ah needs to get permissin' from my daddy.'

CHAPTER 2

A hot August day in 1951 simmers in Stillmore, Georgia, as Reverend Jones stands on the front steps of his church waiting for young James Walker. Tall and slim, the preacher has a regal bearing while still projecting a humble demeanor. He examines the exterior of the building where the white paint is peeling off the fascia board of the eaves. He muses.

It's so hard to keep our house of worship looking good. This year has been particularly damaging with hot, humid weather and so many storms battering the building. Then there's those awful termites eating at the foundation. I wish we could afford to keep our church in better condition. It means so much to the congregation. There's just never enough money.

As he turns to look down the entry path to the church, here comes James walking slowly, gazing down at the ground, deep in thought.

'James, thank you for coming. Please join me inside.'

He opens the door for the young boy, and they enter the unlit space with the slanting rays of late afternoon sun beaming through the two windows on the west side of the building.

'Have a seat, son.' The reverend gestures for James to sit in the rearmost pew. He positions himself next to the lad. The boy hangs his head. There is a blank expression on his face that Reverend Jones knows he must penetrate.

'James, anyone who witnessed what you did would be deeply troubled, especially when that victim was someone they loved. It's a difficult thing to talk about, but son, the memory of this tragedy will eat you up inside unless you release some of that awful feeling deep in your heart by talking about it. I'm here for you, James. Please open up and tell me what happened.'

The far-away look on James' face changes. A tear trickles down his right cheek. His expression twists into a contorted look, as painful memories of that fateful day flood his mind.

'It's all right, James. Let it all out.'

'Okay, Reverend. Ah tell you best Ah can.

'My friend Zeke and Ah was walkin' home after helpin' Uncle Amos pick cotton all day on his tenant farm 'bout a mile from our house. We took a short cut through de woods. As we reach de clearing, dere be a strange white light shinin' from de east. We come out o' de woods, and de sun be settin' in de west, but dat other light come from a bunch o' men all dressed in white cloth with each o' dem holdin' a torch. Ah knows right away, it be de Klan.'

James stops talking and begins to sob. Reverend Jones hands him a handkerchief.

'You're being very brave, James. Continue your story.'

The boy begins again.

'Dey was whoopin' n hollerin', so Ah knows somethin' 'bout to happen. Dat's when Ah saw Billy. He be standin' there bare-chested with just his pants on, no shoes. And, dey had his hands tied behind his back.'

James stops his story and begins convulsing with tears. The pastor holds him close and strokes his head.

'I know this is hard to talk about, son, but try to finish your tale.'

Gradually, young Walker composes himself and continues.

'Dey pushed Billy up 'til he be standin' under a sideways limb of a big oak tree. Then, one of doze men throws a thick rope over dat branch and forces de noose over Billy's head and roun' his neck. He was fightin', shakin' his head and screamin'. Dey puts a rag in his mouth and' tied it roun' the back of his head.'

James' talking turns to yelling.

'Why dey do dis to Billy? He be only askin' fo' what be right fo' all us people.'

The reverend tries to calm him down again.

'Most everybody knows what they did to Billy was wrong, son. Deep down, even decent white folk know that.' Reverend Jones faces the boy with a look of empathy in his eyes swallowing emotions of his own. 'Keep talking, James.'

Young Walker gulps in air trying to restrain his feelings, but as he regains control, another wave of emotion wells up inside him. He explodes again into convulsive sobbing.

'It's all right, James. It's all right, son. Let it all out.'

Finally, nearly drained, James begins again.

'Ah don't knows what got hold o' me then, but Ah done stood up from where Ah be crouched down and started runnin' toward Billy, tryin' to save him. My friend Zeke, he done tackled me and said, "Git back here. Don't you know dey only kill you too?"'

'De Klan din't see me. We was lucky. Doze men was listenin' to de boss man talk 'bout how Billy was a trouble maker who din't know his place and had been warned many times befo' 'bout rousin' up de nigger folk.'

'Den, wit' all de Klan screamin' loud, two big men done pulled on de rope and sent Billy up in de air kickin' his legs and makin' a gurglin' soun'. Dat was the mos' awful thang Ah evah done see.'

Reverend Jones hugs James and tries to soothe his troubled mind.

'Son, I pray that we live to see the day when something that terrible can never happen again.'

James looks up at the preacher.

'Dere's one more thang that's troublin' me, Reverend Jones.'

'What's that, son?'

'When Billy's body be raised up by dat rope, he be lookin' straight at me, like he was askin' me with his eyes to come save him. Ah keep seein' his face in my sleep. It bothers me awful.'

'You had a powerful experience, son. But, you shouldn't feel guilty. Your friend Zeke was right. There was no way you could have saved your cousin. But, I'm going to tell you, James, there are things you can do to honor Billy's memory.'

'How's dat, Reverend?'

'Get yourself a good education and grow up to be a man of peace and a leader in your community. Billy would be proud of you for that.'

'Thank ya, Reverend Jones. Ah be glad to come talk with you.'

'Any time, James. Any time.'

They walk out into the early evening sunlight with the preacher's arm around the boy's shoulder and the young lad's arm around the minister's waist.

CHAPTER 3

'Wake up, Tom. Uncle Leon is outside waiting for us. Your mother laid out your new hunting clothes for you. Hurry up and get dressed. I'll be putting our shotguns and supplies into Leon's pickup. Rex is coming too. Don't forget to brush your teeth.'

Young Tom Stirling is about to venture out on his first hunting experience with his dad, Tom Senior, his Uncle Leon and their dog, Rex. Although he is only 10 years old, this day is going to be a rite of passage into manhood. Little Tom, called TJ by his parents, has looked forward to this day for weeks. He has seen his dad and uncle venture off many times before bringing back stories of bravado along with some edible trophies for the dinner table.

TJ isn't used to getting up at five o'clock in the morning. He rubs his eyes dazed by his abrupt awakening. Then, it dawns on him how special this day is. He flings off his pajamas and dives into his new duds including the hunting boots with the rubber bottoms and the leather tops. He can hear the truck revving outside on the semi-circular driveway in front of the house. He pulls on his red and black checkered hunting jacket and excitedly runs out the door, impatient to start the hunt.

'Did you brush your teeth?' his father asks. TJ stops abruptly making a look of disgust. 'Get back in there and brush them real good.'

The custom-ordered clock on the dash of the brand-new forest green '51 Chevy pickup reads 6:00 a.m. as they finally pull away. Leon drives along a dirt road that forms the northern perimeter of their family thousand-acre peanut farm in Cordele, Georgia. It's a cool autumn day mostly overcast with the sun trying to peak under the canopy of cloud cover in the east.

'Tom, I've asked three of the negras who help us with the farm to come along with us this morning. You know Abner and DeWayyne. Abner's son, Onzell is also coming. You remember him. He's out there with his pa sometimes helping in the fields.'

'Yes Daddy, I know that little pickaninny. He's always laughing and happy. Why isn't he sad about being so poor?'

'He's just a simple negra boy, son. Don't take much to keep 'em happy.'

Leon pulls up in front of the tin roofed shack where Abner and his son live. All three are standing out front.

'Get in the back with the dog, boys,' shouts Leon. 'Mr. Stirling here has an extra gun that one of you can shoot with. Y'all ready?'

'Yussuh, Mr. Leon Sir, we's ready,' answers Abner as he steps on the shiny chrome rear bumper and over the rear tailgate. Then Abner lifts little Onzell over the side and onto the wood-floor truck bed, sitting him between DeWayne and himself. The broad smiles on those black faces tell how special this day is for them too.

They drive about another mile to an open grassy field where Papa Stirling and Leon have had a run of good luck bird hunting before.

'Okay, everybody out of the truck. Time to go shoot some birds,' says Uncle Leon.

Leon, Big Tom and TJ strap on their shooting vests fitted with special pockets for ammunition. They put on their red caps. Then, Leon hands out the guns. Little Tom is given a Winchester 12-gauge pump-action shotgun. Abner takes the old side-by-side shotgun that Tom Senior's father had handed down to him by his daddy. The guns are loaded up, and they are ready to hunt. DeWayne and Abner wear knapsacks on their backs to carry the prized birds.

Leon leads the group out into the field. He motions them to fan out and advance slowly while he blows on his decoy whistle. There's no wind, so the only sounds are the brushing of their clothing against the tall grass and their boots slurping into the ground still soggy from recent rains.

After 15 minutes, they are part way across the wide field when Rex flushes a covey of bobwhites, 25 yards in front of them. Bam-Bam! Bam! Bam! All four guns are fired and three birds drop from the sky.

'Son, I think you missed,' notes his father.

'Oh no,' sighs TJ. 'I wasn't too sure 'cause I closed my eyes when I squeezed the trigger.'

'Well, I can't be sure either, but I'm sure I shot the one on the left, and that was the only bird to fall when we both fired at the same time.'

Rex sprints after the birds and returns with two in his mouth.

'Go get the other one, Rex,' commands Leon.

Within two minutes, the English pointer finds the third quail and retrieves it.

'Tom Senior corrects a couple of his son's shooting mistakes and they continue wading through the grasses.

'TJ, you must keep your eyes peeled on your target until you see that bird drop from the sky,' his papa advises.

An hour passes. Then, a second covey of quail is flushed. Bam! Bam! Bam! Bam! This time four birds drop from the sky.

'Congratulations, son. You just bagged your first bird.'

'Yahoo, my first one! This is great, Daddy.'

By noon, they have made it across the entire field to the pine woods on the other side.

'We've bagged a dozen quail,' notes Uncle Leon. 'I think we should take a break and eat some lunch.'

'Good idea, Leon,' says Big Tom. 'Let's spread the tarp on the ground over there between those two trees.'

Myrna, TJ's mother, has made a dozen sandwiches for the hunters including chicken salad, roast beef, and peanut butter and jelly. Those staples along with apples, boiled peanuts from the farm, and a dozen Dr. Peppers are consumed by the famished hunters in thirty minutes.

'I got a little surprise fer dessert' Abner pipes up. 'My woman Nessie, she done made us some sweet potato pie.' He reaches in his knapsack and pulls out six pieces wrapped in wax paper handing one to each person.

'Oh boy, Daddy, that's my favorite thang to eat in the whole world,' says Onzell.

'I thought you smelled a little better than usual today, Abner,' jokes Leon. The white men laugh, and the black men make nervous smiles. 'Please thank Nessie for us.'

Then, it was time for Papa and Uncle Leon to tell a couple of hunting stories before heading out again.

'Tom, do you remember the time we found that little boar piglet?' Leon asks.

'I'll never forget it,' Tom fires back. 'You went to catch that thing and almost got skewered by the onrushing tusks of its 150-pound mother. You were lucky I was ready to shoot that sow, but those poor piglets lost their protector that day. In fact, that happened not too far from where we're sitting right now."

'Are there still wild boars out here, Uncle Leon? TJ asks.

'Oh yes, young Mister Sharpshooter,' replies Leon. 'They're out here.'

They pack up all the waxed paper wrappers and empty soda bottles along with the tarpaulin, and head into the pine woods.

'Listen up men… and boys,' commands Leon. 'We've got enough quail to last us for a while. Let's try to bag us some grouse!'

Tom Senior's watch reads 1:00 p.m. Another 3 ½ hours of daylight can help guide their way before darkness sets in. They trudge through the woods for nearly an hour with Rex sniffing for their prey in front of them. No luck. Finally, Rex stops and assumes the pointer position. Two grouse fly up. Leon shoots and misses. Then, Abner pulls the triggers for both barrels, and the second shot fells one bird.

'Good shot, Abner,' yells Big Tom. 'That will be some good eatin' for your family tonight.'

Onzell is so excited, he runs after Rex to help retrieve the bird.

'Son, get back here. De dog will fetch de bird back to us.'

Onzell stops short and returns. They continue hunting in the woods for another half hour with no luck. Then, Leon orders everyone to head back toward the truck before it gets too dark.

When they reach the field half an hour later, the light in the sky is becoming faint. Gray stratus clouds layer across the sky with streaks of sunlight beaming bright rays down the ground at the far western end of the field. It's about 3:30 in the afternoon, and they've walked halfway across that grassy terrain. Unexpectedly, a covey of quail flies up right in front of them. TJ steadies his gun and fires. Shortly after, DeWayne lets go a blast. Two birds fall, and Rex sprints after them.

Rex returns with both birds and drops them at Papa Stirling's feet.

'Those aren't for me, Rex. Young Tom and DeWayne earned these little beauties,' Big Tom correctly notes. 'I'm proud of you son. And, DeWayne, that old gun still shoots straight, don't it?'

Just then, a fast-moving creature comes rushing towards them through the grass. Leon takes aim and fires at the oncoming mass.

'Ahhhhhh', a high-pitched scream comes from that grass and then its body tumbles to the ground. They all rush to see the fallen animal.

'Oh, my God, it's Onzell!' screams Abner standing wide-eyed and not knowing what to do.

'Leon, give me that first aid kit in your vest,' demands Papa Stirling.

Leon is frozen in disbelief by what has just happened. Big Tom rushes over to Onzell, position him on his back and tears open the jacket and shirt the little boy is wearing. The blast has covered the boy's chest in lead shot, and he is bleeding profusely. Breathing is difficult and the wounds are dangerously close to his heart.

'Leon, I said give me that first aid kit from your vest. DeWayne, I need one of those wax paper wrappers from the pie.' Papa Stirling opens the first aid kit taking command of the situation. He first mops the excess blood off Onzell's chest. Then, he uses tape from the kit to secure the wax paper over a sucking wound in Onzell's chest. The boy begins breathing somewhat better.

'DeWayne, help me carry Onzell,' directs Big Tom. 'We need to get him to the hospital as soon as we can.'

Dazed and in a state of disbelief, the group follows his orders. In ten minutes, Onzell has been placed in the back of the Chevy pickup before being rushed to Crisp County Hospital in Cordele. His Daddy and DeWayne lie close to him whispering encouraging words in his ear and saying prayers to themselves.

'You gonna be all right, Onzell.'

'Hold on. Help's acomin.'

'Relax and breathe easy, son.'

Please God, my son is a good boy. He ain't never done nobody no harm. Please, save his life. He too young to die.

Leon races the Chevy to the front entrance of the emergency room. Big

Tom runs in and notifies the receptionist they are bringing in a gunshot victim who needs immediate care. DeWayne and Abner carry Onzell in seconds later.

A gurney is quickly brought out to the reception area, and the transport staff wheel Onzell back to the ER surgical area.

'I'm sorry, but you all need to stay here in the reception area,' says the lady at the front desk. 'I also need someone to fill out paperwork on the boy. And, because the boy's injury is a gunshot wound, I must call the police.'

Everyone waits anxiously in that room for over an hour. Papa Stirling helps Abner fill out the paperwork. That takes ten minutes. The longer they wait, the more anxious and awkward everyone becomes. Tom Senior tries to ease the tension at first with some encouraging remarks like, 'I think he's going to make it,' and 'they tell me the doctors here are real good.' After a while, Big Tom has used up all his thoughts to comfort everyone, and the tension grows greater with the silence. DeWayne and Abner sit quietly next to each other with Abner nervously fidgeting with a cigarette lighter and De Wayne rubbing his friend's neck. TJ snuggles up next to his dad burying his head on his father's chest. Leon sits alone staring at the floor.

Finally, the doctor comes out in his scrubs with his mask dangling down on his neck. He has a furrowed brow and a downcast look on his face.

'I'm Doctor Young. Which one of you is the boys' father?'

'Ah am,' Abner says in a quavering voice.

'I'm sorry. We did everything we could. Your boy didn't make it.'

Just then the on-duty Cordele police officer walks in the door.

CHAPTER 4

'James, please pass me doze sweet patatas,' Daddy Walker kindly requests.

The Walker family sits around the dinner table on the day after Billy's funeral. Father Estes, a tall slim, dark skinned man has assumed his position at the head of the crudely hewn, slab oak eating surface. Mother Hattie, an attractive light complected woman, occupies the opposite end with their four children sitting between. James, as the eldest son, is positioned next to his father. On the table are wooden bowls filled with typical fare for poor black families in the South; collard greens, sweet potatoes, corn on the cob, and chitlins.

'JDubya, did you heah me?' His father repeats his request with some irritation in his voice. 'Please pass doze patatas.'

James is abruptly jarred into the present. 'Sorry Papa, here's de patatas.'

A burning question stirs inside James.

'Daddy, can Ah ax you somethin'?'

'Sure son, what ya wanna know?'

'Is dey gwine to find out who kilt Billy an' take 'em to prison?'

The other family members turn toward Mr. Walker and James. The only sounds are the clunking of dishes and open-mouthed chewing of food.

'Son, de law aroun' heah be different fo' white folk than fo' us'n. You saw what happen when one of us try changin' thangs. And, don't you go and try to be like Billy or you be just as daid.'

'But Daddy, it ain't right we be treated like dat.'

'Ah knows dat, son. Dat's jus' de way thangs is. We try to do de best we can with what we got, and try not gettin' dem white folk too upset with us'n.

'Ah shore wish thangs was different, Daddy.'

'You jus' be careful, an' don't git de white man mad at ya.'

'Daddy, do ya really think Billy died fo' no reason?'

'Dey is hundreds of coloreds just like Billy that done been lynched. And nobody 'members them 'cept for dere families 'n friends.'

'But Daddy, Reverend Jones say if somebody like me gets a good education, dey could become a leader in the community an' help make a better life fo' us colored folk.'

'Reverend Jones is a good man, but he ain't seein' de world like it really is. The white man ain't gonna give up his power over us black folk. And, if one of us'n tries, he be kilt, just like Billy.'

'Dat's terrible, 'cause dat means nothin' ever goin' to get better fo' us.'

'James, all of us want a better life. Just learn to acept what we got, an' make de best o' it. like Ah say before'.

JDubya stops questioning his father. He wants to hear him say how life for coloreds can get better, and his daddy disappoints him. Reverend Jones was saying there was hope. When he goes to bed that evening, he makes up his mind that he is going to change his life by trying harder in school.

CHAPTER 5

TJ stays in his room after dinner that fateful day and doesn't come out to watch television with his parents like most Saturday nights.

'Tom, I think you need to speak to your son,' suggests Myrna to her husband. 'I can tell he is very shaken by that terrible accident today.'

'You're right, dear. I'm going to have a talk with him right now.'

Papa pushes himself up from the living room couch and walks down the hallway to his son's room. He knocks on the door.

'TJ, I need to talk to you.'

The father waits for an answer, but there is none. He opens the door and pulls up a chair next to young TJ, who is curled up side lying on his bed still wearing his hunting clothes except for the shooting vest and hunting boots.

The father begins. 'I wanted this day to be the best one of your young life, son. And, it ended up probably being your worst. I know that right now you must be scared, confused and maybe some other feelings a boy your age might have. I feel real bad too. But, I just want you to know that tomorrow will be a better day, and little by little, you will get over that awful pain eating you right now.'

The young boy remains silent and unmoving while his father waits for a response.

'I also want to speak more about what happened today. Are you okay with that?'

Big Tom pauses, and finally his son nods his head.

'The big question all of us have is whether Onzell's death could have been prevented. The answer is yes and no. That tragedy isn't one person's fault. Abner could have made sure Onzell was there beside him the whole time. And, he could have gotten him a bright colored hat and jacket. Leon could have made sure what he was shooting at before he pulled the trigger.

'But, there's good reasons why those things didn't happen. First of all, Abner is poor. He can barely afford to clothe his family, so for him to buy special clothing for Onzell was out of the question. As for keeping watch over his son for ten hours, that's impossible. Distractions are happening all the time. What with Abner shooting or the rest of us firing our guns, looking for birds, listening for sounds, there's hundreds of times that his attention is directed somewhere else besides his son, and I know he was dedicated to keeping Onzell safe. It was just another moment of distraction during that last instance that allowed Onzell to escape his attention.

'And, what about Leon?' Papa Tom continues. 'Bottom line, he was trying to protect all of us including himself from some attacking animal, possibly a wild boar. His mistake was that he should have identified what he was shooting at before pulling the trigger. Now I know that Leon has had a bad previous experience with boars, and that might have caused him to shoot too quick. And, the light. The light was so dim that he might not have been able to identify what was coming until it was too late.'

'What I'm saying, TJ. It wasn't anyone's fault what happened today. It was an unfortunate set of circumstances. I talked to Leon after leaving the hospital, and we agreed to show our respect to Abner and his family. The two of us are going over to Abner's house tomorrow to express our sympathy to him and his woman, Nessie. They're not rightly married. We're going to bring some food, pay for Onzell's burial and give Abner $1,000.'

The day's experience has made the young boy more curious about the divide between white and colored people. He questions his father.

'Daddy, what makes white people and colored people different?'

Tom Senior gathers his thoughts and responds.

'Son, God made us two different people for a reason. He created white people with smarter brains so they could lead others and make good decisions for running things like our farm and our government. Coloreds do not have that same intelligence. They need to be led and trained to perform physical work. And, as sad as it was to see that little boy die today Tom, we need to be strong and keep things between coloreds and whites the same for the sake of our future. Always remember that.'

'Thanks for talking with me, Daddy. I feel a little better now.'

The father stands and pats his son on the head. Before leaving, he has one more thing to say.

'You get dressed for bed now and have a good night's sleep, son. Going to the early church service tomorrow. We'll pray for little Onzell's soul.'

CHAPTER 6

'Well, look who's here. It's my handsome nephew James, all the way from Stillmore. Come on in, son.'

James has just arrived at his Aunt Violet's home in Savannah. He is dressed in his Sunday best, an ill-fitting black suit handed down from his father, white shirt and skinny black tie worn threadbare on the left side from being pulled through into a knot too many times. His left hand grasps a cardboard suitcase while holding a bouquet of roses in his right.

'Deez is fo' you, Aunt Violet. Youse real nice to take me in like dis.'

'James, I can see you've been brought up to be a respectful and polite boy,' she replies. 'But, I will not tolerate such bad English to be spoken in my house. You will learn it's a command of the English language that will allow you to get ahead in this world. Do you understand me?'

'Yes, ma'am. I does.' answers James.

'No, say yes Aunt Violet, I do,' she corrects.

'Yes, Aunt Violet, I do,' he parrots.

'That's better. Now bring your things into the house, and I'll show you to your room.'

Aunt Violet is a teacher in the Chatham County school district and has taught sixth grade for ten years to black children. She lost her husband to lung cancer a few years before and has no children of her own. Billy's father was her brother, and their family has grown to place a high value on education. She wears a full length white chiffon dress befitting her ample figure with shiny white shoes, burgundy rouge and red lipstick. Her body gives off a scent of roses similar to the flowers from her nephew. A touch of grey at her temples completes the look of a distinguished lady.

When Violet heard her nephew was determined to advance his schooling beyond elementary school, she wholeheartedly supported the idea and encouraged her cousin, Estes, to send James to live with her to attend high school. There is no secondary school for coloreds in Stillmore. Truth be told, she is also lonely and anxious for the company of family.

'Here's your room, James. There's a dresser over there for your socks and underwear. That door in the back goes to your closet.'

She walks over to the door and shows him the inside. The young boy has never had a closet to use before, let alone a room just for himself.

'You can hang your suit, shirts and pants on the hangers in there. The space on the floor is for your shoes.'

'Aunt Violet, you sho are being nice to me. You make me feel impotent.'

'The word is important, James. And, you are important. Always remember that. Now, put your things away, then come down to the kitchen. I've got a special treat for you.'

James is impressed with his aunt. She is much more positive and energetic than the other older women in his family. And he knows he can learn much from this educated lady. He had been told by his mother that when Violet was a little girl, she would always badger her parents. Why this? Why that? Why is the sky blue? Why is it so hot? Why do we pick cotton all day, and the white folk don't? Why do the white folk talk different than us? At school, she revered her teachers and vowed to become one.

After putting away his meager belongings, James walks from his room into the dining room.

He gazes around the room in amazement. There is a circular table in the center covered with a white linen tablecloth and two plastic placemats positioned where the two of them would sit. Polished silverware is set with a fork on the left, knife and spoon on the right. A white linen napkin rests at the top of each placemat rolled up and held by a shiny wooden napkin ring.

A large double sash window brightens the room from the outside wall; decorated with a valance surrounding the top portion and white lace curtains flowing down to the window sill, yoked in by sashes on either side. It is the fanciest window the boy has ever seen. In the corner next to the kitchen, is a wooden china cabinet with a glass door. The inside is filled with hand painted cups and saucers and glass bowls carved with intricate patterns.

'Here's a cup of tea and a fresh cruller from our local bakery.'

James has never been served food and drink in such a formal setting before, so he waits for his aunt to start so he can mimic everything she does. Violet takes the top off a china vessel and plucks one sugar cube from inside with a small pair of silver tongs. Then, she daintily releases the sweetener into her cup. She looks up at her nephew.

'Would you like some sugar in your tea, James?'

'Unsure he could duplicate his aunt's deft handling of the tongs, he replies, 'No, tank ya, Aunt Violet.'

'James, say no thank you, Aunt Violet.'

'No thank you, Aunt Violet.'

'Much better. Just listen to me, nephew, and you will be speaking proper in no time. By the way, you needn't be so formal with me. From now on, call me Auntie.'

The boy nods, 'All right, Auntie.'

James observes his auntie raise her tea cup slowly all the way to her mouth with her pinkie finger positioned outward away from the cup. Her posture is ramrod straight and her head is held stiffly erect as she keeps her eyes looking straight ahead at her nephew. Then, she places the edge of the cup to her lips, tilts it toward her mouth and takes a small sip.

'Lovely,' she comments as a practiced smile briefly forms on her face. 'Do try some, nephew.'

James then attempts to emulate his aunt. He pinches the handle of the cup between his first three fingers. Then, he awkwardly tries to spread his little finger out to the side in fits of spasm while raptly staring at his hand giving added emphasis to do his bidding. Auntie's face breaks into a broad grin as she observes his mighty effort. She quickly erases the expression as he regains control of this task and brings the cup to his lips looking at Auntie for approval. She subtly nods. James is determined to maintain a dignified composure imagining her expectations.

James takes a sip of the beverage. The bitterness of the teas assaults his taste buds immediately. He unwittingly screws up his face into a scowl, bends forward and spits the tea back into the cup.

'Ohhhh, Auntie, Ah apologize.'

Violet breaks into a peal of laughter, as she can no longer contain herself.

'Nephew that was the funniest exhibition of proper manners I have ever seen. Maybe next time, you will take a cube of sugar.'

They both laugh and laugh. The formality between them has been broken.

CHAPTER 7

James and Aunt Violet are walking along the sidewalk toward church that first Sunday after the young teen's arrival. As the building comes into view, James stops and looks in amazement.

'Oh my, I can't believe colored folk go to such a fine church, Auntie.'

The First African Baptist Church is a huge stone building with stain glass windows and a cupola gracing the top of the stone steeple.

'Yes nephew, we're mighty proud of our church. Let's go in. I want to find a good seat up front so we can better hear what Reverend Gilbert has to say in his sermon.'

'Yes ma'am. What our Reverend Jones wouldn't give to have such a fine place of worship like this back in Stillmore.' The nephew and his aunt take their seats in the middle of the front pew.

'Oh, after the service, there's several people I want you to meet. Remember I taught most of the students in your class. I'll introduce you to some of them and their families.'

James is looking good in the new suit Auntie had bought for him during the week. She also made him go to the barber to tame his wild, long curly hair with a short trim, cut close to his head. The new look gives the young lad a confidence in his appearance that he never had before.

The inside of the church shines like a polished jewel. The deep colors of the stained-glass glow in the morning sunlight. Varnish on the solid oak pews glisten in the light of an ornate chandelier hanging from the center of a high open nave.

'Auntie, how can colored people afford to have such a fancy church?'

'Shhh, James. The service is about to begin.'

The first part of the program seems familiar to the boy with readings from the Bible and singing from both the choir and congregation. James is impressed by the church organ with its powerful vibrations that seems to penetrate his insides. Finally, Reverend Gilbert rises to the pulpit to give the day's sermon.

'Today, on the Sunday before Labor Day, I want to recall the voices of our ancestors. They toiled mightily and suffered unjustly during their lives. Most of them died without knowing freedom, without receiving the dignity they deserved, having only hard work and oppression to characterize their existence day after day, week after week, month after month, and year after year.'

'If they could speak to us today, what would they tell us. Would they say, "You've got a better life than ours? Be thankful for that."

'Tell me brothers and sisters, is that what they would say?' The reverend holds his hand up to his ear.

'No!' shouts the congregation in unison.

'I believe you are absolutely right. I can hear those voices echoing up from the holes in this church floor saying, "Don't accept being second class citizens. Don't accept hard labor jobs with poor pay. Don't accept police brutality or the hateful acts of the KKK. Don't accept that community leaders must be white. Don't accept an inferior education system for negroes, and don't accept white people telling you that you're not qualified to vote.'

'This church stands on a foundation of freedom and human rights. And the underpinning of this sanctuary is not the stone and timber that lies beneath this floor. No, the foundation is the spirit of hundreds of slaves who hid in the cramped space below these planks of wood, waiting for the

Underground Railroad to guide them northward towards freedom. They weren't satisfied with their lot in life then and they wouldn't be satisfied with the conditions today either.'

The preacher goes on to rally the congregation to register to vote. By the time the sermon ends, he has deputized several of his parishioners to lead a voter registration drive. The entire church is electric with energy as the service concludes, and the congregation filled with hope and purpose streams out of the pews and into the vestibule.

'James, come with me. I want you to meet some friends of mine.'

They walk over to the corner of the room where a man, woman and teenage boy smile as Auntie approaches.

'Good morning, Mr. and Mrs. Washington, wasn't that a fine talk Reverend Gilbert gave this morning.'

'My yes, that man could inspire me to love pickin' cotton.' Mrs. Washington answers. 'Thankfully, he's not asking for that.' The group shouts with laughter at her remark.

'I want you to meet my nephew, James,' Auntie begins. 'He'll be staying with me while he attends Beech High.'

'Hi, I'm David,' says the young Master Washington. 'We heard you were coming to live with Mrs. Walker. Welcome to Savannah.'

'Thank you, David. Ma' whole name is James Lincoln Walker. Ah be comin' from a country town called Stillmore. It sits 'bout 25 miles from here.'

'How did you like our pastor's sermon this morning, James? He sure got the congregation fired up, didn't he?' David notes.

'He's a right powaful speaka, David. Ah neva' heard no one talk so bold befo'.'

Aunt Violet cringes at James' use of language and forces an embarrassed smile at the Washingtons. They exchange pleasantries before Auntie takes her nephew's hand and leads him over to meet other families with boys his age. As they move on, she whispers in his ear.

'James, notice how well young David speaks. In a couple of months, I want you to be speaking just like him. Do you understand?'

'Yes'm.'

Auntie introduces her teenage nephew to several other families as well, the Jeffersons, the Tates, the Robinsons, and the Reeds. In two-hours time, James feels a sense of community that he has never felt before. These are people making a better life for themselves, and they seem to accept him as one of their own.

Finally, Auntie looks at her watch. It's time to go.

'Nephew, we need to leave here now so we can catch the 1:00 bus back home.'

'Okay, you'se de boss, Auntie.'

CHAPTER 8

'Hey Tom, look at that colored boy walkin' over there. He doesn't belong in this side of town. Let's give him die-rections.'

Tom and his friend, Miles are leaning against a wall drinking Nehi grape sodas outside a local café in downtown Cordele. It's a hot, summer day in 1958. Miles yells out.

'Hey boy, if youse lookin' fo' watermelon, youse on de wrong side o' de tracks.'

The young colored boy stops and turns to face Miles. His jaw tightens and anger radiates from his eyes. As his body stiffens, he clenches his fists.

'You lookin' for a fight, boy. Well, you come to the right place.'

Miles stands erect, his muscular six-foot three-inch torso straining against his white tee shirt. He takes two steps toward the colored boy. The black youngster briefly stands his ground facing Miles and locking eyes with him. Then, better judgment takes hold. He turns and walks away.

Miles looks back at Tom and speaks loudly so the colored boy can hear.

'Tom, I wasn't sure of the color of that boy. Was he black or was he yellow?'

The colored boy stops in his tracks at that remark, then continues walking away.

Miles pipes up. 'You know. I think he was both....black and yellow.'

The colored youth continues walking away while Miles and Tom laugh like hyenas.

Miles Trousdale is the son of a Ku Klux Klan leader in the Cordele area. They say apples don't fall far from the tree, and that certainly is the case with Miles. His hostility toward coloreds is disguised by a sense of humor that other white boys in town find amusing. He is physically imposing with a biting tongue, and, not the least of all, he is captain of the Crisp County High School football team.

Tom, as editor of the school newspaper, became friends with Miles by interviewing him after football games. They both loved fast cars and pretty girls. While Miles has the cheerleaders mooning over him, Tom has a souped-up red '55 Chevy Biscayne that his daddy bought for him. They double date using that car and often end up parking next to Williams Lake outside of town.

'How far did you get tonight, Tom? Miles asks after they had brought their dates home one Saturday night.

'Same as last time, second base. How about you? I heard a lot of moaning back there.'

'I was rounding third base and heading for home, but she was blocking the plate with her hand. We made a little mess in your back seat.'

'Don't you mind that, Miles. I was rootin' for ya to cross that plate when I realized I was stopped at second. I'll clean that up in the morning.'

Tom would regularly get home late after these weekend ventures with Miles, and his parents would be waiting up for him. This night, his father is angry. He confronts TJ as soon as he comes in the front door.

'Son, I told you to be home by eleven. Here it is past midnight, and you're now just walking in. Your mother has been sick with worry. Did you ever consider that? What have you got to say for yourself?'

'I'm sorry, Daddy. We went to the movies. Then afterwards, we went out to Williams Lake and watched the moon reflecting off the water. It was beautiful.'

'Well, for the next two weeks, you can watch the moon from your bedroom window 'cause I'm grounding both you and your car.'

'Aw Daddy, Miles and I have plans for next weekend. How about if I cut the lawn tomorrow and wash and wax your car?'

'No deal, son. And, I want you to stop hanging around with that Trousdale boy. I hear he's nothing but trouble, and his father has done some awful things.'

'But Daddy, Miles is fun, and he's done some good things for me.'

'Like what? Fix you up with trampy girls. You heard me. Stay away from him.'

It's Halloween 1958, and the Cordele Fire Department has just put out a blaze that destroyed the front porch and a portion of the main front wall of the home of Abner Jackson. Father Stirling has gotten his son released from the local police station and is driving him home. The irate look on his face speaks loudly to his son.

'We meant it as a little joke, Daddy. No harm intended,' says young Tom attempting to calm his father's boiling temper.

'Of all the coloreds that you could play a sick joke on, you picked Abner, my lead farmhand. What's wrong with you, son? Are you some kind of sadist?'

'Daddy, let me explain.'

'I'd like to believe that my own flesh and blood isn't some kind of demented criminal.'

'Please, Daddy, listen to my side of the story.'

'This better be good. Go ahead.'

'Abner's oldest boy, Rastus, was spreading rumors about Mr. Trousdale saying he led a group of KKK men to burn a cross in the front yard of a new colored family that moved into Abner's neighborhood.'

'So, Miles wanted to let Rastus know that he wasn't about to tolerate anybody taking trash about his daddy. Being Halloween, we decided to send a message by filling a paper bag with cow dung, putting it on the Jackson's front porch and lighting it on fire. As soon as Miles lit it, I rang the doorbell and we ran across the street to my car.'

'Then what happened,' Tom Senior smugly asks.

'Well, at first, nobody answered the doorbell and the front porch started to catch on fire. I jumped out of the car and tried to put out the flames, but the fire was getting out of control. Abner opened the front door, and I yelled to him to call the fire department while I kept trying to beat down the flames with a small carpet that was lying on the porch. The kids finally came out with buckets on water which helped some, but the fire wasn't put out until the fire department arrived about 15 minutes later.'

'How did the police get involved? Mr. Stirling asks.

'One of the firemen asked how the fire got started, and I had to admit that I instigated with my friend. Then when I looked over to the car where Miles had been sitting, I noticed he was no longer there. He had taken off on foot to go home.'

'So, let me get this straight. That friend of yours, who came up with this lame brained idea, lit the fire, and refused to help you put out the fire, ran away to place all the blame on you. Can't you see that this so-called friend of your is really not a friend, but just somebody who is dragging you down?'

'I admit it turned out to be a big mistake, but really we didn't intend to harm anybody.'

'Here's what you're going to do. First of all, you're going over to the

Jackson home tomorrow and apologize to every member of that family. Second, you're going to pay for all the repairs to the house. And, thirdly, you are going to provide your labor to help fix that place. Do you understand me?'

'But Daddy, you know I don't have the money to pay for fixing that house.'

'Yes, but you're going to earn it by getting a part-time job, doing odd jobs for me, and helping Abner put his house in good repair. In the meantime, I'll front you the money and expect full repayment with 5% interest. And, believe me, I know how to keep an accurate accounting.'

'Daddy, that's going to ruin my whole senior year in high school. You know how many committees I'm involved with at school, plus my homework. I won't have any time for fun.'

'You should have thought of that before you burned down part of Abner's house.'

Back in school two days later, Tom approaches Miles in the hallway outside his locker.

'Miles, I ended up in a lot of trouble for the Halloween prank we played on the Jacksons. You didn't stick around, and I ended up at the police station.'

'Hey Tom, sorry about that. I guess I just panicked when the fire started, and I also didn't want to give any assistance to that jerk, Rastus after what he said about Daddy.'

'Well, Miles, my father made me make a formal apology to the Jackson family yesterday, plus I have to pay for the damages. You need to help me out on that one.'

'You're right, Tom. I owe you big time. Listen, in good conscience, I can't help you work on the house, but I'll come up with money for the repairs. How's that?'

'I appreciate that Miles. If you can give me half the expenses, I don't mind doing the work. And, I understand your situation with Rastus. He's a trouble maker.'

That fall, Tom helps Abner tear down the burned portion of the front wall and board up the exposed structure with plywood. They make a temporary door for the front entry and try to seal the cracks as best they can with caulking. A finished repair can't be completed until next spring when there is enough good weather and daylight. Unfortunately, the Jacksons have to remain living in their home as they can't afford to live anywhere else while restorations are being done.

One day shortly after temporary repairs had been made, Tom pulls up to the Jackson house in his daddy's pick-up truck with a big box loaded on the back. He knocks on the door and Abner opens up.

'Can you give me a hand with this thing, Abner? It's a little heavy and bulky for me to carry.'

'Whatchu got, Masta Tom?'

'It's called a Franklin stove. We can set it up in the front of the house to give you some more heat this winter.'

'Why that's right thoughtful of ya, Tom.'

TJ and Abner open the box and spread out the contents next to the temporary front wall. Tom reads the directions while Abner and Rastus put it together. They use a hand drill to make a pilot hole in the plywood where the vent will go. Then, the opening is cut to the correct size with a small saw. The stove is completely assembled in three hours. TJ thinks to himself, *These coloreds may not be able to read, but they sure have good mechanical skills.*

'Thank you fo' this, Masta Tom. We be ready fo' ole man winta now,' crows Abner with a big smile on his face.

'It was the least I could do under the circumstances, Abner. Now you and your family keep warm this winter, hear?'

Tom leaves the Jackson home that day feeling good about himself. He knows there is more to be done before he fully pays for that mischievous trick, but he can see how what he already contributed makes the Jackson family safe for the winter. And, ironically, they are in his debt. His guilt is assuaged, but he is now disillusioned with his friend, Miles, who hasn't yet contributed one cent of the promised money.

Miles approaches Tom a few days later at school. He holds up his hand overhead fanning out four tickets.

'Guess what I got, Stirling ole boy?'

'Four tickets to the Daytona 500? Tom says sarcastically doubting Miles could have anything that would interest him besides money. He has begun to agree with his father about Miles' poor character.

'No, four tickets to the Little Richard concert and dance down in Albany next week. And, I talked to Susie Thompson. She would love to be your date. Whataya say?'

'No kidding. How can I stay pissed at you with an offer like that? I hear that nigger singer can make a crippled old school marm hot to trot. I'm in, Miles. What time do I pick you up?'

In a flash, Tom's resentment toward his friend disappears like a rabbit from a magician's hat. He had tried to make time with Susie Thompson a few times before, but she had refused his advances staying true to her boyfriend, David. Recently, however, the couple had fought over some remark David made about a close friend of hers. Susie became infuriated and said she was going to start dating other boys. When Miles caught wind of that, he knew he could mend his relationship with Tom if he could get Susie to go out with him.

Susie Thompson is one of the prettiest girls in school. Flaxen blond hair pulled back into a ponytail that frames her high forehead, creamy white skin, penetrating blue eyes and pouty red lips. She is tall, slim, and often wears tight pants that show off her perfectly formed buttocks. Susie likes to have fun too. Tom is almost drooling with anticipation at the prospect of his upcoming date.

The night of the concert, Tom pulls up with his Chevy in front of Miles'
house announcing his arrival with a blast on his horn. Da-da-da-da-da-da-
da-da-da-da-da-da. Tom had a special feature installed that plays the first
twelve notes of that Southern anthem, Dixie. He is looking like a cool cat.
Pink shirt, skinny gray tie, gray tailored pegged pants, dirty white buck
shoes, and his brown hair combed back in the requisite "DA" slicked into
place with BrylCreem. The added touch of Canoe cologne makes him
believe his is sexually irresistible.

In truth, Tom's looks are something less than handsome. He has a
protruding chin with an indentation where his two jaw bones join, and the
short space between the bottom of his nose and upper lip make him appear
as if he's lost his upper teeth. The remainder of his body is slim but
unathletic, and his skin is the Caucasian whiteness of someone who spends
too much time indoors. He makes up for his physical shortcomings by
being openly friendly, as well as generous with his time and possessions.
He also has the gift of a quick wit and being an engaging conversationalist.

Soon the four teenagers including Miles' date, Melanie are driving the 30+
miles southwest along Route 91 to Albany. Little Richard has been
entertaining white audiences for about two years after producing the cross-
over hit, "*Tutti Frutti*". The black singer made a giant step up from the
chitlin circuit he had been working. And, the young white kids seem to
love this new music, rock and roll.

Little Richard gets the show rocking with his rendition of "*Lucille*", and
afterward, the master of ceremonies steps to the microphone.

'You are all invited to get groovy and hit the dance floor for the rest of
Little Richard's set. Enjoy yourselves.'

'Susie, let's show Little Richard what white kids can do on the dance floor.'
Tom stands from his table beside the bandstand and gazes imploringly into
the eyes of his date.

'Sure Tom. I know how to shake my bottom to this rock and roll music.
Are you man enough to keep up with me? I can get pretty wild out there.'

'I'll have no problem staying up with you. The question is, are you woman enough to keep up with me.'

They both smile. Susie takes his hand and he guides her to the center of the dance floor. The room is a rectangular auditorium with a raised stage at one end where the band is stationed, and enough room on the floor below for 10 tables along the sides having four chairs each. A parquet wooden floor forms the center of the room. At first, Tom and Susie are the only couple dancing.

'I hope you're good', Susie notes. 'Cause everyone is looking at us.'

'Just keep up with me girl, and we'll be fine,' counters Stirling.

The singer begins screeching out his newest hit.

'Long tall Sally, she's built for speed. She got everything that Uncle John needs. Oh baby. Yeaaaaaah baby. Ooooooooh, baby. We're havin' us some fun tonight. Yeah.'

As Little Richard belts out that number with its infectious beat, Tom grabs Susie's hand twirling her into his arms and dipping her svelte young body almost to the floor. The audience jumps to their feet and shouts their approval.

After putting on an exhibition for a minute or so, several other couples join in, creating an orgy of white energy following the primal syncopations of the black entertainer. Miles is reticent to dance as he feels he can't complete with the moves of Tom and Susie, but eventually Melanie coaxes him out.

Tom is becoming more aroused as he rocks around the hall with Susie. He is thinking his comely date is like Sally in the lyrics, and he imagines himself as Uncle John. His anticipation rises as the evening continues. They're both aware of being the best dancers on the floor.

By the time the show is over, the crowd is exhausted, sweaty and happy. Driving home that night, all four teenagers exude excitement about their cross-cultural experience.

'Those coloreds may not be able to do much that requires their brains, but they sure know how to make foot stompin' music,' Stirling remarks.

'Amen, brother,' agrees Susie.

'You're right, Tom,' concurs Miles. 'But what I don't like about tonight is that those uppity niggers will start to think they're as good as us just because we're together in the same place.'

'I don't see it that way,' Stirling disagrees. 'They're only hired to entertain us.'

Tom begins driving with only his left hand on the steering wheel. His right hand reaches over and holds Susie's hand squeezing it gently. She lets him take her hand but doesn't give any reciprocating signs of amorous intent.

About 20 minutes into their drive back to Cordele, Miles starts kissing Melanie. Soon, their reflections are missing from the rear-view mirror with soft moans and heavy breathing emanating from the back seat. When the sounds become louder and undulating movements start rocking the car, Susie lets go of Stirling's hand.

'Tom, when we get into Cordele, I want you to take me directly home,' she demands.

'But why, Susie, I thought we were having a great time tonight.'

'Just because,' she coldly replies.

For all his efforts at impressing Susie tonight, all he gets is a little peck on the cheek at the front door. While Miles circles the bases, Tom gets thrown out trying to get to first base. What started out as a great evening with seemingly escalating opportunity to satisfy teenage fantasies, in the end turns out to be a precipitous disappointment for young Stirling.

Next week at school, he sees Susie in the hallway between classes. As he walks over to talk to her, he realizes she's arm-in-arm with David. He stops. Ignoring Tom, she walks right by without so much as a 'hello'. Miles comes up to him and says, 'Did you hear, Susie and David are back together again. Sorry old sport. I guess you and she weren't meant to be.'

As disappointed as Tom was, he lowers his expectations and starts dating girls that are more responsive to his advances. He and Miles remain friends throughout their senior year despite repeated objections from his father. When springtime rolls around, it's time to select a college.

'Hey Miles, I just got accepted to University of Georgia.' Tom exclaims.

'So did I, buddy. Hey, we can be roommates.'

CHAPTER 9

'Mr. Walker. In 1877, the State of Georgia passed a law requiring males over the age of 21 to pay what was called a 'poll tax' in order to vote in elections. Men who had voted before the year 1865 and their male descendants were exempted from this tax. I want you to present an argument in support of this law.'

Mr. Thomas Adams, the civics teacher, requires his students to debate political issues of the day. He is a slight, middle-aged man who always dresses formally in a three-piece suit and insists on strict discipline in his classroom.

James is in his senior year at Alfred E. Beech High School. With the support of his Aunt Violet and his new urbanite friends particularly David Washington, he had begun to perform well academically. He nervously stands up at this desk to respond to Mr. Adams' request. After pausing to collect his thoughts on what might be a plausible argument, he begins.

'The State of Georgia needs to be sure that elections are determined by voters who understand the issues and candidates presented on a ballot. The consequences of electing individuals and passing ballot measures can affect the future of Georgia positively or negatively. In general, poor men of voting age are illiterate and form opinions on election choices based on hearsay and not on a responsible examination of the pros and cons of each choice. By requiring a poll tax, the state is ensuring a more informed electorate eliminating uneducated persons not able to make intelligent decisions.'

'Boo! Boo! Boo!' James sits down to a chorus of rejection from his classmates.

'Quiet down class,' the teacher commands. 'Mr. Washington, do you accept Mr. Walker's argument?'

'No, I do not,' replies David.

'All right then, Mr. Washington, make your rebuttal,' instructs Mr. Adams.

'The United States of America was founded upon a constitution that granted liberty to all its citizens. When the 14th Amendment was approved by Congress in 1866, black men were granted citizenship, which included the right to vote. To counter this newly created voting electorate, some state legislatures passed laws restricting the voting rights of these new citizens by establishing qualifying conditions such a literacy tests. The federal government, in turn, enacted the 15th Amendment to the constitution, which guaranteed the right to vote for all male citizens over the age of 21. The Georgia legislature again undermined the intent of this new federal legislation by creating a poll tax. That measure was clearly passed to prevent colored citizens from voting and gaining any political power within the state.'

Applause breaks out as David takes his seat. Mr. Adams then asks the class to critique the two speakers.

'Class, tell me in your minds who won this debate and why.'

Several students comment. All of them support David. Then Mr. Adams sums up the exercise.

'I asked James to support a position that would be extremely unpopular within this class. If I asked that same question to white students, what would have been their response? Most likely, they would have agreed with James' points of view. As people of color, we are fortunate today that this poll tax has been repealed, but has the fight for equal treatment under the law been won? That's a subject for our next session. You are dismissed.'

James and David leave the civics classroom and walk to the school cafeteria. They slide their plastic trays down the horizontal chrome railings in front of the food set on glass shelves above. Piling dishes of cornbread, fried chicken, milk, cooked vegetables, and fruit onto their trays, the cashier tallies up their tabs at the end of the line. They sit down with two of their friends from Mr. Adams' class at a table for four.

'James, I thought Adams was a little unfair putting you in such an unpopular position, but your response was good,' David comments.

'C'mon David, my answer was lame. I thought even a white person would have been embarrassed by my statement.'

'Did he really think anyone could make a believable argument for a poll tax?' replies Julius, one of the other classmates.

'I must admit, I felt like a hypocrite trying to say something convincing about a poll tax,' James offers. 'But strangely, I could sense the threat that white people must feel with the idea that colored people could gain power over them through the ballot box.'

'I can't believe you feel sympathetic toward the white man after he's been persecuting us for centuries,' states Horace, the other classmate at the table.

'No negro is going to tell another colored that he is being treated as equal to a white person,' David declares. 'But when you understand how the white man thinks, you can at least begin a discussion with him from his point of view.'

'That just sounds like an Uncle Tom way of looking at things,' counters Julius.

'That's where you're wrong,' David disagrees. 'If you don't know where the other guy is coming from, there's very little chance to get what you want with anybody, not just white people.'

'David, I bet you're going to end up being a politician because that's exactly how they need to think,' concludes James.

'My parents would be very disappointed with that choice, James. They have the idea that I'm going to be a professor at Morehouse or some elite school like that. By the way, my folks have me participating in a voter registration drive this weekend. Can I count on you three fellahs to help me out?'

'Sure, I'll do it,' responds young Walker. Julius and Horace remain silent looking down at their lunch trays pretending not to hear David's request.

CHAPTER 10

The following Saturday morning, David and James stand outside the Wage Earners Bank in downtown Savannah each with a clipboard in one hand and voter registration handouts in the other. David walks over to the first bank customer who has arrived a couple minutes before the bank opens at 10 a.m.

'Sir, hello, my name is David Washington. My friend James Walker and I are here this morning to assist negro residents in voter registration. Are you a registered voter?' The man shakes his head. 'If you can spare a moment, we have some important information for you. And, we would also like to have your name, address, and phone number so we can further aid you as well as keep a record of new voters in Savannah.'

'Well, young man,' the bank patron remarks. 'You can sign me up. In fact, when you get a little older, you should run for office yourself because you surely have the gift of gab.'

Minutes later, a second customer approaches the front entrance to the bank.

'Good morning, sir,' James begins. 'I have information here to help you....'

'I'm in a hurry, son,' he replies brushing by young Walker to enter the bank just as the front door unlocks.

'James, you need to get right in front of the person, make eye contact, and speak like you're an authority on voting,' David advises.

'Okay, I'll try to do better with the next customer.'

James takes David's advice and gradually gains confidence with his approach. More than half the people entering the bank this morning are not registered voters. Some stop and listen to their spiel; others pass by seemingly too busy to stop. Despite a mixed response, after three hours, they acquire a list of over 30 names.

The bank is located at a busy intersection, and several white passersby give them looks of disdain. A few make derogatory comments.

'Niggers don't belong in the votin' booth,' shouts one middle aged lady after observing David handing out a pamphlet.

Then, about one in the afternoon, a group of four white teenagers in jeans and leather jackets come around the corner in front of the bank and see David and James standing there with their clipboards. They walk right up to the two boys, and the leader asks a question.

'What are you coloreds doing loitering on the street corner?'

'We're taking a survey,' young Washington answers.

One of the other boys grabs James' clipboard.

'These coloreds are trying to register nigger voters,' he exclaims.

Incensed, the white boys throw away the clipboards and rip up the flyers, scattering pieces to the wind. They rough up the black youths pushing them to the ground. As the gang walks away, the leader turns and makes a parting comment.

'You niggers got to understand where you belong…and it ain't in the voting booth.'

After they leave, James notices David bleeding from the head. He takes out a handkerchief from his pocket and offers it to his friend.

'Are you all right, David?' he asks while observing blood running down his forehead and into his eye.

'It's only a scratch. I'll be okay,' replies David mopping his brow.

David holds the cotton cloth for another minute until he's sure the bleeding has stopped. As they get back on their feet, a police officer approaches them.

'Did you boys throw these papers all over the sidewalk?' he inquires in an accusatory tone of voice. Then, before either one can answer, he demands. 'Pick up every last piece of paper right now, before I ticket you both for littering.'

The two boys scurry around the area shoving bits of paper both large and small into their pockets. An afternoon breeze is blowing some of their materials further down the sidewalk and into the street. More than five minutes pass as the boys gather every shred they can find. The officer stands in one place the entire time, his feet spread wide apart with his nightstick pulled, slapping repeatedly into his left hand. Walker stops for a moment and glances at the cop. He senses they could be beaten if they don't pick up every last scrap.

'All right, now you boys git! And, if I ever see you two around here again, you'll be arrested for loitering.'

The two youths nod and walk away from the bank, holding their clipboards with the list of names attached. As they leave, James realizes something he witnessed and whispers to his friend.

'You know, David, I saw that officer near the corner just before those white kids showed up. He saw those punks messing with us and did nothing to stop them.'

'James, that's all the more reason why us coloreds need to get out the vote.'

CHAPTER 11

The front doorbell rings at Aunt Violet's home

'I'll get it,' James calls to Auntie, who is busy in the kitchen. He opens the door, and his jaw drops.

'Reverend Jones, what a surprise. I had no idea you were coming. Please come in.'

'You're looking good, James. Life in Savannah apparently agrees with you.'

'It's been a great opportunity for me here. So nice to see you. How is everything back up there in Stillmore?'

'Things change much faster in a place like Savannah than they do in Stillmore. But, the reason I'm here is your Aunt Violet invited me down to talk to you about your future.'

They walk back into the kitchen, and the reverend greets Violet.

'Mrs. Walker, thank you for inviting me. I know you're a great cook, so I wasn't going to miss the opportunity to indulge myself for one of your delicious meals.'

'Well, Reverend Jones, I know how much my nephew values your advice. And, now that he's a high school senior, it's time to be making decisions about what comes next.'

'James, how are your grades in school? Are they good enough to get you into college?' he asks.

'When I started at Beech High freshman year, my grades were pretty bad, but with the help I've gotten from Auntie and my friends at school, they've gotten better.'

'He's being too modest, Reverend. My nephew is one of the top students in his class. Now, why don't the two of you go sit and talk in the dining room while I finish getting dinner ready.'

James and Reverend Jones sit across from one another at the dining room table. Auntie had set out her best linen tablecloth with three silverware place settings and two silver candlestick holders fitted with tall white tapered candles. In the center of the table is a silver bowl filled with fresh cut spring flowers.

'James, I hope you're planning on going to college,' the preacher begins. 'It would be a shame to have made the effort to leave home to get a high school diploma here and not go on to higher education.'

Just then, Auntie enters the room with a big, steaming ceramic bowl of fried chicken and places it on the table.

'Can I ask you gentlemen to help me bring in the other dishes?'

The two males stand and walk back into the kitchen to assist Auntie. All the food is brought out and placed on the table according to her direction. There's creamed corn, mashed potatoes, black eyed peas, and a pitcher of mint iced tea, all served with style as Auntie puffs out her chest and proudly admires her work. Finally, the three of them sit down.

'Reverend, I would appreciate it if you would say grace.' Auntie requests.

'I would be honored, Mrs. Walker.' The reverend pauses for a few seconds, clears his throat, and begins. 'We are gathered together today to guide one of our fine young men toward a future of promise for himself, his family, and all those whose lives he will touch. May this delicious food prepared by his caring Aunt Violet symbolize the nourishment provided by those who love and support James. I ask this in Jesus' name. Amen.'

They pass around the delectable dishes each taking a generous serving. The young boy is beaming. Two of the most important people in his life are there just for him. The reverend speaks again.

'James, I know how you must feel knowing your family is toiling hard in the fields to put food on the table and keep a roof over their heads. But, if you leave school now to return and live with them again, you will only be perpetuating that existence. You have the opportunity to go to college and learn a white-collar trade where you could help your family much more. Can you see that?'

'I understand what you're saying, Reverend Jones, but it still makes me feel bad, having a life of plenty here, and seeing how little my family has when I visit back home. That would only stay the same if I went on to college.'

Auntie, visibly upset, pipes in. 'Nephew, if you don't go on to college, all your efforts to get an education will have been wasted. As a colored boy, you can't get a good job with just a high school diploma. The only job you're prepared for right now is picking cotton. Is that what you want?'

'No ma'am,' responds James afraid he has disappointed his Auntie with his last remark.

'Have you thought about which college you might be interested in attending, son?'

'Well, I guess Georgia State makes the most sense. Auntie went there, and if she was willing to have me continue living here, I could take the bus to school.'

'Georgia State is a good school, and it's affordable,' Auntie adds. 'I wouldn't be where I am today without my training there. And, nephew, it would be my pleasure to have you stay here with me during your college days at State.'

Reverend Jones has come to Savannah with an alternative suggestion.

'If you want to consider another option, James, I have some influence at

Morehouse College up in Atlanta. I am an alumnus of the Baptist Seminary there, and have participated as a member of the selection committee for incoming freshmen in the past. I would be more than happy to recommend you to some people I know there. Are you interested?'

James looks surprised to think he might be qualified to attend such a prestigious school and is lost for words.

'Say yes, nephew,' Violet blurts out. 'Morehouse is the best possible school for a young negro lad like yourself.'

'All right, sir, if my father will allow me to attend college, I would be happy to attend either Georgia State or Morehouse.'

'Your Aunt Violet and I have already discussed this with Estes, and he has agreed to let you go.'

Food has never tasted so good to the young student, and Auntie caps it off with her fabulous black bottom pie.

Two months later, James goes out to the mailbox to bring in the day's mail. There's a letter addressed to him from Morehouse College. He slowly opens the envelope bracing himself for disappointment.

CHAPTER 12

'Are you going Greek, Tom?' asks Miles

They are standing in their dorm room, a non-descript box with spare furnishings and one window overlooking a courtyard. The roommates have just returned from freshman orientation and are considering options for their newly begun college experience.

'Miles, I'm thinking you can't get a well-rounded college education without going Greek. Besides, we'll meet a lot more girls by joining a fraternity.'

'My new buddies on the freshman football team have talked about two houses, SAE and Lambda Chi Alpha.'

'I've heard that SAE is only a jock house, so I know I wouldn't fit in there. What do you hear about Lambda Chi?'

'Apparently, there's a mix of guys; jocks, engineers and business types.'

'That might be okay. Why don't we check it out during rush?'

'I'm going to look at SAE too. Several guys on the team are hoping to pledge there. So, I figure I need to take a look see.'

'Fine. Just don't expect me to go there with you.'

Freshman year at the University of Georgia is an experience Tom had looked forward to since he made a campus visit there the year before.

Athens is located in a scenic area where the Piedmont plateau forms wooded hill country in the northeastern part of the state. The crisp autumn weather has yet to turn leaves of trees from green to bright fall colors; but the cool, moist scent of the season fills the early morning air.

Stirling attends his first class, Econ 101. He's sporting a vertically striped red and white short sleeved shirt, khaki pants and brown penny loafers. He carries a wire bound notebook and clips a PaperMate pen to the inside of his shirt pocket.

As he enters the lecture room inside Millege Hall, he scans over the students already seated and decides to situate himself next to a cute blond coed wearing a tight blue sweater.

'I hear Professor Maloney covers all the questions on his exams in his lecture notes,' he informs her. 'Hi, my name is Tom.'

She turns her head and encounters his smiling face.

'Hello,' she answers curtly, suspecting he is another annoying loser hitting on her.

'What's your name?'

'Sandy,' she offers while looking away.

'Well Sandy, if you ever miss class and need to borrow notes, I'd be happy to loan you mine.'

'I'll keep that in mind.'

Tom is making his first move on a Georgia coed, but he isn't getting the response he hoped for. Still, he isn't ready to give up.

At the end of the lecture, he asks Sandy if she understands one of the concepts the professor had presented. When she indicates she isn't sure, he explains it to her. Then, he follows up with a request for a date.

'Sandy, there's freshman dance at the Tate Center this Friday night. Would you do me the pleasure of attending with me?'

'I don't think so. I don't even know you.'

'Tell you what. You bring a friend and so will I. And, you should know that my friend plays on the freshman football team. He's handsome too.

'Oh, my friend Laurie is really into football. Maybe we could get together.'

'Great. It's a date then. Tell me which dorm you're living at, and we'll pick you up at eight o'clock.'

'No. No. Not so fast, Tom. We'll meet you at the dance.

'Okay. We'll be looking for you.'

The first couple of weeks fly by in a blur of schoolwork and socializing. Tom finds himself delighted with campus life. He has met several classmates with whom he can study or go out for something to eat. His date with Sandy doesn't go well, however. He gets one dance with her, then, she hooks up with a former high school classmate for the rest of the evening. Miles doesn't care for his date. She's overweight and has bad teeth. He excuses himself to go to the men's room and doesn't come back.

Miles is finding that his status at Georgia is a big let down from his standing at Crisp County High. He is the second string running back on the freshman football team, and his boorish personality leaves him desperately dependent on Tom for his social life.

They discuss their early impressions back at the dorm.

'I'm not very happy with things here. The coach is beating our brains in at practice, and I'm so tired afterwards, I don't have the energy to study. As for my love life, it stinks. So far, my only date was that fat friend of Sandy's.'

Tom reacts. 'I'm getting sick of hearing you complain. That's all you've been doing since we got here. Frankly, I think Georgia is a terrific school. You're not back in Cordele anymore, Miles. I think you need an attitude adjustment.'

Trousdale is insulted. 'You have no idea what I'm putting up with, so you can take your two-bit advice and shove it up your ass.'

For the next two days, the two roommates don't talk to each other. Then comes the night of the fraternity rush at Lambda Chi Alpha.

'Are we going together, or am I going by myself?' asks Tom.

'All right, I'm coming.'

Miles visits SAE with one of his football teammates the following day, but he feels more comfortable with Tom.

The two roommates decide to pledge together. They are accepted along with four other classmates. They endure the requisite hazing during the following six weeks and become indoctrinated with Lambda Chi's innermost secrets. The culmination of the pledge period is the initiation, which takes place in late October.

The pledges trudge down to the frat house basement as a group dressed only in their underwear. The ritualist of the house recites Greek phrases then details the qualities that a pledges must possess to be ordained as a brother on this day-of-judgment.

'Each of you will now be interrogated thoroughly to determine if you possess the lofty character required of a Lambda Chi Alpha brother.'

Tom and Miles are taken into separate rooms as were the other pledges. Stirling is pretty sure he can handle anything the brothers throw at him based on talking with Big Brother John the day before. Miles has been less enthusiastically received and wasn't given any encouragement by his big brother, Phil.

Miles is directed to sit upon a spare wooden chair in the middle of one room with four brothers standing menacingly close to him.

'Tell me pledge Trousdale, who is the president of our chapter?' one brother asks.

Miles' mind freezes. He mutters several names under his breath, but he can't come up with the right one. He furrows his brow and begins to stammer.

'Umm, umm, umm.'

'Mister, do you think we should allow a pledge to join our exalted fraternity, to which he is making a feeble attempt to become a member, when he doesn't even know the name of our Chapter President? Huh, do you?'

'I know who it is. He's the guy with the glasses and short blond hair.'

'Does he have a name? Should we go and tell him now that you don't know his name and ask him if we should allow an ignorant, nobody on the freshman football team to become a brother? Should we? Huh?'

'I'll think of his name. Give me a minute, damn it.'

'Don't use profanity, boy. Just answer the question.'

Another brother jumps in.

'Word has it that you cheated on your recent math exam. That's not the kind of behavior we accept for a brother. How do you plead?'

'I wasn't cheating. I was only confirming one of my answers.'

'Oh, and that's not cheating.'

Meanwhile in another room, Tom was receiving different treatment.

'Do you think the brothers at our fraternity are good looking, pledge?'

'Oh, yes sir.'

'And, Mr., have you looked in the mirror lately and can honestly say you are handsome enough to be a brother in this house?'

'I can only hope you see me that way, Brother Zack.'

'Mirrors don't lie, pledge. You are below our standard of attractiveness.'

'I can only hope to improve my image to your satisfaction, sir. Do you think growing a beard would be an improvement?'

'No!' Brother Zack replies.

'Pledge, several brothers have made the observation that you try to ingratiate yourself to them. Some describe you as a 'kiss ass' or a 'brown nose'. Do you think that is a positive attribute for a brother to have?'

'No sir. I believe a person should always be forthright and honest.'

Both men continue to be badgered with negative observations about their character. After an hour of unrelenting verbal abuse, each pledge is told to wear a black robe and follow their brothers of inquisition back down to the basement. One at a time, they are confronted by the ritualist, who is now donning a ceremonial robe while candlelight provides the only illumination in the cellar. After reciting liturgical passages, he hands a candle-lit lamp to the pledge with these words, 'Choose your path wisely, lest you fall into error.'

Brother Coe tells Tom, 'Bring me thy lamp, O pledge.'

Stirling hands him the lamp and is immediately excoriated by all brothers in attendance and shepherded back to the interrogation room.

During his session with the ritualist, Trousdale refuses to give up the lamp as if warding off defenders while attempting to score a touchdown with a football. He too was roundly denounced by his group of brothers and rudely escorted out of the basement.

After completing their degrading interrogation, the brothers for each pledge, bring them back individually to the cellar. Tom is uncertain whether he did well enough to be accepted. Miles is convinced he has failed. When they finally arrive back in the basement, everyone is congregated there still in their robes. The president stands before them and makes an announcement.

'Congratulations, all six of you are now brothers in the greatest fraternity in the world, Lambda Chi Alpha.'

The pledges are dumbfounded. Stirling overcomes the surprise quickly, turns to Miles and gives him a hug.

'Hey buddy, we made it.'

Trousdale stands there unable to move in shocked disbelief.

Shortly after their initiation into the brotherhood, there is a house party on a Saturday night in November. Tom and Miles arrive separately with their dates. The action this night is downstairs in a big open room that doubles as the brothers' dining room. The folding tables have been put away in a closet, while stack chairs line the walls creating a large open space in the center for dancing. Soft music is playing through the loudspeakers located in the far corners, and a bar is set up and manned by two of the brothers at the near end.

Tom is speaking to his big brother John with their dates for the evening listening intently to his story.

'When I was a pledge, John sent me over to the SAE house with a full grown pig on a leash. I was charged with letting it loose inside their building. It was two in the morning, so I assumed all the brothers would be asleep in bed. Since all of them are jocks, nobody is burning the late-night oil studying. Right! However, without my knowing, John had conspired with two SAE brothers about this stunt. As soon as I snuck through the unlocked front door, those guys bound and gagged me, tying my arms and legs to a chair. Then, they took the pig and left without a word. About twenty minutes later, they returned with one of them carrying a sandwich on a plate.'

'If you want to get out of here, you must eat this sandwich,' one of them says. 'We made it from the liver of the pig you just brought.'

'I was terrified, but I agreed. I would have done most anything to escape that place. They first shoved the plate under my nose. Feces had been rubbed around the edges. The smell was overpowering and nauseating. I thought they were demanding me to eat a pig shit sandwich. So, I refused to take even one bite. Then they threatened to strip me naked and leave me tied up on the doorstep of Kappa Kappa Gamma.'

'After considering the two choices, I nodded in submission and girded myself for the most revolting experience of my life. One of the brothers shoved the sandwich toward my mouth. I scrunched my face, held my breath, and took the first bite.'

'It wasn't half bad. Turns out they had put a glop of lime Jello between two pieces of Wonder Bread. I was able to finish the whole sandwich. Then, they untied me and pushed me out the front door. I ran as fast as I could back to my dorm and locked the door.'

'Later, I heard they had an exchange supper with Chi Omega the next week and served roast pig.'

Miles has just entered the room with his date and overhears the end of Stirling's recount of the hazing incident.

'Tom, you never told me that story before,' interrupts Miles.

'Oh, there you are Miles,' responds his roommate. 'By the way, this is Jasmine from Kappa, and John's lady friend, Kim, also from Kappa.' They all make nods of acknowledgement.

'This is Marie from Dalton,' Miles responds. There was a pause with the expectation that Miles would further inform them to which sorority she belonged. An awkward silence follows with the two Kappa girls taking notice of the excessive makeup caked on Maries' face and the strong scent of cheap perfume suddenly assaulting their noses. John breaks the ice.

'How about some refreshing punch for the ladies? Tom, Miles, give me a hand with the drinks. Ladies, we'll be right back.'

John Baxter is a fraternity brother first and a college student second. He believes in all the traditions and rules of Lambda Chi Alpha and is determined these new brothers will follow them as well. John has declared himself a business major carrying a barely passing 2.0 GPA. Despite his less than mediocre academic record, he has been elected house treasurer and is regarded by fellow chapter members as a leader and example of a true Lambda Chi brother.

'Let's show these girls a good time, boys,' John advises. 'That means treating them with respect while at the same time getting them to let their hair down, if you know what I mean. Remember how you treat women is a reflection on our house. Of course, if your date has an interest in going all the way, there's nothing in our charter that says you must refuse her.'

'Thanks for that fatherly advice, John,' responds Tom with a sly smile and twinkle in his eye.'

'I already know what interests my date,' notes Miles. 'And, I must say, we share the same one.' The three brothers erupt in a lascivious laugh at that remark, then return to their dates with drinks in hand.

The evening unfolds predictably. John and Tom find much to discuss with their dates. There is small talk about classes, the Greek life, and the Brothers brag about how much booze they can handle. Miles and Marie however, don't fit in. He has some insights about the pigskin scene but Marie has nothing to say except, 'Can I have another drink?' They split off and begin dancing to the music being played on a turntable by Brother Jason, the frat deejay. He gets everyone's attention first with rock and roll hits of the day, then later in the evening, slow romantic songs like Pat Boone's 'Love Letters in the Sand'.

When the slow ballads begin, Miles disappears with his date into the upstairs bedroom of his big brother Phil. He closes the door, turns off the light and stands facing her. Without warning, he pushes her backwards. Marie collapses onto the bed without resistance. In an instant, Miles is on top of her, kissing her lips, rubbing her breasts with his left hand and removing her panties with his right.

He lowers his trousers below his knees and has his way with Marie. Five minutes later, she lapses into unconsciousness. He shakes her several times, but when she fails to respond, he panics and rushes downstairs to beg Tom to rescue the situation.

Stirling is sitting next to Jasmine with his hand on her shoulder and his face close to hers talking in a soft, hypnotic drawl to which she is clearly responding. Miles comes up beside him and whispers in his ear.

'Tom, I need you, man. Marie is out cold upstairs, and I don't know how to wake her up. Help me.'

Stirling leans back and turns toward Miles with a look of irritation. After a few seconds contemplation of his own situation versus Miles', he recognizes the urgency of his friend's predicament and excuses himself.

'Jasmine, don't you move, you sweet thing,' commands Tom. 'I'll be back in a flash.'

When they arrive at Brother Phil's room, Marie hasn't moved. She is lying spread eagled on the bed with her hot pink panties lying on the floor.

'Oops,' Miles reacts quickly stuffing the underwear in his pants pocket.

Tom shakes her several times, attempting to wake her, but she's out cold.

'What do we do now?' Miles looks to Tom in desperation. He sees his night's plan of wild sex turning into a potentially embarrassing spectacle.

'We need to try to wake her up. Jeez, Miles, how much did she drink?'

'She kept guzzling that fruit punch down like she'd been out in the desert without water.'

'Oh, not good,' responds Stirling. 'I know John keeps some ammonia capsules in his dresser. He's used them in the past on a drunken brother. I'll go get one of those.'

Tom quickly leaves, while Miles wallows in his predicament. 'How could that dumb broad get herself that loaded,' he thinks to himself. 'Now, everyone's going to think I raped the bitch. Great.'

Tom returns with the capsule.

'Let's sit her up first,' Stirling advises. He grabs both legs while Miles curls his arm under her shoulders and together they swing her into a sitting position.

Tom holds the ammonia capsule under her nose and cracks it open. Marie suddenly jerks her head back and moans. Then, without warning, she turns her head aside and heaves a huge quantity of punch colored fluid onto the bed along with a red cherry.

'Shit, now what do we do, Tom?'

'I'll go get a new set of bedding from the hall closet along with some towels. We can't leave Phil's room like this.'

Stirling returns with the linen, and they clean the room as best they can, remaking the bed with Marie draped around a stuffed chair nearby.

'Next, we're going to stand her up, walk or drag her downstairs and out to your car,' Tom orders.

With Marie wedged between them in a slumped standing posture, they position one of her arms over each of their outside shoulders and hold her around the waist with their inside arms. Little by little, they make their way out of the bedroom and down the hallway. Marie's legs are partially supporting her, and she is making a half-hearted attempt to keep pace with the two new brothers. As they approach the stairs, she goes limp, and he legs stop moving.

'Wake up, Marie. You've got to help us,' Stirling enunciates clearly into her right ear. She emits a rebellious wail and tries to sit down in the hallway.

'What's going on up there,' yells a brother from the base of the stairs. He had taken his date into the darkened living room to make out on the sofa.

'We're okay, Bobby,' Stirling reassures him. ''Miles' date got a little sick and we took her to the upstairs bathroom.'

They are now at the edge of the stairwell and starting to descend. After three steps, Marie's foot slips and she drops down to a sitting position on one of the wooden steps with her legs spread wide apart. By this time, several more brothers with their dates have congregated below. The party is breaking up. As the grandfather clock in the living room strikes midnight, the light in the stairwell shines up Marie's hiked up skirt revealing to the multitude of onlookers the uncovered state of her pelvic area. To make matters worse, her pink panties are protruding out of Miles' right trouser pocket.

'Oh disgusting,' comments one coed while other girls watch with their mouths agape, looking away, then turning back to look again in disbelief.

Several brothers snicker, then stifle that reaction, realizing how this embarrassing moment could smear the house reputation.

Tom and Miles attempt to minimize the damage by quickly hoisting Marie to her feet and rushing her down the remaining stairs.

'I want to lie down right now,' she demands.

The two new fraternity brothers pay no heed to her request and hurry her to the entryway. As they open the door, Marie turns toward the crowd still witnessing the debacle and comments.

'Don't drink the punch, girls, 'cause it's spiked.' She then proceeds to throw up a second time.

When Tom returns from helping Marie into Miles' car, Jasmine comes up to him and yanks on his arm.

'Take me back to the dorm right now. I've never been so embarrassed in all my life.'

CHAPTER 13

Tom never dates Jasmine again. He never dates another Kappa again. In fact, Lambda Chi is black balled by that sorority for the next four years.

As for Miles, he meets with the officers of the house on the week after the unfortunate party incident. The session concludes with the following decree read by the secretary.

'For unseemly and irresponsible behavior unbecoming a brother of the Nu Zeta Chapter of Lambda Chi Alpha, Mr. Miles Trousdale is hereby placed on probation for a period of three months. During that time, the brother in question shall perform KP duty free for five days a week after evening meals. In addition, Mr. Trousdale shall be complicit in no additional incidents considered detrimental to the Lambda Chi Alpha reputation or in violation of the fraternity charter code of behavior during that same period. Failing to comply with these conditions shall be considered cause for expulsion of said individual from the fraternity.'

Miles was resentful of this action. After all, he had only acted precisely as John had advised him and Tom that very night.

'Tom, I just did what any of those supposed "brothers" would do at a house party, and a lot of them have probably done the same thing.'

'I feel for you, Miles. I know they had to do something because that little incident caused a big uproar. But, you don't deserve such a harsh penalty. I'll talk to John. Maybe the officers can reduce the punishment.'

'You're a buddy, Tom.'

Tom confers with John the next day. As an officer of the chapter, John comes up with an idea that he believes will exonerate Miles for the party incident. And, he is sure the other officers will concur. John visits the President, Vice President and Secretary individually. To a man, they fully support his plan.

At 10:00 p.m. on a Tuesday night, John pulls up in front of Busbee Hall with Brother Phil riding shotgun. Miles and Tom are waiting outside.

'Get in, boys,' John says as he rolls down the driver side window and shouts to them. 'We're going on a little adventure.'

'Where are we going?' asks Miles.

'You'll see,' replies John

'John's come up with a plan,' says Phil. 'If you do a good job tonight, all the charges against you will disappear. You'll be a brother in good standing.'

'That's a big relief to me, but tell me what I need to do?'

'You'll find out when we get there,' John states in a tone that stifles further questioning.

They drive for about an hour southeast on Route 78 towards Augusta. John stops for gas at an Esso station near Thomson. Both John and Phil get out of the car while Miles and Tom remain in the back seat.

''Where do you think we're going, Tom?'

'I have no idea, but if it gets you back in the good graces of our brothers, I'm all for it.'

'I'm a little worried they're going to ask me to do something that I really don't want to do.'

'You've got to trust these guys, Miles. They're your brothers.'

Stirling looks out the rear side window and sees John and Phil in a heated discussion. From their body language, he can see that John is insistent on the point he was making, and Phil appears to be relenting in his opposition.

'What were you brothers arguing about?' Stirling asks when the return to the car.'

'Phil was unaware that Lambda Chi has an exclusion clause in the charter that prevents negroes and Jews from becoming members.'

'John, I never knew that either,' Tom replies. 'Well, I guess it doesn't mean much to us since there's no negroes on campus anyway.'

Tom thinks to himself, *I'm not fond of negroes entering our university, but I don't know if I would feel as strongly as John does if they did.*

'I knew that from my daddy,' Miles adds. 'He heard it from a friend who was a frat boy in college. Truth be told, that's one reason I pledged Lambda Chi instead of SAE.' There's a silent pause. Then, he adds, 'Of course, the main reason I joined was I really liked the brothers.'

John starts the engine and drives out of the filling station heading south on Route 25. They continue on for another hour and a half before reaching the outskirts of Savannah. Tom and Miles still have no idea where they are going or what they will be asked to do.

'Here's the deal,' John begins. 'We're going to the campus of Georgia State, a negro college. There's no way those cotton pickin' darkies belong in college. That's just degrading to all us intelligent and deserving white students.'

'This is the plan. Their mascot is a tiger. There's a huge bronze sculpture of that beast within a landscaped circle in the middle of campus. We are going to give it a little makeover. I've got all the tools we need in the trunk. Miles, you have the most important job, and that's dealing with the tiger's manhood. I'll show you exactly what to do when we get there.'

'I'm liking this,' Miles reacts. 'I thought you were going to make me do something I would hate. This is going to be fun.'

The dark green 1950 Studebaker Champion drives through the west entrance to the campus around 1:00 a.m. No traffic and no people can be seen as the car slowly glides its way through the darkness towards the administration building. John circles the oval in front of that structure where the object of their mission is located, and parks his vehicle heading back toward the entrance gate.

'We've got to be as quiet as possible, so no loud talking or making any unnecessary noise, he instructs. 'Phil is going to spray paint the tiger pink. Tom, you can help paint too. Miles, I've got a cutting torch in the trunk. You've probably never used one, so I'll fire it up and show you how it works. Then, you're going to cut off the tiger's balls with it.'

'I love it,' gushes Miles.

'Are you sure we're not going to get thrown in jail for this? Stirling anxiously asks.

'Am I trying to confront a tiger with a bunch of chickens?' John fires back. 'C'mon, I was hoping you all had some balls even if the tiger was going to lose his.'

End of discussion. They exit the car quietly leaving the doors ajar to minimize the noise and expedite their exit after completing their task. John pops open the trunk. Inside are all the tools and supplies they will need; the spray cans of paint and an oxyacetylene torch complete with tanks, hoses, torch wand and sparking device.

John positions the oxygen and acetylene tanks in their wheeled caddy. Then, he hands the hoses, torch and sparking device to Miles.

'Let's go Mr. Pseudo Football Star', mocks John. 'Phil, take those paint cans and give two of them to Tom.'

They walk about 100 feet inside the circle with all their paraphernalia before reaching the statue.

'Look at the size of that thing,' Stirling remarks. 'That's got to be a lot larger than a real tiger.'

'Yuh. And, check out his mouth,' Miles notes. 'That thing could tear you to bits with those teeth.'

Phil instructs Tom to shake the can of pink paint for one minute and then begin painting the head; holding a flashlight in his left hand and spraying with the right. Phil himself starts painting with another can of the aerosol substance on the left flank of the body before shifting to the right side where he plans to assist Tom. Any leftover paint will be applied to the rear quarters after Miles completes his task with the torch.

John has Miles set down the torch equipment he was carrying near the raised tail of the tiger. The two cylinders are positioned upright. John checks the connections to make sure they are tight. Then, he turns on the acetylene cylinder and uses the sparking device to light the gas. He adjusts the flame until puffs of smoke are minimized, then opens the oxygen tank. When the two gases correctly mixed, a small white flame arises just outside the nozzle.

'It's all set,' John informs Miles. 'All you need to do is hold the tip of the white flame next to the base of the tiger's balls and move it slowly across until you've cut all the way through. I'll hold the flashlight on his nuts while you do it.'

'Got it, boss' cries Miles. 'This is the most fun I've had since I shot a nigger for trespassing on our property back home.'

'Keep it down, you sadistic prick. And, get to work with that thing,' John admonishes.

They methodically go through their assigned tasks. When Tom and Phil are halfway through the right flank of the statue, its brass balls drop to the ground making a 'ping' sound on the concrete footing.

'Let's hear the tiger roar now,' says Miles. 'Meowww.'

'All right, hot shot,' advises John. 'Shut that thing off including the tanks and put all that stuff back in the trunk of the car. And, when you come back, I want you to pick up those balls and stick them in the tiger's mouth.'

Before returning the torch equipment, Miles tries to pick up the bronze balls with his bare hands but quickly drops them.

'Owwww,' yelps Miles. 'Jesus, those things are hot.'

'No shit Sherlock,' says John. 'Whaddya expect, dumb ass, you just sawed those balls off with a blow torch. Wait a couple of minutes, then pick them up.'

When Miles finally moves the male genitalia to its new, unnatural resting place, Tom and Phil finish painting the hind quarters.

'Miles, you have one more job to complete, declares John. 'Take this can of white spray paint and write the letters as I give them to you on the left flank of the tiger.'

'Yes sir.'

'Get that can ready, and here we go.' John holds his flashlight on the space where he wants Miles to paint and begins spelling our words letter by letter. N….I….G….G….E….R….S.'

'That's a good start,' chimes Miles.

'Shut up and keep writing, carps John. 'New line.'

G….O….space….B….A….C….K….space….T….O….space…..
P….I….C….K….I…..N…..space….C…..O…..T….T….O….N….new
line…..Y….O….U….space….D….O….N….T….space….
B….E….L….O….N….G….space….H….E….R….E….new line….
W….H….I….T….E….space….M….E….N….space….R….U….L….E

As soon as Miles finishes writing, two black males appear out of nowhere.

'What's going on here,' one of them asks.

'Nothing,' John answers.

'You guys are messing with our mascot, aren't you,' the second student challenges. 'I'm going to report you to the campus police.'

At that point, Tom and Phil rush back to the car, while John and Miles stay back to confront the two students.

'I don't think you're going to do anything,' John counters. With that brief retort, he proceeds to punch the guy in the face and knocks him to the ground. Following John's lead, Miles grabs the second student by the shoulders and thrusts him back against the statue smacking his head against the hind quarters rendering him unconscious.

'C'mon, let's get out of here,' says John as he begins running back to the car. He jumps in and starts the engine.

'Where's Miles?' Stirling asks. He looks back and sees his roommate pummeling the other student who was trying to get back on his feet. Just then, the headlights of an oncoming vehicle shine toward them from about a quarter mile away.

'Miles, run. We gotta get outta here quick,' Tom yells through his cranked down rear window.

John puts the car into first gear and begins to pull away just as Miles approaches the vehicle. He jumps face down onto the flat surface of the trunk holding onto the sides as John accelerates toward the campus exit. Suddenly, a flashing red light shines from the roof of the now chasing vehicle. Its siren begins to wail.

John is able to depart the college grounds before the campus police car can drive close enough to overtake them. Luckily, the chase ends here as the Studebaker engine is whining at full power and smoking oil fumes from the tailpipe are obscuring view of the license plate. They turn right into Savannah city proper and race for a few blocks before pulling over and allowing Miles to climb off the top of the trunk and return inside the car's back seat.

As they drive on, there are hoots of excitement and relief.

'You did all right back there, Trousdale,' admits John. 'Anybody get hurt?'

'I think those two colored guys aren't doing so well,' notes Tom.

'I remember my daddy saying, 'The only good nigger is a dead nigger.'
Miles recalls with a big smile on his face.

Suddenly, Tom feels depressed. He never has had a high regard for
coloreds, but what he had just done makes him feel sick inside. He tells
himself to never take part in something like this ever again. So, as the
others relive with relish the evening's adventures on that long ride back to
school, Tom withdraws into his own thoughts of guilt and remorse.
Visions of little Onzell lying in that field, covered with blood and hovering
near death, flash in his head.

CHAPTER 14

'James, look at this article in today's Constitution,' alerts Tyus, his new dormitory roommate.

The front page photo shows the defaced tiger mascot statue of Georgia State College with a racist message written on the animal's flank. The accompanying article describes two unconscious black students found at the scene who were taken to the local hospital, both in serious condition. Walker puts down the course book he had been studying to see what Tyus is riled up about.

'Tyus, I used to be afraid when I saw that stuff. Now, I get angry.'

James is enrolled in his freshman year at Morehouse College majoring in marketing. He has been diligent in his studies during his first months at school knowing he must keep up with his highly intelligent classmates. But this news story pushes him out of his academic mindset. If he had registered at Georgia State, he might have been one of those students beaten by those sadistic bigots. He remembers the incident where he and David were bullied in front of the Wage Earners Bank. Then, more vividly, he experiences flashbacks of the lynching of his cousin Billy.

'You know, I heard there's going to be a meeting today of the student NAACP at Samuel Graves Hall. Why don't we go?' prompts his roomie.

'We must, Tyus. What time does it start?'

'2:00 this afternoon.'

'Let's go,' insists Walker with resolute firmness.

A group of fifty or more students crowd into the classroom. Four chairs
are positioned facing the student gathering from the front of the room for
the officers of the student organization. The students cram together, some
sitting at desks, others standing around the perimeter of the space. A loud
buzz of conversation fills the air as James and Tyus arrive taking their place
by the back wall. The noise quiets as the student president of the
organization rises to the lectern.

'Thank you all for coming. We are fortunate to have one of the true leaders
of the NAACP with us today, Mr. W.W. Law from Savannah. As many of
you know, Mr. Law has been a guiding light of the non-violent civil rights
movement in Savannah for many years along with the Reverend Ralph
Mark Gilbert. Among their many accomplishments have been the
registration of hundreds of negro voters and the integration of city police.
Without further ado, I give you the honorable Mr. Law.'

A fortyish, thin, ebony skinned man of medium height steps to the podium
amid polite applause.

'As I look around this room today, I feel a powerful sense of energy. The
energy of youth can be a wonderful resource for action. Beyond that, this
college has a proud tradition of developing leaders of the negro community.
Today is a time for both, leadership and action.'

The crowd in the room shouts its approval.

He continues. 'I am here today to speak to you the day after a hateful crime
was perpetrated against our people. By now everyone here has heard the
news of the racist act committed last night on the campus of Georgia State.
As a responsible colored community, we cannot stand idly by and accept
this indignation as status quo. We must take action now and continue in
opposition to these degrading acts against colored people until they stop
and the negro is accepted as equal and not separate.'

At this point, the gathering erupts into cheers lasting nearly a minute.
Then, one of the students shouts a question.

'What can we do, Mr. Law?'

'In this city, there are several restaurants designated for 'whites only'. I encourage this group to organize a plan to integrate these establishments. This must be done peacefully even though there will be threats or even acts of violence against those participating. Do not attempt to retaliate because such a response will only reinforce the prejudice that coloreds cannot behave in a civilized manner.'

'In Savannah, our NAACP chapter unsuccessfully attempted to integrate the 'whites only' diner at Levy's Department Store. The participants were arrested, and that restaurant remains segregated today. To win our fight, we must continue these efforts in an unrelenting crusade until our just battle is won, not only in Savannah, but here in Atlanta, and throughout the South. Are you with me, Morehouse students?'

A vociferous chorus of 'yes, yes, yes' is almost deafening as Mr. Law waves and steps down from the lectern.

The student president follows Mr. Law and lays out a plan to integrate four 'whites only' luncheonettes across the city. Then, he asks for volunteers.

'Tyus, are you ready to get involved with something like this? It could be dangerous, and our folks might get upset with you.'

'If you do this, James, so will I.'

Walker smiles and raises his hand extending two fingers.

'Over there in the back of the room,' the secretary points at James.

'Are you predicting victory for this demonstration, or are you volunteering two people?'

'Two volunteers for now, sir, and hopefully victory later.'

'Please come up to the podium, give us your contact information, and we'll give you your assignment.'

Tyus and James stand in a line of unsuspecting martyrs. One of them light heartedly jokes about the racial divide, acting as a highbrow white person talking about colored people in a sophisticated voice. He spoofs with hand and facial gestures talking in an exaggerated clipped accent.

'You know, Stanley, I find these coloreds to be quite excellent at shining my riding boots. I believe they must secrete some sort of special polishing chemical within their saliva because the leather becomes gloriously shiny when they lick them.'

The volunteers within earshot bust into laughter.

When the two youths reach the head of the line, they are assigned to integrate the Woolworth's lunch counter in Decatur along with another pair of students, Jerome from Waycross, and Herschel from Atlanta.

CHAPTER 15

Coloreds are allowed to shop at the Decatur Woolworth. They just aren't permitted to eat at the 'whites only' diner on the second floor. Georgia segregation laws prevent them.

The enclosed upstairs dining area offers customer service at the counter or at several red Naugahyde covered booths. Ten vinyl covered stools fixed to the floor with chrome metal seatbacks provide seating for the counter side patrons.

James and the three other Morehouse students stand outside the diner entrance looking through the glass door. They have been instructed to wait until four empty stools next to each other become available, enter the diner and sit. Then, it happens.

'That one guy just got up to leave, and there's four seats together at the middle of the counter,' Tyus observes.

'That's our cue. Let's go now,' James commands

Hearts thumping within their chests, the four young men quickly enter and take their seats. Eyes in the room are immediately upon them, and biting remarks about their presence can be overheard.

'Look, there's negras in here,' says one in a low voice. 'They shouldn't be tryin' to eat in a white person's restaurant. Someone should get 'em outta here.'

'Those uppity niggers don't know their place,' says another.

Walker can feel his anxiety building, but he's been trained to expect this reaction and not to panic. A glance into his partners' faces tells him, they're worried too. He nods as a gesture to keep to their plan.

The waitress at the counter maintains her back to the four students wiping the sink with a rag. She is an unkempt woman in her 30's wearing a multi-stained red and white vertically striped dress uniform with a tiara-like cloth headpiece pinned to her messy blond hair. Her oval shaped name tag reads 'Hilda'. The other whites at the counter get up and move toward the cash register near the entrance to pay their tabs, some leaving a nickel or dime for a tip.

There's an aura of nervous calm. Finally, Walker speaks breaking the silence.

'Miss, we're ready to order.'

Herschel loudly repeats James' request addressing her as 'madame' noting the waitress is wearing a gold band on her left hand.

Finally, she turns to face the four colored customers. Looking above their heads to avoid eye contact, she curtly addresses them.

'This lunch counter is for whites only. Y'all will have to leave.'

A brief pause of several seconds follows when no one moves or speaks. Tension in the air is thick, and all the customers in the diner seems to be holding their breath.

'I would like to order a club sandwich and a coke,' James requests.

'Make it two,' says Tyus.

'Three,' adds Herschel

'I'll have the same,' agrees Jerome.

The waitress is nervous and begins to tremble. A few seconds later, she screws up her courage and gives them an ultimatum.

'If you colored boys don't leave right now, I will go in the back and get our manager.'

'We're only asking to be served like any other customer in this diner,' Walker states confronting the woman by leaning toward her.

The waitress' face is now flushed and her neck muscles tense as she grits her teeth.

'You're asking for trouble,' she exclaims as she dashes off to the back office.

The four students look at each other. They don't know what to expect next. The other customers in the diner are getting restless and start making irate remarks to each other; first within the booths, then between them. Finally, one large, burly middle-aged man addresses the boys.

'You heard Hilda, get out of here and go find a nigger restaurant where you belong.'

Other customers voice similar sentiments. The students continue to sit on their stools without responding. Within a minute, the manager appears and confronts the four boys.

'We have segregations laws in this state. You coloreds are in violation of those laws and will not be served in this establishment. Now, get out before I call the police and y'all get in some serious trouble.'

James places his hand on Tyus' shoulder to stay put, and all four students remain seated. Two men rise from their booth and come over to remove the students by force. Unbeknownst to the black youths, the manager had called store security from his back office, and they enter the diner at that very moment.

The boys are grabbed by the back of their collars and physically hoisted off the stools. As they are roughly escorted out of the diner, James yells out.

'We have as much right to be here, as anyone else.'

Outside the restaurant, they are herded downstairs and out of the building by two department store security men. To their surprise, two city policemen are waiting for them just outside the entry doors. One of them stands facing the youths and details their situation.

'You colored boys have committed two offenses, entering a 'whites only' establishment in violation of segregation laws and disturbing the peace. You are now under arrest.'

The students are handcuffed and marched to a waiting paddy wagon parked half a block away. Pushed forcefully into the vehicle by the policemen, they sit on benches facing each other with James and Tyus occupying one side, Jerome and Herschel on the other.

'Seriously, are they going to throw us in jail for peacefully walking into a 'whites only' restaurant?' poses Jerome. 'We didn't start a fight. We didn't request anything another customer wouldn't have asked for.'

'This is called fighting for our rights,' Walker replies. 'As my daddy used to say, "Them white folk ain't gonna give up nothin' to us coloreds."'

The students sit silently for the remainder of the five-minute ride fearing what might happen next.

They are driven to the main police station on East Trinity Place. In a separate room, mug shots are taken, each is fingerprinted, and records are checked for previous arrests. No priors are found.

Led to a security storage area, they hand over their wallets, keys, and loose items in their pockets, sign a paper attesting to the list of those personal possessions, and watch as the officer behind the counter stuffs the list and their belongings into envelopes with their names written in pen on the outside.

'You can make one phone call before we put you in a cell,' the jail officer informs them.

James thinks about whom to call. He doesn't want to upset Aunt Violet. His father doesn't have a phone. So, the choice is simple, he calls Reverend Jones. It is now early evening on a Saturday night.

'How long are we going to be here?' Jerome asks.

'That has yet to be determined,' says the officer. 'But don't plan on eatin' any watermelon for a while.' The officer chuckles. The students rankle at his racist remark.

Walker remembers Reverend Jones' phone number from a previous call he had made to him from Auntie's phone. The preacher answers.

'Hello.'

'Hello, Reverend Jones. This is James Walker. I'm in some trouble along with three of my classmates from Morehouse. We attempted to integrate the Woolworth lunch counter in Decatur today, and we've all been arrested. Is there anything you can do to help us?'

There's a long pause.

'James, sorry for your situation. I hope you're all right. And, yes, I think I can help you. I know a civil rights lawyer from Atlanta who has helped our people before. I'll give him a call as soon as I hang up.'

'Thanks a million, Reverend. Oh, would you please let my father know about my situation. I feel bad about this. It's like I went against the advice he's given me many times over the years.'

'Son, you did a brave thing, so you have nothing to be sorry for. I'll be in touch with you as soon as I have any news. In the meantime, be very cooperative with those police.'

Walker and his classmates are led to a single cell, ten feet by ten feet where there is one single bed and a smelly, dirty commode. Three of them must sleep on the concrete floor and none of them are given any food or water that night. They wait, hoping to be rescued.

Bail is set at $500, as they await arraignment scheduled for the following Monday.

CHAPTER 16

'Son, Ah don't know why ya' do this,' father Estes cries out. 'De whole family is sacrificin' so you can get a college education, an' you get yooahself in trouble with de law. What's wrong with ya?'

'Papa, I know being in jail looks bad, but I believe this is something we need to do. There is hope for a better life for us coloreds. I began learning that living down in Savannah with Auntie, but up here in Atlanta, things are changing even faster.

Estes can't understand and doesn't accept what James is saying.

'What ya did was wrong, son, an' dangerous too.'

James and Estes are sitting at a table across from each other the day after his arrest. It's a windowless room where, upon arrival, detainees are permitted to meet with family or legal counsel. A police officer stands outside guarding the doorway.

He enters. 'You got two minutes,' the officer notifies them.

'I come heah t'day wit' Revren' Jones. He done foun' a lawya who might help ya. Now listen to dat man an' do what he say. You hear me, son?'

'I hear you, papa. And, I'll do what he says. Thanks for coming. I love you.'

Father and son both have tears in their eyes as Mr. Walker rises from his chairs and leaves the room. A minute later, Reverend Jones enters along with a dapper, light skinned colored gentleman dressed in a dark blue suit, white shirt and red tie. The officer leaves the room.

'Good morning, James,' greets Reverend Jones. 'Sorry you're having to go through all this, but I brought you the best legal counsel for coloreds in the South. Meet attorney Richard Cole, Esquire.'

'How do you do, James? Pleasure to meet you. Reverend Jones has said a lot of nice things about you.'

'I'm honored to have you represent me, sir.'

'First of all, I regret to inform you that the City of Decatur has decided to press charges. We were hoping since you and the other boys had no previous record that they would release you without further legal action. However, it seems the city is trying to make an example of the four of you to discourage others from attempting the same kind of segregation busting.'

'Given how poorly we've been treated so far, I'm not surprised,' concurs young Walker.

James is feeling guiltier about missing school than violating segregation laws. He knows how much his family has sacrificed to allow him to advance his education.

'Here's the situation, James. You and your friends are to be arraigned before a judge magistrate tomorrow for violating segregation laws. Bail has been set at $500 each. Conviction is punishable by imprisonment from 30-60 days and/or fines ranging from $100 to $500.'

'Wow. That's much worse than I thought. Any chance of getting us off?'

'I'll make every effort to do that, James. A lot depends on the judge hearing the case. Let's hope we don't get Judge Gerhard. He's got a reputation for handing down maximum sentences.'

The guard reenters the room. 'Time's up, counselor. You're going to have to leave.'

Attorney Cole stands and gives one last piece of advice.

'Stay strong, son. I'll do everything I can to get you back in school where you belong.'

Walker is escorted back to his cell feeling bewildered. Did he jeopardize his future by agreeing to take part in this civil rights act? Is he going to fall too far behind in his classes and end up flunking out? Did he realize these consequences? Was this whole sit-in idea a huge mistake?

When he reaches his cell, Tyus, Jerome and Herschel are anxious to hear how the meeting went with James' lawyer as none of them are able to afford an attorney.

'I'm afraid we're going to be stuck in her for a while,' he says.

'What did the lawyer say?' asks Jerome.

'He said that the local authorities want to make an example of us. $500 bail and we're looking at least at a 30 day stay in this dump and a $500 fine. He's going to try reducing these numbers, but he's not optimistic.'

'What about school?' Herschel asks. 'We have exams coming up next week.'

'I can't say,' James answers. 'I suppose if Morehouse supports us, we'll be allowed some sort of make- up exams. If they are opposed to what we did they might even expel us from school.'

'That's a depressing thought,' notes Tyus. 'Remind me. Why did we do this in the first place?'

'I don't know about the rest of you, but I'm losing my mind living with the three of you in this pig sty of a cell,' complains Herschel. 'It's cold. The food is bad. We all stink. I can't take a crap without three pair of eyes gawking at me. And, James, you're pissing me off being so bossy.'

'Listen, we all did this knowing there could be some bad consequences,' Walker reminds them. 'We did it because we believed what Mr. Law said. To make the South a better place for coloreds, we need to stand up for our rights.'

The other three students stop complaining the next couple of hours after James' chastising remarks, but no one is happy. In his own mind, young Walker remains doubtful himself about his decision to enter this interracial battle. Things are much worse than he envisioned.

One week later, the four students are in court having spent the previous seven days in the squalor of the Decatur jail. None of them made bail.

'All rise for the honorable Judge Henry Trent Gerhard,' the bailiff announces.

The four boys stand facing the judge along with their counsel, attorney Richard Cole. Judge Gerhard climbs the four stairs and takes his place on the rostrum. He is an overweight, balding man in his late fifties with bushy eyebrows and thin lips. The judge offers a piercing stare at the defendants as if he knows they're guilty before hearing their case. He takes off his glasses continuing to look down at the boys, then speaks.

'Be seated,' he commands in a booming voice.

The prosecution and defense take their seats as do ten other people in the gallery including Reverend Jones, Estes Walker and relatives of the other boys. After sounds of sliding chairs and rustling clothes subside, a nervous silence pervades the courtroom. With all eyes upon him, the judge finally begins the proceedings.

'Will the defendants in this case please rise.' The boys stand.

'Tyus Robinson, James Walker, Jerome Wilson, and Herschel Taylor, you each stand accused of violating segregation laws of the City of Decatur and the State of Georgia. You each have plead not guilty during the arraignment. Do you wish to change your plea at this time?'

'No sir, not guilty, your honor,' says Tyus.

'No sir, not guilty, your honor,' echoes James.

'No sir, not guilty, your honor,' parrots Jerome.

'No sir, not guilty, your honor,' repeats Herschel.

The prosecutor, Mr. Willhite calls several witnesses from the scene at the Woolworth luncheonette including the waitress, the manager, and three restaurant patrons present that day. Hilda Callahan, the waitress, is first to testify. As she stands in front of the witness chair, the bailiff asks her to place her hand on a Bible to take the oath.

'Do you promise to tell the truth, the whole truth, and nothing but the truth, so help you God.'

'I do.' She is instructed to sit.

The prosecutor approaches and begins to draw out her testimony.

'Mrs. Callahan, you were the counter waitress at the Decatur Woolworth luncheonette on the afternoon of December 9th, 1959. Is that accurate?'

'Yes, I was.'

'Did you witness four black youths enter the diner at approximately 2:00 p.m. in violation of the segregation code.'

'Objection your honor,' defense lawyer Cole rises to counter that question. 'The last portion of that statement infers the guilt of the defendants which has not been proven.'

'Objection overruled,' Judge Gerhard denies the protest. 'You may answer the question, Mrs. Callahan.'

'Yes sir. Those boys over there came in and sat at my counter around the time you say.'

'Did you recognize them as colored boys who had entered the diner illegally?'

Mr. Cole stands and raises his hand again.

'Objection, your honor. It has yet to be proved that these boys did anything illegal.'

'Overruled again. Please continue Mr. Willhite.'

'Please answer the question Mrs. Callahan.'

'I knew right away they shouldn't be there, and I told them to leave immediately before they got in serious trouble.'

'Did they follow your recommendation and leave?'

'No sir. They just stayed right there on those stools and tried to order some food.'

'What did you do next, Mrs. Callahan?'

'I told them I wasn't going to serve them any food, and I would get the manager if they didn't leave right away.'

'And, did they leave then?'

'No sir. They kept insisting on ordering food.'

'What happened next?'

'I could tell this whole incident was upsetting our white customers as they were talking loud among themselves and getting angry. So, I went in the back and got the manager.'

'Did the manager come out to confront these boys?'

'Yes, and he insisted the boys leave immediately or security would have them removed.'

'And, did they leave then?'

'No, they kept insisting on ordering food. So, the manager finally had to call security to take them away.'

'Did you ever have an incident like that happen at your diner before?'

'Never sir. And, may I say I've never been so disrespected in all my life.'

'No more questions, your honor,' concludes Mr. Willhite.

'Mr. Cole, do you wish to examine the witness?'

'Yes, your honor.'

'Mrs. Callahan, you stated that you felt disrespected by the four accused boys. Tell me, did they make any requests of you different from what any other customer might have made?'

'No.'

'And, did they make any comments to you that would have been considered insulting?' And, if so, what specific remarks were made.'

'I can't recall the exact language they used, but they seemed to have a hostile attitude and were very demanding.'

'So, you can't remember any specific insults directed toward you, and they never spoke to you other than to order food.'

'I guess that's so.'

'Thank you, Mrs. Callahan. You may step down.'

The manager of the diner, Mr. Moore is called next and questioned by Mr. Willhite. He corroborates most of Mrs. Callahan's testimony and adds the boys acted in a belligerent manner. He claims he finally had to call store security to have the students forcibly removed from the premises. Mr. Moore emphasizes that at no time did the boys cooperate, and they left the diner kicking and screaming.

Mr. Cole takes the floor for cross examination.

'Mr. Moore, isn't it true that you called security before you came out from your back office as there is no phone in the service portion of the restaurant.'

'I knew I had a serious situation on my hands when Mrs. Callahan came to me.'

'So, did you call security from your back office?'

'I had to prevent a potential violent conflict in my restaurant. Can you understand that?'

'Yes, I can. But did you call security before you came out to confront the boys."

'I acted quickly and responsibly, so yes I called security from my office.'

'Did you demand the boys to leave when you personally dealt with them?'

'Yes, I wanted them to leave immediately before security came to remove them.'

'And, when they remained in their seats despite your insistence they leave, what happened next?'

'Security arrived on the scene and escorted the boys out of my restaurant.'

'Each of my clients insist that two of the restaurant patrons who were likely upset by the presence of the students, left their booths and grabbed Mr. Robinson and Mr. Walker by their shirt collars, hoisted them out of their seats, and forced them out of the restaurant along the security officers who were removing Mr. Wilson and Mr. Taylor in a similar manner. Is that an accurate description of what happened?'

'To my recollection, that sounds fairly close to what happened, but you must remember that Mr. Walker was resisting and screaming out.'

'Mr. Walker recalls saying that he had as much right to eat in your diner as anyone else. Does that account sound accurate?'

'He may have said something like that, but he was yelling.'

'Mr. Moore, do you condone a patron in your restaurant manhandling another customer and forcing him off the premises?'

'No, I don't unless that person is a police officer.'

'Were the two men who removed Mr. Robinson and Mr. Walker police officers?'

'They were loyal customers of our establishment."

'Were they police officers?'

'No, but they had both served in the United States military.'

'Being as neither of those gentlemen were police officers, did you make any attempt to stop them?'

'I felt the situation was under control.'

'Did you make an effort to stop those men from taking action against Mr. Robinson and Mr. Walker?'

'I felt they were instrumental in getting the disturbance under control.'

'Did you believe the security officers could have controlled the situation without the assistance of your customers?'

'I didn't consider that possibility because the officers together with my two white patrons were putting an end to the trouble.'

'Mr. Moore, do you believe that persons should be denied the right to be a customer at your restaurant because of the color of their skin?'

'I object to this line of questioning, your honor,' Mr. Willhite interjects. 'Mr. Moore's personal beliefs are not relevant to this case.'

'Objection sustained,' concurs Judge Gerhard.

'No further questions, your honor,' states a smiling Mr. Cole. Despite having his last question unanswered, he believes bringing the issue of racial discrimination into the trial was critical to be placed on record. Even though the final verdict in this case might not recognize the injustices endured by coloreds, Attorney Cole senses that the door to equality is being pushed in, if only a small crack.

The testimony of the restaurant patrons follows a similar pattern to the first two witnesses with differing views elicited by the attorneys. In their closing arguments, Mr. Willhite focuses on the audacity of the four students making a blatant violation of segregation laws. Mr. Cole makes the case they had the same rights as any other customer requesting service.

There is a short recess of 20 minutes. Then, the judge calls the parties back into the courtroom. When the entire room is seated, Judge Gerhard reads his decision.

'Based on the testimony presented in this case, evidence has been shown beyond a reasonable doubt that   violations of segregation laws were undeniably perpetrated by each of the defendants. Thereby, the four defendants are found guilty as charged. As a consequence, Mssrs. Robinson, Walker, Wilson and Taylor shall be confined to prison for a period of 45 days to include time already served and each shall pay a fine to the City of Decatur in the amount of $500. This court is adjourned.

James looks over at Attorney Cole and speaks his mind.

'Is that the best you could do? It's bad enough rotting in a cell for 45 days, but how are we supposed to come up with $500 each.

CHAPTER 17

'Hey Tom, are you going to the Pi Phi exchange dinner tonight?' asks John.

'Well, I sure don't have a hot date with a Kappa, do I?'

Tom has started his junior year at Georgia. He is disappointed at having one or two dates with a coed and not developing any long-term relationship. He decides to attend the dinner tonight, not expecting to score with some sexy sorority babe, but because he has nothing else planned.

Lambda Chi is hosting the dinner downstairs in their regular dining room. The décor has been improved somewhat by adding black tablecloths and a vase of flowers on each table. Before sitting down to dinner, the brothers dressed in suits and ties mingle with their female guests in the living room upstairs. Punch is offered out of a crystal bowl, sitting on table near the entry to the room with dozens of cut glass tumblers surrounding the vessel.

Pi Phi is considered a middle status sorority on campus with a few pretty girls, but they are more reputed for high academic performance and community service. The main reason for tonight's affair is two brothers who are dating Pi Phi sisters, one of those ladies being a representative on the Pan Hellenic Council.

Tom notices a cute, slim coed standing alone in the corner and decides to introduce himself.

'Welcome to Lambda Chi. My name is Tom, Tom Stirling. And you are?

'Nancy Gunn. Pleased to meet ya, Tom.'

'Say, can I get you a glass of punch?'

'That would be nahse. Thank you'

Tom returns with two glasses handing one to Nancy.

'Where are you from, Nancy?'

'A little town called Doerun.'

'Oh, I know that place. In fact, my daddy and uncle have gone bird hunting there a few times. I'm from Cordele, not too far from Doerun. Daddy has a peanut plantation.'

'Well, it's a small world. Mah daddy's a farmah too, he goes bird huntin' 'roun near owah home all the tahm.'

'I bet you're sick of eating quail, huh?'

'Oh, you know it. Ah bet my mama has cooked that bird every way imaginable; fried, roasted, grilled, baked, quail salad, quail casserole, stuffed quail, and even quail soup,' Nancy enumerates.

'What I hate most is chewing into one of those bird concoctions and biting on a shot pellet that didn't get cleaned out,' Tom relates. 'I broke a tooth once doing that.'

They both laugh.

'That's the worst, ain't it?' agrees Nancy. 'Ah loved growing up on a farm, and mah parents are great, but Ah sure don't want to spend the rest of mah life back thayah.'

'Neither do I. I'd like to give big city life a chance. Atlanta sounds like an exciting place to live. I can see myself being a successful businessman there with a big house in a suburb like Duluth.'

'Ah like that idea too,' concurs Nancy.

Tom has no expectations talking with Nancy. He just immediately feels comfortable with her. She has a pretty face with soft brown, wavy hair, but she's too skinny to get his libido worked up. They agree to sit together at dinner.

CHAPTER 18

Springtime comes alive on the Georgia campus. Tom and Nancy seem to belong together. She is somewhat frail of health suffering from Crohn's Disease requiring regular medical attention. Tom shows his softer side to her. When that debilitating condition flares up, he devotes himself to comforting her. He often sits by her bedside instead of attending fraternity social functions. She loves him to tell her stories. One in particular describes a visit by Big Brother John to Cordele for a weekend of hunting.

'John, you know, is a city boy from Atlanta. His father owns an insurance agency downtown on Peachtree. For fun, Mr. Baxter would take John and his two younger brothers to boxing matches in the city. If there was a white guy fighting a black guy, his father would stand up and yell insults at the negro. That's how John got his attitude toward coloreds.'

'Anyway, his daddy never took the boys out to the country. So, John knew nothing about hunting before the one time he came with me to Cordele. We outfitted him with a red cap, hunting vest and my granddaddy's ole side-by-side shotgun. Then, we headed out with Daddy, Uncle Leon and me to track down some ducks. I showed him some fundamentals about shooting, and he seemed to understand.'

'When we reached the marshland where the ducks were hiding in the reeds, Uncle Leon flushed a covey of fowl with his caller causing them to fly overhead. John stood straight up, twisted around crossing his legs to follow the birds and fired both barrels. The recoil from the gun sent him flying backwards into the wet marsh soaking him head to toe, and completely immersing the gun in water and muck. We had to stop the hunt, go back to the house, and get him into some dry clothes listening to him whining the whole way 'bout being cold and wet. Daddy spent a month cleaning that gun before it would fire again. I said to myself, "Never again. Let John stay up there in the big city where he belongs".'

Nancy loves these stories and begs Tom to tell her more. Stripling is the first male who shows understanding toward Nancy's down times, and she feels herself under the spell of his caring ways. For him, she is someone he has become closer to than any other person in his life. But, something is missing for Tom….sex. She doesn't believe in intimate relations before marriage.

Miles and Tom are no longer roommates in their junior year, but they are still brothers at the fraternity and see each other almost daily. Miles can sense Tom is sexually frustrated; the way he looks at the other brothers' dates, the comments he makes seeing an attractive coed walk by, and his increasing use of sexual innuendos in conversation. While they are sitting next to each other at dinner one evening, Miles makes a proposal.

'I'm taking Lucille to the beach this weekend over at Tybee Island. She's got a friend coming with us. If you're interested, you're welcome to join? Lucille tells me her friend is extra friendly, if you know what I mean?'

Tom thinks to himself for a second. *Man, I really need to get away. And, this sounds like fun.* He tells his buddy, 'Sure Miles, I could use a little diversion. Count me in.'

Tom feels guilty not being with Nancy on a late April weekend, but he convinces himself he needs a break from her for a couple of days when he can think about his own needs. He makes the excuse that Miles wants him to go so Tom can drive back to school as his friend plans to get wasted on cheap booze.

Driving down on a warm, sunny Saturday, Miles is at the wheel of his 1955 two-tone Desoto Firedome V-8 with his skanky date, Lucille by his side. Tom is relaxing in the back seat with Lucille's friend Doris. She has sidled up against Tom glancing flirtatiously into his eyes while placing her left hand on his right thigh.

Tom smiles at her with a knowing look. He has read this body language before, and there is no doubt in his mind where this new relationship is headed. He swallows his saliva in anticipation. Doris has one eye that wanders off chameleon-like, and her face is dominated by a broad flat nose. Tom looks past these unflattering features. He has much more interest in her large, pendulous breasts, clear tanned skin and toned, shapely legs. He begins breathing heavier just thinking about what will soon likely happen.

When he places his right hand on her left shoulder, she shifts her hand higher on his thigh. Stirling becomes immediately aroused, pulls Doris close to him kissing her first on the neck, then French kissing her mouth. She moves her hand directly over his stirred manhood and begins slowly rubbing rhythmically up and down.

'Do you have the right time, Tom?' Lucille blurts out unexpectedly from the front seat. 'I don't think my watch is right.'

The mood is broken in the back seat. Stirling separates himself from Doris, looks down at his watch, and replies.

'Ahhhh. I have 9:17.'

Tom still knows he has a hot weekend ahead. He is just going to have to wait a little longer.

'You must be thrilled, Nancy!' exclaims her sorority sister sitting to her left.

Nancy Gunn is seated in a wide circle inside the living room of her sorority house with all 40 of her sisters clad in white dresses surrounding her. She is wearing a necklace called a lavaliere composed of a sterling silver chain highlighted by a silver pendant hanging in front with the Greek letters lambda, chi and alpha embossed over it.

'Oh yayes', responds Nancy. 'This is the biggest day of mah life.'

Deep down, she is apprehensive. Tom has been wonderful to her, almost too wonderful. Then, there have been those gaps in time when he was gone for seemingly innocent reasons, but was he telling her the truth? She had been cruelly lied to by other boyfriends before.

Elizabeth Sorensen, the chapter president is grasping a brass holder decorated with a blue and silver ribbon. A long, white tapered candle is inserted into the holder. She removes a Bic lighter from her small black purse and lights the candle. The flickering wax symbol is raised up above her head as a signal for the entire gathering to begin singing, 'Ring Ching Ching', a Pi Phi national song. As they harmonize, the candle passes around the circle until it reaches Nancy. She continues passing it to Elizabeth and the singing continues until the object reaches Nancy a second time. At that point, she blows out the flame to the cheers of everyone.

The front door opens. In walks Tom dressed in a blue blazer emblazoned with the Lambda Chi Alpha cross and crescent over the left breast pocket. He smiles and nods to the ladies at each side of the room. He is allowed inside the circle by two of the sisters moving aside. Tom turns and faces Nancy. She looks up at him beaming with anticipation but shaking inside. She knows many of her sisters are envious of her caring relationship with Tom now culminating in this dramatic moment. He approaches her and lowers himself on one knee.

'Nancy Gunn, you are the light of my life, the hope for my future, and the love that nourishes my soul. I pray you accept this token of my devotion, the pin from my treasured brotherhood, Lambda Chi Alpha.'

Nancy is overcome with emotion hearing these words in the presence of all her sorority sisters. Her lips tremble. Her heart begins to thump rapidly against her chest. Sweat begins to form on her forehead, and she becomes uncomfortably hot over her entire body. Before she can respond to Tom's heartfelt plea, she feels herself losing control. She desperately attempts to fight that feeling and express to Tom how she feels the same way toward him. The occasion overwhelms her. She begins leaning to the right and abruptly faints into the arms of Elizabeth, her president and big sister.

'Oh, my God,' gasps one of the sisters. 'Is she all right?'

The sisters stand as one and move in closer to Nancy. Tom rises off his knee and takes control of the scene.

'Stand back! She needs air. Someone open the window over there.'

He lifts Nancy's body from Elizabeth and lowers her to the carpeting placing a pillow under her head and elevating her legs on a couple of nearby cushions. Her skin is pale and clammy. He looks intently into her face and surprisingly, she opens her eyes.

'I accept you into my heart, Tom,' she weakly whispers.

His expression changes from furrowed brow worry to a beaming, wide grin. The sisters scream with relief and support.

Two weeks later, Nancy is walking through campus on her way to class when she bumps into Miles.

'I guess I should congratulate you on your recent pinning, Nancy.'

'Thank you,' she replies. 'You know, Miles, Ah've been meaning to ask you a question.'

'Shoot,' he says.

'When you went down to Tybee Island with Tom, was thayah two girls goin'?'

'Well, since you weren't goin', I thought Tom needed some company so he wouldn't feel like a third wheel, you know.'

'And, did this person you call company get along with Tom?'

'Well yah, who wouldn't get along with Tom? He's such a nice guy.'

'Miles, I know somethin' that could get you in trouble if I squealed. You remember that night down at Georgia State where you messed up their mascot and a couple of colored fellahs? Tom told me about that. Did you know one of those coloreds you beat up was in a hospital for two years in a coma with a head trauma? In fact, the authorities down thayah still have a warrant for somebody's arrest.'

'You wouldn't do that, would you?'

'Not if you told me what happened with Tom that weekend. And, I'll know if your lying.'

'Well, when we got down there, we found a good spot on the beach kind of away from everyone else, put down our stuff and went swimming. That water was pretty cold, so we didn't swim too long, we played Frisbee on the beach.'

'What happened at night? Did y'all go to some motel?'

'No, we actually slept on the beach.'

'Ah'm not talking about sleepin'. I want to know if Tom had sex with that tramp.'

'Umm, you know, I was so busy with my girl, Lucille, I really don't know what Tom was doing with Doris.'

'You're lyin'! I know you're lyin'! I guess you want me to talk to the police down at Georgia State.'

'All right. All right. Tom had sex with Doris. Is that what you wanted to hear?'

Nancy sits down on a nearby bench, and starts to cry.

'It was no big deal,' reassures Miles. 'It was just a one night stand. They never saw each other again. You know, Nancy, you're just being a naïve, spoiled little princess. Every guy does that kind of stuff. He was only being red blooded Georgia boy. Get over it.'

Miles walks away, shaking his head. Nancy sits devastated, sobbing on the bench for the next half hour.

CHAPTER 19

'Whatever you do in life, strive to do it so well that no man living or dead, and no man yet to be born can do it any better.'

Dr. Benjamin Mays, president of Morehouse completes his commencement speech with that advice. The students and audience applaud loudly. His words reflect the sentiment of many of the family members attending as well as the graduating students.

The Dean of the Division of Humanities and Social Sciences follows Dr. Mays to the podium to award diplomas to students deserving of a Bachelor of Arts degree.

'Graduates, you may now place the hoods in your possession over your gowns with help from the fellow student standing next to you.'

He begins calling names in alphabetical order. The W's are near the end of the procession. After what seems like hours, James hears his name called.

'James Lincoln Walker, Cum Laude.'

Walker climbs the stairs of the temporary platform in his black cap and gown topped with a yellow tassel hanging from the right side of his mortarboard. He follows a queue of classmates accepting their diplomas from the Dean. As he reaches the end of the platform holding his treasured diploma, a smiling face greets him.

'Congratulations, Mr. Walker. We appreciate your dedication to equality,' compliments President Mays. James shakes hands with him, the last of the college dignitaries on the stage. The new grad smiles and nods in acknowledgement of that high praise.

He descends the stairs on the far side and returns to his place among the graduates. As the last of his classmates receive their diplomas, the Dean of Arts and Letters steps to the microphone.

'By the powers vested in me by the College Board of Trustees, I now declare each of you graduated from Morehouse College possessing all rights, privileges, and responsibilities accorded thereto. Gentlemen, you may turn your tassels. Congratulations, you are now Morehouse men.'

With that announcement, the graduates fling their mortarboard caps high into the air and scream with delight.

The recession ensues led by an African drum corps, followed by faculty then students. They proceed in ranks of two through an access road to the Westview Terrance gate before disassembling. James seeks out his friends; Tyus, Jerome, Herschel and several others he had befriended during his four turbulent years at college. They hug, wish one another good luck and promise to maintain their friendship in years to come.

Walker seeks out his family to continue celebrating the day. He finds them waving frantically at him from inside the convocation arena. Father Estes, Mother Hattie, and his three siblings are there along with Aunt Violet and Reverend Jones.

'Ah neva' thought you finish, son. Ah be proud o' ya,' his father declares beaming with a big smile revealing two missing front teeth. 'Now whatcha gonna do?'

'Well Daddy, that's a complicated question. I do have two interviews scheduled here in Atlanta, but I've got to worry about the military too.'

'James, I've made reservations for all of us at a restaurant near here,' interjects Auntie. "Let's go there, and we can talk in more comfortable surroundings.'

They walk several blocks to Mary Mac's Tea Room, reputed to serve the best Southern cooking in the city. The hostess shows them to a table for eight with Estes sitting at one end and Hattie at the other. His brother and sisters are in their late teens now. James can see the tired look in their faces seemingly resigned to a life of endless toil with little hope for the future. Aunt Violet can't stop smiling. James' graduation is a triumph for her. Reverend Jones is also delighted for the young graduate. He has seen a ten year old, lost and frightened boy mature into a confident young man ready to make his mark in the world.

'James, we are all proud of you,' Auntie gushes. 'You've learned what courage and perseverance does for a black man in the South. Here you are, a graduate of the most prestigious black college in the country.'

'Thank you, Auntie. I wouldn't be here today without your help.' The Morehouse man realizes the others surrounding him were also invaluable to his achievement. 'And, thanks to the rest of my family and Reverend Jones. I wouldn't be standing here today without your help either. I owe a debt of gratitude to each and every one of you.'

'James, look at you, speaking like a black Demosthenes,' comments Auntie.

They all laugh as his younger brother parrots James' remarks with an attempt at proper English. Then Jasper continues.

'How kind of ya, budder James, to compliment us wit' such humble words comin' out o' de mouf of someone who looks down on de rest o' his family.'

'Jasper, you could have chosen the same path as James,' counters Auntie. 'Jealousy and resentment will only make you a bitter person as you get older. So, get over it, and get on with your life.'

The atmosphere at the table is becoming testy. Reverend Jones stands to quell the ugliness in the air.

'I can see how the circumstances allowing James to reach the success he has attained today can seem unfair to you younger siblings. It's true that you all sacrificed so James could pursue his education. He knows that. I've had many conversations with him in the past, and I believe he will repay you many times over in the coming years. You might believe James saying that to you is just an empty promise, but I know the commitment to his family is heartfelt. He is a giving not a selfish person.'

The table goes quiet. The waitress comes to take their order. When the food arrives 15 minutes later, Estes makes a request.

'Revren' Jones, we would preshate you blessin' de food.'

'My pleasure, Estes.'

He pauses, clears his throat and gestures for the family to hold hands with the persons next to them.

'Whether everyone here today realizes it, this is a pivotal day in all the lives of the Walker family. What James has accomplished should be a example to everyone here. Think positive. Dream big. And, with god's blessing, good things will come to pass. May this food nourish our souls and provide us with the energy to rise above our differences. And, may the bond that holds us together at this moment through the holding of hands symbolize the love and support we have for one another. I ask this in Jesus' name. Amen.'

They pass around the bowls of fried chicken, mashed potatoes, collard greens, corn on the cob, corn bread and creamed spinach.

'Oh, my goodness. This chicken is better than mine, and mmmmm-mm, the creamed spinach is like something from heaven just like the Reverend here,' exclaims Auntie laughing.

'Now that youse graduated, son. I guess you be workin' somewayah, but what about the military? Is they gonna be comin' fo' ya?'

'Yes sir. My draft status is pretty high, so the Army will be looking for me as well as my classmates.'

'Can't you use your education to become an officer in the military?' Auntie asks.

'Yes ma'am. My counselor at Morehouse suggested I apply for Officer Training School in the Air Force. So, that's what I plan to do.'

'You know, James. I couldn't be no offica in the military like you,' reacts Jasper. 'If dey come fo' me, I be one o' dem grunts in de Army.'

'I understand that, my brother,' responds James. 'You could enlist in the Navy or Air Force. That way, you could choose to train for some specialized job. You might even get an education that will lead to a good civilian job when you get out. On top of that, you'll be eligible for education assistance with the GI bill after discharge.'

'Dat's all a bunch o' recruiter talk. They just gonna send you someplace where you get killed like dat Vietnam country.'

'I'm serious, Jasper. Take advantage of the military. That can lead you to a better future,' adds James.

'Jasper, I believe James is right,' agrees Auntie. 'The military could be a good opportunity for you.'

'We all knows James be youah favorite, Aunt Violet. Course youah gonna agree with him,' complains Jasper.

'Let's stop all this arguing,' the pastor interrupts. 'We're here to celebrate not berate one another. This is a time to bond together as a family at a joyous occasion.'

'Reverend's right,' adds Auntie. 'In fact, I just ordered a black bottom pie for dessert. Now isn't that something to put a smile on everybody's lips?' Their faces light up. 'Yes, I thought so.'

James can understand why Jasper is resentful of his situation. The world is opening up for him while his younger brother remains stuck in the cotton fields. He can also sense Jasper's antipathy toward Auntie. Why didn't she offer to help him with his schooling?'

'I plan to come home this summer and help with picking cotton,' James volunteers.

'You needs to be cayahful, son. Ah hear de Klan back home knows all about yowah demonstratin'. Dey be on de lookout fo' ya.'

'He's right, James,' agrees Reverend Jones. 'There were some rumors going around town after you were put in jail a second time that you were becoming like your cousin, Billy. You would be safer staying in Atlanta until you enter the Air Force.'

'Thank you for that warning, but it's a sad day when a person risks his life trying to return home.'

They finish their meal and depart. Young Walker is staying in town with a classmate at his family home. He has an interview at a black business tomorrow. The rest of the family piles into the reverend's 1953 black Buick Super for the ride back to Stillmore. Reverend Jones is driving with Auntie and Estes in the front seat while Hattie and the three grown children squeeze into the back.

'Thank you so much for everything,' says James. 'I love every one of you.'

CHAPTER 20

Ms. Gunn angrily strides up to the front entrance of the Lambda Chi house, jerks open the door and slams it shut without knocking or ringing the doorbell. Climbing the stairs to the second floor, she barges into Stirling's room. He is studying at his desk and quickly pivots around at this unexpected intrusion.

'Nancy, what a surprise. I had no idea you were coming to visit me. What's the occasion?'

'You sneaky, low life bastard. How dare you cheat on me right before declaring your devotion at the pinning ceremony!'

'Don't be mad, darlin'. I can explain.'

'Don't you darlin' me.' She holds out her pin, then rears back and throws it at him, stinging his chest.

'That's what I think of your phony promises of devotion.'

She turns and storms out of the room. He is flabbergasted. After recovering from the shock of the moment, Stirling chases after her.

'Wait, Nancy, come back!'

She stomps out the front of the building leaving her ex-boyfriend befuddled.

Stirling thinks to himself. *That backstabbing Trousdale must have told her about that little interlude with Doris. Damn him.*

Throughout the next month, Tom tries everything he can think of to win Nancy back. He sends her a dozen red roses, a box of her favorite chocolates, love notes, and romantic poetry. An invitation to attend a campus play is left in her mailbox. No reply. After three weeks, he decides to confront her directly after class. He corners her as she exits the building.

'Nancy, stop! We need to talk.' She begins to walk away, but he hovers alongside.

'We don't have anything to talk about. You betrayed me, and that ended our commitment to each other.'

'Oh come on, with everything we've shared in the last year and a half, you're going to kick me to the gutter for one little indiscretion?'

She stops and faces him.

'What I've learned about Tom Stirling is that I can't trust him. And, that was no little indiscretion. That was our relationship breaking into pieces.'

He continues to beseech her to come back to him, but she rushes at a fast pace, walking all the way to her sorority house. Upon reaching the Pi Phi entrance, she slams the door in his face.

A week later, he receives a phone call.

'Is this Tom Stirling?'

'Yes, who's calling?'

'I'm Carol, a sorority sister of Nancy. She's been pretty sick the last few days and told me she would like to see you. Could you come over?'

'Oh yes. I'll be right there.'

Stirling rushes over and is led to Nancy's room, finding her sitting up in bed.

'I can see that you don't feel so good, Miss Gunn. Maybe a story will cheer to up.'

'I do miss your stories, Tom.'

He spins a tale about a young woman and a young man from rural Georgia who fall in love. Then, an unfortunate incident occurs that drives them apart. Finally, after being separated for a time, they realize how much they need and love each other. They reunite and live happily ever after.

Nancy begins to cry. 'Ah hate to admit it, you dog. But, Ah really have missed you.'

'Does that mean we can get back together again?'

'Maybe. But only if you cross yooah heart and promise never to cheat on me again.'

'I so solemnly swear.' He pulls out a shiny object from his pocket. 'Will you take my pin back?"

'Du you still love me?'

'I never stopped."

'All right, Tom. Ah believe you, and yayes, Ah'll take your pin back.'

'Do you love me?'

'Ah do.'

CHAPTER 21

'You're gonna like my mama's cooking. But please don't talk about Daddy's farm.'

'Why not?'

'Papa's greatest hope when I was a boy, was to have me take over the plantation when he retired. So now that I've decided to become a white-collar businessman, I think he's disappointed in me.'

Tom and Nancy are driving over from Doerun to Cordele for her first meeting with his parents. They both have recently graduated from Georgia, but she was unable to attend the ceremony due to a flare up of her Crohn's Disease. They pull up into the driveway and enter the foyer. Tom Senior and Myrna are there to greet them.

'Mama, Papa, I'd like you to meet Nancy Gunn from Doerun.'

Having been informed about his steady girlfriend, Myrna insisted Tom invite Nancy over for dinner this summer. Tom agreed but warned his mama not to prepare a meal that included quail. Myrna decides on broiled trout.

'Well, don't you look lovely, Nancy,' Myrna exclaims. 'I love youah drayess. Welcome to owah home.'

'Thank you, Mr. and Mrs. Stirlin'. Pleased to meet you both.'

'I'll get drinks for everybody,' TJ says. 'Gin and tonic okay? I'll get you an apple juice, Nancy.'

They enter the cooler living room where a window air conditioning unit is humming in a low register.

'Nancy, have a seat over thayah on the love seat,' directs Myrna. 'Tom, offer her some peanuts.'

'Mama, Nancy can't eat any kind of nuts.'

'You have a raht nahse home here, Mr. and Mrs. Stirlin',' remarks Nancy as TJ hands her a drink.

'Why thank you, Nancy,' Myrna replies. 'But tell us about yourself.'

Nancy describes her upbringing in Doerun, her fight with Crohn's Disease, and how she met Tom. Big Tom and Myrna become impressed how their son has been so sensitive to Nancy during her serious health setbacks.

'That's a side of our boy we didn't know about before,' offers Mr. Stirling. 'You've done right by Nancy here, son.'

The young couple glance at each other, she with a furrowed brow and him with a nervous smile, each recalling Tom's indiscretion.

Myrna withdraws to the kitchen to put the final touches on dinner. She returns minutes later.

'"Y'all come on into the dining room. Food is on the table.'

They saunter in with TJ leading the way. Myrna directs each one to her predetermined seat assignments having Tom next to Nancy.

'There's a knock on the side door.

'I'll get it,' offers TJ.

He opens the door surprised to see Rastus dressed in bib overalls with his hands covered in white dust.

'What the hell are you doing here?'

'Sorry to bother ya, Tom. Please tell Mr. Stirlin' Ah brought the lime fertilizer from the stowah and stacked the bags in the shed. 'Y'all have a good evenin'.'

Young Tom nods his head, closes the door and returns to the dinner table.

'Papa, I didn't know you had Rastus working for you.'

'Yes, son, he started coming over to help Abner a couple of years ago. He's doing all right.'

'Be careful, Daddy. That boy's a trouble maker.'

'He's been a good field hand, son.'

'I'd keep a close eye on him. He can be an uppity colored.'

Big Tom serves up the fish from the platter while the others pass around the mashed potatoes, green beans, corn on the cob, and gravy.

'Delicious, Mrs. Stirlin',' compliments Nancy. 'My mama never cooks fish at home like this. It's so flaky and flavaful.'

The women prattle on about the food for a while. Then Father Stirling changes the subject.

'Tom, have you ever thought about military service. Leon and I were both in the Army before World War II. My daddy was running the farm back then, but he took sick shortly after I was discharged, and I've been the head farmer around here ever since.'

'Well, Daddy, I wouldn't want to join the military so you would get sick and force me to run the farm. But yes, I'm seriously considering joining the Air Force before the Army gets me like they got you.'

'How long would you be gone?' Nancy asks.

'When you volunteer, they got you for four long years,' TJ answers.

'That's a long tahm for a girl to wait for a fellah,' remarks Myrna.

'Yes, it is,' agrees Nancy glaring intently at Tom and poking him in the ribs.

'The fact is, one way or another, you're gonna be in uniform whether you volunteer or get drafted,' notes Papa.

'I know that, Daddy. The only way out would be if I was 4F or married with kids.'

Tom glances over at Nancy. He has gotten hints before. She doesn't want to wait around too long with no promise of getting married. That harsh look in her eyes tells him he'd better get her an engagement ring real soon.

An idea strikes him. He excuses himself from the dinner table and sneaks into the living room where Big Tom keeps a silver humidor full of Cuban cigars. He slips the band off one of them, puts it in his right pants pocket and returns to the dinner table.

As they finish eating their main course, TJ makes a suggestion.

"Mama, could we have dessert served in the living room?'

'Certainly dear. It'll take me a few minutes to get it ready. Y'all go in there and relax.'

A short time later, they are all seated comfortably finishing their homemade blackberry cobbler and ice cream, when Tom stands and makes an announcement.

'I've got something important to say.'

The others give a perplexed look at one another to see if they were the only one who didn't know what Tom was up to. TJ steps in front of Nancy and gets down on one knee.

'Nancy, you are the love of my life and you complete me. Will you marry me?'

She looks stunned. Yes, she wants to become engaged to Tom. He has been a true companion to her like no other man had before. She has forgiven his sexual transgression, at least the one she knew about, and some level of trust has been restored. Nancy has expected Tom to propose to her, just not in his parent's living room, but she can't refuse him in front of his mother and father. And, she can't ask him to propose somewhere else a little more romantic. There is only one answer she can give.

'Yes Tom, I will marry you.'

'Congratulations,' says Papa.

'That's wonderful,' gushes Myrna.

'Hold out your left hand,' commands Tom. He reaches in his pants pocket and pulls out the crumpled paper band from the cigar.

He slides the brown band with gold printing depicting a tobacco leaf and the lettering, 'Hecho i Cuba' onto her left ring finger.

'This is only symbolic. We can go together and pick out a diamond one real soon.'

'You betta get me a nice ring, Tom. This one's a little insultin',' she replies with a smile and a twinkle in her eye.

He smiles back and gives her a short peck on the lips.

CHAPTER 22

Suspense hangs over Walker's head in the summer of 1963. He has already seen several of his Morehouse classmates called into active military service. Unless he is accepted into the Air Force officer training program, he will likely be inducted into the Army as an enlisted man.

James interviews for two different civilian jobs that first week after graduation. One is a sales position for hair products used in negro barbershops and beauty salons. The other is a management position for a negro owned, city-wide trash collection company in Atlanta. Both firms agree to place his application on file and invite him to interview again after fulfilling his military obligation.

He spends the summer working at the Morehouse College bookstore, stocking shelves and working the cash register. It's a waiting game. Will he be accepted into officer training before getting that dreaded invitation from the Army? In late August, he receives a letter in the mail from the United States Air Force. He opens it with trepidation.

"Congratulations, Mr. Walker. You have been accepted into the United States Air Force Officer Training Program. You are to report for duty beginning 20 December. 1963. He smiles and breathes a sigh of relief.

The months pass quickly, and in late December, he boards a C-97 military plane out of Atlanta's Hartsfield Airport bound for Kelly Air Force Base (AFB) in San Antonio, Texas. The aircraft is crowded with recruits like himself. While maneuvering his way through the tangle of young men to take a free seat, he accidentally bumps into a fellow recruit who happens to be white.

'Watch where you're going, boy,' says the affronted person.

'Didn't mean to offend you,' Walker responds. 'Remember, we're both on the same team now.' The light skinned man glares at him.

James muses to himself. *Another white guy who thinks he's superior.*

Upon arrival, an Air Force bus picks them up and drives to Lackland AFB where Walker is to begin twelve weeks of officer training. He is directed to take a second bus which drops him at the base barbershop for a depersonalizing haircut. Next, he is taken to a warehouse building where a heap of GI clothing is doled out; dress blues with accompanying oxford blue dress shirt and dark blue tie, dress hat, 505 khaki uniform, officer cap, fatigue uniform, epaulets, metal uniform insignia, raincoat, field jacket, pair of brogans, pair of dress shoes, blue web roll belt with silver buckle, white boxer shorts, white tee shirts, black socks, jock strap, blue exercise shorts and a duffle bag.

Finally, settling into their barracks, the new recruits are kept awake for over 24 hours, exposed to a long list of military protocols and expectations. OT Captain Smithers, is the upper classman trainer for Walker's barracks. He stands in front of Walker while the new recruit attempts to make his bed military style.

'Move outta the way, Walker. Let's see if you've learned anything yet.'

He drops a quarter on the middle of the bed. It lands with a thud remaining imbedded in the blanket.

'You're a piece of work, Walker. You don't know how to make a bed. You got 'woolies' crawling out of your uniform buttonholes, and you put your clothes away in the closet like you were late for a hot date. Let me advise you, officer trainee, your only date for the next six weeks is me. And, if you want me to stop nagging you like some bitch on the rag, you had better shape up. Do you understand me?'

'Yes sir.'

Smithers takes a special interest in Walker over the following six weeks. He singles him out and drills him relentlessly with marching maneuvers in front of the barracks. In rapid succession, he barks out commands.

'Tench hut, foh-ward harch, right oblique harch, left oblique harch, company halt, habout hace, pah-rade hest, tench hut. All right Walker, I want you to march in place and, at the top of your lungs, start singing the Group Two song from start to finish.'

'Hey, look me over, lend me your eyes, we're proud of Group Two and here's the reason why....'

'You screwed up that last line, sing it again.'

During his time as an underclassman, Walker is regularly harassed by Smithers in an attempt to break him. James, however, is even more determined; not only to survive, but to excel. When the first half of OTS is completed, Walker has become an expert drill instructor. His shoes are the shiniest and his uniform the most perfect. And, when Smithers drops a quarter on Walker's bed, he could catch it in his teeth because it bounces so high.

During the second six weeks, James has been selected as trainer for the underclassmen taking Smithers' place. In a turnabout of social justice, he is commanding a group composed entirely of Caucasian troops. He fully understands the irony of his position and debates with himself how to employ his newfound powers. The underclassmen are gathered together on their first day, surrounding James. He lets them know what to expect.

'We are all training here to be warriors, ready to defend this country. My job is to prepare you to be tough, disciplined and able to support one another in difficult and possibly life-threatening circumstances. Know that what you may feel is unnecessarily demanding, is meant to shape you into Air Force officers capable of fulfilling any mission you are called upon to perform. And, to that end, I promise to be fair in this process to each and every one of you.'

The looks on the underclassmen range from accepting to defiant. A week later, one of the insolent troops challenges his authority.   Walker is redressing him for failing a white glove inspection.

'Dust on the windowsill, Jacobsen.   That warrants a demerit.'

'I bet I can get more dirt than that just from wiping your face, OT Captain Walker.'

'That disrespectful comment will cost you two additional demerits.'

'You think you're King Shit around here.   Don't you, sir?'

'Two more demerits, Jacobsen.   And, I advise you to hold your tongue.'

'You're on some kind of power trip, aren't you, Walker,'

'That's it.   You are confined to barracks for the next 24 hours.'

Word spread quickly among the underclassmen.   You don't mess with OT Captain Walker.   His remaining time as the trainer for his troops is uneventful.   For the record, Jacobsen is later discharged from the Air Force without completing his training at Lackland.

After 12 weeks, James receives his gold bars and his commission as a second lieutenant.   He is assigned to Keesler AFB in Biloxi, Mississippi for an additional 10 months of training as a communications electronics specialist.

CHAPTER 23

Tom devotes most of the summer of 1963 to Nancy. He does buy her that diamond ring at Reeds Jewelers in Albany.

'Mama, look at the engagement rahng Tom bought for me. Isn't it the most beautiful thang you've evah seen? One carat, princess cut and flawless.'

'Yayass, it's lovely, deeah.'

'Ah can't wait to show it to all mah frayends.'

Stirling stands next to her smiling. He loves seeing her happy.'

That July and August, they go waterskiing at Lake Blackshear almost every weekend, picnic with their friends and family, and see all the latest picture shows.

When the two are alone, they coo, cuddle and kiss, but no sex.

'Stop! That's as far as you go, Tom. Ah want our weddin' night to be special.'

Near the end of August, Tom receives a letter from the United States Air Force. He tears open the letter with anticipation and scans down the page to see if he's been accepted.

'Congratulations. You have been selected to join the Officers Training Program at Lackland Air Force Base. You will begin your tour of duty on 20 December 1963.'

'Look Daddy. I'm going to be an officer in the Air Force.'

'Good for you, son. That's great. But, what are you going to do with yourself between now and the end of December? You've been lazing around all summer. Time for you to do something useful.'

His father knows the postmaster at the local post office and cajoles him into hiring his son for the remaining months before joining the service.

The Stirlings celebrate Christmas early this year as Tom is leaving for San Antonio before the holidays. Myrna invites all their relatives within thirty miles over to the house on the Saturday before he departs. Most show up with some gift for Tom to take with him; a hand knitted scarf, Kiwi brand black shoe polish, a Dopp kit filled with toiletry items. Uncle Leon presents him with a jar of 5-day deodorant pads to give his shoes that mirror-like shine. Some gifts are generous but wholly impractical for him to take into basic training. Grandma Stirling crochets him a six-foot by four-foot Afghan spread in the red and black Georgia Bulldog colors. That item stays home folded neatly at the bottom of Tom's bed.

Big Tom and Myrna drive TJ to Hartsfield Airport with his mother double checking with him to be sure he has everything the military requires as well as all those 'must have' items given by his relatives.

'Son, Ah want you to write me every week youah gone,' says his tearful mother.

'TJ, make friends with the leaders of your unit. And, whatever you do, don't get in with the gambling crowd,' advises his father.

They both give him big hugs as they hear over the loud speaker, the plane is ready to board.

He climbs up the portable stairs rolled in place for the C-97 military transport plane. Inside, the aircraft seems to be half full of colored enlistees much to Tom's surprise. As he take his place next to a fellow white recruit, a colored youngster bumps into him.

'Watch where you're going, boy,' Tom snarls.

'Didn't mean to offend you,' the young man replies. 'Remember we're both on the same team now.'

Tom thinks to himself. *Another uppity nigger. How much of that stuff am I going to put up with?*

At Kelly Air Force Base, all the passengers are herded into two awaiting USAF buses and driven to Lackland. That same negro sits across the aisle from Tom again. When they reach the officer training section of the base, a captain riding in the front of the bus stands and reads off a list of names alphabetically.

'When I call your name, grab all your belongings and fall out.'

The officer gets to the S's and the name Stirling is not called. Not only that, there are only four recruits left on the bus, and one of them is that same negro.

Oh, my God, that colored could end up being my roommate. Stirling reasons to himself. *Grandpa will roll over in his grave if that happens.*

The captain calls the next name. 'James Walker, get your things. The rest of you are assigned to the Medina Annex. That's a couple of miles from here.'

Tom breathes a sigh of relief. At least he'll probably have a white roommate. The bus drives on for ten more minutes and enters the gates at Medina. Stirling exits the bus and enters the arena of military training.

He is rounded up with the rest of his class from the second bus and taken to the annex barbershop where his long, slicked back hair is quickly transformed into a military flat top with a few strokes of electric clippers. Next, the group is bussed to a warehouse where GI clothing is issued. He receives the full complement of clothing and insignia that he will wear over the next twelve weeks.

OT Captain Malm greets the new class in the barracks meeting room with a mixture of upbeat enthusiasm and perfectionistic expectations. He is a stickler for detail. The correct donning of the Air Force uniform is of utmost importance to him.

'The placket edge on your shirt should line up exactly with the zipper cover on your pants and the silver belt buckle is set precisely over the center of that line.'

He continues. 'I expect to see the reflection of my face in your shoes, and I don't ever want to see a rooster tail in your flight cap.'

He demonstrates the dreaded 'rooster tail'.

'The military salute must look like this.' He snaps his right arm into the desired position.

'Upper arm parallel to the ground, fingers fully extended and touching the bill of your cap. All right, line up at attention and give me a salute exactly as I showed you.'

Malm confronts each airman and makes corrections. When he approaches Stirling, no changes are needed. He calls him out to stand before the others.

'OT Stirling is performing as I requested. I look forward to all of you doing likewise by tomorrow when we start military drills in earnest. You should also be aware, when you approach an Air Force member of superior rank, you salute that officer first. Do I make myself clear?'

'Yes sir,' they shout in unison.

Tom has always been fastidious with his clothes and keeps his room neat and uncluttered. He adapts to Malm's demands easily. He also realizes that doing precisely what his trainer or any other upperclassman demands leads to preferential treatment.

Despite his reputation as a 'kiss ass' trainee by his fellow barracks mates during the underclassman period, Tom is promoted to OT Major for the final six weeks. He has been touted as a superior underclassman by Malm and other high ranking upper classmen concur. His charge will be training the entire corps of trainees at Medina for the final graduation parade.

He gains a reputation for being relentless, demanding precision for each and every drill command. At the final parade, presented before the base commander, a contest for the best marching group is won by OT Major Stirling and the Group One Medina Marines. Afterwards, several of the trainees express their thanks to Stirling. Group One will now have a yellow streamer attached to their blue marching flag signifying winner of the commander's competition.

At graduation, Tom receives his second lieutenant bars and his next assignment. He is ordered to attend training at Keesler AFB in Mississippi for communications electronics. That pleases him as he will now be able to make a five-hour drive back home to Georgia on long weekends to see Nancy and his family.

CHAPTER 24

Tom is milling around his newly assigned classroom at the Keesler AFB Annex introducing himself to new classmates before the start of the communications electronics orientation session. He is chatting with Purdue graduate, Phil Tribbett when a lone negro student enters the room.

Tom nudges Phil, 'Guess they'll let anyone be an Air Force officer nowadays.'

Tribbett just smiles.

The orientation officer calls out to the students in the room.

'Would everyone please take a seat?' He pauses while everyone settles into his place. 'Before I get into a review of the course material and our expectations of you over the next 40 weeks, I would like each person to introduce himself giving your name, where you come from, and which college you attended.'

The students are called alphabetically. Finally, Tom's name is called. He rises from his chair.

'I'm Tom Stirling from Cordele, Georgia, watermelon capital of the world and home to my daddy's peanut plantation. I graduated from University of Georgia and proud to be a rabid Bulldog fan.'

There's a mixture of cheers and boos from the class.

Two more names are called. Finally, the last student is asked to introduce himself.

'James Walker.'

Walker stands from the back of the room smiling confidently.

'Good morning, my name is James Walker from Stillmore, Georgia. I grew up near a cotton plantation where my family worked as sharecroppers. Graduated from Morehouse College in Atlanta. I'm looking forward to the challenge here and getting to know all my classmates.'

Tom turns to Phil, who is sitting next to him in the middle of the room.

'You know that guy looks familiar, but then all those coloreds seem to look alike. I bet that boy doesn't make it past the first exam in this course.'

'I'm not so sure,' Phil replies. 'He must have some smarts or they wouldn't let him in here.'

'Hah. You'll see,' assures Stirling.

James is glad to see three Vietnamese officers as members of the class. Since he is the only negro, at least there are other students of color to blend in with the twenty Caucasians.

With introductions completed, the orientation officer drones on about the upcoming class schedule and the course grades that students are required to maintain. A civilian tutor is available for students having difficulty with their studies.

As the orientation ends, Tom can't resist questioning James' qualifications for this training. He approaches and taps him on the shoulder.

'Say there, Walker, isn't it?' James nods.

'Glad to meet a fellow Georgian. Did you study electronics at that negro college you attended?'

'No, I studied marketing and business administration, but when I took the Air Force aptitude test, I scored a 99 percentile in electronics.'

'Very impressive, I expect you'll be at the top of our class then,' Tom replies, tongue in cheek. He is positive Walker is either lying or cheated on the test.

'Oh, I doubt that,' replies James. 'There's a lot of bright officers taking this course. By the way, you look familiar, Lieutenant Stirling. Have we met before?'

'Oh, I think I would have remembered that. You're likely confusing me with someone else.'

At that moment, a revelation strikes both men as each recall the less than friendly encounter on the flight to San Antonio several months before. James considers bringing up the incident but decides against the idea.

'You're probably right. Well, see you in class tomorrow,' says James.

Tom meets two of his classmates, Phil Tribbett and Duane Kallo for breakfast the next day. They get together at Dinah's Diner off Route 90 between the main base at Keesler and the Annex.

'Youah table is ready, y'all,' the hostess announces.

As they sit waiting to order, there, in front of each of them is a paper placemat depicting the major battles of the Civil War. Tom is irritated by this reminder that the South had been defeated in that conflict. He takes his fork from the table setting and obliterates Sherman's March-to-the-Sea by scouring it back and forth.

'I hear they have great grits here. Don't care much for their placemats though,' states Tom half joking. Phil and Duane, surprised by Tom's outburst, glance at one another with puzzled looks. But, as Yankees from north of the Mason-Dixon Line, they refrain from comment.

When the waitress brings their orders: coffee, fried eggs, grits, biscuits and gravy, Tom changes the subject.

'Yesterday, I looked at a big house in Gulfport where the widow who owns the place has three bedrooms for rent in a nice white neighborhood. I don't know about you two, but I hate living in base housing. Too much like the barracks back at OTS. Would either of you be interested in joining me? That way we could make a deal to reduce the rent.'

'Sounds like a good idea to me, Tom,' say Phil. 'I'd like to take a look at the place first.'

'I'm okay staying on base right now,' replies Duane. 'I'm trying to save money to pay back my college debt. But, I might be interested later.'

Barracks life cramps Tom's style. He likes to get out on the town and have some fun. He can tell Tribbett is on the same wavelength.

Tom and Phil move into the Gulfport house by the end of their second week in Mississippi. Later, when a third student from their class joins them, taking the third available bedroom, Mrs. Pernice, the owner, reduces Tom's rent by $5 a month. Combining that savings with his income as a new second lieutenant, Stirling splurges buying a brand new yellow Chevy Impala SS with the 409 engine and factory air conditioning. He knows the young ladies will be looking when he drives through town.

'I'm handing back your exams for the first test on electric circuitry,' Mr. Schnagel, the instructor announces. 'If you scored below 75%, you will need to take a make-up test. Congratulations goes to Mr. Walker who attained the highest grade in the class.'

Tom has a stunned look on his face. He is handed his test shortly thereafter. 90% is written in large red numbers at the top of his paper. That makes him feel a little better.

Phil elbows him in the side. 'Hey, you did well, but I guess it will be the second test before they drum Walker out of this program,' he comments facetiously.

Tom isn't about to accept that Walker received the highest grade legitimately. He confronts him after class.

'Walker, wait up,' calls out Tom as the group leaves after the lecture. James turns around near the classroom door and sees Stirling walking towards him.

'Hey, you did great on that test,' Tom comments. 'Congratulations. Now, tell me, how did you do that?' Did you get a copy of the exam before?'

'Stirling, you insult me,' answers Walker.

'Didn't mean to upset you,' counters Tom. 'I was just a little surprised that a colored boy educated at a colored school could do better than a guy like Jim here, who went to Purdue, a prestigious white university.'

'I probably put in more time studying my notes,' explains Walker smiling.

CHAPTER 25

James lives on base for the first six weeks of school. During that time, he finds his way to the First Missionary Baptist Church in downtown Biloxi where he meets Reverend Theodore Washington. Coincidentally, Pastor Washington knows Reverend Jones. They had befriended one another at a summer conclave for the Southern Christian Leadership Conference two years before and have kept in touch by letter.

The Biloxi preacher takes a liking to James introducing him to several church members including attractive young ladies. One of these women, LaShawndra 'Peaches' LaFitte, approaches him after church one Sunday.

'Lieutenant Walker, my friends and I would like to invite you to a little party we're having over at my house this Saturday night. We sure would appreciate it if you would come.'

Peaches is an attractive lady of color sporting straight hair with streaks of blond. She also is wearing a tight dress that leaves little to a man's imagination.

'I'd be delighted, Peaches. Tell me what I can bring.'

'Just your handsome self, James. Here's the directions.' She hands him a folded note with the address and time of the party, squeezing his hand in the process further arousing his curiosity.

'Now, don't be late,' she teases.

As he walks away toward his car, he opens the note. '321 Delauney Street,

Biloxi, telephone: (228) 492-8711. 8:00 p.m. Saturday nite. Be ready to party and bring some protection.'

Walker thinks to himself. *Protection? Does she mean like a gun or a bodyguard?....Oh, stupid, I know what she's saying.*

James arrives at Peaches' home a few minutes after eight o'clock. He doesn't want to seem too anxious. As he gets out of his car parked in front, he can hear blues music wafting out the open window of the living room. He straightens his blue dashiki shirt and checks the fly on his khaki pants before ringing the doorbell. Two packages of protection have been slipped into his wallet back at his room.

The smiling face of Peaches appears in the doorway. He looks down at the white bandeau top she's wearing revealing the deep cleavage between her ample bosoms. Glancing further down, he sees her hard, flat midriff exposed, and a short, magenta colored, flower print skirt. James starts breathing a little heavier, and a band of sweat begins to form on his forehead.

'Welcome James. Please come in. There's several people I want you to meet.'

He follows Ms. LaFitte into the living room where guests are engaged in animated conversation. A few of them he recognizes from church. Peaches introduces the rest, but she doesn't let him out of her sight.

'Would you like a drink, James?' she asks.

'Whatever you got,' he replies.

'C'mon in the kitchen. I'll fix you a rum and coke.'

'I can make it,' James counters. 'Let me make you one too.'

Peaches smiles and observes James dropping two ice cubes from a chilled silver bucket into two glasses, pour in a jigger of Bacardi's white rum and fill the glasses with Coca Cola.

'Here you go,' he says handing one drink to her.

They each take a sip with Peaches not taking her eyes off James.

'That's a good drink, James Walker,' she comments. 'I can see you know how to take care of a woman.'

With that remark, she closes in on him pulling his head toward her by grasping his neck and plants a wet French kiss in his mouth.

'Wow,' reacts Walker. 'You sure know the meaning of Southern hospitality.'

They go back into the living room where everyone is standing around. Peaches turns the dial on the radio to a slow music station.

'Lieutenant Walker, would you dance with me?' Ms. LaFitte asks.

'How could I refuse the most beautiful girl in the room,' he replies.

They dance for one song as the only couple moving to the music.

'It's too early in the evening for this slow stuff,' notes one male guest. 'Let's liven up this place.'

He turns the dial to a local rock and roll station ramping up the volume and the mood is transformed.

'Do you know how to fast dance, James?'

'No, but I'm willing to learn if you'll teach me.'

Walker isn't about to say no to Miss LaFitte and mess up any chances for late night romance. He wants to impress her how fast he can learn, but instead, he pulls and pushes her out of sync with the music nearly dislocating her shoulders.

'How'm I doin', yells James over the loud music.

'Well, you need to change a couple of things. First, try to move in time with the music. Feel that beat. Then, remember, we're supposed to move together on the dance floor. You're not trying to beat me in a wrestling match. Try again. This time let me lead.'

Walker is slowly getting it. Peaches nods every time he moves the right way and busts out laughing when he doesn't. There are ten people in that room trying to impress the others with their dance moves. The hot, humid summer weather has sweat soaking their clothing. The rum, whiskey and beer are being quickly consumed. The conversations become louder and the dancing more furious until around eleven o'clock there's a knock at the front door.

Peaches opens it. Standing in the entrance is a tall, overweight white Biloxi police officer glowering down at her.

'May I speak to the owner of the house?' he sternly asks.

'I am the owner, officer. What's wrong?'

'Your neighbor called in a complaint about excessive noise. And, walking up to your house, I don't understand why the whole neighborhood doesn't make the same complaint. If you don't tone down this racket, I'm going to cite you for disturbing the peace.'

'Sorry for the trouble, officer. I'll quiet things down.'

She closes the door after he leaves and retreats back to his cruiser. Peaches returns to her guests and explains the reason for the lawman's visit. The radio station is changed and the volume lowered.

'That's bullshit,' one of the male guests complains. 'Let's wait 'til the cop drives away, then we can get back to real dancin'.'

They listen for the officer's car to drive away then time five minutes on the clock.

'Okay, you can change back to the rock and roll station,' announces Peaches. 'But, keep the volume down. And, somebody close that front window.'

After one raucous song, another knock sounds at the front door. The same officer reappears. He had driven around the block and parked in the same space across the street. Walker answers the door this time.

'Okay folks, party's over,' he declares. 'Where's that lady homeowner? I'm taking her down to the station to issue a citation.'

'Officer, we're sorry that things got a little out of control here, but Miss LaFitte has no record with the police, and you can see that the guests are getting ready to leave. How about I give you 25 dollars and you forget about that disturbing the peace citation?'

'Finally, someone here is talking some sense,' the policeman replies in a low voice. 'By the way, how did that young lady become the owner of this place?'

James pulls out his wallet and removes a twenty and a five.

'She inherited it when her grandmother died. Here you go officer, and thanks for understanding our situation.'

'I'm glad we see eye to eye. By the way, you dropped something on the floor you might need a little later.

Walker looks down at the floor and sees one of the condoms had accidentally fallen out of his wallet.

Meanwhile, Peaches notifies her guests that the party is over. They gather their belongings and leave shortly after the officer.

'James, you are my hero now. How did you get that cop to drop the charges?' the lady of the house inquires.

'Peaches, I've met a few policemen in my time. Learned how to speak their language.'

'Well James, you realize we're the only two people left in this big house. Now, you're not gonna leave me all alone tonight, are you?

James knows this is his moment. He picks up his new girlfriend in his arms and carries her into the bedroom. That night James finds use for both his protection devices. He also discovers Peaches had more of those security items in the nightstand next to her bed. He awakes late the next morning exhausted with a big smile on his face.

Peaches enters the room all dressed in her Sunday best. He looks confused.

'You stay here and rest up. I'm going to church to atone for both our sins. When I get back, we'll start on some new ones that we can worry about praying for next Sunday.'

She puts her fingers to her lips, then reaches over and touches James on his. As she turns to leave, he collapses back into the featherbed feeling the morning heat building through the bedroom window. He likes this new town of Biloxi.

CHAPTER 26

During the long 4th of July weekend, James decides to drive back to Stillmore and spend the holidays with his family. He leaves Biloxi on a Friday afternoon after class. Traveling along US Route 90 toward Tallahassee, he remembers the warnings given him by his father and Reverend Jones regarding the hometown Klan and wonders if his return is a good idea. He turns northeast on US 84 out of Valdosta hitting US 1 in Waycross. Ninety more miles heading north takes him close to Stillmore.

The house is dark when he arrives home long after midnight. A bare light bulb outside the front door has been left lit for James as the rest of the family has gone to bed. James finds a blanket and settles down for the night on the living room sofa. The next morning finds someone tickling his feet.

'Leave me alone,' he moans. 'I need more sleep.'

'Time to rise and shine, nephew.'

'Auntie,' he bolts up to a sitting position. 'I didn't know you were going to be here this weekend. Nice to hear your voice.'

Looking around, James can see his parents and two sisters are already dressed and helping to prepare the morning breakfast.

'Guess everybody else is up, so I better get ready, I suppose. Where's Jasper?'

'That's why I'm here, nephew. Your brother got drafted into the Army.

He's at Fort Dix, New Jersey. I'm staying in his room for the weekend.'

'Papa, Mama, how come I didn't know Jasper went into the Army?'

'Ah believe Reverend Jones was goin' to write ya, JDubya,' says Papa Walker. 'Guess he didn't get roun' to it yet. Yoouah brotha' left little ova a week ago. Oh, and by the way, real good to see ya made it home, son.'

Violet stays home with Hattie while the others go pick cotton in the morning. Coming back for lunch hot and sweaty, Estes and his children cool down with some fresh squeezed lemonade.

'Sure hope we don't have to go out there again this afternoon,' James pleads. 'I'm not used to working outdoors in this heat.'

'No, son, we is gonna head into town dis afternoon and buy some grub fo' de weekend.'

'I'm buying,' JDubya says.

'Don't think we don't preshate yoowah sendin' money to us'n,' Estes comments. 'We does.'

'Papa, that's the least I can do.'

After lunch, they all climb into the Nash Rambler and ride down to the grocery store near the edge of downtown.

Auntie has written a grocery list of the food needed for the weekend meals including the Independence Day celebration. James pushes the shopping cart while Violet ticks off with a pencil each item placed in the basket. Five pounds of unbleached flour, check; five pounds of cane sugar, check; baking powder, check; corn starch, check; two pounds of butter, check; two dozen eggs, check; one package of Baker's chocolate, check; one box Bisquick, check; one large watermelon, check; two pounds of collard greens, check, two gallons of lemonade, check.

Auntie is directing Hattie and the two girls, sending them off to retrieve each item as she calls it out.

'Auntie, don't forget the most important thing,' nephew reminds her. 'The meat. I've got enough cash for some big cuts of beef and a couple of whole chickens. We can barbecue on Daddy's outside pit.'

'That'll be perfect,' she replies. 'I invited Reverend Jones over to dinner this evening. We're going to need to prepare that meat too.'

'Yes ma'am, I'm going with Papa right now to get the ingredients we need to make his famous barbecue sauce.'

When the Walker family completes finding all the items on Auntie's list, the basket is piled high above the sides. As they are checking out with the cashier, a suspicious male customer with a thin mustache intently watches their movements from an aisle opening several feet away. Estes notices him but says nothing until they're back in the car driving home.

'Did you see dat man lookin' at us near de checkout counter?'

'Who was that, Daddy?'

'He be one o' de Klan. So, son, you stay close to de house 'til you gotsta leave.'

'Thanks for the warning, Papa.'

The sweet smell of grilling meat daubed over and over with a stringed mop soaked in a rich, pungent concoction redolent with southern spices, infuses the air surrounding the Walker home. Estes and JDubya stand over the pit with aprons over their tee shirts and jeans proudly tending to their prized preparations.

Turning into their dirt driveway, a black Buick cruises slowly into a parking slot formed with split logs in front of the house. Out steps Reverend Jones.

'Good day, everyone. Welcome home, James.'

The women folk file out of the kitchen and greet the preacher.

'So glad you could make our little get together, Pastor Jones,' cries Auntie.

'With that smell coming from the barbecue pit, I'm surprised the whole neighborhood isn't sniffing around begging for a taste.'

Estes and JDubya finish the barbecue piling the chicken and beef on two large platters then bring them inside to the big oak table. The ladies have all the other fixins prepared, and they sit down ready to dig in to a mouth-watering meal.

'Reverend, would you do us the honor o' blessin' dis heah food?' asks Papa Walker.

'It'll be my pleasure, Estes.'

The preacher clears his throat and begins.

'Lord, bless this food and the hands that prepared it. We're concerned about your servant, Jasper, who is now in the Army preparing to defend our country. We ask that you watch over and protect him. This gathering is also filled with joy that young James has returned to us if only for a short time. Please watch over him as well, as he performs his leadership role as a member of the United States Air Force. I ask this in Jesus' name. Amen.'

The family along with the preacher dive in and devour the food, smacking their lips with relish. After the main course is eaten, Auntie brings out her specialty, black bottom pie.

'Aunt Violet, you sure know how to spoil us,' remarks JDubya. 'I'm full up to here.' He points to his neck. 'But, I can always find room for Auntie's famous dessert.'

The meal sparks conversation about how several of the young negro males in Stillmore have been drafted into the Army just like Jasper. JDubya tells about his experiences in Biloxi. They carry on 'til about ten o'clock. Finally, the pastor stands to take his leave.

'That was one of the best meals I've ever tasted. Thank you. Hard for me to drag myself away from you folks, but I've got a little polishing to do on my sermon for tomorrow. See you all in church.'

Next morning, the Walker family arrives at the parish early finding seating across the front pew. They recite prayers and join the choir singing along with the hymns. After the collection is taken, Reverend Jones begins the sermon.

'I was going to give a talk this morning about scripture from the Bible. I set that lesson aside for another time. Instead, I want to talk about how fortunate we are to have this humble house of God to meet together every Sunday. Our church has stood on this ground for 40 years. I am the fourth pastor here, and I trust many more will follow bringing the word of God.'

'However, more important than this building is the strength of community that it houses. The members of our church have had a longstanding commitment to Christ, to our work in Stillmore, and to the welfare of each other. As long as we maintain those things, our fellowship will remain strong.'

The Reverend completes his sermon testifying about the contributions made by many of the church faithful. Then, the recessional hymn is sung.

The Walkers are the last to leave the church. JDubya gets an ominous feeling as they descend the front steps. Then, out of nowhere, three white men rush toward the Walkers and tackle James. He fights them by wriggling his legs free and punching one of the men in the face knocking him down. Reverend Jones grabs another from behind and restrains him. The third attacker is confronted by Aunt Violet, who forcefully kicks him in the groin sending him to the ground moaning and clutching his crotch.

'James, get in your car and leave now,' yells Estes.

He sprints to the Nash Rambler, starts the car and spins his tires onto the dirt road as the assailants scramble to follow him. He looks in his rear-view mirror to see if the attackers are behind him. A Pontiac GTO with three men inside is gaining ground. Walker, knowing the neighborhood like the back of his hand, makes several sharp turns onto side streets. Completing one last right turn before reaching Highway 1, he checks on his pursuers again and hears the screeching of tires as the chase car fails to negotiate the turn and plows into a telephone pole. Steam billows from its front end with the metal hood bent skyward. With his chest thumping, James forces himself to slow down as he enters onto the state highway. Being pulled over by the ever-vigilant Georgia Highway Patrol could put him back into the hands of the KKK. He retraces his route back to Biloxi arriving there one day earlier than planned.

The next day, James is sitting at his desk reading his homework assignment from class. It's the 4th of July, and he has no plans to celebrate. He thinks about calling Peaches but remembers she is out of town visiting relatives in Jackson. The phone rings about two in the afternoon.

'Hello.

'James, this is Reverend Jones. I wanted to see if you reached home all right.'

'Yes sir, I made a few driving maneuvers and finally lost those Klan fellahs.'

'I'm glad you're okay, son. By the way, those men who came to get you yesterday and failed.'

'Yes.'

'Today, they succeeded.'

'How do you mean, Reverend?'

'They burned our church down to the ground.'

Walker feels a sudden weight of guilt pressing on his shoulders.

'I'm so sorry, Reverend. I should have known not to come back to Stillmore.'

'No James, it's not your fault. Somehow we'll get through this.'

CHAPTER 27

Tom and Mrs. Pernice are sitting in rocking chairs on the front porch chatting about family when he notices an attractive young woman exiting the front door across the street. As she heads toward her car, she waves to Mrs. Pernice.

'Who's that?' asks Tom.

'Oh, that's Sandra Billings. She's recently separated from her husband and came home last week to live with her mother.'

'She looks real nice. Will you introduce me?'

'Now Tom, you're an engaged man.'

'I know. I know. No harm in being friendly though, is there?'

'I suppose not. I've been neighbors with the family since Sandra was born.'

The young lady must have forgotten something as she climbs out of her car and goes back to the house. When she returns, Mrs. Pernice calls out.

'Sandra, I've got a new boarder I'd like you to meet.'

The comely woman stops. Tom and his landlady step down from the porch and walk across the street. As they approach, Tom can see his new neighbor possesses a creamy white complexion and blond hair. She wears a white blouse and short, Navy blue skirt showing off her slim, tanned legs.

'Sandra, this is Tom Stirling from Georgia. He's one of the Air Force officers studying at Keesler.'

'Nice to make your acquaintance, Tom,' she offers.

'The pleasure is all mine, Sandra,' he replies making no effort to restrain his interest. 'I didn't know we had such a beautiful neighbor.'

'You flatter me, Tom,' she responds. 'Fact of the matter is I've just moved back in with Mother yesterday. My marriage hasn't been working out, and we decided to separate.'

'I'm so sorry to hear that dear,' consoles Mrs. Pernice. 'I remember how happy we were for you when you got married. After all, I've watched you grow up from the time you were a little girl.'

'Thank you for your concern, Mrs. Pernice. But, I'll be okay.'

'If you ever want to go get some coffee and talk sometime, Sandra, I'm a good listener. And, I'd be more than happy to take you.'

He speaks with a look of sincerity and concern. Sandra feels lost at present, but she perceives Tom as an understanding man who could give a fair perspective of her situation from a male point of view. She has only talked to women for advice since her breakup.

'I'd like that. Thank you for that kind offer.'

Tom is restless for the next few days. He finds himself waking up at night thinking of Sandra. During the day, when he has moments to himself, his mind drifts off picturing her soft, Southern sensual presence. Little does he know, she is having thoughts about him as well.

A week later, he invites Sandra out. He is relieved when she says yes.

'I thought we'd go to the Edgewater, Sandra. They've got a café there with a nice view of the Gulf.'

They drive down their road of single story, wood-framed homes on 13th street and turn left onto Beach Boulevard through the center of Gulfport. Hallmarks of segregation are apparent as they pass the movie theater where coloreds can only attend by sitting in the balcony and the Greyhound Bus Terminal with its separate colored and 'whites only' water fountains outside. Driving east out of town, they ride along the less developed parts of beachfront property until reaching the Edgewater.

There's a heaviness in the air laden with scents of magnolia blossoms and salty seaweed from the beach as they exit the air-conditioned car and approach the high-rise hotel. The cool air inside is a welcome relief as they enter the ground floor café and are promptly shown to a window side table.

The waitress approaches.

'What will you have?' she asks.

'Sandra, I'm going to have a powdered doughnut with my coffee, would you like one?'

'Just coffee's fine,' she replies.

Tom starts the conversation by talking about a childhood friend.

'I have this longtime buddy, Miles who got married to a girl before finishing college and is now going through a divorce.'

'What happened?'

'Well, he got his girl pregnant senior year in college, and they kind of got forced into tying the old knot. This guy wasn't ready to settle down. When she got so big they couldn't have relations anymore, he found another girl at a local bar. Now she's bringing up the baby without him.'

'That's so sad. The same kind of thing happened to me. At least I wasn't pregnant, but that lying husband of mine was cheating on me just like your friend.'

Shifting the focus of the conversation, she asks.

'What about you, Tom. Do you have a girlfriend?'

'There's a girl back home that I have an understanding with. We both know that being away from each other for three to four years can make things difficult. So, we'll have to see how things work out.'

'That must be hard for both of you,' she says now feeling compassion for Tom's predicament. 'You must get lonely from time to time.'

'Thanks for your concern, Sandra. I try to keep busy and not think about it too much.'

Tom can sense a growing closeness with Sandra. He gazes into her eyes with a look of understanding. She responds with a look of longing. Tom touches one of his shoes against one of hers. She presses both her feet alongside his foot.'

'Is your coffee okay?' he inquires. She turns her head side to side.

'How about some cream?' He suggests raising his eyebrows.

'I'd love some.'

They finish their coffee without saying more only exchanging wistful looks. Tom rises from his seat leaving money for the check on the table, and assists Sandra from her chair. They step outside and climb into his car.

Turning toward one another, they drink the sentiment in each other's eyes. The temptation is irresistible. In an instant, they are swept away in a rush of passion, kissing with abandon. Lips, cheeks, neck, ears, anywhere on exposed skin is smothered. Abruptly, a sound from outside the car intrudes on their all- consuming lust. Tom looks up.

A wrinkle-faced, elderly woman wearing a full length, shapeless cotton dress knocks on the passenger side window with her cane.

'You two are making an indecent display in a public place,' she declares. 'Stop immediately and leave this property or I will call the authorities.'

Sheepishly, Tom obligingly releases his arms from Sandra and starts the engine. He wants to give that lady the finger, but instead, he swallows his pride and backs up the car to leave the hotel.

'Sorry,' he mouths to the woman as they drive away.

'There's nothing to be sorry for,' says Sandra who is visibly upset. Tom turns on the air conditioning full blast then reaches for Sandra's left hand. The warmth of the day and the heat of their passion has them both sweating through their clothes. A churning relentlessness stirs within both of them.

As they head back toward home or maybe somewhere else, Tom thinks of Nancy. *She'll never know about Sandra, and I know I'll be faithful to her after we're married.*

CHAPTER 28

Tom travels home several times during the year in Biloxi. His parents are always happy to see their only son. Myrna makes his favorite foods, and he goes hunting or fishing with his daddy. The family connection is important to all of them, and Tom does his part to spend time with his folks.

He is also acutely aware that his relationship with Nancy needs nurturing. On long weekends, Tom drives his new muscle car over to the Gunn house to spend one day with his fiancée and her family.

Since becoming engaged, Nancy's life has been a waiting game. She accepted a position as assistant librarian in Moultrie. In her spare time, she reads or goes shopping with her mother or younger sister, Elaine. She also has learned to sew and makes decorative items for family and friends. She is sitting on the living room sofa next to her mother working on a cross stitch pattern in her lap.

'Mama, Ah'm getting' tired a waitin' for Tom to marry me,' she complains. 'What do you think Ah should do?'

'Well', a girl shouldn't be too pushy when it comes to catchin' a mayan,' her mother explains.

'Hmmm. Well, Ah know Ah wouldn't like travelin' roun' like a vagabond wife in the Ayah Force, but three mo' yeeahs is a long tahm to wait for a fellah. Ah might go plum crazy by then.'

'Maybe you should put a little pressure on Tom,' Mama Gunn suggests. 'You could make him a little jealous by sayin' another mayan is sweet on you.'

'Good idea, Mama. That's just what Ah'm gonna do.'

Tom goes over to Nancy's home that second evening back in Georgia. He has been out fishing with his father earlier that day and caught a couple of catfish for dinner at the Gunn's. Stirling is in their back yard preparing the fish with a seasoning rub before grilling the deboned entrée on the Weber barbecue spit. Nancy comes out to check on him.

'Looks real tasty, Tom. Smells good too.'

'Hope you enjoy eating it, sweetie,' responds Stirling focusing on his task.

'Mama and Ah have the rest of the dinner prepared. How long you gonna be?'

'About ten minutes,' Tom guesses. 'Say, what did you do today?'

'I went shoppin' in Moultrie with Mama. And guess what?'

'What?' Tom reacts feigning interest in the exploits of two women shopping.

'I ran into Henry Clark.'

'Who's he?'

'He was voted the best lookin' boy in mah high school class. We got to talkin', and he asked me out on a date to the picture show.'

'And….what did you say?'

'Ah showed him mah diamond ring and said,' "Ah'm engaged, Henry. But if anythang happens between me and my fiancé, Ah would be delighted to go out with you."'

'Nancy,' reacts Tom who is now fully attentive and pissed off. 'Why would you say such a thing when you're promised to me?'

She starts to cry.

'Because you're gone all the tahm, and we don't even have a weddin' day set.'

Stirling thinks to himself, *Oh, so that's the game we're playing now.*

'You know you want to stay living in Georgia. At least I'm stationed close enough to come home on long weekends. I thought you were happy when I got assigned to a base close by in Mississippi.'

'Ah am glad youah heah. But, youah home for such a short tahm.'

'If we got married now, and I got assigned to Minot, North Dakota, would you be happy living in that freezing, flat land a thousand miles from here? No, you wouldn't. You would be running home to Mama in two months.'

'Why do you have to be so negative? Ah might surprise you how well Ah adapt. On the otha hayand, if Ah up and married Henry Clark, Ah wouldn't have to worry about that, would Ah?'

Is this what it's going to be like when we get married? Stirling muses. *I love Georgia. I love Nancy. But, I also don't want to be trapped in this little cocoon for the rest of my life.*

A smile breaks out on Tom's face.

'What are you smiling about, Tom?' Don't you think the future of our relationship is a serious matter?'

'Of course, I do. I'm trying to do what's best for both of us. Don't I come home every chance I get and spend time with my sweetheart?'

'Ah guess. What if Ah came down to Biloxi to spend time with you thayah?'

Stirling thinks for a few seconds. He really doesn't want her to come as that could uncover things with Sandra.

'Nancy, I think you're forgetting that I'm in school all day from Monday to Friday. You would be bored stiff. Plus, I don't have a place for you to stay.'

'Elaine could come with me. She's not doing anythang this summer. We could go to the beach or see the local sights while youah in class. And, Ah'm shuah you could find us a room somewayah.'

Stirling can see Nancy is determined to press this issue so he partially gives in.

'All right, I'll find a room for you and Elaine for one week. Longer than that and you'll both be ready to hitchhike back to Doerun.'

'Thank you, Tom. It'll be fun.'

The fish is now ready. He picks up a pair of long tongs and sets the fish on a large plate next to the grill.'

Nancy has momentarily forgotten her wedding demands, as she is excited about visiting Tom in Biloxi. Their present conversation triggers doubts about his long-distance relationship with his fiancée. He knows he has three more years of service, and chances are he will be assigned much further away than Keesler. Another reservation is his attraction to other women like Sandra.

CHAPTER 29

'Hi Nancy. Hello Elaine. Welcome to Gulfport.' Stirling smiles and opens the driver side door of his fiancee's 1964 Ford Falcon.

His betrothed and her sister have arrived in front of Mrs. Freida Pernice's home for a two week, summer visit.

'So, this is where you live, Tom. Seems like a nice neighborhood and close to the beach too. Ah'm shuah Elaine and Ah will be spendin' tahm there while youah in school.'

'C'mon inside. I want you to meet Mrs. Pernice.'

Tom is uneasy about the possibility of Nancy coming face-to-face with Sandra. Standing around in front of the house or sitting on the front porch with the two Georgia belles are two things he's determined to avoid.

The lady of the house is busy in the kitchen preparing a tray of fruit and a pitcher of mint iced tea to welcome the two young women.

'Mrs. P., here they are. I'd like to introduce you to Nancy Gunn and her younger sister, Elaine fresh in from Doerun, Georgia.'

'So nice to meet you ladies. I've heard so much about you from Tom.'

'Pleasure to meet you, ma'am,' says Nancy. Elaine just smiles.

'Why don't we go out on the front porch to get some air and have some refreshments,' recommends Mrs. Pernice. 'We'll get to know each other a little better that way.'

'I don't think that's a good idea,' disagrees Tom. 'I was bitten by a mosquito waiting out there. Let's just sit here at the kitchen table.'

Freida gives in to Tom's suggestion. They spend the next hour chit chatting about family and comparing the weather between Mississippi and Georgia. When the conversation becomes tedious, he stands and announces his plan for the rest of the day.

'I'm going to show the gals to the motel where they'll be staying. After they get settled in, we can head out to dinner. I made dinner reservations for the four of us at the 'Chicken Ranch' on the back bayou. Best southern fried chicken in town.'

'Oh, you'll love that place, girls. Their food is simply scrumptious,' Freida exclaims.

As they reach the front door, Tom looks out the window and sees Sandra walking toward her car across the street. He quickly retreats.

'Ah, I forgot something. Oh, and let me show you my room.'

They walk down the hallway to the first room on the right. He ushers them inside.

'Tom, you could have at least made your bed before showing us this mess,' Nancy remarks. Elaine snickers with her hand over her mouth.

There are books sitting on the desk and on the floor. Fresh dry-cleaned uniforms are draped over a chair. He reaches into the desk drawer and pulls out a comb. At the same moment, a car engine starting up across the street makes a muffled sound through the glass of the bedroom window before driving away.

'Got my comb. We can go now.'

Nancy gives him a quizzical look.

'He's acting weird,' his fiancée whispers. Elaine smiles.

Blue sky, temperatures in the 80's, a gentle breeze blowing in off the Gulf, a perfect beach day. Tom has invited his friend, Duane from class to accompany Elaine. The four of them help anchor down a blanket with rocks on the warm, dry sand a few yards from the shoreline.

A Coleman cooler full of ice, soft drinks and sandwiches wrapped in wax paper is wriggled into the sand next to them. Nancy pulls out a tube of Coppertone suntan lotion, and the four of them slather the creamy substance over their legs, arms, face and front. The two couples take turns applying the lotion over each other's backs.

After lying there, watching the waves and other sunbathers settling in, a figure, familiar only to Tom, walks along the water's edge, a blond in a white bikini.

'Check that out,' says Duane. Elaine abruptly elbows him in the side.

'You're supposed to be looking at me, not the other girls on the beach,' she complains.

Tom realizing whom it is, immediately turns on his stomach and covers his head with a wide-brimmed hat.

Sandra has made an unexpected appearance.

She stops directly in front of them dipping her feet into the lapping waves at water's edge. Slowly she wades in waist deep. Finally, Sandra plunges into the gently bobbing currents swimming back and forth for several minutes.

Tom, thinking she has passed by, turns on his back and looks around checking to make sure his sunglasses are firmly in place by pressing his index finger against the frame over the bridge of his nose. Not seeing Sandra, he lets out a sigh of relief.

'Whew, it's hot. Elaine, could you pass me one of those co-colas in the cooler?' he asks.

As he pops open the bottle and takes his first sip, Sandra, hair and body drenched in seawater emerges. Walking slowly out of the surf with her feet sinking into the soft sand, she looks directly towards the foursome on the blanket.

Tom coughs, chokes and quickly swivels face down.

'What's wrong with you?' queries Nancy.

'Co-cola must have gone down the wrong pipe,' he replies in a weak, hoarse whisper.

Nancy furrows her brow trying to understand Tom's strange, nervous behavior. Sandra, now standing on dry sand, leans back, jutting out her chest as she attempts to shake off some of the wetness from her hair.

'Get a load of that babe in the bikini,' exclaims Duane. 'Wow1'

'That's okay, Kallo, I need to clear my throat from that last drink I took,' replies Stirling. He forces gutteral sounds from deep in his throat; then coughs again. Nancy gives him a look of disgust.

'Duane, don't encourage him to look at otha women,' reprimands Nancy. 'It's mah job to make shuah he only has eyes for me.'

Sandra walks directly toward them, deftly flicking a lump of sand on their blanket as she walks by.

'That woman is a brazen hussy,' judges Nancy through gritted teeth.

On Saturday, Labor Day weekend, the two-week visit is coming to an end. Elaine needs to get ready for high school in a few days, and Nancy will return to her job at the Moultrie Public Library.

'The girls are coming by in a few minutes, Mrs. P. to say thank you for all the hospitality you've showed them,' Tom informs her in the kitchen.

'Why that's right nice of those girls. But, they don't have to do that. It was my pleasure to make their stay a little more enjoyable.'

Outside, the Ford Falcon pulls up. Tom rushes out the front door to greet them.

'C'mon in, ladies. I was just telling Mrs. P., you were coming over.'

'We brought youah nahse landlady a box of pralines,' informs Nancy.

'She'll love those,' he says. 'Now hurry up, 'cause I know you need to get on the road.'

'Slow down, Tom, We're not in that much of a hurry. Remembah, we're from Gouwgia. We like to take owa tahm and enjoy thangs.'

Tom had met with Sandra the previous night. He chastised her for making such a scene at the beach a few days earlier. She got angry replying that she was no tramp who slept around with men for a cheap thrill. She wanted more of a commitment from him. He reiterated details of his longstanding relations with Nancy, and told her he had no plans of breaking their engagement.

'Engagement,' she shouted. 'You never said anything about an engagement. You said you had an understanding with some woman back in Georgia. You deceived me. You have been using me these past three months.'

'No, I just fell for you. And, I thought you felt the same toward me.'

'You're a sweet-talking two-timer, Tom Stirling. You wait. I'll get back at you for this.'

Sandra had known about Nancy's visit for a month, but she had never been told he had some serious entanglement let alone be engaged. She was enraged and determined to wreak vengeance.

The next day, Sandra sees the Ford Falcon parked against the curb across the street and decides to seize her opportunity for payback. She rushes into her bathroom, puts on make-up, lipstick and brushes her hair straight. Donning a low-cut peasant blouse and short skirt, she strides across the street in heels and rings the doorbell.

'Why Sandra, what a surprise,' reacts Mrs. P. answering the door.'

'I heard Tom had some visitors, so I thought I'd come over and introduce myself.'

'Well, that's very nice of you, but they're about to leave. Another time would be better for you to visit.'

'No! Any friend of Tom's is a friend of mine. May I come in please?'

Not waiting for an answer, Sandra barges by Mrs. Pernice and makes her way into the kitchen. Tom stands there dumbfounded with his mouth open. Nancy and Elaine abruptly stop talking and turn to face this woman with a look of disbelief on their faces seeing this strange person who has thrust herself into their presence.

Tom turns red with embarrassment. He responds to the situation by acting as if he doesn't know Sandra.

'May I help you miss? Are you lost?'

'You know damn well who I am, Tom Stirling, and I'm here to meet your lady friends.'

Tom searches for a response to Sandra, but before he could counter her attack on him, Freida comes to his rescue. She grabs Sandra by the waist and shoulder and forcibly escorts her out the front door and back across the street.

On return home, Mrs. P. addresses the ladies from Georgia.

'Sorry for that intrusion. Sandra has been in and out of mental institutions for several years now. She suffers from fantasies about different people. Poor Tom. She has developed this delusion that he is her boyfriend. So, naturally, when she sees him with another woman, she flies into a fit of jealousy. Sorry, you had to witness that.'

'Ah appreciate youah explainin' that, Mrs. Pernice,' says Nancy. 'That shuah was bizarre.'

They exchange well wishes including a safe trip back to Georgia. Tom and Mrs. P. wave as the Falcon pulls away.

'Thank you, Mrs. P. You're my new best friend.'

As they drive out of town, Elaine turns to her sister.

'Did you believe that explanation Mrs. Pernice gave 'bout that Sandra person?'

'Ah'm not shuah. That was the weirdest thing Ah ever did see.'

CHAPTER 30

Last day of school for Tom, James and the rest of the communications electronics class. Results of the final exams have been posted on the bulletin board outside on the kiosk. Everyone passed.

Stirling decides to have a group celebration with a few of his classmates, spending a night on the town in New Orleans, sixty miles away. Phil from Indiana, Paul from Pennsylvania, Robert from Connecticut and Duane from Massachusetts agree to go with him.

'Hey Tom, why don't we ask Walker,' suggests Duane. 'He's a funny guy, and he can likely show us a different side of town.'

'Yuh. I'm not too sure I want to see that side, but okay, if you guys want me to, I'll go ask him.'

'Give the guy some credit, Stirling,' reacts Phil. 'He did make it all the way through the program despite your misguided predictions he would flunk out after the first test.'

The group laughs.

He walks over and buttonholes Walker, who is saying his goodbyes to the three Vietnamese officers from the class.

'Walker, can I talk to you for a minute?'

The black lieutenant excuses himself from the Asians.

'I know what you're going to say, Stirling. They must have fed you the answers on all those tests so you could pass the program.'

'Not at all. Frankly, you've changed my impression of the capabilities of coloreds. But, I came over to ask you to join a group of us in a little graduation celebration. We're going to New Orleans this Friday to let our hair down, shall we say. You want to join us?'

'Sure. In the interest of improving relations between our peoples, I'd be glad to join you white guys. Just tell me where to meet.'

We'll get together at the Shell gas station on the Route 90/49 intersection in Gulfport. The six of us can fit in my car. Five p.m., and don't be late.'

'I know us coloreds tend to shuffle along real slow, Tom. But, I'm fixin' to sashay by big butt a little faster, so I can be there on time, just for you.'

Tom grimaces and looks to the heavens with open arms as if to say, *Do I deserve this cracker baiting abuse.*'

Early that Friday evening, the six new communications specialists are speeding westward along Route 90. The murky waters of the Gulf are on the left, and, every so often, a southern plantation home comes into view on the right, reminding James of an ugly past. Tom is driving with Robert in the middle and Paul riding shotgun. James sits between Phil and Duane in the back seat.

'Okay, what's the plan once we get to New Orleans,' inquires Paul.

'Well, we could go to dinner an Antoines's or Court of Two Sisters,' suggests Robert. 'I hear both restaurants have great Cajun food.'

'That'll slow us down and make us sleepy,' counters Phil. 'How about we get tickets to see Al Hirt, and maybe cruise a couple of bars on Bourbon Street.'

'Now you're talkin',' concurs Duane.

Tom being well acquainted with the city from many previous visits makes an alternate suggestion.

'When we get there, we'll buy tickets for the Al Hirt late show at 10 p.m. Then, we should get happy at Pat O'Brien's bar. The drinks there will really put us in the mood to celebrate. After an hour or so there, we can go to an oyster bar and down a few of their local specialties before going to see the fat man blow on his horn. Finally, to sober up before we head back, we can walk down to the 'Café du Monde' for some beignets and chicory coffee. How does that sound?'

'You're the man, Stirling. Get ready to party, guys,' says Phil.

The warm, muggy April evening feels uncomfortably sticky as they exit the car at a $2 lot near the French Quarter. All six of the lieutenants had visited the 'Big Easy' before, but Tom has that southern 'savoir faire' that the Yankees lack.

'We'd like six tickets to Al Hirt's late show please,' requests Stirling of the lady at the box office. 'Special night for us. We graduated from school down at Keesler yesterday.'

'Oh, congratulations.'

'And, you look like a sweet person. Would it be possible to get a table up front?' He gives her a big smile and slides a twenty-dollar bill across the counter.

'You're in luck, sir. I happen to have a table for six right next to the stage.'

'Thank you, sweetheart. You're the best.'

As they walk away with their tickets, Paul gushes with appreciation for Tom's suave ways.

'Stirling, old boy, you are some kind of smooth operator.'

The weekend crush of merrymakers along Bourbon Street force the young officers to weave along the pavement avoiding clumps of out-of-towners gathered in front of the girly show bars listening to the sexual fantasy claims of the barkers. Further on, they stop for a few minutes at the corner of St. Peter Street to listen to the old men of Preservation Hall play original Dixieland music from an open-air patio. Smiles break out as they listen to the measured but skillfully played horns melding music together in harmony likely practiced hundreds of times before. When the musicians pause for a break, the officers amble a short distance further entering the brightly lit outdoor courtyard of Pat O'Brien's.

'I remember this place well from the last time I was here,' recalls Duane. 'You've got to order a 'Hurricane'. It's a sweet rum concoction that will put a smile on your face for the rest of the night.'

Paul finds an empty table next to a loud group of men who were already well lubricated. They sit down and order their drinks. James' chair is closest to that boisterous clique.

'I believe I have a nigger sittin' next to me,' comments one of the rowdy men.

The young officers hear the comment, but choose to ignore it. That same man continues to bait James.

'Where I was brought up, the only niggers allowed in a place like this were the ones serving the drinks and food. Now these uppity darkies think they can go anywhere.'

'Pipe down, Lloyd,' says one of his companions.

The situation is like an itch on his back that he can't reach to scratch. He continues his tirade.

'Pardon me, would you fellahs switch seats?' comes a request from the middle-aged, red-faced man speaking in an angry voice. 'I don't want no nigga' sittin' close to me.'

In his mind, James flashes back to that day as a college freshman when he and three classmates attempted to integrate a 'whites only' diner. He wasn't about to move. Tom stands and addresses the bigot.

'He's got as much right to sit in that seat as you do to sit next to him. Get one of your buddies to change seats with you if that's what you want.'

Phil, Robert, Paul, and Duane stand one-by-one in support of Stirling's bold pronouncement. James remains seated and silent. The other men at the adjacent table are in no mood for a fight.

'Turn around and shut up,' says one. 'We're here to have fun not get dragged into some drunken brawl.'

His friends' lack of support fuel Lloyd's hostility further. He stands up and turns to confront the colored lieutenant. With his face engorged into a beet-red hue, he draws back his right arm and aims his fist full force at James' head.

As the power of his thin, wiry body generates a forward thrust, an unexpected deterrent diverts his arm forcing Lloyd off balance. He falls to the ground. Tom has used his forearms in a crossed position to block the blow and shield James' head.

For a moment, the men at both tables stand in disbelief while Lloyd lies stunned on the ground. Conversation in the patio around them stops. All attention turns toward the scene of the altercation.

'Time for you to leave, buster,' Tom barks out standing over the instigator. 'This is no place for a sick racist pig to be hanging out. You're an embarrassment to all men from the South.'

'Come on. Let's get out of here,' suggests one of Lloyd's companions. Two others grab the troublemaker from underneath his armpits and drag him outside with the others following.

'Here's your 'Hurricanes',' announces a solidly built raven-haired waitress as she sets down her heavy tray of drinks.

Each of them grabs one glass. But, before anyone starts to take that first sip,' James has something to say. He stands and salutes his friends.

'I've never had as much support from five white guys as I did tonight, especially you, Tom. What you did took a lot of guts.' He raises his glass high overhead. 'Here's to white guys stickin' up for black guys.'

'Hear, hear,' they cheer raising their red punch filled tumblers.

The toast gets the whole bar acknowledging them. Robert stands on his chair and begins leading them in song with index fingers and thumbs held upside down at the tips simulating open cockpit airplane goggles.

'Up in the air, Junior Birdman,
'Up in the air, upside down,
'Up in the air, Junior Birdman,
'With your noses off the ground.

'When you hear that grand announcement,
'That your wings are made of tin,
'Then you know that Junior Birdman,
'Has turned his box tops in.'

The place erupts in laughter and cheers as Robert steps down.

They leave O'Brien's a few minutes before nine toting their now empty complementary 'Hurricane' glasses. A feeling of omnipotence fills their heads as they stroll toward the Acme Oyster Bar.

The oysters taste sweet. Al Hirt rocks. And, the beignets and coffee at Café du Monde leave the memory of the evening sitting softly and sweetly on their brains. There's not much conversation of the ride back to Mississippi, but the bond between the young lieutenants feels much stronger than when they left Gulfport earlier that evening.

In a couple of days, each officer will be leaving for different bases across the country. Tom has been assigned to Pease AFB near Portsmouth, New Hampshire. James is heading to McClellan AFB in Sacramento, California.

CHAPTER 31

Leaving the South is unsettling for Tom. An assignment in the heart of Yankee territory is cause for a new outlook on the country. True, he has made several friends from north of the Mason-Dixon Line at Keesler, but they were in his territory. Now he is moving to New Hampshire where their citizens fought against his rebel compatriots in the most divisive conflict in U.S. history.

Driving north along Route17, he tries to imagine being away from his parents and Nancy for the next two years. Tears were shed when he left Georgia knowing that the separation would be longer than ever before.

His car is packed with food and gifts, reminders of home and the affection held for him by his family, friends, and of course, Nancy. She gave him an 18x24 inch photo of the two of them hugging each other standing in their bathing suits with Lake Blackshear in the background. He thinks about her and smiles. When she was ill and feeling down, Tom had that gift of storytelling that made her laugh and bring her out of a self-pitying funk. Then, when she was feeling good, there was that surprising wellspring of energy bugging him to go dancing, waterskiing, shopping, anything to get out and be active. In truth, he needs both sides of her.

After two days of reminiscing on the road, Tom approaches the entrance to his new base on the western outskirts of Portsmouth, New Hampshire. Upon receiving directions from the guard at the front gate. He locates the communications building. Arriving there, he is escorted to the office of his supervisor, Captain Gary Wilgus. He knocks on the door and is called in.

'Lieutenant Stirling reporting for duty, sir.'

'Have a seat Lieutenant. We've been expecting you. How was your trip up from Keesler?'

'It took me two days. I need to get used to turnpike driving. We don't have roads like that down South, and people seem like they're more in a hurry up here.'

Cutting short the introduction formalities, the Captain turns to the basic orientation of his new lieutenant.

'Well, you made it here safely, and that's the important thing. Lieutenant, I'm sure you're aware this is a SAC base. So, in general, there's more security here than a base with a small flying mission like Keesler.'

'Yes sir, I've received some general information on that.'

'Cut the sir stuff. Call me Gary.

'Okay, Gary.'

'You'll find that we are conscientious about getting our work done around here.   We do handle a lot of confidential, secret and top-secret communications. So, we need to be thorough with our procedures for processing classified information.'

I fully understand the importance of that, sir er Gary.'

'I also run his unit with the understanding that staff morale is very important. We do our jobs right. Then, when we're off-duty, we go out and enjoy the attractions in the area. Do you like water skiing?'

'Oh yes, sir er Gary. Down in Georgia, my fiancée and I go waterskiing every chance we get.'

'Well, I'm from the state of Washington. We may not have the best weather in the world, but we have lots of water and places to ski. We'll have to head up to Lake Winnipesaukee sometime soon. That's a great place to ski, and there's a boat I rent every so often out of Wolfeboro.'

'I'd love that, sir er Gary.'

'How about alcohol? Do you drink?

'I've been known to have a beer or two.'

'Good. I know this great bar downtown in Portsmouth that I think you'll like. Let's head over there after work today. And, we can get to know each other a little better.'

The new lieutenant from Georgia is assigned as officer in charge of maintenance for base communications equipment. He is introduced to the staff in his department and shown his new office. The base telephone system, teletype machines, short haul radio gear and cryptography apparatus will now be his responsibility to keep up and running.

'We learned something about all this gear down at Keesler, but I need to bone up on it.'

'I'm confident you'll do just fine,' reassures Wilgus. 'Any questions can be answered by Master Sergeant Frost over there. He's got 20 years' experience and knows this stuff like the back of his hand.'

Gary Wilgus is a 30 year old officer with a casual attitude toward military protocol. Still single and fun loving, his main priority in life is completing his required duties as quickly as possible, then departing the office for more pleasurable pursuits.

Flanagan's is an Irish pub located on Congress Street in the early 19th century brick building section of downtown old Portsmouth. A long wooden bar runs the length of the spacious tavern along the right side as you enter. The remainder of the space is dotted with small oak tables except for a small stage in the back with an adjacent dance floor. Lively music imported from the emerald isle plays nightly from Thursday through Sunday.

Gary and Tom find an empty table in the middle of the room and gesture for the waitress to take their order.

'I'll have a Guinness draft,' says the Captain. 'Shall I make it two, Tom?'

'Sure.'

The waitress brings their pints and a bowl of cashews. Tom still feeling a little uncomfortable in his new surroundings lets Gary lead the conversation.

'So, you're from Georgia. I've only been to Biloxi and never really traveled much around the area when I was in training there. Tell me about life in the South.'

Being in Yankee country, Stirling is a little hesitant to talk in much detail. He begins with some generalities.

'I guess things down home are pretty much similar as anywhere else. I enjoy water skiing just like you and we see the same movies everybody else in the country watches.'

'I know that, but tell me what's different down there from up here in New England?'

'What I know about New England is from one day's experience and hearsay. I know our food is different. I tried to order grits at a Howard Johnson's off the Jersey Turnpike. The waiter looked at me like I was from a different planet.'

'I think you'll get to like some of the food here. Maine lobster and New England clam chowder can be out of this world.'

'That sounds great. I see they have chowder on the menu here. Can we order some?

'Good Idea,' Wilgus summons the waitress, and she makes her way to their table. 'We would like to each get a bowl of your clam chowder. And, bring us a couple of packets of those little saltines to throw in.'

'Comin' right up, two chowdahs.'

'We hear there's been a lot of trouble down in your neck-of-the-woods, especially in Alabama and Mississippi. What do you think of all that turmoil?'

'I can say that our family believes the newspaper and TV people are blowing the problems way out of proportion.'

'What about the Voting Rights Act that Congress is now debating? Isn't it a good thing to make sure all eligible citizens have the right to vote?'

Stirling is starting to feel uncomfortable, but he still wants to make a good impression on his new boss.

'Well, sir er Gary, the colored people where I come from have been able to vote for some time now.'

'That's good,' respond Wilgus. 'But it seems like in many parts of the South, the negroes are having trouble registering to vote.'

'That might be happening in some places. In certain areas of the South, people believe that a person should be able to read and write before being allowed to vote.'

'Do you believe that, Stirling?'

'Well, I do see the legitimacy of that argument. It's difficult for a person to be adequately informed on election issues important to the public welfare without being able to read and write.'

Unexpectedly, a woman at the next table interjects herself into the conversation.

'I couldn't help but overhear your statement regarding the qualifications for voters in the South. I'm sorry, but if that isn't the most thinly disguised argument I've ever heard for white supremacy. You should be ashamed of yourself.'

'Who are you, lady?' Tom reacts. 'I don't remember the Captain and I starting a conversation with you.

The woman stands up and glares imperiously down at the lieutenant.

'I believe that our national government has finally decided the time has come to eliminate the injustices of slavery from our lives.'

'Have you ever lived in the South, Miss?'

'No. I don't need to live there to know how pervasive the attitude of racism still festers. How else could George Wallace and Ross Barnett be elected governors of Alabama and Mississippi?'

Now, Tom stands and faces the woman.

'Excuse me, Miss Know It All. Until you've moved to the South and understand what it's really like to live there, you have no cause to judge our people.'

'I beg your pardon, President Jefferson Davis. I am a reporter for the Portsmouth Herald. It's my job to know what's going on in the world. And, what I know about how negroes are treated by your white people doesn't paint a rosy picture of race relations.'

Undeterred, the Lieutenant moves closer to his attacker. He notices that she smells of lavender perfume. Looking her up and down, he discovers that she is quite physically attractive in her low-cut blouse and tight black slacks.

'My name is Tom, by the way. And, your depiction of every white person in my part of the country being a bigot is 99 percent wrong. You probably have more of that kind up here.'

'Well, my name is Phoebe. And, I didn't say every white person. But, you supposedly have a democratic system of government down there, and yet, there's still enough of those bigots to elect a white supremacist governor every four years. So, who did you vote for 'Dixieman'?'

'You know, if you weren't so hostile to people with a different view of the world than your own, you might learn something and get an insightful interview. You could write an article for your paper that wasn't a bunch of biased crap.'

Captain Wilgus has now heard enough. Before the argument could heat up any further, he decides to speak up.

'Say good night to the nice lady, lieutenant. We're leaving.'

'Good evening, ma'am. Pleasure talking to you. Best of luck keeping your job at the paper.'

'Oh, you're such a Southern gentleman. Go on back behind the fence with all the other warmongers.'

Tom gives her a military salute with his middle finger raised above the others. He has a devilish smile on his face. Phoebe grits her teeth. Her face flushes red.

CHAPTER 32

The drive to California marks the first time James has traveled beyond the Southern states. He reminisces on his affair with Peaches while riding through Mississippi. She provided many nights of pleasure during his tour in Biloxi. He'll miss her, but they're both moving on. The Tennessee hills and Kentucky bluegrass come into view before reaching the transcontinental highway, US Route 40 in Illinois. The flat plains of Kansas open up the biggest sky he has ever seen. Walker swerves to avoid tumbleweeds blowing across the highway outside of Fort Hays and nearly causes a head on collision with a semi. Upon reaching the border with Colorado, he expects to see the Rocky Mountains but views only a flat horizon. A hundred miles go by before dramatic snow-covered peaks come into view, framing the city of Denver.

There ain't no hills in Georgia like that,' he effuses awestruck by the beauty.

As Walker begins climbing into the Rockies, he discovers his 1961 Dodge Dart has very little power. Other cars zip by as he sputters up the incline. He pulls into a gas station to have his engine looked at.

'It's the altitude, fellah' says the mechanic. 'You need to have your carburetor adjusted.'

With a tweak of a screwdriver to change the fuel-oxygen mix, Walker is back on the road keeping up with traffic and enjoying the vertical landscape surrounding him on both sides.

By the fourth day of his trip, James has made it across the arid spaces of Utah and Nevada. He crests Donner Pass in California and cruises down the four lane Route 80 into the outskirts of Sacramento. Pulling up to the main entrance to McClellan AFB, he presents his orders to the guard at the gate.

'Welcome to California, Lieutenant. Take a left at the stop sign, then pass by two more stop signs. The 2049th Comm Group will be the next big building on the right. You can park across the street from the front entrance.

'Thank you, Airman.'

The 2049th is no little outfit. It's the major military communications hub of the west coast handling all messages between Washington and Vietnam as well as smaller USAF facilities in the western United States. Included in the operation are long range radio transmitters and receivers, a Plan 55 teletype message center, Air Route Traffic Control, as well as local base communications systems. He is escorted to the commander's office.

'Colonel LaFrenz, I'm Lieutenant Walker reporting for duty.'

'Welcome to the 2049th, Lieutenant. I believe you will find the mission of our unit here both challenging and rewarding. I have assigned you to work in the Plan 55 teletype section as assistant to Captain Eastland. He's on his way up here right now to meet you.'

The ruddy face Colonel has put Walker at ease.

'Colonel LaFrenz, I feel fortunate to have been assigned to your organization. I look forward to doing my best to serve you and the unit.'

'I like your attitude, Lieutenant. Oh, here's Captain Eastland.' He pauses while the captain closes the door behind him and approaches. James smiles at his new boss, but his new superior officer, gaunt faced and short, glares glumly at him.

'Jim, here's your new assistant, Lieutenant James Walker. Lieutenant meet Captain Eastland. I trust it won't be too confusing having two officers with the same name down in Plan 55.'

Walker recognizes the Colonel's attempt at humor with a smile. Eastland retains a grim countenance.

The younger James offers a firm handshake to his new boss with only a brief, limp response in return. A coldness projects from the captain, and the smile disappears from the lieutenant's face.

'I trust you're familiar with our equipment from your training down at Keesler,' Eastland growls. 'I expect you to be able to 'hit the bricks running'.'

'I'll need to refresh my knowledge and observe the operation first hand, sir. But, I'm ready to work hard and get up to speed as soon as possible.'

'I expect hard work. The question I have is whether you have what it takes to handle your job to my expectations.'

'Whoa, whoa Jim,' interrupts the Colonel. 'Lieutenant Walker just arrived. Give him some time to settle in.'

'I only want him to have a clear understanding of the importance of our mission here and his role in making sure it happens.'

James is now having second thoughts about how rewarding working here is going to be.

Plan 55 is a complicated system of electro-mechanical machines. The mechanical portion is prone to frequent malfunction. Operators need to quickly recognize such problems and seamlessly switch to a properly operating device and notify maintenance. Maintenance workers are kept steadily busy troubleshooting, repairing or performing routine maintenance. The room housing the system encompasses the entire basement level of the building. The atmosphere is loud and frequently chaotic.

'Walker, get in here,' yells Captain Eastland through the glass partition dividing their two officer cubicles. The Lieutenant hurries into is boss' office. 'There's an entire bay of equipment down. Run out there. Find out what happened, and report back to me ASAP.'

James hustles onto the floor and finds Master Sergeant Stratton on the scene. Five other bays are operating normally, but the one in question has no electricity feeding into it. Its lights are out and there's no chattering of the keys stroking the paper strips.

'What have you discovered, Sergeant?' the lieutenant asks.

'Power cord isn't working. We need to call in an electrician to fix the problem.'

'Any possibility of switching out power cords to get things up and running sooner.'

'A good idea, Lieutenant. Unfortunately, there are no extra power cords.'

James rushes back to inform Eastland of the situation. He explains what he learned from Sergeant Stratton.

'God damn it Walker. We can't sit around twiddling our thumbs waiting for some incompetent electrician. What other solutions do you have?'

'Sir, I've only been here one week. I thought with your experience, you might know other alternatives.'

'Lieutenant, that's the kind of 'pass the buck' attitude that I can't stand. Go back and talk with the sergeant again. And, don't come back here unless you have a better solution than waiting around for some lame brained electrician. Do you understand me?'

James thinks to himself, *If this is such a crisis situation, why isn't the captain out there helping to solve the problem.'* He holds his tongue.

'Were you about to say something, Walker?'

'No sir. I'm on my way.'

With that rebuff, James wheels around and heads straight back to the lifeless equipment where the sergeant is huddling with a group of airmen. When Sergeant Stratton hears the lieutenant approaching, he turns and gives him good news.

'The electrician just arrived. He located a short in the power cord. Says it will take five minutes to repair.'

A cheer rings out a few minutes later. Lights on the bay come on, and the teletype feeder begins punching chadless holes in the paper tape. The electrician, Sergeant Kantala, has fixed the problem. Smiles all around. Walker thanks the men and dashes back to tell Eastland of their success.

'Sir, the bay is back up. The electrician, Sergeant Kantala fixed a short in the power cord.'

'I hope you learned something from this little challenge, lieutenant.'

'I did, sir. I learned we have some very competent airmen working in Plan 55.'

'You know, I didn't get myself involved in this mini-crisis because I wanted to see what kind of metal you have. All I saw was that you depended on other people to bail you out. I expect better next time.'

CHAPTER 33

Intrigued by his contentious encounter with the female journalist at Flanagan's, Stirling reads the daily Portsmouth Herald for the following two weeks to examine the content of his attacker's articles. He finds an investigative series written by reporter Phoebe O'Connor.

'That must be her,' he mumbles to himself.

The articles describe conditions of a local nursing home. Along with the detailed inspection of the facility performed by her team, interviews with patients, families and employees reveal a pattern of abuse and neglect to the elderly residents.

'That lady has some spunk,' he concludes.

The spurned lieutenant decides to revisit Flanagan's bar on a Thursday night with hopes of seeing the firebrand Ms. O'Connor again. Arriving there around 9:00 p.m., he intends to apply a different tack when approaching her. He will exude Southern charm.

The place is crowded and loud with the Irish band rousing up the patrons to sing along to 'Danny Boy'.

As he surveys the room from the bar, he catches a glimpse of Phoebe drinking cocktails at a table with three female friends. He walks over and stops, standing next to them. The lieutenant waits for a lull in their conversation then interrupts.

'Miss O'Connor, I want to congratulate you on your series exposing the nursing home. You did a great job.'

'Well, if it isn't the Southern boor who has a distaste for reporters and negroes. What would cause you to flatter me like this?'

'I think you've misjudged me, and I'm out to prove that I'm a pretty nice guy.'

'Well, from that first impression you made, I would say you've got an uphill battle on your hands to convince me you're anything but a Southern bigot.'

'I can understand how you may think that, but I believe you unfairly jumped to a simplistic conclusion about me.'

Phoebe turns her chair around and faces him. She is intrigued by his boldness.

'Oh really, and exactly how do you plan to change my opinion of you?'

Tom was hoping for that reaction.

'For starters, the next round of drinks for this table is on me.'

'That's a good first step, lieutenant. But, that's really not going to change my take on you one iota.'

He motions to the waitress in a circular motion and points to the table of women. The waitress nods. He pulls up a chair from the empty table next to them and scooches up beside the reporter.

'I trust you women could use another drink. After all we are in an Irish bar, and there's a great tradition among the Gaelic citizenry for community drunkenness in the local pub.'

'I think your Southern friend knows how to have fun, Phoebe,' says one of her companions.

'I see at least one of you knows how to have a good time,' replies Stirling.

With that vote of confidence, Tom launches into his storytelling persona recalling the episode with James at Pat O'Brien's bar. Phoebe's friends are wide-eyed with admiration for this Southern defender of negroes. The newspaperwoman, however, is unconvinced of this professed valor, believing the Southern rebel is only trying to impress them with made up poppycock.

'How do we know that story isn't a bald face lie?' cries Phoebe in a cynical tone.

The lieutenant places his hand over the left side of his chest.

'Cross my heart and hope to die. That story is the God's honest truth.'

Just then the waitress brings their drinks and Tom gives her cash and tells her to keep the change.

'I think you're being too hard on this guy, Phoebe,' says another of her friends. Tom raises his glass and makes a toast.'

'Here's to a spirit of understanding between North and South.'

'They clink glasses and move on to small talk. Minutes later, the band is back on stage and invites everyone to come up and dance the Irish jig.

'I don't know how to do this,' cries Stirling.

'Just follow me,' says Phoebe as she pulls him toward the dance floor. 'It's in me blood.'

The lieutenant starts clumsily, but soon begins to catch on to the crossing of legs and hopping in rhythm. When the crowd calls for an encore, the reporter's friends return to the table leaving the floor to the Irish woman and the Southerner. She begins to be impressed, more with his dancing than with his social mores. They go back to the table smiling and sweating.

'That was fun, Reb. You're catching on. By the way, I could use another drink.'

'Coming right up.'

Around 11 o'clock, the friends of the reporter decide to call it a night leaving the two alone. By that time, both the lieutenant and the Irish lass have had several drinks, and their dueling barbs turn more light- hearted.

'You're dancing much better. Too much on your toes though. A little effeminate if you ask me.'

'Are you calling me a queer?'

'I don't know. Do you like boys?'

'I like boys....when they help me find girls.'

Tom wasn't sure whether Phoebe was teasing or coming on to him. He decided to order one more drink then make his move.

'Two more scotch/rocks please,' he requested. The waitress looked at them with some concern as they were swaying around and slurring their speech.

'Are you sure. You two have had quite a lot to drink tonight.'

Tom stands and balances on one foot. Phoebe does the same.

'Okay, I guess you're both in control.'

As the barmaid leaves, the reporter excuses herself to visit the powder room. While she walks away, Stirling notices her gait is a little unsteady. Upon her return, he makes a declaration.

'You're not driving home tonight because you can't walk straight.'

'I don't need to drive because I live two blocks from here in an apartment.'

'Well then, I insist on walking you home.'

12 o'clock. The band is packing up their instruments. The lieutenant walks up to the waitress, cancels his last order and pays the tab.

'Get your coat, you're going home.'

She makes a mild protest.

'Who do you think you are, Reb, trying to boss me around?'

'I'm only making sure you get home safe.'

'Well okay, but you're not getting into my apartment.'

'At least, I can walk you to the front door.'

They leave the bar with Tom shepherding Phoebe with his arm around her shoulder.

'Stop! Can't you see there's a red light?' he pulls her back onto the curb avoiding a late-night cab passing by, which nearly strikes her.

She turns quiet and they make it to her apartment building and up the outside staircase to her second-floor flat.

'You need some coffee before you try to drive back to the base,' she insists.

'Okay thanks. That will help.'

She opens the door. They enter. Tom turns her toward him and plants a kiss on her lips. There's a pause. He isn't sure if she is going to slap his face or try to push him down the stairs. She pulls him closer and covers his face with hungry kisses. In the dark, they shed their clothes while bumbling down the hallway to her bedroom stopping intermittently to clench each other in paroxysms of passion.

Coming in an hour late for work the next day, the lieutenant explains his tardiness.

'Captain Wilgus, I want to apologize for my tardiness this morning. My car didn't start last night and I got stuck downtown. I'll make every effort to make sure that doesn't happen again.

Gary gives him a knowing smile.

'I've had that happen myself, Lieutenant. Maybe it's time you took that car in for a checkup.'

'Good advice, Captain. I'll do that.'

CHAPTER 34

'Happy Birthday, Colonel,' offers Captain Eastland with a forced smile.

Lieutenant Walker has now served six months at the 2049th Comm Group. James and ten other officers of the unit are assembled around a rectangular table at the McClellan Officers Club to wish their commander a happy 42nd. In truth, each of them knows by missing this event, their annual performance review might be affected. That is of particular importance for the Captain from Mississippi.

'Thank you, Jim. You didn't need to go through all this trouble for me, but I appreciate it.'

'My pleasure, Colonel.'

Eastland has an ulterior motive. He is up for consideration of promotion to Major. For this to happen, he needs an outstanding performance evaluation from LaFrenz. The Captain has been passed over once before. A second rejection will result in him becoming a riffed officer. As such, he would be reduced in rank to Staff Sergeant, forcing him to complete five additional years as an enlisted man to receive retirement benefits.

As a young lieutenant, Walker is sitting at the far end of the table with Jerry Hicks from Personnel. Jerry, a freckle faced and amiable cohort from Alabama, whispers in his ear.

'How do you put up with Eastland? He's a sadistic creep who will never let up on you.'

James nods, then turns to face Hicks responding in a soft voice.

'I've been dealing with his kind of treatment my whole life. I've learned to never give in. Hopefully, things will eventually turn in my favor. It's like trying to win a staring contest. Who's going to blink first?'

Jerry has heard stories about Eastland from other staff in his office. He sympathizes with Walker's situation and has a suggestion for his fellow lieutenant.

'Look, I'm going to a meeting of the Sacramento Jaycees next week. You should come along. Right now, you're getting beat over the head every day by Eastland. This would give you a chance to get involved with something positive.'

Just then, James' boss saunters down to the end of the table where the two lieutenants are sitting.

'Walker, have you gone up to wish the Colonel a happy birthday?'

'Not yet sir. I was waiting until you finished giving your supportive comments to him.'

'Are you implying I'm 'brown nosing' our commander?'

'Not at all. I'm only aware that you are very much in agreement with the decisions he makes for our unit.'

'Maybe if you were more observant about how the command structure functions around here, you would be more effective in your own position.'

'I'll take that suggestion to heart, Captain.'

After two rounds of drinks, tongues are set wagging about certain individuals who aren't performing their jobs up to snuff. The murmured name of Eastland is mentioned more than once.

Half hour later, a set dinner consisting of green salad, baked potato with all the fixings, creamed corn and prime rib is served. Following the main meal, a celebratory dessert is placed in front of the Colonel; carrot cake topped with vanilla crème frosting and a single birthday candle.

Captain Eastland stands preparing to lead the group in a singing tribute to their leader.

'All right, everyone rise, and we'll toast the Colonel with a chorus of a song I know you're all familiar with.

Chairs squeak against the wooden floor as the officers rise to their feet and gaze down at the smiling commander who remains seated. Eastland raises his arms like an orchestra conductor, then abruptly lowers them to begin the song.

'For he's a jolly good fellow. For he's a jolly good fellow. For he's a jolly good fe-he-low. That nobody can deny.'

Clapping and shouting follows. After the cake is cut and consumed, each officer approaches LaFrenz and pays his respect individually. As the most junior officer, Walker is last to express his good wishes.

'You must be proud of all you've accomplished during your time in the Air Force, Colonel,' James surmises.

'Lieutenant, in my career as I'm sure in your brief one, there's a lot of ups and downs. You just learn to keep going when times get tough.'

'I'll remember that, sir.' In that moment, Walker believes Colonel LaFrenz understands his challenging relationship with Captain Eastland.

As officers begin heading out, James buttonholes Hicks.

'Jerry, I'm going to take you up on attending that meeting next week.'

'Great James. I think you'll get something valuable from it.'

'Well, Lieutenant, how did you like the meeting tonight?'

Jerry Hicks has introduced Walker to Pete Fetros, President of the Sacramento Jaycees.

'I'm impressed that your group puts on so many activities that benefit the city.'

'Would you be interested in joining our group? We would like to have you as a member. We're always looking to have the military community get involved in our organization.'

'Jerry told me some exciting things about the Jaycees, and the enthusiasm I saw in this room tonight convinces me. Yes, I would like to join.'

'Great. We meet in this restaurant every second Tuesday at 7:30. To get yourself involved, you should volunteer for one of our committees. You could team up with Jerry and our committee for the Miss Sacramento Contest. Would you be interested in that?'

'Sounds like I could meet some pretty ladies. Sure, sign me up.'

'Great. Jerry can fill you in on the next meeting for Miss Sac. Nice to meet you, James. And, welcome to the Jaycees.'

As they leave the meeting, Walker turns to Hicks.

'Hey, thanks a million for inviting me tonight. This Jaycee stuff is a real shot in the arm for me. I owe you, pal.'

'Don't mention it. Glad you liked the group. It's a great bunch of guys.'

Jerry and James are selected to be escorts for the Miss Sacramento Fashion Show at the Mansion Inn downtown. Donning their ceremonial black mess dress uniforms, they enter the large ballroom inside the hotel. Over 150 chairs are set up facing the stage at the end of the room. Six judges have their seats reserved in the front row.

'Hey handsome, you're looking good in that uniform,' comments Shirley Stone, a blond contestant awaiting to be escorted up the stairs to the stage.

Walker is taken back. His is awestruck at being surrounded by all the beautiful women, and Shirley is certainly one of them; tall, pretty and with a figure that would make Elizabeth Taylor jealous. He takes her hand and leads her up the two steps to the runway. She wears a form fitting ball gown with a plunging neckline.

'Ahhh, thanks, Miss. Good luck up there,' responds James making a flustered response. Polite applause greets Ms. Stone as she reaches the center of the runway, stops and turns, posing for the audience.

Walker ushers several more of the lovely contenders to the stage alternating duties with Hicks. At the conclusion of the show, the two huddle.

'What do you think, Jerry? Do we stand a chance with any of these girls?'

'Sure. You just need to have confidence approaching them without appearing too cocky. I've got my eye on Janet, the brunette with the face of an angel.'

'I can see why you like her, but I've got my hopes up for Shirley. She gave me a look and a smile, but I'm not sure if that means I have a chance with her.'

'Go for it brother. She's probably interested in you.'

After waiting a couple minutes more, the young ladies emerge from backstage in their street clothes. Jerry straightens his jacket of his uniform and walks toward Janet, stopping in front of her.

'I think the judges really liked your gown,' he comments. 'And, I must say, you looked terrific. By the way, my name is Jerry Hicks.'

'Thank you, lieutenant. Nice of you to say that,' she responds. 'You look swell yourself in that uniform.'

'Thank you. Say, I wanted to ask you, have you ever been to the Officers Club at McClellan?'

'No, I haven't, but I have a friend who said she had a great time there a while back, when she was dating one of the pilots on base.'

'Well, there's a big dance at the club next Saturday with a live band. Would you do me the honor of attending with me?'

'I don't know, Jerry. We just met.'

'How about if we double date. My friend James over there would like to go too. He wants to ask Shirley, one of your competitors, to go with him.'

'If we could double date, I would feel much more comfortable.'

'Wait here, I'll be right back.

Jerry rushes over to James standing a short distance away.

'James, she's willing to go out with me next week if I can get you to double date with Shirley.'

They both look around for Shirley and see her exiting the outside door heading for her car.

'I'm going back to Janet. You hurry and track down Shirley. Trust me, James, this could be a dream date for both of us.'

Walker nods and races for the exit.

When he gets to the parking lot, he spots Shirley unlocking the driver side door to her vehicle and getting in. The engine starts as Walker reaches it. She begins backing up when he knocks on the hood of the car. The vehicle stops and she rolls down the window.

'I didn't know you were supposed to escort me to the parking lot, lieutenant.'

'I've got something else in mind,' he blurts out trying to catch his breath.

'Yes,' she says waiting for his suggestion.

'There's a dance at our officer's club next Saturday night. I was hoping you might consider attending with me along with my friend, Jerry and his date, Janet, from the Miss Sacramento competition. Oh, and my name is James Walker.' She pauses for a few seconds.

'Well, Lieutenant Walker, it just so happens I'm free next Saturday night. So, if you promise to be a gentleman, I'll go out with you.'

'Miss Stone, I am duty bound to be a gentleman.'

CHAPTER 35

'Air show. Air Show! Why the hell would I want to go out and cheer for my tax money being wasted on criminally overpriced killing machines?'

'Look, you may think you can solve the world's problems by smoking pot and attending peace rallies. But, sister, you should get down on your knees and thank the United States military for keeping this country safe and allow a bunch of misguided hippies like yourself to exercise their constitutional rights by demonstrating against true patriots.'

'Tom is standing in Phoebe's apartment wondering how he could get involved with someone so diametrically opposed to his view of the world. Then, it hits him. She's a little spitfire who's great in bed.

'Wow. Check out the great American flag waver bleeding red, white and blue for his imperialist government.'

'Look, Jane Fonda. I'm asking you to come with me to a local event benefiting the city of Portsmouth. It's your civic duty to attend.'

'I'm going to go with you just so I can make you aware of how the military-industrial complex has made this country a land controlled by warmongers.'

'Oh please. By the way, do you belong to the Communist Party?'

''I suppose if I said yes, you would get the base commander to firebomb my apartment.

'Now I'm convinced. You are ready for the loony bin.'

Crisp, clear autumn air blesses Portsmouth on the day of the Air Show. The flight line at Pease Air Force Base is choked with warplanes dating back to the Eddie Rickenbacker days of World War I; Sopwith Camel, P-51 Mustang, B-17 Flying Fortress, B-24 Liberator, F-86 Sabrejet, F-104 Starfighter, B-52 Stratofortress, and the B-58 Hustler are all there. A crowd mills around each one taking photos of themselves with pilots dressed in the uniform of its era. Tours of the insides of the B-24 and B-52 are open to the public with roped off areas to protect the sensitive equipment.

Tom and Phoebe decide to wander through the insides of the World War II and Vietnam era planes.

'Well, what do you think? Pretty impressive, huh,' says Tom guessing that his date should be overwhelmed by a sense of aviation history there before her eyes.

'I think those World War II flyers were very brave going into Nazi Germany and risking their lives flying through flak and ground fire. But those B-52 pilots carpet bombing innocent Vietnamese civilians from 40,000 feet with sophisticated protection against SAM missiles, is totally different. They are committing mass murder against faceless victims.

'Wait a minute. You're saying the B-24 pilots were heroes and the B-52 pilots are terrorists, but they're doing the same thing.'

'No, because during World War II, Nazis were the embodiment of evil. In Vietnam, the evil doer is the United States military.'

'I can see nobody's going to win this argument. Let's get a good seat in the stands before the show begins.'

As they make their way through the crowd toward the temporary bleachers, the base Air Force band begins playing in front of the flight operations building. With American flags waving up and down the flight line in the afternoon breezes, they break into the heavy beat of John Philip Sousa's 'Stars and Stripes Forever'.

'Must they be so heavy handed with the flag thing,' says Phoebe. 'It makes me want to throw up.'

The smell of fresh made popcorn wafts under their noses as the couple reaches the event seating.

'I'm getting a bag of popcorn,' says Stirling. 'I figure if you're chewing on something, there's less chance of you embarrassing me out here.'

'You've never dated an Irish girl from New England before, have you? We're all pretty headstrong. Get used to it.'

Tom spots Wilgus sitting in the third row near the aisle.

'Gary, good to see you. Oh, this is Phoebe O'Connor. You might remember her from Flanagan's.'

'How could I forget? But, from what I can recall about that evening, I would never have guessed you two would be dating.'

'Sometimes opposites attract. Right Phoebe.'

'If you say so.'

Tom turns his head side-to-side grimacing at the same time as if to say, *There she goes again.*'

'Say, why don't' you both sit next to me for the show?'

'Sure, Gary. Thanks for asking.'

As they plop down, the band finishes their last number, and an announcer comes to the microphone.

'Ladies and gentlemen. Thank you all for attending the 15th annual Pease Air Show. We've got some exciting acts to thrill you this afternoon. We'll start off with some aerial aerobatics by two P-51 Mustangs piloted by Captains Brian Mulroy and Philip Mitchell. Let's hear it for these two outstanding fly boys.'

A roar from the crowd follows and one plane takes off followed by the other seconds later.   They do formation flying over the field with synchronized barrel rolls and hammerhead stalls. Then, they pass over the runway at full throttle skimming above the tarmac in opposite directions.

Finally, the two planes land, taxi up in front of the stands and park. The two pilots climb out of their respective cockpits, remove their headgear and wave to the applauding fans. The reporter takes note that Captain Mitchell is a negro.

'At least the Air Force has one negro pilot,' she snidely remarks.

'Phoebe, you might be interested to know there's over 100 negro pilots in our service,' Gary informs her.

'I guess picking cotton is good preparation for preparing pilots.   Right, Reb?'

'When are you going to leave this race thing alone?'

'When you admit negroes are just as smart as whites.'

Tom sighs and scratches the back of his head.

Gary decides to change the subject before the next aerial act.

'Miss O'Connor, have you ever been water skiing before?'

'No, I never have. I was a competitive swimmer in college, and I love the water. But, I never had any friends that did waterskiing.'

'How about the three of us go up to Lake Winnipesaukee for some skiing before the weather gets too cold? Between Tom and myself, we can teach you.'

'Well, that's the first pleasant invitation I've been offered today.'

'That'll be fun, Gary. I haven't skied since leaving Georgia.'

The second flying act begins, and the threesome settle back to watch. Phoebe starts eating popcorn. Tom smiles as she suddenly becomes quiet.

They stay seated throughout the afternoon observing several more exhibitions. Between each aerial act, the Irish redhead continues to berate Stirling for whatever reason pops into her head. The Georgian is not about to let her get the upper hand in this verbal jousting and rebuffs each accusation with a stinging reply.

The final act features the Air Force Thunderbirds. After a display of high speed formation flying, the crowd is thrilled, all except the reporter for the Portsmouth Herald.

'Well, Tom, Captain Wilgus, from what we saw today, you must be proud of the superiority your Air Force has over the North Vietnamese. What I don't understand is why, with all the technological advantages our military has over the Viet Cong we haven't won that war.'

'It's complicated,' Gary answers.

'Maybe it has more to do with the North Vietnamese having more motivation to unite the country than that sham government and army in the south have to protect their side of the 17th parallel.'

'Miss O'Connor, first of all, I seriously doubt the accuracy of that statement. And secondly, there's a lot more factors involved than what you are supposing,' says Gary becoming more perturbed with Phoebe's strident anti-military rhetoric.

'What seems obvious to me is that the U.S. is trying to win a guerilla war with high tech gizmos that only serve to pad the coffers of the military industrial complex. Do you really think you'll win by trying to bomb North Vietnam back to the Stone Age?'

'There's some things you don't seem to understand,' replies Stirling. 'We're not only defending South Vietnam against invasion by a foreign country, we're also fighting the spread of Communism in Southeast Asia.'

Gary raises his hand as a signal to end the discussion.

'Sorry, you two, I have an engagement with a lovely lady this evening, and I need to get ready. Nice seeing you again, Miss O'Connor. Maybe next time we can talk more about waterskiing than the war. Let me know when you two are available.'

With that remark, Gary takes his leave and the other two head back to Phoebes' apartment.'

'I want to show you how to make southern fried chicken. Let's stop at Star Market and get what we need for dinner at your place.'

'Presumptuous of you, Reb. Okay, I guess I owe you dinner for taking me out today.'

'I'm happy you've accepted your obligation to be nice to me for once.'

'Don't get used to it,' she answers with a sly smile.

The lieutenant manages to talk his way into spending the night. He's falling for this woman, and he begins to question his commitment to Nancy.

CHAPTER 36

A nervous cough rumbles from James' throat as he pauses at the front door of Shirley Stone's family home. He feels uncomfortable standing in this middle-class neighborhood of modest sized two-story houses in Carmichael, California.

Walker mutters to himself, *What am I doing here? I've never dated a white girl before, and I don't feel I belong here surrounded by white families with their manicured lawns bordered with perfect flower beds and brand-new cars like the Pontiac GTO sitting in the driveway of this place.'* He looks back at his dull brown Dodge Dart parked on the street with the paint peeling off the roof and cringes at its ugliness.

The lieutenant braces himself, clears his throat and presses the button to the side of the decorative glass surrounding the entry. A bell-like sound chimes inside. Within a few seconds, the door opens. A 40 something male with a white T shirt hanging over his bulging belt line gives James a quizzical look.

'If you're here to sell me something, you can leave now before you even open your mouth.'

At this moment, Walker feels he's made a big mistake agreeing to this date. Prior to meeting Shirley, he had thought interracial dating could be a bad experience for him. He is now becoming convinced.

Before James can respond to Mr. Stone, a woman's figure enters the doorway.

'Brent, don't be such a jerk,' she admonishes her husband. 'This is James, Shirley's date for the evening.'

She turns and faces Walker.

'Hello dear, forgive my husband. My name is Marge. Please come in and make yourself at home.'

Brent grumbles under his breath and moves aside allowing James to enter.

Marge motions for the young man to have a seat on the living room couch. She sits on an adjacent stuffed chair and begins making polite conversation while Brent retreats to the kitchen.

'Shirley tells me you're an officer at McClellan. What do you do there?'

Walker, who is beginning to feel more comfortable, begins answering questions about himself.

'And, where are you from?'

'Home is a small town in Georgia. Long way from here.'

'Isn't that nice.'

Suddenly, loud audio of a baseball game begins blasting from the TV in the kitchen.

'Will you turn that down, Brent,' Marge shouts. 'We can barely hear each other talk in here.'

The volume remains high for about 10 seconds while Mrs. Stone and Walker stare at each other. Just as Marge gets up to go out and chastise her husband, the sound level drops. She sits back down as Shirley emerges from her room smiling, dressed in a fuchsia print cocktail dress.

'You look lovely, dear. I've been learning interesting things about this handsome lieutenant here.'

'Very nice meeting you Mrs. Stone. A good evening to you and your husband.'

'You two have a nice time, and don't stay out too late.'

The audio from the kitchen continues as father Brent remains out of sight.

The second couple of the double date, Jerry and Janet have been waiting in the back seat of the car.

'That took a while in there,' Jerry notes. 'How did it go?'

'Well, let's say that Mrs. Stone was very hospitable. But, I don't think I won over Mr. Stone.'

'Now lieutenant, don't judge my father too harshly. He's only being a papa bear.'

They arrive at the Officers Club and look for a table. A hostess guides them to one of the few tables still available at the back of the room. The large ballroom encompasses one end of the club. Tonight 30 tables are arranged facing a bandstand with an adjacent dance floor.

The band has begun playing their first set. A waiter arrives at their table to take the order for drinks.

'My lady friend would like a Vodka Collins, and I'll have a Budweiser,' James tells him. The server gets requests from Jerry, and the four remain at the table until their drinks arrive. Looking around the room for familiar faces, Jerry spots two couples from the Comm unit.

'Look, James. There's Colonel LaFrenz and his wife sitting with Captain Eastland and his old lady.' Walker sees where Hicks is pointing and winces.

After a few sips of their drinks, Shirley suggests they dance. Jerry and Janet agree, but James is reluctant. With some prodding, he finally relents.

The band breaks into the cha-cha version of 'Cherry Pink and Apple Blossom White' as they reach the dance floor.

'I have no idea how to dance to this,' complains Walker.

'C'mon, I can show you. It's fun,' implores a smiling Shirley.

Jerry and Janet are already immersed into the Latin rhythms stepping around the floor with a knowing confidence. James realizes he has no choice but to give in. He moves awkwardly, several times in the wrong direction despite Shirley guiding him with her hands entwined around his forearms. They stop and start again and again until he finally learns the basic 1-2-3 steps at the end of each bar.

'All right, you've got it,' she says beaming at him. He manages an unconvinced frown as the song ends.

'Lieutenant Walker,' cries a familiar voice calling from a nearby table. 'Come on over here.'

'Colonel LaFrenz, nice to see you. Hello captain, ladies.'

The lieutenant is now in a situation where he needs to be extra polite. At the same time, he thinks. *How could I be so stupid to bring Shirley here on our first date?*

'I saw you dancing out there,' notes the Colonel. 'Looked like you were working pretty hard.'

'Sorry you had to witness that, sir. Shirley here was trying to teach me some new steps. Afraid I'm not a very good student. Oh, by the way, this is Shirley Stone.'

Shirley, standing behind James, steps to the side and nods toward the group. The Colonel and the two women acknowledge Shirley's presence. Captain Eastland sits unmoved with a scowl on his face and his arms folded. The lieutenant takes his leave as the band strikes up Chubby Checker's 'Let's Twist Again', with Shirley pulling him toward the gyrating couples on the dance floor.

'Nice to see you all. Enjoy the evening,' James remarks as he escapes a scene he was dreading. He waves to the table. Colonel and his wife smile back. Mrs. Eastland turns to her husband whispering something in his ear.

When the two young couples return to their table, Shirley comments.

'That one man at the table you visited seemed unfriendly. How well do you know him?'

'That's my boss. He's from Mississippi.'

'Oh, I think you're telling me he doesn't approve of dating between whites and negroes.'

'Right. But please, let's not have that spoil everything. Heck, I just learned how to cha-cha. I never dreamed I could do that.' Walker takes his glass of beer and raises it up and waits until the others hoist theirs. 'Here's to a fun evening.' They clink glasses and gulp down a few swallows to quench their thirst.

The two couples stay through three sets with the band. They head home around midnight. Janet is dropped off at her apartment in Del Paso Heights. When Jerry leaves to accompany her to the door, James asks his date about the evening.

'Shirley, I hope tonight wasn't too much drama for you with your father and Captain Eastland.'

'Are you serious? I thought we had an exciting night. And, don't you worry about Daddy. He'll come around.'

'So, the race thing isn't a big deal to him?'

'He's a little traditional, but I have no reason to think he's a racist.'

'That's good. I've learned to be cautious around white males.'

'Does that Captain Eastland give you a tough time at work?'

Before Walker can answer, Jerry returns.

'Janet had a good time tonight, Jerry,' Shirley remarks.

'"I think she did,' responds Hicks.

When we went to the ladies-room together, she told me she really likes you.'

'That's great. I did make a date with her for next week.'

'Ain't lettin' no grass grow under them feet, eh Jerry.'

'I'm a lucky man,' he replies.

They drive back to Shirley's place. James parks the car and walks her to the door.

'I might try to kiss you, but I'm afraid your father would open the door and hit me over the head with a frying pan.'

'You could try that and find out, but I think you have the wrong impression of Dad.'

James leans over and gives her a restrained kiss on the lips. She lingers with her lips against his.

'I would like to take you out again,' he nervously states. 'Maybe we could go to a movie or something.'

'I'd like that. Give me a call.'

She smiles then turns to open the front door. Facing her, he retreats backwards, stumbles and nearly falls down the front step. Waving to her with a sheepish grin, he runs to his car where Jerry is waiting for the ride back to base.'

CHAPTER 37

'Watch Gary carefully,' Tom instructs Phoebe. 'There he is floating with his ski tips pointing up out of the water. He's facing our boat with his arms extended; his hands firmly gripping the tow bar, and the rope between his legs.'

'Okay, now the boat is moving slowly. When that line gets taut, we accelerate….RRRRRRRR! Here he comes. He's up. Now, for him to maintain control, he needs to keep his legs flexed and body extended slightly backwards. See how comfortable he looks. He's leaning to the left now so he can cut across our wake to the left side…. Gary's shifting his weight toward the right ski and you can see him gliding through the wake to the right side. Looks like fun, huh.'

'Got it,' Phoebe states in her cocksure manner. 'I'm ready when he's finished.'

Captain Wilgus gives the cut sign to slow down the boat. Stirling revs down the 50-horsepower inboard engine powering the 18 foot Chris Craft. Gary drops the tow bar slowly sinking down until only his head and shoulders are above the water. The boat swings into a sharp turn and eases to a stop a few feet from the skier.

'Climb in, Gary. The Irish lassie wants to go next. How about I give her instructions while you pilot the boat?' Wilgus spryly clambers his tanned, athletic body onto the craft.

'We're a team, Stirling.'

Phoebe attaches the clips on her life preserver and jumps into the water feet first. Gary eases the boat ahead until she can reach the floating bar at the end of the tow line.

'Get the tips of both skis out of the water, and wait until we line up the boat with you. Keep your legs bent and your arms straight. Good.'

The sound of the motor changes from a barely audible, low pitched, stuttering drone to an eardrum piercing whine as Gary shoves the throttle lever forward. The confident Miss O'Connor quickly pops up on top of the water with a knowing smile on her face. Soon, she is traversing the wake with ease. After a few minutes, Stirling makes the cut sign to her, but she shakes her head and motions with one hand to keep going.

'She's doing fine,' notes Wilgus. 'Let her have a good time out there.'

Phoebe begins making her turns more sharply as she becomes increasing more comfortable with her body riding over the smooth water of the lake. Tom gives her the settle down signal with both hands, palms downward. She tosses her head back laughing.

Instead of skiing more cautiously, she lets go with one hand each time she changes directions leaning at sharper angles to the water's surface.

'That crazy Irish wench is risking serious injury now,' cries out the lieutenant to his boss. 'You need to slow down the boat so she has to stop skiing.'

Just as Tom makes that request, a large, rogue speedboat veers toward them at full throttle from the opposite direction. Phoebe makes a turn and is heading toward the onrushing craft.

Stirling screams out and gestures with his right arm, 'Turn the other way.'

Gary cuts the power, but it's too late. O'Connor skis directly into the right side of the oncoming boat. While that vessel barrels onward, the Irish reporter is knocked unconscious floating on her back with red blood billowing into the water surrounding the edges of her yellow life preserver.

'Oh my God!' cries Stirling rubbing his face in disbelief. 'Turn this thing around and get her NOW!'

The boat idles up next to Phoebe. Tom dives in to float her to the edge of the craft. He knows she might have a fractured spine, so he summons Wilgus to assist him. At Tom's request, Gary slides a six-foot board over the side for Stirling to place underneath her frame.

'I need you to keep her head in line with her body while we hoist her into the boat,' advises Tom recalling what he learned in a first aid class.

'I've had training before, Stirling. I know what to do.'

They slowly glide her onto the boat and lower her down to the floor with one life preserver under her head and another under her legs. A gash oozes blood from her forehead and two more cuts bleed from her thighs. Gary finds a clean cloth in a side hatch and tosses it to Tom. He rips the cloth in three pieces covering her open wounds and applying pressure to the cut on her head.

Gary starts the engine and cautiously guides the craft back to the boathouse. Stirling stands over his date checking her pulse and breathing. Fortunately, they are both functioning normally. He begins a one- sided conversation.

'You crazy, stubborn redhead. Couldn't you hear that boat coming? All right, what's done is done. We've got to get you to a hospital as soon as possible. You just keep that Irish temper up and fight.'

When they arrive at the dock. Wilgus rushes up to the home above the boathouse and knocks on the door. Luckily, someone is there. He calls for an ambulance. Ten minutes later, the emergency vehicle arrives. The crew rush down to the boat where Phoebe remains. She is carefully transferred to a trauma board, carried up to the vehicle, and driven to nearby Huggins Hospital.

Tom is pacing back and forth in the waiting room outside the surgical suite.

'She's been in there six hours now. What could they be doing that takes so long?'

Wilgus tries to ease his anxiety. 'She had a lot of injuries, Reb. Sit down. I'm going to get you something to eat.'

He returns a few minutes later with a Snickers candy bar and a cup of chamomile tea from the cafeteria.

'Here, drink this. It'll calm you down.'

No sooner does Stirling take a couple of sips than the doctor enters the room to give the news on Phoebe's condition.

'She's going to live, but we had to patch up numerous injuries. She's has four fractured ribs, a fractured left orbital bone, fractured left femur, two severely sprained ankles, multiple lacerations, some internal bleeding and a concussion.'

He continues. 'She did pull through okay on the surgical table, but she will need to go through an extensive recovery period before she's ready to resume her normal life.'

'At least she's going to survive. We were worried about that when it happened,' replies a relieved lieutenant.

Miss O'Connor is wheeled into an ICU room, and her two companions set themselves down in the cubicle waiting for her eyes to open.

CHAPTER 38

'We're planning an international track and field meet to be held at Hughes Stadium this summer. How about joining our committee?'

Pete Fetros is speaking to James before the beginning of the monthly Jaycee meeting.

'I'd like that, Pete. I ran track in college. Love the sport.'

'Great, I'll have Ray Clark, the committee chairman, get in touch with you later. It's going to be a joint venture with the AAU.'

'Thanks for thinking of me.'

'They're about to start the 220-yard dash, Shirley. Watch the guy in the middle. That's Tommie Smith,' informs James.

'Who's he?' she asks.

'Only the fastest man in the world.'

'Oh really?'

'Watch and see.'

A mid-spring dual meet is underway between San Jose State and Fresno State. Seven black male sprinters adjust their starting blocks at the near end of the cinder track. At the San Jose State facility, an extension on one side of the oval track provides enough length to run a straight away two twenty. The sprinters settle into their blocks, and the starter standing on the infield grass just ahead, raises his pistol. He calls out.

'Ready....Set....BANG!'

For the first thirty yards, the pack is nearly even. Then, the runner in the middle begins to pull ahead, at first by a yard. At 100 yards, he is 5 yards in the lead powering forward like a gazelle on amphetamines. As a group, they appear to be striding in unison, but with each step the man in the middle extends his lead.

The crowd is now standing. A cry of 'Oooooooh' emanates from the three hundred or so fans in the stands.

At the finish, the winner is clear of the field by 12 yards as officials at the line click their stop watches. Smith briefly raises his arms in victory then walks back to shake hands with his fellow competitors. After a short huddle, the timing officials check and recheck their watches, then give a final result to the track announcer. He activates his microphone.

'Winner of the 220-yard dash is Tommie Smith of San Jose State. The winning time is....19.5 seconds, a new world record.'

The crowd lets out a roar, and Smith jogs back down the cinder surface to acknowledge the applause of the fans.

'Are you impressed?' asks James.

''My word, that man is amazing,' cries Shirley. 'Do you have him signed up for your track meet?'

'You know, I'm not sure. I think the AAU is supposed to get a commitment from him.'

'Well, you should go down and talk to him about that.'

'But, I don't know him. Don't you think he would just dismiss me as some pesky fan?'

'No, you're involved in organizing an international track meet. You have plenty of reason to approach him.'

Shirley finally convinces him to make the contact.

'Tommie, Tommie,' James yells as the new record holder reaches the stands near him. Smith turns and comes closer to the bleachers, but Walker is obscured by other fans standing and cheering. He works his way along with Miss Stone down to the fence separating the fans from the track. As the sprinter begins to head back toward his teammates, Shirley shouts out his name.

'Tommie, Tommie Smith, fastest man in the world, please come over here.'

Smith turns his head and spots a beautiful blond woman gesturing to him with her arms raised overhead. He stops and walks over. The crowd reacts again moving closer to the runner and pinning James and Shirley against the fence.

'Tommie, Lieutenant Walker here needs to discuss your participation in the AAU meet in Sacramento this summer.' James manages a sheepish smile realizing his girlfriend had accomplished something he had made a feeble attempt to do.'

'Okay. We can meet, but not here. Meet me in front of the Phys. Ed. Building after the last event.'

Smith looks less superhuman dressed in a tee shirt and khakis. At six-foot three, he is tall but not unusually so. His clothes conceal the steel strength musculature that powers him beyond the efforts of other mere mortals. He seems polite but somewhat impatient.

'Remind me why I'm meeting with you.'

James attempts to justify himself.

'Thanks for giving us your time, Mr. Smith. My name is Lieutenant James Walker. I represent an organizing group for the international track and field competition coming up at Hughes Stadium in June. We're working with the AAU to stage this event, and we would very much like for you to participate.'

'Where are you from, Walker?'

'Georgia.'

'Well, I'm sure you know how us black men are being used by the white establishment for their benefit and detriment of our people. I refuse to be part of a black pony show that profits a bunch of rich white 'fat cats'.'

'I hear you, brother. Look, I'm not a front man for some capitalist group. I'm with the Sacramento Jaycees. We're a non-profit organization conducting events that benefit the city. I believe that your participation in an event like ours is a showcase of your talents to the world and a cause for black pride.'

'Let me think about it.'

'Here's my phone number in Sacramento.' James hands Tommie a slip of paper with his number. 'Call me any time.'

'I just remembered. There's a meeting of the 'Olympic Project for Human Rights' coming up next Wednesday evening. If you can make it, you'll get to meet Harry Edwards, the organizer.'

'I'll try to be there.'

'Sorry, Miss. No white people.'

Smith excuses himself and leaves with a group of other runners who had come out of the building while Tommie and James were talking.

'What are you doin' to run so fast, Smith?' asks one as they walk away.

'Just usin' my God given ability.'

'You are some kinda' freak, man,' says another as he playfully slaps him on the butt.

Driving back to Sacramento, James admits to Shirley that he is apprehensive about getting involved with this Harry Edwards group.

'I'm not sure what this 'Olympic Project' thing is, but I'm concerned it will get me mixed up in some racial politics that could get me in trouble.'

'You need to go. Getting Tommie Smith for your track meet is a must. He's the world's fastest runner. Remember?'

'I know you're right. But, I also know I'm sticking my neck out. Eastland will jump down my throat if he finds out.'

Harry Edwards lives in a second story, one bedroom apartment within a large complex about a mile from the San Jose State campus. The site of the meeting is his living room. James knocks on the front door at 7:30 p.m. A large black man with a close-trimmed beard, piercing eyes and an angry scowl answers the door.'

'Who the hell are you?' He asks.

'James Walker,' he replies, wishing he had talked himself out of coming. 'Tommie Smith invited me.'

Inside the room behind Edwards, Lee Evans is arguing with John Carlos in an agitated voice. Smith is nowhere around. He waits for a response from the man barring the door, who seems to be looking around for someone else.

Just then, the pinging sound of someone running up the outdoor flight of metal stairs interrupts the front door confrontation. Down the hallway from the top of those stairs emerges the figure of Tommie Smith.

'He's okay, I invited him,' yells Smith.

Edwards give them both a look of contempt.

'You're supposed to clear it with me before you ask any stranger to come to our meetings.'

'I did ask you, and you gave me the okay.'

'You must have caught me when I was preoccupied with something. What do we know about this guy? He might be an undercover black reporter from some right wing white supremacist newspaper.'

'He's not. I checked him out. He's with an organizing committee for the upcoming track meet in Sacramento this summer.'

'That's different. C'mon in Walker. Maybe you can shed some light on our dilemma.'

Smith introduces Walker to the other athletes. They briefly interrupt their conversation but appear disinterested in the intruder. Quickly dismissing him, they restart their argument. Edwards launches into a harangue with Smith about the need for secrecy and discretion for their activities. Sensing the hostility in the room, James gets the distinct impression that he doesn't belong there.

Finally, Edwards calls the meeting to order.

'All right, everybody shut up and listen.'

He gives Evans and Carlos the evil eye, and they stop talking.

'Being one of the top athletes in the world should make a difference in how society treats you. But does it? No. On the track, you are idolized as America's best. But, when you're looking for an apartment next to campus, you're just another nigger trying to bust into a white neighborhood. We've got to break that barrier down. I want to get out of this rat-infested building, and none of you are living any better than me.'

'So, that's our challenge. How do we finally get decent housing for our black brothers and sisters?'

James now feels even more out of place. He is living in a comfortable Bachelor Officers Quarters apartment with a white roommate from Brooklyn.'

'I say we boycott the AAU track meets until they come around to support our housing concerns and do something to change things,' demands Evans.

'And, what exactly do you think the AAU can do to change anything,' remarks Carlos.

James interjects. 'I guess I don't understand. How does boycotting help with the housing issue?'

'Media attention,' responds Evans. 'You invite the media to interview you in dumps like this place to see why you're boycotting.'

Walker scratches his head then reacts to Evan's statement. 'But you're giving up the spotlight of competing in a nationally televised event. Wouldn't you get more media attention by making your point in an interview after winning a race watched by millions of viewers?

The discussion continues without agreement for another hour when James decides he needs to leave.

'Thanks for letting me make my pitch. I truly hope to see you all at our meet in June.'

He gets blank stares from the group except for Smith who smiles and accompanies him to the door.

Driving back to Sacramento that evening, Walker feels frustrated that he has no commitment from Smith or any of his cohorts for competing at the Hughes Stadium meet.

CHAPTER 39

'Where am I?'

Phoebe opens her eyes and speaks for the first time. Tom is slumped in a chair next to the hospital bed. Startled, he struggles to stand up from the saggy backed chair where he has dozed off for the past several hours. Peering down, Stirling attempts to orient his lover.

'You're in the hospital. You were in a waterskiing accident and have been unconscious for two days. How do you feel?'

'Got a really bad headache.'

'I'll call the nurse. I'm sure the doctor prescribed something for that. Great to see you're finally awake.'

'I'm supposed to be at work. Help me get out of here.'

'Are you nuts? You're not going anywhere. For one thing, you're strung up in traction for a fractured femur. And, that's just one of your injuries. We contacted the Herald. Your boss says he'll be in to visit you later today.'

Several weeks have passed. Phoebe is leaving the hospital ambulating on crutches. Tom assists her into his car by first sliding the passenger seat all the way back, then lifting her left leg while she gingerly slides in. He attaches the lap belt and places her crutches in the back seat. As they're driving back to her apartment, Stirling begins the conversation.

'So, you plan to return to work next week. Will you be able to function okay?'

'Reb, you can't imagine how good I'll feel to be me self again. You've been a real friend during this tough period, but I need to get back to my feisty Irish ways.'

'You need to realize you're no way near 100% recovered. It takes time to regain your energy and stamina.'

'You sound like my mother. God bless her soul. I know how to take care of myself. I'm tired of being dependent on other people. Can't you understand that?'

'What I do understand is that you are reckless and overestimate your abilities. Furthermore, you're impetuous and prone to make judgments without all the necessary information.'

'You're talking like some old 'fuddy-duddy'.'

'Okay, what's going to happen when your boss gets a lead for a breaking story on a factory fire and wants to send you out on site.'

'I can get a driver and head out there. No big deal.'

'I don't think you realize how difficult it's going to be to handle the high stress of a situation like that. Just because you've done similar stories before does not mean your body is ready to deal with that kind of pressure in your present condition.'

'And, just what do you recommend, Doctor Stirling?'

'Go back to work part-time and stick to desk duty until you're able to walk like a normal person.'

'Okay, that might make some sense, but you've got to understand that chaining me to a desk is like putting me in prison. I need to be where the action is.'

Two weeks later, Tom gets a phone call at work.

'Lieutenant, there's a lady on the phone for you. She sounds pretty upset,' the airman states.

Tom picks up the phone with a sense of foreboding.

'Phoebe is that you?'

'Who's Phoebe? This is youah fiancée, Nancy. Rememba me? I haven't heard from you in three weeks.'

'Nancy, what a surprise. I guess I owe you an apology. I've been taking care of a friend up here who was in a bad accident with broken bones and other injuries. I know I've been remiss not calling you. I'm truly sorry.'

'So, is this so-called friend a mayan or a womayan?'

'Tom knows he is trapped. He has no choice but to lie.

'His name is Stan. He went waterskiing with Gary and me and ran himself into another boat. He got banged up pretty bad, and was in the hospital. He needed help when he got home.'

'Well, Ahm sorry for Stayan, but you coulda at least called me, and let me know what was goin' on. Ah've been sick with worry about you. And, tell me, who is Phoebe?'

'She's somebody I work with,' he states then quickly changes the subject. 'I'm sorry, honey. I promise to call you every week for the rest of my time here. I miss you.'

'I miss you too, Tom. When are you headin' back down heah to Geowgia?'

'I'm hoping to get back there for Christmas. That's only a few more weeks. Right now, I got to get back to work, sweet pea. You take care of yourself, hear.'

'Say hello to Stayan, and, don't you forget to call me again.'

Stirling smacks himself on the forehead. *Jesus, how can I be such a jerk? I know how much Nancy needs me. Deep down, I need her too. The truth is I can't resist Phoebe. She's like no woman I've ever been with before.*

Tom heads over to Phoebe's apartment that same evening to check on her. She comes to the door using only one crutch.

'Hey, look at you. That leg must be getting stronger.'

'Yes, I can almost take my whole weight on it now.' She tries to stand on her bad leg, winces and quickly shifts back to her right side.

'Have you eaten? I brought a bottle of wine.'

'I just had some Chinese takeout delivered. Wanna join me?'

'Sure.'

They go into the small dining room where several cartons of hot Asian delights are lying on the table.

'Have a seat,' commands Tom. 'I'll get the plates, utensils and a couple of glasses.'

Lemon Chicken, Mongolian beef, sweet and sour pork are spooned onto two plates along with a generous serving of rice. They gorge themselves, and end up finishing the entire bottle of chenin blanc.

'How are things going at work?' asks Tom.

'You know I hate being stuck in the office. There was a call to go out and investigate a drowning down at the pier. Of course, the boss wouldn't let me go and sent Cooper instead. That's frustrating for me. How about you? Anything out of the ordinary?'

Tom thinks about his surprise call from Nancy, but decides to not bring that up.'

'Nothing unusual.'

'Okay, I opened my fortune cookie, before I tell you mine, read yours.'

'Mine says, "You will travel to exotic places." Okay, now your turn.'

'I don't believe this one, "Romance is in your near future."'

Tom opens his arms and pleads, 'Romeo is right here.' She gives him a quizzical look.

'By the way, is that left leg still swollen? I can give you a little massage. Maybe that will help the circulation.'

He tries to rub her leg while sitting in a dining room chair. It's too awkward.

'Let me have you lie down. That way I can really get deep into that inflammation. Got any skin crème? That will make it easier too.'

Tom retrieves some lotion from the bathroom medicine cabinet and begins massaging her leg while she lies in bed.

'Oh Reb, that feels really good.'

Taking that remark as a cue, he begins rubbing a little higher on her thigh above the swelling. One thing leads to another, and they're soon making love for the first time since the accident. Afterward, they lie on their backs in the dark and begin talking.

'I got a call from my old boyfriend today,' she informs him. 'He heard about my accident and wanted to know if I was okay.'

'You still see him?'

'Broke up about a year ago. We were constantly fighting.'

'Why doesn't that surprise me? Coincidentally, I had a call from an old girlfriend down in Georgia today.'

'You weren't in an accident. Why was she calling you?'

'Well, she hadn't heard from me in a while, and asked how I was doing.'

'She's still your girl, isn't she? You've been cheating on her with me.'

'We broke up before I left down South. I knew my assignment here was two years, and that was going to be too long away from each other. We agreed to go our separate ways.'

'I don't think I believe you. But, I commend you on being a convincing liar.'

CHAPTER 40

'Walker, get in here!'

Captain Eastland's face is beet red, ready to explode. James hears the anger in his voice. He quickly rises from his desk and hurries into his boss' office.

'I overheard Hicks talking to Lieutenant Morin. He said you have been meeting with Harry Edwards and a group of radical negroes. Is that right?'

'It was in regard to a track meet that I....'

'Stop, Lieutenant. Did you or did you not attend a meeting run by Harry Edwards? Yes or no.'

'Yes, sir.'

'Are you aware that Mr. Edwards is considered a subversive by the United States government and a leader of the black power movement?'

'No sir, I was not.'

'How do you think it looks for a United States Air Force officer to be associated with a known revolutionary in his own country? Answer me?'

James recoils at Eastland's insinuations. 'Not very good, sir.'

'Not very good? No, much worse than not very good. It appears that the officer is acting as a conspirator against his own country. If I hear of you associating with Mr. Harry Edwards again, I will recommend you for court martial as a traitor to the oath you took as an officer. Do you understand me?'

'Yes sir. But, I can explain the circumstances to you.'

'No, you are dismissed. Consider this a verbal warning. Now go back to work.'

James is stunned by the severity of Eastland's reaction. He knew it would be bad news if his boss did discover his meeting with the San Jose athletes. But, the threat of a court martial; that was something far worse than he imagined. He did vow to the Captain he would have no further contact with Edwards, but now he feels conflicted by making that promise. The only person he feels safe talking about his dilemma is Shirley. He meets her at Sambo's pancake house. They locate an out of the way booth in the back of the restaurant.

'I don't know what to do. Eastland is going to recommend me for a court martial if I have any more dealings with the San Jose athletes. Now I'm afraid any influence I have with Smith and his teammates will be totally lost. And, the Jaycees are counting on me to have those guys commit to the Hughes Stadium meet. What am I going to do?'

'You can't just totally cut off your relationship with those runners. The fact is, you need them, and they need you. Don't you believe that boycotting events like your track meet is the wrong tactic?'

With a look of resignation, Walker nods his head.

'Well then, you owe it to yourself and to them. You need to stay in contact and convince them of the benefit for their participation.'

'But how? How can I do that without risking the wrath of Eastland?'

'Okay, tell me specifically, what did you promise your friend, the Captain?'

'I agreed I would have no further contact with Edwards.'

'Great. So, you will have no further contact with Mr. Edwards. But, nothing was agreed to that prevents you from associating with Tommie

Smith or his teammates. Right?'

'Now that you mention it, no. But, what if Eastland gets wind of my discussions with Smith?'

'Think about it. The only way he found out the last time was through your friend, Hicks.'

'Your right, Shirley. All I need to do is keep my trap shut. I'll tell Jerry about my confrontation with Eastland, and let him think I've cut off all contact with the San Jose runners. And, that's partially true.'

'Good. I think you're finally seeing the light.'

'Thanks Shirley. I think I can see how this could work out now.'

Walker soon realizes his next step working with the runners isn't going to be easy. He paces back and forth in his BOQ bedroom talking to himself.

Should I call Tommie and let him know the situation with my boss? No, that might tell him I'm not fully committed to work with his group. Maybe I should make excuses to avoid attending their meetings. But, he might conclude the same thing and my influence on them would be zero. What if I did attend the meetings and made sure Hicks or anyone else at work, doesn't find out? Then, I would be taking a risk, violating my promise to Eastland. Man, this is going to be more difficult than I thought.

He considers calling Shirley to help him make the decision. Then, the lieutenant walks into the bathroom and looks into the mirror.

I know what she would say, he tells himself. *And, it's the best chance for me to convince those guys of the right decision. To hell with Eastland's threats.*

CHAPTER 41

Nearly two years have passed since Stirling arrived at Pease. His orders have just come through channels for his next deployment, Tan Son Nhut Air Base, Vietnam. He pulls up a chair at the desk in his BOQ quarters clad in white boxers and tee shirt, staring at his life changing papers.

Okay, we all knew when we signed up, this day could come. Things would be worse if I was wearing Army camo fatigues and carrying an M16. Calm down. Take a positive attitude, and make the best of it.

Time for one last trip to Georgia before heading to Southeast Asia. As he drives the yellow Chevy southward, Stirling ponders the quandary regarding the two women in his life.

I can't imagine leaving Phoebe and never seeing her again. On the other hand, Nancy has been there for me like a rock. I know she expects to walk down the aisle once I get back from 'Nam. How did I get myself into this mess?

Tom had returned to Georgia several times during his tour in Yankee country. While ties to his parents remain close, relations with Nancy have become strained. Time apart, gaps in communications, waning interest in the other's day-to-day activities and unconfirmed suspicions on her part have eroded their bond. He knows he must take the initiative to patch things up.

They're sitting on the sofa in the living room at Doerun.

'"Whatcha get me, honey.' She opens a large box covered in pink wrapping paper and a large white bow. 'Oh, you devil, Tom. Do you expect me to wayah this?'

She's holding up a pink cotton mini-dress with the hemline above mid-thigh.

'Sure, you've got nice legs. Go try it on.'

Nancy takes the dress into her bedroom returning minutes later to model her new outfit. She giggles. 'Well honey, whattya think?'

'You look like one hot mama!'

'You mean thayat?'

'You bet. In fact, why don't we go dancing tonight? There's a live band playing over at Warner Robbins officer's club, and you can wear your new dress.'

'Ah don't know.   Ahm a little tahd.   Why don't we watch some TV? Beverly Hillbillies are on tonight.'

'C'mon, sweetie, we haven't seen each other in months. Time to do a little steppin' out and havin' some fun.'

'Ah wish Ah felt up to it, but Ah'm exhausted after workin' awl day.'

Tom sighs. Phoebe wouldn't hesitate at an offer like that. Still, he knows making Nancy happy is important.

'Okay, you win, dear. Maybe we can go dancing when you feel a little more zip.'

Saturday morning. Nancy feels good, and the couple head out to Lake Blackshear to water ski. The late spring weather has turned sunny and warm. Tom cruises up Route 300 feeling confident his fiancée has warmed up to him as she moves over and snuggles her head against his shoulder.

'Ah missed you, honey. We've had so many good tahms together with our frayands and just by ourselves too. Did you miss me?'

'I thought about you every day. So nice to be back together again, sweetie.'

Abruptly, she moves back away from him.

'Do you still love me?'

'Of course, why would you ask me a question like that?'

'Because you didn't call me enough.'

'How can you say that? I called you every week except when Stan got injured.'

'That's when Ah thought you mighta got a new girlfriend. 'Cause Ah know you aren't no homosexuayl.'

'I told you Stan got hurt real bad waterskiing, and I felt a little responsible. So, I went to see him every day until he got well enough to take care of himself.'

'Ah can't believe you couldn't find the tahm to call me. Are you shuah Stayan isn't a womayan?'

'Of course not. Would I lie to you?'

'Ahm not shuah. Ah remember that time you and Miles took those floosies down to the shore.'

'Now you're dredging up ancient history. That was years ago. And, didn't I do everything possible to win you back?'

'You did. But Ah always hayave a little doubt in mah mind about you since then.'

Stirling backs the car and boat trailer onto the concrete ramp leading into the water. He helps Nancy into the boat and slowly unratchets the winch cable until the boat is floating. He parks the vehicle locking their personal belongings in the trunk and joins her in the boat.

Soon, Tom is piloting the pink fiberglass craft into the center of the lake.

'You should go first, sweetie.'

'Aw right, honey. Hope Ah rememba how to do this. It's been a while.'

'You're a good skier. You'll do just fine.'

Minutes later, Nancy is gliding along in perfect form on her slalom ski. The winds are calm and the water is glassy smooth. Stirling looks back and sees a big smile on his fiancee's face. For the moment, all is right between the two. Then, the high-pitched sound of the motor is pierced by a distressed woman's voice. Tom looks back again and sees Nancy frowning and signaling him to stop.

He slows the boat allowing her to let go of the tow bar. Circling around, he approaches the sad faced skier bobbing in the gentle wake.

'What's wrong?'

'We need to stop, Tom. It's mah tahm of the month. And, Ah'm getting some awful cramps.'

Stirling now realizes this will be his future with Nancy; bending to an unending series of her needs. He really doesn't mind when she has her flare-ups of Crohn's Disease. They've experienced some of their closest moments then. These petty complaints are what now grates on his nerves.

Two days before the lieutenant plans to drive back north, Nancy has a flare up of her chronic ailment. He comes to take her to a movie they both want to see. Mrs. Gunn informs him she is in bed with a temperature of 101 degrees. He enters her darkened room and sits on a wooden chair next to the bed.

'Sweetie, are you awake?' He waits several seconds for an answer. A soft, moaning voice replies.

'Honey, is that you? Sorry 'bout the movies. Ah don't feel so good. Got a temp, stomach pain, and Ah been to the bathroom several tahms.'

'Hurts me to hear that, babe. We'll go see that movie another time.'

'You know what will make me feel bettah? Tell me a story. Can you do thayat for me?'

'Sure, sweetie. This about the time I took my first flight lesson in a small plane. I got asked to go flying by a friend of Captain Wilgus. I had been interested in getting my own license since joining the Air Force. So, I jumped at the chance.

'It was a euphoric feeling when we lifted off the ground. We circled the field climbing to about 3,000 feet. Then, he said, "Take the yoke." At first, he had me just hold a straight course trying to watch the gauges and looking out the windshield. When I got comfortable with that, we began performing turns to change course headings. I was getting cocky thinking I was in full control of the plane.

'After half an hour or so, he told me we were going to practice some landings. He performed three touch and goes, then coached me through the final landing. As we approached the runway, I was too high, then I was too low. I finally got the plane on the glide path at the correct speed right before we touched down. One problem. The nose of the plane was pointing a little to the right side of the runway. He yelled at me to press on the left rudder pedal to correct my roll out. Unfortunately, my seat was too far forward, so when I hit the left rudder, I was also hitting the left brake, which was on the top of the pedal.

'We ended up performing a maneuver called a 'ground loop'. The plane abruptly swerved left rolling off the runway; plowing through the grass and dirt of the infield. When my instructor finally brought the plane to a halt, we were facing 180 degrees from our intended direction smack in the middle of the airport.

'The air traffic controller in the tower growled, 'Nancy 987 get that aircraft back on the runway and over to the taxiway, STAT!' He had to route all the air traffic coming into the field into a holding pattern until we got over to our hangar.

'Wilgus' friend never asked me to fly again.'

'Youah funny, Tom. You know how to make me layaff. Ah feel bettah already.'

Tom stays over that night at the Gunn house sleeping in a guest room. The next morning after breakfast, he says his goodbyes to Nancy.

'Wish me luck, sweet pea. I'll miss you.'

'Ah'll miss you too, honey. And, you bettah write me every week.'

'I will. And, you stay healthy, hear.'

They kiss and hug looking affectionately into each other's eyes. Tom drives off in his Chevy beeping his horn while the whole Gunter family stands on the front stoop and waves.

The lieutenant spends his last day in Georgia with his parents.

'We're concerned about you, son,' Papa Stirling confesses. 'Those Viet Cong are a nasty bunch. So, don't take any foolish risks. Stay safe and come home to us in one piece.'

'Tan Son Nhut is a well-guarded place, Daddy. And, I'm not going off base trying to kill the enemy. I'm going to be behind protected walls in a secure building.'

'Your mother and I are looking forward to seeing that fiancée of yours in a wedding dress once you get back.'

'Yes sir. I'm looking forward to that myself,' Tom replies with a conviction meant for both his parents and himself.

Tom takes leave from the only real home he has ever known, early on a rainy June morning. Myrna makes sure he has enough food to last the two-day trip up the coast. She packs a full cooler full of sandwiches, chips, drinks, and several of her son's favorite chocolate chip cookies.

He opens the driver side window to wave to his parents as he pulls away. 'I'll be back before you know it,' he yells.

'Don't forget to write,' Myrna shouts back.

He beeps the horn and the sight of his car soon disappears into the foggy wetness of early daylight. Romantic visions of Phoebe fill his mind on the long drive north.

CHAPTER 42

'Here's how I look at your choices. The more you compete, the more you are in the public eye as the best runners in the world. And, you can appeal for changes within the system during TV interviews. By boycotting, you become marginalized; painting a negative picture to the public by associating with groups perceived as radical and dangerous.'

James is speaking at Harry Edward's apartment on an evening in early May, 1966. Lee Evans and John Carlos stand listening to Walker restlessly shifting their feet and turning their heads toward one another with looks of disdain at each assertion.

'That ain't nothin' but an Uncle Tom point of view, Walker,' counters Evans. 'Trying to work with 'whitey' on our problems gets us sympathy from some no-count group like the hippies. And, what do we get from the honky establishment….nothin'.'

Becoming impatient with the split among the members, Edwards takes control of the debate.

'All right, all right, we've heard the same arguments several times on both sides of the boycott issue. It's time to make a decision. We'll now take a vote. Those in favor, say yes.'

'Yes', says Evans

'Hell yes,' says Carlos.

'That's two for the boycott. Now, who's against it?'

'I am,' says Smith. The lieutenant also raises his hand.

'You don't count, Walker. Remember you're just a guest, not a member of our group.'

'That leaves me to decide,' says Harry. He strokes his beard then begins to pace the room. Stopping as if struck by a thunderbolt of inspiration, he turns to face the group.

'I support the concept of refusing our participation, but I don't think we're big enough yet. We need the support of a lot more athletes than just the ones in this room. So, until that happens, we should delay any action.'

'I hear what you're saying, Harry, but that leaves us at a stalemate,' says Carlos. 'So, what do we do next?'

'I recommend delaying the boycott until we sign on at least twenty world class track and field athletes to unite behind this effort,' concludes Edwards.

'Good plan, let's start recruiting,' agrees Carlos.

'Can you tell me what that means for our Hughes Stadium meet?' asks James.

'Right now, we'll participate, but that status could change before your event actually happens,' states Edwards before turning his back on Walker and addressing his runners. 'Okay, we've reached the decision we came here for tonight. Time to get busy recruiting other athletes. We'll make a list right now, then divide up the names among the four of us.'

'Wait a minute,' cries James. The group stops talking and each turn around. 'You're asking me to leave here with no guarantee you'll participate at the Hughes Stadium meet. C'mon, the least you can do is give me a commitment for that. It's only a month away.'

Edwards give him a cold stare.

'What makes you think we owe you anything? You don't seem to understand our situation. We're poor. Whitey's got us living like animals, and we're trying to change that. You're up there in Sacramento living in a nice apartment furnished by the Air Force while we're down her surviving in dumps like this. Sorry, but you're not one of us.'

'Look, Mr. Edwards, I got to where I am by fighting for negro rights since I was picking cotton and the fields as a small boy. So, don't disrespect me. I'm not trying to sell you out to the white establishment. I'm working to make things better for all of us. So, please don't reject me by boycotting our meet next month, because if you pull out, that event will disappear and so will others, like crops in the Okie dust bowl.'

'You've got your one little problem, son. We've got bigger fish to fry.'

With that rebuff, the lieutenant engages the sympathetic eyes of Smith, then turns to leave.

He mumbles to himself as he walks to his car.

Harry's on a misguided crusade.

CHAPTER 43

Tom returns to Portsmouth after two weeks in Georgia. He enters his quarters finding a stack of mail waiting for him, mostly bills and a letter in an international envelope. It's from Miles. He opens the note from his old friend. He had enlisted in the Marines without graduating from college and is now serving in Vietnam.

'Stirling:

'Been over here six months now and seen lots of action. Several firefights with the Cong and NVA. On one mission, I snuffed six gooks with my rifle and slit the throat of another in hand-to-hand combat. What a rush, better than sex. Looks like I'm going to get out of here alive because I took a bullet in the ass from Charlie. They tell me I'll be heading stateside in a month or so.

'Hey, maybe we could get together for a couple of drinks when we both get back home. Drop me a line and tell me how things are going in the wussy Air Force.

'Miles'

Jesus, he's crazier than I thought,' thinks Tom. *'To think he has been my close friend for all these years.*

He readies himself for a meeting with Phoebe where he intends to propose ideas for continuing their relationship. He has convinced himself his future would be more exciting with her than with Nancy. As he drives toward her apartment, he rehearses his speech.

You and I have been through good times and tough times over the past two years. I feel we've developed a bond, which will only grow stronger in the years ahead. We've come to a crucial juncture due to my upcoming assignment for one year in Vietnam. I know for myself, I will miss our numerous discussions and many adventures. But, most of all, I will miss the closeness of you.

I hope you will agree to hold on to the bond we have built and commit to growing in new ways during my absence. When I return that connection can grow anew. I will miss you very much, and I plan to write you every week.

He arrives at her place at about 6 p.m. on a weekday after work. As he knocks on her door, he can hear two people talking loudly inside. Phoebe's voice is clearly recognizable, but the other is some male he doesn't know. Reb decides to let himself in and is met by his lover just inside the door.

'Let's step outside. I need to talk to you.'

Stirling is confused.

'Who's that guy in there? He sounds like he's threatening you. Are you okay?'

'I'm fine. Let me explain.'

'When you were gone down South, Curtis, my old boyfriend, came back to see me. He's changed. AA got him sober, and he's been holding down a steady job for the past several months.'

'What has that got to do with you and me?'

'I'm sorry, Reb. You're going to be leaving for a year. And, I realized when Curtis came back I still loved him. You're a nice guy, Tom, but I don't see a future for us together.'

'But, we've done everything together for almost two years. I thought you felt the same way toward me as I do for you. I love you, Phoebe.'

'I knew this would be hard for you to accept. I'm sure you'll find someone else soon.'

'So, just like that, we're through, finished, kaput? And, we'll never see each other again?'

'Thank you for everything. You were so good to me after the skiing accident. I'll always remember the kindness you showed me during that time.'

There's a voice from inside.

'Babe, finish up with that loser, will ya. I need to show you something.'

'Sorry, Reb, I gotta go. He gets mad when I make him wait. Good luck over there in Vietnam, and stay safe.'

She stoops down to where he is standing next to the top step and gives him a peck on the cheek. Without saying more, she closes the front door disappearing from view.

Tom is shocked. He never anticipated this kind of rejection. He had been ready to break his engagement with Nancy. He feels hurt and confused. As he turns and descends the stairs toward his car, a slow, burning anger rises in his chest.

That bitch. After everything I did for her, she tosses me out like a wad of used toilet paper. I should go back right now and give her a piece of my mind.

He pauses for a moment. That insult was too much. He pivots around and heads straight for her front door.

'Bang, bang, bang!' Stirling pounds on the door with his fist. Seconds later, the door is forcefully opened. A tall, slender man in a tee shirt and jeans looks down on him with a cigarette dangling from the right side of his lips.

'Whattya want?' he gruffly blurts out.

'Tell Phoebe to come out here. I got something more to say to her.'

'Didn't you get the message, punk? She's finished with you. So get lost.'

Stirling attempts to push the man aside and enter the apartment, but he underestimates Curtis' strength. They scuffle attempting to push each other backwards. The old boyfriend soon prevails. Tom tumbles down the staircase. Failing to stop himself by attempting to grab the railing, he lands on his back in the middle of the sidewalk below.

'Go back to your mama, boy. And, don't let me catch you around here again.'

Tom feels defeated. He crawls to his feet with a searing pain stabbing him in the back. Staggering and limping back to his car, he drives back to base.

I can't believe what just happened. We were so close. We needed each other. I know I fell for her, but maybe I was only fooling myself thinking she loved me. But, she must have some feelings for me. It's just that this jerk shows up and messes with her head. What can I do about it? I leave for Vietnam in three days.

Maybe I should call? Write? Visit her at work? Go back to her apartment after that bozo leaves? Am I fooling myself into thinking I still have a chance to win her back? It certainly didn't look good for me back there.

No, I made the extra effort to reach out to her. If I mean more to her than a temporary fling, she needs to come to me.

He waits by the phone for the next 72 hours. No call. Depressed, he boards the plane to 'Nam with his connection to Phoebe severed.

CHAPTER 44

The crowd begins buzzing before the race begins. Word has spread; something special could happen tonight. The gun goes off. Eight elite athletes uncoil their legs springing forward like cheetahs rocketing after their prey. As the runners round the turn and sprint toward the finish line, thousands of fans stand and roar their approval.

June 11, 1966. The winner has bolted across the finish line with a clear lead over the field at Hughes Stadium. The track announcer leans up to the microphone.

'Winner of the 200-meter run, Tommie Smith from San Jose State in a new world record time of 20.0 seconds.' The crowd erupts again, louder than before.

Shirley, sitting next to James, shakes him by the shoulders.

'You did it, honey. You should feel proud.'

'Relieved is a better word. Relieved and happy. Tommie ran a great race, didn't he?'

Ray Clark, Pete Fetros and several other Jaycees sitting nearby come over to congratulate Walker on his successful effort to recruit the San Jose stars.

'Look at this place, Lieutenant,' exudes Fetros. 'It's packed thanks to you. And, what a show with a world record at our event. Good going. Let's do it again next year.'

Ray bends down and whispers into James' ear.

'Fetros doesn't understand what you went through to get these guys. Congratulations, you did a fantastic job.'

'Thanks Ray. I'm glad it worked out.'

Smith comes over to the stands where Walker and the other Jaycees are sitting and motions for James to come onto the field. The lieutenant works his way down, and once on the track, shakes Smith's hand.

'This is a great day for you, Tommie. Thanks for participating.'

'I'm the one who should be thanking you. Appreciate your time working with our group.'

Captain Eastland bursts into James' cubical holding up the local sports page on Monday after the meet. 'Lieutenant Walker, explain to me how this photo appeared in yesterday's Sacramento Bee.' Pictured is James shaking hands with Tommie Smith on the track at Hughes Stadium.

Walker can see the malicious glint in his boss' eyes.

'Sir, you told me to have no contact with Harry Edwards, but you didn't mention anything about Tommie Smith. I have developed a friendship with him, so we kept in contact by phone.'

'Oh, a little phone call to Smith made you such a good friend that he calls you down on the field after a world record run to have your picture taken with him. Is that what I'm supposed to believe?'

'Captain, I was the one member of the Jaycee organizing committee who knew him personally.'

'I smell a rat, Walker. And, I'm going to look into this further. In my mind, you violated my order not to associate with black power radicals. If I can prove it, you're going to be court martialed.'

'Would you like more roast beef, Lieutenant?' Mrs. Stone inquires.

'Thank you, ma'am. I've had plenty.'

James is a guest for Sunday dinner in the family dining room with Shirley, Father Brent and Mother Marge. Mrs. Stone continues to be openly hospitable to him, while Brent is less than enthusiastic regarding his daughter's choice of a boyfriend.

'Pop, you should know if it wasn't for James, that international track meet last week would have been a huge flop.'

Brent Stone is more than a little skeptical that a young, negro lieutenant could have made such an impact. He can't resist prodding Walker with a few questions.

'That's an impressive claim my daughter made for you. Okay Lieutenant, exactly what did you do to make that event such a success?' Brent puts down his fork and stares directly into the eyes of his company.

'Well sir, I was the only black member of the Jaycee committee involved with the track meet. So, they wanted me to convince some of the top negro runners to compete.'

'I don't understand,' Brent comments. 'Why was it so hard to get those athletes to participate?'

Shirley jumps in.

'They are being influenced by black power advocates who are trying to use them to demonstrate against the white establishment. By boycotting major athletic events, they hope to gain their demands. James fought against their ideas and won, at least for now.'

'She gives me too much credit, sir. I had the support of Tommie Smith who really made the difference.'

'Lieutenant, help me to understand why you negroes do these hostile actions. We have a constitution in this country. We have the 'Bill of Rights'. Why do your people take to the streets and riot, loot, bomb and shoot people? How is that going to make America a better place for your people and everybody else?'

The table becomes dead quiet. James can tell that Shirley's father is not a big supporter of civil rights or the plight of the black man in the United States of America. He rankles at this attitude and is tempted to blast Mr. Stone for being so blind to reality. But, he catches himself and pauses until his anger subsides.

'Mr. Stone, I can see how you believe the actions of negroes are being destructive not only to the community but even to themselves. Please remember, these are people whose ancestors came to this country as slaves. No matter what they have done in their everyday lives, they feel the freedom, rights and opportunities that are supposed to be theirs as citizens of the good ole USA, have, in reality, been denied. They are acting out of anger and frustration at this century-long contradiction.'

'Look son. Don't get me wrong, I've never thought slavery was a good thing for anyone, but I don't see where being destructive is going to make things better. You're only alienating white people even more.'

James looks down at the table in front of him gritting his teeth, not sure how to react to Brent's last remark. A silence lasts several seconds before Marge can't stand it anymore.

'Who wants dessert? I've got home made apple pie and ice cream.'

'Let's go for a walk,' suggests Shirley after dinner. 'I think we need to talk.'

They excuse themselves from the table and head out the front door. The intense summer heat has relented in the late Sacramento afternoon.

'How did you end up agreeing to date a black guy when you grew up with a father with those kinds of beliefs?'

'Don't you go criticizing my father! He's a good person. He just lives in a conservative white world where things are fine the way they are. He sees black people rioting on television and believes they are lazy individuals who aren't willing to work to make their lives better.'

'You didn't answer my question.'

'There was a black family that moved into our neighborhood when I was 10 years old. They had a girl my age, and, of course, we went to the same school. Being the only black girl in the class, the other girls tended to ignore or make fun of her. I remember talking to my mother about this. She suggested I try to make friends with her.'

'Go on.'

'The girl's name was Melissa. She told me she came from a place where only black children attended her school, and she never had a white friend before. I said I wanted to be her first white friend. She broke down and cried. I held her and said not to cry. The other kids would like her when they got to know her better.'

'Didn't you feel different from her; the way she talked, the smell of her nappy hair, the darkness of her skin, or that maybe she wasn't very smart. After all, she grew up in a very different environment from you.'

'No, I only saw a lonesome girl who needed a friend.'

Walker wasn't buying Shirley's story. He had rarely met a white person who didn't have some negative feelings toward coloreds. Even honky liberals often expressed fear of getting beaten or robbed by coloreds encountered in a dark alley.

'C'mon. There had to be some things you didn't like about Melissa.'

Shirley is getting pissed about James being so negative.

'Don't you think you're being overly cynical about me? Didn't I agree to date you without knowing much about you at all?

'Okay, you got me there. I thought you were excited to date me 'cause I looked so good in my uniform.'

'You flatter yourself, Walker.'

'All right, I believe you were sincere. Say, let's leave here and head over to my place. I can use some comforting after being rejected by your father.'

'You're getting a little too full of yourself. You go back to your apartment. I'm going to have a talk with Pop about whether white girls should date black men.'

CHAPTER 45

On arrival at Tan Son Nhut, Stirling has been assigned to coordinate maintenance of the extensive array of communications facilities on base; a job similar to the one he had back at Pease only bigger. He directs the efforts of 168 personnel with the assistance of a senior master sergeant and other non-commissioned officers from a central control room. He relies on their expertise honed from many years of experience to keep communications up and running.

'Lieutenant, we've got a problem with the radio maintenance shop,' Sergeant Sillers reports. 'The men working there have no respect for Sergeant Buckles, and their poor performance is causing line outages.'

'We can't have that,' Stirling concurs. 'What do you recommend, Sergeant?'

'Tech Sergeant Moore, runs the receiver shop. When he says jump, his men jump. I suggest we kick Buckles upstairs to a tech advisor position and move in Moore.'

Stirling can see the wisdom of that move. In fact, his new supervisor Captain Ross Pedersen had already briefed him about the deficiencies in the radio shop.

'Excellent advice, Sergeant Sillers. Let's make that change ASAP.'

Back in his office one morning after his arrival, Tom phones Captain Pedersen.

'Hey boss, I have an old friend lying in the hospital over in Cam Ranh Bay. How do I get over there to visit him?'

'Stirling, you need to hitch a ride on a Med-Evac chopper. Check with Air Ops. There's usually a couple of Hueys heading there every day.'

Tom feels guilty for not seeing his old friend Miles. Stirling has been stationed in 'Nam for three weeks now, and he knows Trousdale is slated to be sent home soon. Early on Saturday morning, he wraps up some cookies his mother had sent and heads down to air operations.

'Any chance of catching a lift to Cam Ranh Bay today, Sergeant?' he inquires. 'I got a close buddy in the hospital over there, and I'd like to visit him.'

'You're in luck, Lieutenant. We've got a chopper leaving in half an hour. I can put you on the manifest.'

He remains in the waiting room until finally the NCO gives him the okay to board the big Huey. Climbing in, he takes a jump seat on the side of the aircraft.

Three wounded soldiers are the reason for the flight; two marines and one army corporal, each lying on a litter. One marine has his mangled left arm wrapped in bandages with blood seeping through. The other leatherneck has dressings wrapped over his face and upper torso. The Army GI has lost both lower legs from a 'Bouncing Betty' land mine. His feet are missing, and the girth of the bindings around the remaining bones appear to indicate he's lost a lot of muscle tissue as well. One Army medic attends the three men who are all being sedated on morphine.

The gruesome reality of the scene is Tom's first taste of the real war. He develops a queasiness in his belly from the sudden closeness of combat. His mind turns to his own mortality with fears of this helicopter being shot down.

The whirlybird revs up and within seconds they have lifted off the tarmac, thrusting northeastward beyond the confines of Tan Son Nhut and over the dense palm jungle below. He breaks out in beads of sweat on his forehead while tightly squeezing the sides of his seat. The low-pitched thump-

thump-thump of the rotor seems to make the aircraft an easy target for some sniper below. The co-pilot turns his head and sees the look of panic on Stirling's face.

'Relax, Lieutenant, we've been briefed on a safe route to get there.'

In 25 minutes, they arrive at the airfield located on the coast of the South China Sea.

Tom doesn't know what to expect when he sees his old roommate. From the content of Trousdale's last letter, he suspects the battlefield encounters have changed him in some profound way.

He bids goodbye and good luck to the medic with his three wounded soldiers and follows the signs to the front entrance of the hospital. Inside, he approaches the Navy petty officer manning the information desk.

'I'm looking for a wounded Marine, Lance Corporal Miles Trousdale. Can you direct me to him?'

The swabbie looks through his directory of patients.

'You said Trousdale, Miles, right?'

'That's him.'

'He's in Building D, bed 13.'

'Thanks, now where do I go from here?'

The hospital is composed of several wood framed buildings adjacent to each other. All the structures have sand bags piled ten high around the entire perimeter. The main building contains a reception area, administration offices, recreation area, and a dining hall/kitchen. A second building houses several surgical suites. The remaining ones are for patient beds and include one ICU unit and a physical therapy department.

'Go out this door, turn right and follow the walkway to the third building behind this one. You should find him in there.'

He leaves the main structure and finds his way to Building D. Bed 13 is empty.

'I'm looking for a jarhead named Trousdale,' he asks the soldier in Bed 14. 'Any idea where he might be?'

'Your buddy is a pool shark,' says the young man whose mangled right leg is hoisted up in a skeletal traction frame. 'Most of the time he hangs out in the rec room down at the main building.'

'Thanks for the tip. Take care of that leg.'

He returns to the front of the complex and locates the recreation room. Sure enough, there's Miles lying prone on a gurney with a large, puffy bandage over his buttocks protruding from under his pajamas. He's propped with a pillow under his stomach holding a cue stick in his right hand, ready to hit a shot.

'You always were the biggest ass in our fraternity,' shouts Stirling. 'I guess over here that makes you a target.'

'Well, if it isn't my junior birdman buddy from Georgia,' replies a surprised Trousdale. 'Good to see you, Stirling, even if you did join that namby pamby Air Force.'

'So, tell me about your wound. Are they going to send you home soon?'

'Wouldn't you know, I got some shitty infection. They need to keep me here 'til that gets under control.'

'That's too bad. I bet it sucks being stuck here longer.'

'I hate to admit it, but I love being out there killing those fuckin' gooks. I would go out there right now if they'd let me.'

'Maybe you've been here too long, buddy. It'll be good to get back to Georgia where you can go coon hunting to satisfy your need to kill something.'

'I think that's too tame for me. Maybe I should go to Africa and hunt lions....or maybe African niggers.' He laughs out loud.

'That's sick, Miles.'

'So, Stirling, are you still engaged to Miss Nancy, the virgin?'

'Yes, I am. We're looking to get married when I get back.'

The two go on talking for the better part of an hour. Then, Tom is informed the chopper to Tan Son Nhut is scheduled to leave shortly.

'Miles, great to see you. Take care of that ole butt infection. If you end up being here a few weeks, I'll try to get back up to see you again.'

'Dear Nancy:

'I arrived here three weeks ago, and I'm already homesick. Vietnam is   hot and humid, just like Georgia in summer, only worse because there's no chance to go water skiing. My new boss, Captain Pedersen has taken me under his wing showing me the ropes. My job is similar to the one I had at Pease, only there's a bigger sense of urgency to get things done here. The generals become very upset when their communications get botched up.

'The base here at Tan Son Nhut is big, busy and safe. Besides Air Force troops, there's units from the Army, Marines and even South Vietnamese forces. Soldiers here talk about how the war is going. Some think we're winning, others are convinced otherwise. I'm sure you're getting lots of different opinions in the news back there. We hear about those anti-war demonstrations.

'I've been down to Saigon once. You wouldn't believe the traffic there, a death-defying tangle of scooters, cars, bikes, and bicycle drawn rickshaws, all trying to avoid one another. The roadside markets feature vendors selling produce and Vietnamese dishes to the crowd of locals that jam together with pungent smells filling the air, some tempting and others repulsive. We had a couple of beers at a bar where Americans hang out and walked around a little afterwards.

'The Vietnamese people I've met seem quite friendly. They are generally short, thin and energetic. We've been cautioned not to get too buddy-buddy with them as you can't be sure who to trust.

'That's about it from here. I look forward to your letters. So, write and let me know how everything is back home. I miss you, Sweet Pea. Take good care of your health. Next time I'll write you a story to make you laugh.

'Love you, Tom'

Stirling knows he can't say anything in his letters that would alarm the folks back home.

CHAPTER 46

'Lieutenant Walker, you've been ordered to appear here today to give a deposition regarding your involvement with an individual by the name Harry Edwards. He has been declared a subversive by the United States government. You should understand if you are found culpable of colluding with Mr. Edwards in actions detrimental to the United States of America, a charge of 'Aiding the Enemy' under Article 104, will have been established for court martial hearings under the Uniform Code of Military Justice.'

James is sitting in a conference room at the 2049th Comm Group across the table from an Air Force officer named George Zimmer. Walker is the sole person of interest for an Article 32 inquiry. James is convinced he has done nothing wrong, but this investigation makes him fearful there are forces against him. A JAG lawyer, Alfred Szumski sits beside Walker as his defense counsel.

Captain Zimmer checks the demographic information on Walker, then launches into the crux of the matter.

'Have you ever met an individual by the name of Harry Edwards, a black professor at San Jose State University?'

'Yes.'

'Was your interaction with Mr. Edwards substantive regarding any planned activities?'

'Yes.'

'Did those plans involve actions to be taken that would undermine or disrupt events scheduled to occur within the United States of America?'

'Yes, but I can explain.'

'Please answer the questions with a yes or no response only. You will get the opportunity to respond in detail at a later time.'

'Did you continue to meet with Mr. Edwards despite a verbal warning from Captain James Eastland that disciplinary action would be taken against you should you have any further contact with said individual?'

Walker is now beginning to feel the heat. He has been advised if he gets caught in a lie, grounds for perjury will have been established. He decides to be straight honest and accept the consequences.

'Yes.'

'Did you agree with the goals and objectives established by Mr. Edwards and his associates?'

'Yes.'

'Did you know Mr. Edwards has connections with the Black Panther Party?'

'Not at first.'

'Yes or no.'

'Yes.'

'That completes my inquiry, Lieutenant. Any question?'

'I thought you were going to allow me to explain my association with Mr. Edwards and his group.'

'You may get that chance later.'

Shirley is in the middle of final exams at Sac State when James gets out of that meeting. He needs to talk with someone, so he convinces Jerry Hicks to have lunch with him at a little Mexican take-out place just outside the base. They sit on a bench outdoors under the eaves.

'I love the tacos here,' Jerry remarks. 'Great salsa.'

'Hicks, I need to talk to you about something serious. Did you see that officer I was meeting with before lunch?'

'Yuh, what was that about?'

'Eastland finally did it. He's trying to get me pinned with a court martial for working with those San Jose State athletes.'

'You've got to be kidding. All you were doing was trying to get those sprinters to the Jaycee sponsored meet.'

'That's exactly what I was doing, but my captain is trying to frame me for associating with a known subversive in violation of my oath as an officer.'

'That's a pile of horseshit. They can't make that stick, can they?'

'You would think it's all a bunch of bunk, but you never know what kind of security priorities are driving the brass in Washington.'

'James, if you want me to testify about your character and your role on the Jaycee track and field committee, I'd be proud to stand up for you.'

'I really appreciate that, Jerry. Right now, I hope it doesn't come to that.'

One week after meeting with the investigating officer, Colonel LaFrenz calls Lieutenant Walker into his office. The unit commander normally greets Walker with a smile, but today, his furrowed brow portends something serious.

'Have a seat, Lieutenant.'

Walker settles onto the black leather upholstered chair across the desk from the Colonel. He feels his body stiffen. Something is wrong.

'I have some unfortunate news for you, Lieutenant,' Colonel LaFrenz pauses. 'The Convening Authority, General Westerman has determined there is enough evidence in your case to proceed with a trial.'

He continues. 'I can't say I know all the facts involved. The FBI has declared black power groups to be the greatest threat to national security, and our military is in lock step with them. You are being charged with violating Article 104, 'Aiding the Enemy'.'

'Oh my God, I was afraid this could happen. Sir, how do I prove my innocence?'

'You already have a JAG lawyer, Captain Szumski to defend you. If you are innocent, honesty is always the best policy.'

Walker concludes his meeting with LaFrenz, his head spinning in disbelief. Walking downstairs to his cubicle, he reaches his desk and glances through the glass to Eastland's office. His boss is leaning back in his chair, hands behind his head, sporting a big grin.

James know Shirley will hit the roof when she hears the news. She has a vengeful side to her, and he is sure she will want to get back at Eastland. They meet for dinner at a small Italian bistro on Folsom Boulevard.

'How could they consider this a crime? All you did was try to talk them out of a boycott.'

'They're considering my behavior as contact with a known subversive who has conspired against the United States.'

'That's ridiculous. If anything, you were attempting to prevent action that could be considered anti-American.'

Shirley is becoming flush with anger.

'With all the turmoil going on in the states right now, the government is looking to crack down on protest groups. I may end up being a victim of a witch hunt.'

'What does that mean?'

'I could be facing a year or more in jail and discharge from the Air Force.'

'That's absurd. And, they call that justice?'

Walker finishes his plate of meatloaf and mash potatoes washing it down with a glass of milk. Shirley picks at her Cobb salad with a fork. She is clearly upset.

'I can usually give you advice, but I am dumbfounded this time. If you want, I can get one of my father's guns and go shoot Eastland, that bastard.'

Don't even think about doing anything to him. That will only make matters worse.'

'Lieutenant Walker. I need to discuss plans for your defense,' informs Captain Szumski.

They shake hands, then sit at a desk across from each other in a small conference room at the 2049th. The Captain appears young with a baby-faced complexion but speaks with an assuring, strong deep voice.

'I've got to tell you. I'm shocked to be accused of what they're saying is an act of treason. My sole intention has been to recruit runners to a track meet. How that can be viewed as aiding the enemy is beyond my understanding.'

'I'm pleased to hear you speak convincingly of your innocence, Lieutenant. However, we must craft a defense that makes crystal clear the reasons for your actions."

'However, before we develop a strategy, I need to inform you of the witnesses subpoenaed by the prosecution. Take a look at this list.'

James is handed a sheet of paper and scrolls down line by line. Eastland's name is first, but there on the bottom, to his surprise, is Harry Edwards.

'Edwards?'' How in the world did they get him to testify?' queries Walker.

'I don't know all the details, but the prosecution likely offered him some kind of immunity to avoid being turned over to the FBI.'

'The military couldn't try him?'

'No. And, if his testimony indicates he is not an active member of a black power group, he'll be getting less heat from civilian and government law enforcement.

The officers continue for another three hours covering all aspects of court martial proceedings. As they part, Szumski warns his client.

'Lieutenant Walker, you need to understand, in a court martial, it's not reasonable doubt that you're trying to prove, it's any doubt at all.'

CHAPTER 47

The trial of First Lieutenant James Walker is taking place in the conference room of the base commander, General Westerman at McClellan Air Force Base. On advice from his lawyer, the accused officer opts for trial by panel members rather than decision by a lone judge.

'Order in the court,' Judge Coughlan demands, hammering the gavel against its sound block. 'We are convened here today to try the case of "The United States Air Force versus Lieutenant James Walker. The defendant is accused of violating Article 104, 'Aiding the Enemy'. He has plead not guilty.'

After opening statements, the prosecution calls its first witness, Captain Eastland. The Plan 55 department head produces a written document dated 15 May 1966.

'Captain Eastland, please read the last sentence of the verbal warning to Lieutenant Walker.

'If evidence is produced indicating you have had any association with Mr. Harry Edwards again, I will recommend you for court martial as a traitor to the oath of office you took as a United States Air Force officer.'

Walker recoils at that statement. He whispers to Szumski. 'How incriminating is that?'

'Eastland has no grounds to make that threat.'

The most potentially damning witness is next, Harry Edwards himself.

The imposing figure of Edwards proudly steps to the witness chair sporting a black suit with black shirt, matching the color of his hair and beard.

'Mr. Edwards, are you now or have you ever been a member of the Black Panther Party.'

'No, sir.'

'Have you ever met Bobby Seale or Huey Newton, leaders of the Black Panther Party?'

'One or two times.'

The prosecuting attorney then submits into evidence several photos blown up to 12"x18" showing Edwards interacting with either Seale or Newton or both during six different occasions.

'Is that you meeting with Huey Newton in this photo?

'It does appear to be the two of us together.'

Five more photographs are shown to Edwards eliciting the same question and answer.

'For a casual relationship, you seem to have had a considerable amount of contact with these Black Panther leaders.'

'What can I say? We are all interested in improving the welfare of the black citizens of this country. We just go about it differently.'

'For the record, it should be noted that the FBI has positively ascertained Mr. Harry Edwards is indeed a member of the Black Panther Party.' The courtroom stirs. The prosecution continues.

'I want to shift our attention to your relationship with Lieutenant James Walker. Did you and your Olympic Project for Human Dignity group meet with Mr. Walker at your residence after 15 May of this year?'

'Yes, at least twice.'

When queried about the activities of the Olympic Project for Human Dignity, he indicates his group is willing to take all means necessary to attain the goal of equal rights and opportunities for black people.

'Would those measures include acts of violence, Mr. Edwards?' asks the prosecuting attorney.

'We have never, to this point in time, discussed employing acts of violence.'

'Have you ruled out the possibility of using any acts of violence?'

'No, we have not.'

Walker is taken back. *We only ever talked about boycotting, never violent demonstrations,* he mumbles to himself.

On cross-examination, Mr. Edwards is asked whether he was aware the FBI considered him a subversive and a danger to the country.

'Yes, I have been told that.'

'Are there grounds for you being listed as such?'

'No. I have no formal association with any activist group other than the Olympic Project for Human Dignity.'

'No further questions.'

Judge Coughlin calls for a short recess.

'Captain Szumski, you may now present your first witness,' informs the judge.

'The defense calls Tommie Smith.' The sprinter appears nervous as he takes the stand.

'Mr. Smith, in your experience, has Lieutenant Walker ever advocated actions to be taken by your Olympic Project group which could be construed to be detrimental to the United States of America?'

'No, sir.'

'Can you describe the nature of the relationship between Lieutenant Walker and the Olympic Project group?'

The Lieutenant was attempting to recruit elite athletes from San Jose State to participate in the Hughes Stadium track meet. At that time, we were considering boycotting that event and several others.'

'Do you belong to the Black Panthers or any other group having plans to disrupt or destroy events or institutions within the United States of America?'

'Yes and no.'

'Would you explain what you mean by answering yes and no?

'Our group, the Olympic Project for Human Dignity was considering boycotting upcoming track and field events. Personally, I stood in opposition to this plan.'

'Are you aware of any affiliations Mr. Harry Edwards has including the Olympic Project for Human Dignity, which advocates violence against American society?'

'No sir.'

'No further questions, your honor.'

The prosecution then attempts to discredit Mr. Smith as a witness by presenting court evidence he had been convicted of a felony while a resident in Texas.

Other witnesses for the defense are called to testify including Ray Clark and Pete Fetros. Their knowledge of any direct interaction between Lieutenant Walker and the Olympic Project members is later revealed by the prosecution as hearsay evidence supplied by Walker himself.

In closing arguments, the prosecution reaffirms that Walker did violate the terms of the verbal warning issued by Captain Eastland and concludes that Edwards is indeed a subversive based on his frequent association with Black Panther Party members and by being so designated by the FBI.

Alfred Szumski approaches the jury for his closing statement. 'Neither the prosecution nor the FBI have ever proved Harry Edwards is a subversive. No evidence has been presented demonstrating he has taken actions against the United States of America. Furthermore, evidence presented to this court makes irrefutable, Lieutenant Walker's sole motive was to convince the San Jose State athletes to compete in the Hughes Stadium meet.'

Szumski's final statement attests to the character of Tommie Smith.

'Regarding the felony cited regarding Mr. Smith, the jury should know his crime, committed while a teenager was for stealing food from a local grocery store to help feed his family which included eleven siblings.'

As Szumski takes his seat, Judge Coughlan directs the next stage of the trial.

'The panel will now be sequestered in the adjacent office until a verdict is reached.'

'You sounded convincing?' Walker comments to his counsel. 'What do you think?'

'I'm sure you're going to win.'

Thirty minutes later, the somber-faced panel returns and sits. The judge addresses them.

''Mr. Foreman, has the panel reached a verdict?'

'We have, your honor.'

'How do you find the defendant?'

'Guilty as charged.'

Walker faces Szumski with a look of disbelief.

'This can't be real. I thought you told me there was no credible grounds to convict me.'

'In my mind, there is a paucity of evidence to support a conviction and considerable reasonable doubt. We will appeal this decision.'

James' mind is racing. *If they could convict me on such flimsy evidence in this trial, they could certainly do the same in an appeals process.* He is stunned by this nightmarish turn of events.

'The panel will now convene to consider the punishment phase of this trial,' orders the judge.

James sits crestfallen alongside his counsel and waits. As he looks around the conference room, he sees Lieutenant Paciano Morin. A thought strikes him and he motions for Morin to approach.

'Pac, I have a wild idea that might free me from this insanity. Do you know where Colonel LaFrenz is right now?'

'I was just going to see him. He's waiting in the lobby for me to give him the jury's decision.'

'My only hope may be for him to close down the proceedings of this trial. I'm not certain how that works, but I believe he may have the power to do that.'

Szumski overhears Walker and reacts.

'James, you may be correct. The officer who brought this case to trial has the authority to stop the process, but he will need to convince the judge.'

'Pac, please find the Colonel and let him know if he believes in my innocence, close down this trial.'

Morin nods in agreement and hurries from the court to locate LaFrenz. He finds him pacing nervously in the foyer.

'Colonel, they found Walker guilty.'

LaFrenz turns away and winces trying to disguise the remorse he feels at this moment. Having examined the circumstances surrounding the case more carefully, he has spent a sleepless night ruing his choice to move forward on Eastland's recommendation for a trial.

'Walker says you may have the power to stop the trial proceedings if the judge can be convinced.' LaFrenz ponders for a moment, then nods his head.

'Lieutenant Morin, I want you to return to Judge Coughlan immediately, and persuade him to come meet with me here before the panel returns. I have urgent information for him. Do you understand me?'

'Loud and clear, sir.'

Morin returns to the courtroom and approaches the judge.

'Your honor, if it pleases the court, Colonel LaFrenz asks for a moment of your time to confer with him about this trial. He's presently in the lobby and claims his reasons for speaking with you are of the most urgent importance.'

'This better be good. I'm not in the habit of interrupting the proceedings of a court martial.'

'Thank you for honoring this request, Judge. Please follow me to Colonel LaFrenz.'

They step outside and down the hallway to the front foyer. The Colonel smiles as Judge Coughlan approaches. His countenance quickly changes to a serious demeanor.

'Your honor, I must admit I made a dreadful mistake recommending to General Westerman that this case proceed to court martial. I believe the judgment rendered is a miscarriage of justice. An innocent man has been convicted. Please step into the General's office. We have just conferred on the case and both agree this trial should be stopped immediately, and its records expunged.'

Judge Coughlan appears shocked at this request. He pauses briefly before responding, then begins lambasting Colonel LaFrenz.

'I hope you understand, Colonel. You will have wasted the time and efforts of numerous members of the armed forces with this request. In addition, you have exacted an emotional toll on all participants in this trial. Your action at this point in the proceedings will not reflect positively on your military career.'

'I understand full well what you are saying. However, I could not live with myself for allowing an innocent man to be unjustly punished because of my decision.'

'You should have foreseen this possibility before recommending trial to the General.'

'You are absolutely right. Unfortunately, I was misled and acted without fully examining the circumstances surrounding Lieutenant Walker's actions.'

The judge steps into the General's office and confirms Colonel LaFrenz's request. Duty bound, he returns to the rostrum.

'Bailiff, you will now ask the panel members to return to the court room.'

Minutes later, they are seated in their appointed chairs.

In a loud voice, he gains the attention of the court.

'I have an important announcement.'

The judge waits 30 seconds for the buzz in the room to die down.

'Order in the court,' shouts the bailiff.

'Due to an appeal from the individual who brought this trial forward, all records and decisions taken heretofore during this court martial hearing shall be expunged.' He lifts the gavel and pounds it down.

'Case dismissed.'

A collective gasp fills the room. Lieutenant Walker stands and screams in delight. He slaps hands with his defense counsel. They envelop each other with hugs of joy. Walker triumphantly walks out of the court an exonerated man. He meets the Colonel as he passes through the building hallway and stops.

'I believe justice was served today. I hope you feel the same. Have a nice day, Colonel.'

LaFrenz smiles.

'I agree with you, Lieutenant. Justice has been served today.'

CHAPTER 48

A spontaneous celebration takes place at the officers club the evening after the trial. Shirley sits by James' side while Jerry and his steady girlfriend, Janet attend as well. Many well-wishers from the 2049th are in attendance with the notable exception of Colonel LaFrenz and Captain Eastland.

They sit at a long table composed of several small tables butted together and covered with linen table cloths to accommodate the size of their group. As the waiters complete the beverage service to each person, a grateful Lieutenant stands and clinks a fork loudly against his glass.

'I want to make a toast,' he announces raising his glass. The conversation dies down and all eyes turn to James.

'This is for everyone who supported me throughout this stressful ordeal. You gave me hope when the world I thought I belonged to appeared to rise up against me. Yesterday, I was plucked from the depths of misguided human judgment and raised to the bright light of salvation, reinforced by the smiling faces of friends looking at me this very moment. Thank you from the bottom of my heart.'

Chairs squeak against the wood floor as the gathering rises to their feet.

'Hear, hear!' they shout in unison thrusting their glasses toward Walker.

The awkwardness of working together at Plan 55 is palpable. The Captain no longer holds a threat over the Lieutenant's head, and he seems resigned to let Walker complete his remaining time at McClellan without harassing him.   In fact, he initially avoids any possible contact with his assistant, taking 14 days leave immediately after the trial.

James awaits new orders.   He knows he is obligated to serve a one year overseas assignment before being eligible for discharge.

In April, Hicks comes downstairs to visit him in his cubicle holding an envelope in his hand.

'This came across my desk, and I opened it without checking the addressee. It's for you. You're going overseas in June.'

'You've got a lot of nerve opening my mail.' He snatches the envelope and looks at the letter inside. 'Oh my God! I'm going to Vietnam. Where is this place, Tan Son Nhut?'

June 4th, Walker's last day at the 2049th. He steps into Eastland's office.

'I have a gift for you, Captain.'

His boss looks up with a quizzical expression. James present him with an unwrapped, cardboard box about 6 inches long by 10 inches wide and 6 inches high.

'Go ahead, open it.'

Eastland narrows his eyes suspecting Walker of getting back at him with some malicious prank. Seconds later, he lifts the cover of the box and pulls out the contents.

'My lady friend, Shirley made this.'

The Captain holds up a wooden carving of two hands clasped in friendship, one white and one black.

'This is what I was hoping for between the two of us.'

They hold each other's gaze for several seconds. Then, Eastland's eyes start fluttering and shift downward. A burning rage begins to well up inside the

Captain. His whole body stiffens. Clutching James' gift in his right hand, he rises from his desk.

'Aaaargh!' he screams as he violently flings that symbol of reconciliation into his waste basket. Walker calmly turns and walks out of the office.

On a bright, sunny day in June, James stands on the tarmac waiting to board a C-141 Starlifter en route to Vietnam. Shirley has driven him to his debarkation facility, Travis Air Force Base. She looks tempting in a yellow summer dress. He looks wistfully at her.

'Are you going to write to me?' she asks.

'I will if you will.'

She gives him a passionate kiss, looks deep into his eyes and issues a warning.

'Now you stay away from those trampy Vietnamese girls.' He smiles.

James climbs aboard the plane not knowing what lies ahead. He has strong feelings for Shirley but isn't sure if they have a future together. And, Vietnam. All he knows, it is one scary place.

CHAPTER 49

'Captain Pedersen, thanks for taking me down here. The ambience is great. I love the view and the drinks aren't watered down. This is sure a nice escape from the base.'

Tom is sitting at a table with his boss from the Comm Unit at the rooftop bar of the Rex Hotel in downtown Saigon. GI's and reporters both hang out here trading stories about the war and politics.

'We all need a break from Tan Son Nhut, Stirling. Doesn't take long before you feel trapped in that place. The waitresses here are pretty cute too.'

'I was going to ask you about that, boss. A year is a long time to be away from any sort of physical satisfaction. If you know what I mean?'

'A common complaint, Lieutenant. Just to let you know, the military considers paying a prostitute for sexual favors a punishable offense.'

'You must be kidding. I bet there's a lot of guys in trouble for violating that regulation.'

'Let's say it's not enforced very often. You can take your chances finding a loose lady in Vietnam, but what many GI's do is go out of country. Thailand gets rave reviews.'

'How about you, Captain. Have you ever considered a little tryst with some local attraction?'

'Like a lot of guys, I've got a girl back home. When you come here, you plan to be true to your woman. But, as time goes by, a man can get pretty horny. And, some of those Vietnamese girls look really good. I've been here eight months now.'

'So, have you done it? Did you give in to temptation?'

'Even if I had, I wouldn't tell you. You might leak something that the Colonel finds out about, and my goose would be cooked.'

Tom has his curiosity peaked now. He pursues the subject further.

'So, how do the troops get hooked up?'

'There is always a few airmen on base having connections with women of ill repute on the outside. Typically, these ladies have had some tragedy strike in their family due to the war, and they need money to survive. Prostitution allows them to live more comfortably, and they know GI's have money.'

'How common is this?'

'As the war drags on, drugs and sex are becoming more and more of a problem.'

'I haven't been here that long, but I suspected drugs are a big issue. Hard to walk around base at night without smelling weed.'

'You're catching on, Lieutenant. Keep yourself on the straight and narrow, and you'll get out of this hell hole with your head on straight.'

Tom doesn't care about taking any drugs. A good stiff drink at the bar is welcome and often stirs interesting conversation like with his boss right now. Sex is a different matter. He can't imagine lasting an entire year without it. Thailand sounds tempting, but he won't be able to get there for a while. As he looks across the rooftop at all the people there, one thought strikes him. *Jesus, those barmaids look good.'*

'Lieutenant, we've got a new officer coming in today from the states. If I remember right, his name is Jonas Welker. I want you to meet him at Base Op and show him to his quarters.'

'Okay, what time does his plane come in?'

'Scheduled to land at 10:25 this morning, but check before you head down.'

Stirling leaves Captain Pedersen's office. Returning to the desk in his building, he calls for information about the flight and learns it's landing in 10 minutes.'

'Holy shit, I better get down there now.'

He jumps into a 1964th Comm Group jeep and buzzes down to the flight line. As he enters the base operations building, there, standing beside his bags is Lieutenant James Walker.

'Oh crap! Have you come all the way over here to give me grief about segregation?'

'That's a nice greeting, Stirling. Are you here to offer me a hand with my stuff or just be your old obnoxious self?'

Tom stuffs his mixed reaction at seeing his ex-classmate again.

'C'mon. I'll get you settled into the BOQ. It ain't luxurious but you'll have everything you need; bed, desk, shower, sink and toilet. Food at the officer's mess is good. There's also a commissary. So, you can buy snack food or grub to make a meal on the hot plate in your room. We have a base exchange as well, where you can expand your wardrobe as well as buy gifts for the folks back home.'

'Thanks for the info, Stirling,' replies Walker as Tom seems to shift into a more helpful attitude. 'Say, are we going to be working together?'

'Christ, I hope not. I couldn't take looking at your ugly mug every day.'

'You've got no room to talk about ugly mugs, pale face.'

James gets a short tour of the base from Tom. Afterwards, they swing by the 1964th to meet his new superior officer.

'Captain Pedersen, this is Lieutenant Walker just in from McClellan.'

'Welcome, Lieutenant Jonas, isn't it? Jonas Welker.'

'No, it's James, Captain, James Walker.'

'I trust you're a little tired from your flight. Stirling, let's get Welker here back to his quarters for some shut eye.'

'Thanks Captain. See you bright and early tomorrow.'

'C'mon Walker. I've got more to do than drag you around like some lost puppy dog.'

The first few months of Tom's tour of duty in Vietnam have been hectic. The day after Walker's arrival is typical. He gets ready in the morning, fixing himself a little breakfast with a mug of black coffee to perk himself up. Arriving at work a little before 0800, he consults with the night shift supervisor.

'What's the backlog look like, Sergeant?'

'We had our transmitter go down last night, Lieutenant. We've got at least a two-hour backlog.'

'Has maintenance got it back on line yet?'

'No, we don't have the right spare part.'

'Get Chief Master Sergeant Toyn in here right away. Pedersen will be jumping down my throat if we don't get that transmitter back up stat.'

'Yes sir.'

Tom's phone rings.

'Stirling, I just got my ear chewed off by General Goff.' Pedersen is calling. 'He was waiting for a response to his request to the Joint Chiefs and found out his top-secret message hasn't even been sent yet. What the hell is going on over there?'

'Yes sir. We had an equipment outage last night. I'm expecting Sergeant Toyn to get the problem fixed ASAP.'

'Look, we're trying to win a war here. Communications glitches are not helping. Get that problem fixed now. Do you hear me, Lieutenant?'

'Loud and clear, boss. We're on it.'

'And, you call me as soon as the general's message goes out. Got it?'

'Yes sir.'

Within a minute, Toyn enters Stirling's office. He's a seasoned pro who has seen it all.

'Sergeant Toyn, I presume you've been briefed on the transmitter problem. Can you get it fixed?'

'I've got a sharp young airman cannibalizing the part off a piece of down equipment in the maintenance shop. We should be up on line in minutes.'

'Thanks Sergeant. I owe you a beer.'

In early October, Stirling receives a call from a personnel officer at Long Binh.

'We've got a marine up here who says he's a friend of yours and wants you to visit. His name is Lance Corporal Miles Trousdale.'

'Oh yes, he's a long-time friend of mine. But, I thought he went stateside weeks ago.'

'He was scheduled for a transfer a couple of months ago, but he got into an altercation at Cam Rahm Bay and broke another jarhead's leg. The general sent him down here for confinement in the base stockade pending a court martial hearing. He's slated for trial next week.'

'Why am I not surprised? Trousdale has a quick temper. I guess that finally got him in trouble this time. Tell him I'll do my best to make it up there next Saturday.'

By 1968, the stockade at Long Binh has become a powder keg of hostility. Conditions for prisoners have worsened dramatically. Known unaffectionately as LBJ for our president, overcrowding is heightening tensions. A series of tents designed to house eight prisoners now holds up to 14, each man fighting for space in their mildew ridden leaky canvas quarters. Control of these miserable and dangerous men has been assigned to 90 mostly inexperienced custodians, one-third the authorized staffing. With an equal mix of hostile blacks and angry whites, a racial explosion appears only a lit match away.

Long Binh Army Base in only a few miles from Tan Son Nhut. Stirling is able to requisition a motor pool vehicle to drive over to see Trousdale. The base stockade houses almost all U.S. military prisoners in Vietnam. He is directed at the main entrance to the base toward the rectangular barbed wire fence surrounding the mud-laden grounds of the detention facility. He parks outside the entry gate and approaches the guard.

'I have written permission to visit with an inmate Lance Corporal Miles Trousdale today at 1400 hours.'

He presents papers and is escorted to the administrative building. Entering a small, wooden building with a tin roof, Stirling is accompanied to a spare room with a metal table and two metal chairs. There, with a uniformed MP standing behind him, is Trousdale.

'Well, looky here, my Dawg frat brother. Did you hear what the base commander did to me? 60 days in this friggin' rat hole right before discharge.'

Tom joins his friend at the table. 'What happened?'

'I was batting on the softball field. A big fat pitch come up toward me like a grapefruit. I'm ready to belt that ball clear down to Saigon, but the catcher tips my bat with his glove. I am totally pissed. So, I turn around and yell at him. Does he apologize? No, he stands up and hocks a loogie right on my shoe and says, "Whattaya gonna do about it?" That's when I wind up and slug him on the shin with my bat. I'm perfectly justified to do that, right. So, what happens? The base commander ships me down to this God forsaken place and I end up spending two months in this hole.'

'That does sound unfair. What happened to the other guy?'

'Nothin'. They felt sorry for him.'

Tom can see that Trousdale has gotten worse. When he talks about the softball incident, his face turns crimson. He stands pacing the room with his hand balled up into a fist like he's ready to punch a hole in the wall. The guard twice grabs him by the shoulders and shoves him back into his seat. Tom looks at Miles' arms and sees what looks like needle marks.

'Are you doing heroin?'

Trousdale doesn't answer the question. Instead he goes off on a hostile diatribe.

'Do you see how we live in this pig sty? 12 guys in a cloth tent built for 8. When it trains, it leaks like a sieve. And, they put me in one with six angry niggers. I'm ready to kill each and every one of them.'

'Take a chill pill, brother. You get into a fight and it'll only make things worse for yourself.'

'Fuck you, Tom. Why did you think I asked for you to come over here? I want you to tell these goons I need to be in a tent with all white guys.'

'Miles, I think you need some help to control that temper of yours.'

'Get lost, Stirling, I don't need your two-bit advice.'

'Time for me to leave, buddy. Good luck and stay cool.'

'Go screw yourself, Stirling. And, thanks for nothin'.'

Stirling takes his leave from Trousdale and is about to exit the confines, when his escort guard tells him the full story.

'He didn't get thrown in here just for breaking that guy's leg. He also hit the umpire over the head with that same bat.'

Tom's head drops. He now has a fuller understanding of the extent of Trousdale's sad downfall.

'Look Trousdale's right. If you don't get him separated from those negro prisoners, there's going to be trouble.'

CHAPTER 50

'Hey Walker.' A voice calls from a few tables over at the officer's club. 'C'mon over here and join me.'

James looks up and sees Stirling waving to him. He picks up his drink and dinner bussing them over toward his old Biloxi classmate. Tom has a half-eaten sirloin steak sitting on his plate along with the remains of a baked potato and green salad on the table in front of him.

'Hey, you and I have the same date of service, right? That means we're going to be promoted to captain next week.'

'You're right. Wow, we'll get a nice raise too. A little more money to put in the credit union. How about you? Saving a lot of dough since you got over here?'

'Well, at first, I was putting nearly all of my check in the 10% credit union. Lately, however, I found a new way to invest my money.'

'Really, how's that?'

'Gambling. I got suckered into betting on poker and football pools. Lost a lot more than I won.'

'I can understand. You do need to find diversions over here.'

Stirling changes the subject as frittering away his money is a sore subject.

'Walker, how are you liking your assignment here so far?'

'Okay, but I do miss some things from back in the states. How about you?'

'Do you mean women?'

'Yah. That, my family, and some outside things I had going.'

'There are WAFs over here and some lady nurses too, but I haven't had any luck with any of them. For you, though, very few of the women are negro. So, you would need to go off base and find a local babe. Have you thought about that?'

'Well sure, I thought about it, but I haven't done anything? How about you?'

'Not yet, but one of my airmen tells me he can get me hooked up if I'm interested.'

'Are you going to do it?'

'I'm considering it. Hey, look over there at that table next to the bar, a WAF sitting all by herself. Let's go over and introduce ourselves.'

James doesn't really want to go, but he plays along with Stirling. As they approach, Walker can see the WAF is tall and gawky looking with a considerable amount of dark facial hair.

'Hi. My name is Tom, and this is James. Do you mind if we sit down and join you?'

Before she can answer, Stirling pulls out a chair and sits. Walker, seeing no other alternative, follows suit. The WAF looks down at her food without responding. Stirling tries to bridge the awkwardness of the moment by beginning a monologue.

'We're communications officers over at the 1645th. Been here a few months now. Like everybody over here, we're just doing our jobs and hanging out until we go back to the states. That's about all you can do, try to make the best of it. Right?' No response. 'Among other things, a guy misses a little female companionship. How about yourself? I bet you'd enjoy having some friendly guy take you to the movies or something like that. How about it, interested?'

There's a pause of several seconds. The WAF seems frozen. She doesn't try to eat. She doesn't move. And, she doesn't speak. James figures the lady is upset or depressed about something and tries to ease out of her space by making a parting comment.

'I can see you want to be alone with your thoughts, so we'll leave now. Maybe we can talk some other time. I hope you feel better.'

As James pushes his chair back and stands to leave, she looks at him and speaks.

'Thank you for understanding.'

As they walk away, Stirling whispers in Walker's ear.

'Jesus, are all the women around here as fucked up as that broad?'

'Stirling, you don't know. Maybe she heard about someone close to her that was killed over here. Maybe she saw some guys who were med-evacked in here all disfigured. Or, she might have had an ugly experience with somebody like you hitting on her.'

'Okay, maybe you're right. I guess I was a little forward with her. It's just that I'm so damn horny, and beating the meat a couple times a day doesn't help much. In fact, you look pretty good to me right now.'

Walker gives him a look of disgust.

CHAPTER 51

'Where am I supposed to meet this chick?'

'Be outside Gate 51 tomorrow night at 1900 hours. There's a local guy named Vo. He will meet you there and take you to the girl. You'll meet her in an empty building. I've seen this babe. She's prime. Her name is Mai Li.'

'Got it. You better be right about this fox. I'm paying you a lot of money, and I expect big time fireworks with this broad.'

'You'll be thanking me tomorrow morning. Rest assured of that.'

Tom is receiving instructions on hooking up with a local call girl. He is in his office talking with Airman Second Class Norwood, a fast talking, wheeler-dealer enlisted man. The door is locked as Stirling wants no one walking in bearing witness to this arrangement.

Norwood collects his money in advance from his clients to pay for the girl, her escort, incidentals like birth control protection, and, of course, his fee. From his boss, he receives a cool $200. The young entrepreneur is likely putting more money in his credit union account than anyone else on base. Business is booming.

Tom looks at himself in his BOQ mirror. He wants to look good for this girl. Shaving for the second time today, he sprinkles some Mennen aftershave in his hand and slaps it on his face; combs his hair leaving one lock rakishly draped down over his forehead and adds a little Vitalis. He dons a blue print, short-sleeved shirt with images of Polynesian dancing girls wearing it outside his khaki slacks. Before he steps outside his BOQ room, he pulls open the top dresser drawer, reaches in and shoves five Trojans into his right front pocket. Now, he's ready.

At precisely 18:55 hours, Stirling approaches the MP guard at Gate 51 who allows him to exit the base. Reaching outside, he looks around for his contact, Vo. There's a muscular Asian man wearing a black jacket, smoking a cigarette standing 20 yards away. Stirling walks up to him.

'You know Mai Li?'

'Forrow me,' he replies

They walk silently along the outside walls of the base then turn up a muddy side street continuing for another five minutes. Three more turns and they finally arrive at an abandoned shack next to a rice paddy. Light glows from inside.

Stirling opens the door of the one room structure and enters. A girl who was sitting on a bed stands. In the light from the kerosene lantern behind her, he sees the silhouette of a young girl with long dark hair clothed in a blouse and skirt. He wants to examine her more closely, but first he announces himself.

'Xin chao, Mai Li. My name is Reb. I will treat you well.'

She nods her head and bows. He walks behind her and picks up the lamp. Facing her, he can see she is very young, maybe 17 or 18. Her face is fair skinned with high cheekbones and full lips. She looks into his eyes, and his pulse quickens.

Coming closer, he gently places his hands on her shoulders and instantly the world outside disappears.

She's a vision, he thinks. *This has got to be the best reason for being in this God forsaken country.* He pulls her slowly towards him and kisses her softly on the lips. She surprises him by inserting her tongue into his mouth. With that gesture, he begins to undress her, unfastening one button at a time on her blouse stopping to look into her eyes, resuming their embrace after each undone fastener. Finally, they are standing naked facing each other. He can't believe how totally beautiful she is, her face, her body, her sensuousness. He remains frozen for seconds drinking in this moment. Then he reaches down, picking her up by the legs and shoulders and carries her to the bed.

The Lieutenant senses this moment is more than the mere satisfaction of reaching a climax with a woman. With the war raging nearby, the act of sharing relations with the most desirable female he has ever been with needs to be savored.

She lies on her back as he softly caresses her from head to toe. Mai Li responds to his touch by pressing herself into his searching hands uttering soft, breathy moans. He is now fully aroused and wants to take her, but she stops him with her hand and motions for his to lie on his back.

Her hands are magic; kneading, stroking his flesh and covering him with wet kisses. His head is spinning with pleasure. Finally, he can't remain still any longer. He rises up and envelops her with unbridled passion taking total control of this love creature.

'Vo, wake up. Take me back to the base.'

Nearly three hours have vanished in a blur of ecstasy. His escort had fallen asleep outside the hut having waited much longer than expected. Now, the reality is Tom needs to return to base before the midnight curfew. He is walking on air after the most sensational love rendezvous of his life. Does he love her? He mulls over the possibility.

I couldn't love her because I have no idea who she is. And, who can believe that a set-up like this could produce a lasting relationship. But, ask me if I want to see Mai Li again. O, my god, yes.

He reaches Gate 51 and the MP passes him through. Upon arriving back at his BOQ room, he sits at his desk for a few minutes before turning in for the night. On top of the writing pad is a letter. It's from Nancy. He opens the folded paper and rereads it a second time. He is struck by the closing sentence.

'Remember, honey, you are the only man in my life, and you always will be.'

A pang of guilt strikes his chest. The feeling of euphoria from this night's blissful encounter is shattered.

Why does life have to be so complicated?

CHAPTER 52

Reverend Jones has been corresponding with James since the time the eldest Walker child left Stillmore to live with Aunt Violet. Because his parents aren't able to read or write, the pastor relates news about the family as well as other developments around town. His latest letter concerns Jasper.

'Your brother has been transferred overseas to Vietnam with his army unit. He is stationed at a base called Camp Holloway. You should try to contact him.'

The minister lists his address at the bottom. Jasper's base is in the central highlands near Pleiku. James reflects on the relationship with his brother. *I feel really sad. The two of us have never been close since my move to Savannah.'* Placing the letter inside his desk drawer, he makes a promise to himself. *'I swear I will get together with my brother while we're both in Southeast Asia.*

Because Camp Holloway is smack in the middle of a combat zone, visiting there is discouraged. He writes to Jasper suggesting an R&R trip out of the country. Two weeks later, he receives a response.

'James:

'You don't know how lucky you are sitting down there inside your big ass base with your swimming pools, baseball fields, cooked to order meals and nobody shooting at you. We're out in the jungle half the time looking for Charley, sleeping in the rain, wading through murky waters, and battling the NVA, mosquitoes, leeches, red ants, and the two-step snake.'

'As for your suggestion, we should go on leave together, I'm only interested if you're paying. Remember, you owe me. And, even if you do agree to cough up the money, I can't say when I can get off. I'll put in for leave and let you know. A lot of guys here like Thailand, mostly for the babes. They say the women there will do just about anything and everything.'

'Write me. It helps to hear from family, even my candy ass brother.'

'Jaz.'

Private First-Class Walker receives permission for five days of R&R in Bangkok during January of 1968. He is able to contact his brother and they arrange to fly seated next to each other on a commercial flight out of Tan Son Nhut. James and Jaz were last together in Georgia over two years before. They begin catching up on lost time.

'You're looking good, Jaz; a little more muscle, a little more filled out. I guess Army life agrees with you.'

'You have no idea,' Jasper replies with a hint of contempt.

'So, what's it like out on a mission in the highlands? Have you seen any action?'

'It's scary as hell. Even when you don't run into any NVA, you're tense all the time. Every sound, any movement you see or hear in the jungle, you know it could be Charley with his rifle barrel pointed straight at you.'

'Go on.'

'About a month ago, we were briefed about NVA units and supplies sneaking into the highlands off the Ho Chi Minh Trail. We knew their whereabouts, and I was sent with a small detachment to stop the infiltration. We were close to our objective when our point man messed up by failing to identify a pit with punji sticks. He fell in and was skewered by razor sharp bamboo. He screamed in pain, and before we could rescue him, we began receiving heavy enemy fire.

'Eight of us dropped to the ground and started shooting back. We really couldn't see Charley, but kept blasting away. The sergeant called in for a Chinook. We could only hope it would get there quickly. Meanwhile, two more of our guys were hit.'

'Did you have any medical supplies to help those troops?'

'One of the wounded was right next to me. I pulled a sulfa powder pouch from my pocket and spread it over his neck wound. Blood was gushing all over, but that stuff finally stopped the bleeding. I was so shaken, I threw up all over him; couldn't control myself.'

'Awful, what happened after that?'

'We began using our M203 grenade launchers, and continued to rake them with both our M16s and machine guns. After 30 minutes of fighting, we heard the sounds of two choppers coming in. Turns out there was both an attack Cobra as well as a med-evac Huey. That first pilot unloaded big-time on the gooks and we were able to get all three wounded guys on board the Huey. Made it back to base from there. When I took my fatigues off afterward, I realized I'd shit my pants. Boy, did we get drunk that night.'

'Jesus, that's frightening stuff. Please take care of yourself, Jaz. No heroes needed just live brothers.'

Jasper is irritated by his brother trying to advise him.

'You know what really sticks in my craw, bro. I worked my ass off all those years in the cotton fields to help put you through school. And, now my neck is on the line every day in this shit hole, while you're down there sippin' cocktails with your lazy ass cronies in the officers' club. Shit James, It's just not fair. I resent you for that.'

'Jaz, I only wish good things for you. What I've learned in my 26 years is that you got to make the best outta what you got. And, for you right now, that means having a great time in Bangkok and getting yourself home in one piece.'

'Hi, my name is Took. If you're looking for companion, I available.'

The Walker brothers are standing at a bar in the Patpong District. A young Thai girl dressed in a tight blouse and short shorts is propositioning Jaz. She has the number 7 attached to her pants.

'You like me. I show you good time.'

Jasper notes that she is wearing a lot of makeup, but the girl looks pretty.

'Whattya think, bro. Should I take a chance on Took?'

'She's as cute as any of the girls I've seen. If that's what you want, go for it.'

'How much? Oh, and you need to find a girl for my buddy here.'

'I have good friend for your boody. He will like very much.'

'Before we agree on anything,' James interjects. 'How much?'

'I give good price. You each give me $65, and we do everything. At the end, if you like, you give me tip.'

'That sounds okay, but I want to see other girl first.'

'You stay here. I go find Kanita.'

Took leaves them standing at the bar and goes into the street. Less than two minutes later she returns with her friend.

'This my friend, Kanita.'

Her pal is even more lovely than Took. She seems reserved but pleasant.

'What are your names?'

'My name is Jackie Robinson,' answers James. 'And, this is Larry Doby.'

'You like my friend, Mr. Jackie?'

'Yes, she seems very nice.'

'Okay, now we need to sign contract.'

'Contract, we're not going to sign a contract, are we James?'

'Everyone must have contract,' Took declares. 'Government say so.'

'I'm afraid we have to. They told us about that at the R&R Center.'

'No contract, no girl. No good time in Bangkok. '

An older, overweight mamasan comes over to ensure the transactions are done correctly. James and Jasper sign the paperwork using their fake names from the baseball world.

'The Thai official make big money from contracts,' says the big mama.

Took then makes suggestions for the days' activities.

'Many things to see in Bangkok. We have many beautiful palaces. Shopping very good at cheap price. I take you to best shops. Thai food have good flavor. At night, we take you to Muy Thai boxing match. Then, we sleep with you. You like?'

Jaz has no girlfriend back home. He has no qualms about sleeping with Took as long as he doesn't catch VD. James, on the other hand, has reservations. He has been true to Shirley even though they have no formal commitment to each other.

They explore the magnificent temple of Arun Wat, save the Sleeping Buddha temple and the Grand Palace for another day. Afterwards, the girls take them to an outdoor restaurant to eat Pad Thai and Tom Yum soup. Shopping will wait until the last day. Both brothers want to see Muy Thai boxing.

Took procures four ringside seats next to the blue corner. The stadium is vast, maybe 20 rows deep climbing high above the ring. Rowdy fans pack the place, screaming loudly for their favorite fighters.

During the first round of a match, the crowd is somewhat subdued as the two pugilists jab and shuffle around the ring, feeling each other out. The action picks up in the second round, and crowd noise increases. In the third and final round, the fighters appear to be battling for their lives. James and Jaz are caught up in the excitement and cheer for their man in the blue corner. The energy in the building rises to a crescendo that sends shivers down their spines.'

A fist to the stomach. A kick to the head. The fighter in the blue trunks is down. The referee finishes counting; 8, 9, 10. He's out. Red trunks wins. He raises his arms high overhead in celebration. But, blue trunks remains on the canvas unmoving. In less than a minute, two men slide a stretcher onto the ring floor and carry the fighter out of the arena.

'How you like?' Took asks Jaz. The young brother is slumped into his chair and has turned pale.

'I was back in Vietnam and saw myself fighting against red trunks, only in my mind, he was wearing the red North Vietnamese flag. I lost.'

'Let's have a drink,' Took suggests to Jaz. 'Make you feel better. Then we go to apartment.'

James looks at Jasper and smiles. 'You're in Bangkok, and you're having fun.'

'Let's go,' says Jaz snapping out of his frightening fantasy.

When they finish their drinks at the bar and arrive at their assigned apartment, the two couples split up and go into separate bedrooms. Jaz is euphoric. He has spent the whole day seeing new places with a beautiful young woman. Now, he gets to have sex with her. Vietnam seems like a distant memory.

James, on the other hand, has serious reservations. He never slept with a prostitute before. Thoughts of Shirley keep invading his conscience. Kanita seems like a pleasant person, but they have no past and no future together. As she begins to remove her blouse and shorts, he's tempted by the soft curves of her body and her flirtatious glances. He takes off his shoes and socks, shirt and trousers.

She climbs into bed naked and beckons him to join her. He stands there in his boxers frozen with confusion. Something inside is stopping him from having sex with this beautiful Asian girl.

'What's the matter, Jackie? You no like me?'

The entire day had been building toward this moment, and now, an unseen force was holding him back.

''No Kanita, you are very beautiful and very sexy.'

'Then, why you no make love to me?'

The unmistakable sound of rhythmic thumping reverberates from the adjacent room. James can sense that Kanita is becoming upset.

'Let's just lie together in bed,' he suggests.

'Okay,' she replies with a renewed sense of anticipation.

They snuggle in bed with their arms around each other. She begins to caress him, but he doesn't respond. Several minutes pass. She becomes discouraged and turns away.

'Maybe you like boys, not girls.'

'No, I can assure you, I like girls.'

'Then why you no make love to me?'

'I have lady friend in U.S. I remain faithful to her.'

'But she thousand miles from here. She can no give you sex. I can give you sex.'

James knows Kanita being unhappy with him can ruin his brother's time with Took. He tries to calm her by telling a story.

'I come from a poor black family in Georgia....'

He talks for 30 minutes before she falls asleep from boredom. The gyrating noises from the other room continues.

With some reassuring talk and an agreement to switch their Thai mates, the brothers make it through their five-day furlough. Jaz is euphoric. James is relieved. On the plane ride back to Tan Son Nhut, they discuss their experiences.

'I can't understand you, brother. Two hot women who want to have sex with you, and you refuse them both. What's wrong?'

'I know it sounds crazy, but I can't be disloyal to my girl back in Sacramento.'

'You're right. Crazy is the right word.'

James changes the subject.

'What are you going to do with yourself when you get out of the Army?'

'I got a buddy over here whose Daddy owns an auto repair shop in Missouri. He said if I was interested I could join him there in the family business.'

'Something like that could be great for you, Jaz. You need to get away from those cotton fields. You got no future down there.'

'I sure can see that now that I'm away from it all. Still, there's Daddy, Ma and our two sisters. Can't forget them.'

'No, I think about them all the time and wish I could find a better life for them too.

The plane touches down in Vietnam.

'I'm glad we got together, bro. For me, that was the most important part of this trip.'

Jasper smiles and shakes his brother's hand.

He later catches a lift on a Huey back to his base. James waves as the chopper takes off.

CHAPTER 53

'I'm going over to meet with Pedersen this morning.' Stirling tells his secretary. 'He's called a special meeting for all his department heads. I should be back in about an hour.'

January 31st, 1968. Rumors about increased NVA and Cong activity has been spreading. But, it's time for New Year's celebrations, a holiday called 'Tet' in Vietnam. In past years, the occasion has been a cause for cessation of hostilities.

As Tom steps out the front door of his building, he can hear gunfire in the distance. *'Probably some skirmish on the perimeter,'* he surmises. Taking precaution, his pace quickens as he hustles the 100 or so yards to his boss' building.

A screaming sound approaches getting louder by the millisecond. The new captain tries to run, but an explosion occurs right in front of him. He's down, dazed and unable to move.

'Jesus, oh my God,' he cries lying helpless on his back.

Walker sees his fellow officer blown backward to the ground by the blast. He is on his way to the same meeting when the incident occurs. Instinctively, he rushes to Stirling's side and sees blood oozing through the shirt front of his 1505 khaki uniform. Not trained to apply first aid, he thrusts his arms under Tom's body, lifts and carries him as fast as he can toward the base hospital.

'Stay with me, Stirling. We're going to the hospital to get you fixed up. I want you to talk to me until we get there,' he speaks in gasps as he totes his wounded comrade's 170-pound frame toward the help he desperately needs.

'What's your name?'

'Reb,' he blurts out between stabs of pain.

'Where are you?'

'In a fuckin' war zone, you idiot.'

'Okay, save your energy, we're almost there.'

Walker hauls him up the front steps of the hospital and into the reception area.

'I need help here, quick. The captain here has just been hit by a mortar round, and he's bleeding bad!'

An orderly and a Medic are summoned to the front by the receptionist. They quickly retrieve a gurney and assist Walker, transferring the Captain onto the wheeled stretcher.

'Get a packet of TraumaDex stat,' yells the Medic to the orderly. 'He's losing a lot of blood.'

Walker hears the staff conversing loudly about emergency procedures as they roll the gurney down the hallway. He follows them. The leader of the team shouts back.

'Captain, you'll have to wait in the reception area. Several personnel will be working on your friend, and you'll be in the way.'

James feels frustrated he can't do more to help. Then, it hits him. He and Stirling are both supposed to be attending an important meeting with Captain Pedersen. He hurries out the door and goes to inform his boss about the unfortunate incident.

Two and a half weeks later, the wounded captain opens his eyes not realizing where he is. His brain is in a fog. A dull pain throbs through his body below his neck. As he stares in front of him, he makes out the blurry visage of a dark face.

'Stirling, Stirling, wake up. It's me Walker. Listen, you're gonna fight like hell and walk out of this place. You had a mortar shell blow up and penetrate your abdomen. The doctors did surgery to stop the bleeding and sewed you back together. You are looking at me inside Tan Son Nhut Hospital. Okay, let's see if you're with it or not. Tell me, what's my name?'

No response. The black captain tries again.

'What's your name?'

He realizes Tom is having difficulty processing his questions.

'Let's try again. How many fingers am I holding up?' Walker extends his index and middle digits.

Again, no verbal response. Walker's face reflects disappointment. He starts to look away and notices something moving. Following with his eyes down the right arm toward Stirling's hand, he observes his palm with two fingers extended.

'Hey buddy, welcome back to the land of the living. If you can understand me squeeze my hand.'

He reaches down and grasps Tom's right hand. A weak response follows.

'Great, you're with me. I've got a letter here from Nancy Gunn. Do you want me to open it and read it to you?'

Another weak squeeze follows. Walker opens the envelope and begins reading.

'My dearest Tommy:

I was so sorry to hear about your injuries. And, to think you were on a so-called safe base when the bomb came. Awful. I still can't believe it happened to you.

Everyone back here is praying for your swift and complete recovery. I talk to God every night and demand him to make you all better. I'm knitting you a sweater in your favorite red and black colors to remind you of Georgia. I'll send it to you when I finish it in a week or so.

Well, things around here are the same. I've been over to see your folks a few times. They are very worried about you as am I. You get better soon, you hear. And, come home to us. We miss you so much.

Love, your sweet pea, Nancy

P.S. I'm sending you pictures of Elaine and me waterskiing at Lake Blackshear.'

Walker supports Stirling's head so he can look at the photos. Tears are streaming down both cheeks. He begins sobbing uncontrollably.

'Let it out, buddy. Let it out. You're coming out of a coma from the blast concussion.' James waits until Tom finally gains control. 'Hey, I gotta go to work, but I'll be back to see you later. Start flirting with the nurses. That'll make you feel better.'

The attending nurse whispers to Walker. 'He's going to need a lot of therapy and likely more surgery.'

James reacts, 'Right now, keep talking to him until he starts yapping at you.'

Walker drops by again late that afternoon. To his surprise, he finds Stirling sitting up in bed wide awake.

'Thanks for coming by, Walker.'

The black captain is stunned by the changes he can see since that morning. His mouth drops open.

'You can talk? That's great. What happened? This morning you couldn't say anything.'

'That nurse has been jabbering at me all day to say something. Finally, I said, "Shut the fuck up." That got me started.'

James smiles.

'I don't think you realize how worried everyone has been about you. Good to see you're back to being your old obnoxious self.'

'Time to go for a walk, Rebel Bulldog man.'

'Don't feel up to it, Walker. I'm gonna read. So, get lost.'

Stirling has been in recovery for six weeks. He's lost 35 pounds and his energy remains fleeting. In his mind, Tom can feel his whole life slipping away. He doesn't feel he's capable of doing anything let alone finding that big job back in Atlanta after he gets out. And, what woman is going to be attracted to a guy with a torn up, disgusting looking body? Even Nancy will probably be repulsed.

'No excuses, you pantywaist. Get up. We're gonna do 30 minutes.'

Walker has been challenging him every day since the shelling event. He retrieves Stirling's PT shorts along with a tee shirt and socks out of the dresser drawer. Then, he drags out a pair of brogans from the closet and delivers an ultimatum.

'Get dressed. You're gonna get your ass moving if I have to kick it all the way to Saigon!'

The road outside the barracks is dotted with puddles from the frequent rains. They start out slow with Tom taking short, halting steps to avoid stepping in the water. James looks perturbed.

'Let's walk like you're more grown up than a two-year old mama's boy.'

'Easy for you to say. You never had your insides ripped to shreds.'

'Oh, a pity party. Is that what you're asking for?'

'What are you trying to be, some kinda drill sergeant?'

'That's exactly what you need right now, Stirling. I don't think you realize, if you don't push yourself, you're gonna end up like some pathetic old fart who has done nothing with his life except scrounge off welfare. Is that what you want?'

'I want to go waterskiing.'

'Then, start showing these puddles who's boss, damn it. I want to see some grit instead of hearing your tired, lame excuses.' They pick up the pace.

CHAPTER 54

'What are you going to do when you get home, Stirling?' Walker asks.

They are standing in the white captain's BOQ room near the end of March. Tom has received orders to Brooke Army Hospital for additional corrective surgery. He expects to be discharged from the Air Force upon leaving there.

'I have some friends in Atlanta. I'm hoping they can set me up with a job in sales or marketing. A position at Coca Cola would be great.'

'You feel up to working a full-time job?'

'That might take a while, but I think I could handle something part-time. What about you? Any plans when you get out?'

'I'll go back to Sacramento first to see if I have anything still going with Shirley.'

Tom's face grimaces at that remark.

'I'm sorry, Walker. I don't believe any colored man should be with a white woman. You need to stick to your own kind. Stay away from those pale skinned foxes. Can't you see you're asking for big trouble? Look at all the news about coloreds rioting back in the states. A lot of angry rednecks are out there ready to kill a black man with a white chick.'

James ignores the sermon and turns the conversation back to Tom.

'What about you and Nancy?'

'Everyone expects we'll get married. That's the plan.'

'That girl has been true to you all these years. And, you've been stepping out on her with a lot of different women. Are you sure you can be faithful to her after you're hitched?'

'I will do my darnedest to be the best husband I can. You can't ask for more than that.'

'I'm no expert on marriage, but I do know getting a little action on the side is probably the quickest way to ruin a relationship.'

'You're right….You're no expert.'

James can see he and Tom are never going to see eye-to-eye regarding women. So, he bids goodbye and returns to his own quarters.

'Oh good, a letter from Reverend Jones.'

Walker always looks forward to news from home. He feels blessed to have his pastor maintain an interest in him. He does get correspondence from Aunt Violet as well. But, the Reverend is the one person who could fill him in on everything happening back in his hometown.

As he stands over his desk ready to open the envelope, a strange feeling comes over him as he had received a letter from the pastor only one week before. He unfolds the two creases in the paper and begins to read.

'Dear James:

I don't know if you have been informed, but there's some sad news to tell. Your brother, Jasper has been reported killed in action over there in Vietnam.'

Walker reads that sentence twice in disbelief, then collapses into his desk chair. His heart races, and he begins to hyperventilate. Two minutes later, he composes himself enough to continue reading the letter.

'According to the information given to your parents by the Army officers who came to their home, his unit was on a mission to capture an enemy outpost in the central highlands when they were ambushed close to their objective.

Three soldiers were killed and six others wounded. Jasper was one of those who didn't make it. He died sacrificing his life so the rest of us could live in peace and freedom. We are erecting a stone memorial for him on our church grounds. God bless his soul.

I am truly sorry to convey this tragic news of your brave brother. Your parents are heartbroken. They wanted me to let you know what happened to Jasper. We pray you remain safe and return to us soon.

With deepest sympathy,

Reverend Jeremiah Jones'

James rises from his chair and crumples onto his bed. Tears flow. He feels cold and empty. Minutes later, his mind races with feelings of anger and remorse. He stands and starts pacing the floor shouting to himself.

'We were only beginning to relate like true brothers. I was so glad we had that time in Thailand; I believed that was just a start for us. He had a whole new life ahead of him that would have freed him from those humiliating and degrading ways of the South. This is too cruel.'

The next day, Walker calls in sick to work letting them know why he wasn't coming in. He crawls into bed and curls up with his sober thoughts.

In the late afternoon, there's a knock on his door.

'Go away. I want to be alone.'

'Walker, I need to talk to you,' says a familiar voice from the other side of the door.

'Leave. I don't want to talk to anybody.'

'Hey, it's Stirling. Look, I heard about your brother. That's gotta hurt bad. But, remember what you told me. There ain't no time for a pity party.'

James realizes he's acting as bad as Stirling was after his blast wounds.

'Hate to admit it, but he's right.' he thinks to himself.

Walker unlocks the door and lets Stirling in. His eyes are swollen, lips pouted and he's only wearing boxer shorts and a tee shirt.

'You look like shit,' the white captain notes.

'Thanks, but I still look better than you. What do you want? Can't you see I'm in no mood for entertaining guests?'

'What you need is a good stiff drink and some uplifting conversation. Get dressed. We're going to the officers' club.'

Walker grumbles but finally relents and puts on his fatigues. They walk along the rutted toad about a quarter mile and enter the club heading straight for the bar.

'Two Southern Comforts on the rocks,' requests Stirling.

'I can't believe my brother is gone,' bemoans Walker. 'He meant a lot to me, and I feel like I failed him. I never sacrificed for Jaz like he did for me, and I was too selfish to realize that.'

'You're being too hard on yourself, Walker. The decision you made to get out of those cotton fields was the best decision of your life. If your brother wanted to follow in your footsteps, he probably could have. After all, you paved the way for him.'

'Maybe. But, that doesn't take away the hurt I feel right now for his sacrifice. The fact is, as his brother, I never gave him the kind of guidance and support I should have.'

'James, James, I'm sure you gave him that kind of attention whenever you were together. You're that type of guy. The sad part is that you two were separated for several years. That's hard on any relationship.

'Yuh, I guess you're right.'

The two young captains have three rounds of drinks and eat dinner together afterwards. The dark cloud over James is slowly lifting. Leaving the club, they walk back to their quarters arm in arm.

'You feeling any better now?'

'Yah, some. Thanks.'

'A little booze with a friend usually helps.'

Stirling's remark strikes them both. They turn to look at each other and simultaneously say, 'Are we really friends?'

Tom erupts with a full-throated laugh that makes his chest hurt. He doubles over in pain before starting to laugh again. James finds Stirling's reaction hilarious and can't stop guffawing.'

The hulking C-141 Starlifter sits next to the runway fueled for takeoff. The crew is receiving their pre-flight briefing before heading out to the aircraft. Stirling stands by the Base Ops building with his duffle bag ready to board the plane. Walker is there to see him off.

'I'm sure you're going to miss this place. So many fond memories especially those days lying in a hospital bed.'

'I guess picking cotton back in Georgia made you a cynical SOB. Plus, I think that made you a vindictive bastard who likes bossing white guys around.'

A flight crew member enters the room informing passengers the plane is ready for boarding. The mood suddenly changes between the two Georgians.

'Walker, I gotta thank you for being there for me. I needed a good kick in the ass, and you didn't hesitate to give it to me.'

'I couldn't stand and watch you degenerate into some pathetic vegetable.' At least now, you're a step above a rutabaga. Good luck with those surgeons down at Brooke. I'm sure they'll do their best to make your scars look pretty for that fiancée of yours.'

'Well, I don't know if I'll ever see you again. So, good luck and thanks for your abuse. A word of caution. Stay away from white women.'

'And, you stay faithful to Nancy. She obviously loves you.'

Tom nods his head, smiling at Walker as he turns and steps toward the plane with the big green sack slung over his shoulder.

CHAPTER 55

'Hello, Shirley, it's James calling you from 'Nam. Can you hear me okay?'

'I hear you fine. This is a surprise.'

Walker isn't sure if the pretty blond from Sacramento is still interested in him. He hasn't received a letter from her in over a month despite having written her two times recently. He tries to play it cool.

'Hey, I'm going to be discharged from the Air Force in a couple of weeks. I thought since I was flying into Travis, we might be able to get together. Whattya say?'

James holds his breath as there's a long pause.

'I'd like that. You tell me when you're coming in, and I'll meet you there.'

He turns away from the telephone speaker and exhales a sigh of relief. Smiling, he does a little jig with his feet.

'Great. But, I should warn you, my flight is scheduled to land at 2:00 a.m. on July ninth. That's a crazy hour. Are you sure you want to do this?'

'Yup, I'm sure.'

'You know I've been in a war zone for nearly a year. You might notice that I've gone a little psycho.'

'I'll take that chance. I think the guy I knew was pretty okay. So, I'm willing to bet he hasn't changed that much.'

'Just a little okay, huh. Is that what you think of me?'

'Well, maybe a little better than okay.'

'Thanks, I'll take that as a compliment. So, how have you been doing? I haven't heard from you in a while.'

'After I graduated from Sac State, I took a job working for an Assemblyman downtown.'

'That sounds exciting. You probably meet a lot of fast talking guys down there.'

'Oh yah. I've learned to read men pretty well. I can tell when they're only interested in that one thing. So, what about you and all those pretty Vietnamese girls?'

'Nope, that wasn't for me. I behaved myself very well.'

'If I find out you're lying to me, I just might call Eastland and report you for violating the officer's code of conduct.'

'You wouldn't do that, would you?'

They go on talking for half an hour before finally saying their goodbyes. Walker is feeling much better about his chances after their conversation. He now has added expectation for his return to the States.

The day finally arrives, July 8th, 1968. Captain Walker says goodbye to his troops and fellow officers of the 1645th before boarding the C-141 Starlifter back to the USA. As the plane climbs to cruising altitude, he soberly looks out his window at the outline of Vietnam coast against the blue South China Sea and ruminates about his time there.

My brother's death still feels like a millstone that will always be hanging around my neck. In my one year here, I've seen the morale of our troops go down the tubes. There's almost no talk of winning now. The primary preoccupation for soldiers is counting down the number of days until they escape from this deathtrap.

Martin Luther King and Bobby Kennedy shot to death. LBJ refusing to run for election. The war turning from possible victory into probable defeat. All that negative news just gives GIs a sense of futility. Why has so much money, material and human life been sacrificed? Is there any worthwhile end to this madness or is futile waste its only legacy?

He falls asleep to the hum of the jet engines. When he awakes, the pilot announces over the loudspeaker they'll be landing in 30 minutes. Thoughts of Vietnam fade. A sense of anticipation rises within him for being back in his home country and seeing the only woman he can imagine being with.

'Yeahhhh! Scream several soldiers as the plane touches down on U.S. soil. Soon the aircraft door opens and stairs to the tarmac roll into place. As James exits the plane, he looks out and sees a radiant blond woman waving at him. His heart starts thumping, and he wishes the men in front of him would get the hell out of the way. Finally, he reaches her.

'Oh my, it's so good to be back home especially with you standing out there like the evening star in a dark sky.'

'Well, you look like all your limbs are intact. I feel so bad for those boys who come back injured. We see them all over town.'

'I'm very impressed that you came to meet me. You must be a night owl. Hardly anybody comes to the airport at this hour to meet someone.'

Shirley grabs him by the arm and leads the way to her car, a 1966 white Chevy Biscayne.

'Let's go someplace where we can talk.'

'Ah okay,' says James. 'I know we have a lot to talk about. Where do you suggest?'

'There's a 24-hour café near here called "The Milk Farm". C'mon. Throw your stuff in the trunk and we'll head over.'

Walker is disappointed and thinks to himself. *She didn't kiss me. I'm a little afraid where this is going. And, to think I refused two gorgeous babes in Thailand because of her.*

They drive off base for about 15 minutes finally reaching the mostly empty restaurant. A big overhead sign outside depicts a cow jumping over the moon. Inside, one derelict looking man; unshaven with long, scraggly hair and dirty clothes, sits at the counter. Another couple is talking animatedly in one of the booths.

'Sit anywhere you like,' says the lone waitress on duty.

James looks at his watch. *It's 0300 on a Tuesday. Is she going to work after this?'*

They find a booth and sit down.

'Shirley, I'm confused. You came all the way out here to meet me in the middle of the night, but I feel like you're holding back something. Am I right?'

'There is something I need to tell you.'

Walker braces himself for some bad news.

'Okay, let me have it.'

She squirms in her seat and pauses.

'I have been seeing another guy.'

He sighs and with a look of resignation responds.

'That's what I suspected. So, the real reason for meeting me here was to tell me that. Now I understand.'

'Don't be upset. I delayed seeing anyone else for months after you left.'

'Let me guess. Then, you met a white guy who your daddy approves of.'

She drops her head looking down toward the floor for a few seconds. Then, she lifts her gaze to him.

'He's actually a guy from my father's work. We've been dating for about a month now.'

'Well, I wanted to see you to find out if we still had feelings for each other. I guess that's ancient history now.'

Shirley looks imploringly into James' dark eyes.

'No, that's not it. I need to decide whether to go against my father's wishes or agree with him to keep peace in the family.'

'Does that mean you still do have feelings for me?'

'I do.'

Walker puts down his coffee cup and stands in the aisle. She does the same seconds later. They kiss, first softly. Then, as their emotions well up., they embrace each other passionately. The couple in the nearby booth stop talking and look. The disheveled man at the counter, who has been eavesdropping shouts out.

'It's all good, honey. If he really loves you, take a chance.'

She drops off Walker back at base housing and drives home after their late-night revelations. In the morning, he completes the administrative paperwork for an honorable discharge from the Air Force. At home, Shirley mulls over how she is going to split up with her new boyfriend and break the news to her father.

Walker catches a lift into Sacramento and takes a room in a cheap downtown hotel waiting to see what develops with Shirley. She visits him after work, a day and a half later.

'Let's go for a walk,' she insists. James can see clearly, she is distraught. He puts on his sneakers.

They walk a couple of blocks to Capitol Park and begin strolling on the macadam walkway beneath the eucalyptus trees and beside the manicured rose gardens.

'Daddy is angry with me. He told me if I left Andrew to be with that negro, I have to leave the house.'

'Oh no. I care for you Shirley, very much, but I don't want to be driving a wedge between you and your family.'

'I love both my parents, but Daddy can be really stubborn. I know he sees me as his princess daughter who should only live the fairytale life he fantasizes for me.'

'Do you think he could ever come around to accepting someone like me?'

'Not any time soon.'

'Maybe it's best if I drop out of the picture for a while.'

She bristles at that suggestion.

'No, you've been gone for a year already. Don't you think that's long enough?'

'Yes, I do. But, it sounds like my presence is stirring up a hornet's nest.'

'That's not going to change. It's something I have to deal with sooner or later.'

'Man, I hate this idea of putting you through this agony. Is there anything I can do?'

Shirley sits down on a bench near a thicket of rose bushes. A perfume fragrance fills the air around them. He settles down next to her and places his mocha complected right arm around her ivory white shoulders. She turns to look at him. And they are soon drawn into a tearful embrace. As they hold each other, an elderly white couple pass by.

'I think that is utterly disgusting. Why don't those negroes stick to their own kind,' says the man.

Overhearing that remark, the young couple separate.

'You're going to hear a lot of that if we stay together.'

'I don't care. A person has to decide what's important to them in life.'

'I love you, Shirley. I didn't know how much until I was in Southeast Asia. I realized I wasn't interested in other women, just you.'

James knows some big decisions need to happen soon. His family is expecting him to return home in the next few days. He has no reason to remain in Sacramento except one. Shirley is also well aware of the urgency of their situation.

'Shirley, can you see yourself in a long-term relation with me?'

'Yes, I can.'

He pulls out his Swiss Army knife, cuts off a single red rose from a nearby bush, then gets down on one knee. Extending the flower toward her, he makes a fateful request.

'Will you marry me?'

A broad smile fills her face. 'Yes, I will.'

He stands, places the rose in the hair behind her ear, and kisses her again.

'I know I'm supposed to give you a ring. Can you wait until tomorrow?'

'Don't worry about a ring,' she states.

'When I was a girl growing up, I imagined myself having a big church wedding with a fancy reception. All my friends and relatives would be there, and my father would give me away. That doesn't seem possible now. The only way we can get hitched around here is by a Justice of the Peace.'

CHAPTER 56

The sun drops behind the Capitol Building. Daylight begins to fade.

'C'mon, we have a lot to talk about. Let's go back to my room to figure things out.'

Shirley nods. They slowly begin the short walk back to the hotel hand-in-hand. Neither says a word on the way. James can sense the conflict his new fiancée must feel as she lowers her head lost in thought.

They enter James' room, and she begins to softly cry. He turns on a desk lamp and notices the wetness in her eyes. He removes a handkerchief from his pocket and gently dries her tears. She looks up at his face and submits to the intensity of his gaze. His hand caresses her cheek.

'Shirley, talk to me. That split with your dad must have you aching inside.'

She regains her composure and begins to reveal the depth of her dilemma.

'Ever since I was little, I've always been daddy's girl. Back then he would sit me on his knee and read me stories. My favorite was 'Beauty and the Beast'. We went shopping once and I found a dress that looked exactly like Beauty's; bright yellow with a voluminous skirt and an off the shoulder bodice. I wanted that more than anything in the world.'

"Can I have his dress, Daddy? Please, please, please."

'He looked at me with a frown and said, "That's more expensive than any of your mother's clothes."

"I promise to be a perfect daughter if you buy this for me." I looked at him with pleading eyes.'

'His expression changed from a hard, strict father to a soft, cuddly teddy bear.'

"Okay, but you better keep your room neat and finish all your chores."

'When I tried on that dress and stood proudly in front of Dad, he said to me, "From now on you will always be my little princess."'

'I was five years old.'

They sit on the end of the bed and hold hands. James is moved by Shirley's close relationship with her dad.

'We must find a way to bring him into our lives.'

She looks at James with an expression of doubt.

'He's not a Dad that a daughter can wrap around her finger. There's a stubborn side to him. I'm well aware how strongly he feels about his daughter marrying a black man.'

Walker believes he can change Brent's views.

'If he sees how much we love each other, maybe he'll come around. Let's meet with him.'

'You would do that?'

'We must do that.'

Shirley squeezes James' hand. Her whole body begins to tremble. He pulls her toward him, his dark arms embracing her porcelain white shoulders. As her tears moisten his cheek, he leans back to look at her face. Her blue eyes emote a hunger for his touch. The only sound becomes heavy breathing first from her then him.

'They softly kiss and fall back on the bed. The heat between them becomes unbearable. Impetuously fumbling with their fingers, they clumsily remove each other's clothes flinging items carelessly to the floor. Pausing briefly, they lie facing one another. James' taut, muscular body glistens in the dull light. The glow from Shirley's luminescent hair lends an ethereal silhouette to the willowy curves of her torso.

The primal forces of lust soon overcome them, and they are irresistibly drawn together. Entwined in a passionate embrace, they drink the life-giving love from each other. A sense of belonging and oneness fills them as they move like an undulating sea. An hour passes. The ardor ebbs succumbing to exhaustion unlocking their hot sweaty limbs.

Lying supine looking at the expanse of whiteness in the textured ceiling with a sense of contentment never experienced before, he softly pronounces, 'Shirley, you'll always be the only girl in the world for me.'

She turns to him and commits herself, 'James, I love you more than anything.'

Inspired by this joyous moment, a thought triggers in his head. He suggests to her.

'What if we had two weddings, one little one here and one big one in Georgia?'

'Oh James, is that possible? I would love that.'

CHAPTER 57

James and Shirley are seated on the living room sofa waiting for Brent to drive home from work. Shortly, the purring sound of his Lincoln Town Car pulling into the driveway filters through an open window. The car door slams and footsteps echo on the concrete walkway. Marge has left the couple to meet her husband at the entry. The door opens.

'Your daughter is here with her fiancé. They want to talk to you. I insist that you meet with them in a civilized manner.'

'She knows damn well, I don't want to see her or that negro. Tell them to leave.'

'No, for the sake of our family....and our marriage, you're going to have a conversation with them right now.'

The young couple hear the exchange from the adjacent foyer. Shirley is steamed at her dad for being so pig headed. She balls her hand in a fist and growls under her breath. Walker, on the other hand, is poised to be diplomatic. He knows getting into an argument with his future father-in-law is a losing proposition.

Marge stands behind Brent physically shoving him toward the living room. He turns his head and whispers to her.

'You need to understand right now. I don't approve of this proposed marriage, and if I have any power to stop it, I will.'

Mr. and Mrs. Stone enter the room and come face-to-face with the young couple. James stands and speaks first.

'Mr. Stone, I know you don't support my engagement to your daughter, but before you force me out of your house, may I say something?'

The irate father looks daggers at Walker. Marge jabs her index finger into his rib cage from behind.

''Make it short,' he blurts out.

'Sir, the reason we want to marry is because we love each other. Being apart one full year tested the strength of our relationship. Our feelings and devotion to one another have remained unbroken. Beyond that, your daughter and I both want your acceptance of us as a couple. It would mean a great deal, not only to us, but to bring the family together as a whole. You love your little princess, sir. And, she loves you. Please find it in your heart to accept us.'

Marge nods her head. Shirley smiles at James, then stares beseechingly at her father. He gazes down at the floor searching for a response he can live with. Steely eyed, he faces Walker and begins.

'You're asking me to recognize something I've been against my entire life. Your people have a way of living far different than us whites. I believe our two groups must marry among themselves. My God, think what kind of world you would bring your children into. That's why I cannot agree to this proposed marriage.'

He turns to walk out of the room but stops when Walker responds to his comments.

'I hope and pray you'll learn to accept us, Mr. Stone.'

Brent continues leaving the room and stomps up the stairs to his master bedroom. Marge drops her head in disappointment. James sits back down on the couch, and Shirley falls into his comforting arms whimpering.

'I now pronounce you man and wife,' declares the Justice of the Peace. 'You may now kiss the bride.'

The wedding party stands in a windowless room at the County Courthouse in downtown Sacramento. No festive decorations, only a large photo of Edmund G. Brown, Governor glaring down at the gathering with a stern expression as if to say, "I don't approve of this marriage."

As the ceremony ends, the officiating justice looks at Walker with a sense of expectation.

'Did I forget something?' James asks. Then, it dawns on him. 'Oh, now I remember.'

He pulls out $50 from his pants pocket, two twenties and a ten, handing it to the official.

Walker is dressed conservatively, sporting a blue suit, white shirt and blue tie. Shirley wears a white short-sleeved dress with the hemline above her knees. Marge Stone is there to support her daughter and bear witness for the marriage. A few of Shirley's friends are also in attendance. Father Brent….has refused to recognize the union.

The party departs the courthouse in two cars driving to the Mansion Inn for a luncheon celebration. The bride has reserved a small room next to the main restaurant. The guests and married couple settle into stuffed armchairs placed around two small tables butted together and covered with a white tablecloth. Shirley has chosen chicken cordon bleu with mashed potatoes and green salad with Green Goddess dressing. Before the food arrives, two chilled bottles of Cook's champagne is served. James rises to make a toast along with a surprise announcement.

'Attention everyone. Thank you so much for supporting Shirley and me on the important day in our lives. We are so happy to have you here.' He looks at Shirley and smiles. She erases the serious look on her face and forces a weak grin. 'I also want to announce, you are all invited to the second wedding for the two of us to be held at the First African Baptist Church in Savannah, Georgia. The event will occur three weeks from this Saturday at 2:00 p.m.' He raises his glass. 'Here's to our first and second marriage.'

Everyone cheers and raises their glasses, all except Shirley. She turns to her new husband with her mouth agape. He laughs knowing he has just given her a present that needed no wrapping paper. Sitting down after quaffing the champagne, James whispers to his new bride.

'I've been talking with Reverend Jones back home. He's gotten permission from Pastor Gilbert to perform the ceremony in Savannah, and Aunt Violet is handling the invitations.'

'I'm impressed with this guy I just married,' she gleefully responds.

'I hope you will like it down there. I figured we need to consider both California and Georgia before we decide where to plant our roots.'

Shirley has heard bad stories about how blacks are treated in the South. She's not so sure that a mixed couple could be accepted.

'Do you think we would be safe down there?'

'You need to know people and places to stay away from.'

Overhearing the conversation, Marge Stone fears for her only child. 'That doesn't sound very comforting, James. Always remember, we are entrusting our daughter's safety in your hands. Promise me you'll protect her.'

'Mrs. Stone, I will guard her with my life.' Marge's fears being eased for the moment, her thoughts turn to her husband.

'I'm so disappointed Brent has chosen not to acknowledge this marriage. And, I know my daughter is distressed by her father's decision.' She turns to Shirley. 'This should be the happiest day of your life, dear.'

'Don't remind me, Mother.'

CHAPTER 58

'Auntie, so good to see you.'

The newlyweds have arrived at Savannah Airport on a small commuter plane from Atlanta after transferring from their cross-country flight. James gives his aunt a big hug.

'I'm so glad to see you, nephew. Handsome as ever and all your family is glad to have you home from that awful war. Now, introduce me to this lovely lady beside you.'

'Aunt Violet, I have the pleasure of presenting to you Mrs. Shirley Stone Walker from Sacramento, California.'

'Welcome, dear. We're pleased to have you in the family.' Auntie kisses her on both cheeks. Shirley smiles. 'Let me help you with your things. I've got a taxi out front waiting for us.'

The new bride feels relieved to have an important member of the Walker family greet her in such a friendly way.

'I love your place, Aunt Violet. You've got it decorated beautifully.'

'Thank you, dear. Come let me show you to your rooms.'

'Rooms, Auntie?'

'Well, in my mind, you're not really married until you've had a proper church wedding. So, while you're staying in my house, there's separate bedrooms until after the ceremony at our blessed house of worship.'

'I guess we don't have much choice as long as we're under your roof.'

Violet leads them to their rooms and shows Shirley where she can store her things.

'I want you both to come down to the dining room after you get settled. We can talk about the wedding. And, I have a little treat for the two of you.'

'Have some tea, dear.'

'You are such a gracious hostess, Aunt Violet.'

'Call me Auntie. Everyone else in the family does. But, let's talk about the wedding.'

Violet has her best lace tablecloth spread over the table with plastic placemats for each person to protect the valued covering. She had baked an apple pie that previous day and warmed it up in the oven to serve. The smell of brown sugar and cinnamon permeates the air. She slices a generous piece for each of her house guests and a smaller one for herself.

'So, tell us what we're in for, Auntie,' requests her nephew.

'Well, I'll tell you what's been organized so far, and we can discuss the other arrangements that still need to be made.'

'I do appreciate your doing so much for us, Auntie,' Shirley remarks. 'Our ceremony back in California was quite impersonal.'

'We're going to change that, aren't we? So far, I've got the church for two weeks from Saturday and you know Reverend Jones has agreed to perform the marital rites. Nephew, do you have a best man, and does your bride-to-be have a maid of honor?'

James hasn't given much thought about those decisions because this whole idea happened so quickly, his main concern was convincing Shirley to come to Georgia. Then, a name comes into his head.

'I made a good friend over in Vietnam. Would it be okay if I asked him?'

'Certainly, what's his name?' Auntie asks.

'You need to understand. He's a white guy from Georgia, and his father is a plantation owner.'

'Whooee! Boy, you sure now how to stir up some excitement. But, I'm not so sure that's a good idea. You need to realize the church will be filled with people who look like you and me, and some of those folks have very strong feelings against white people.'

'My buddy's name is Tom Stirling. I don't really have his address, but I know he's from Cordele, Georgia.'

'He's your best friend and you don't know how to get hold of him? That seems odd.'

'We became close due to a couple of difficult circumstances. He was there for me when Jasper was killed.'

'I can understand how you two became close during that troubled time, James. I do. And, you should invite him to attend the wedding, but I feel you need to choose a black friend to be the best man.'

'I suppose I could ask David Washington. We haven't seen each other in a while, but we're still good friends.'

'That's a good choice, nephew. I've always liked David. How about asking your father? Would you consider that?'

'I don't want to put more pressure on Daddy than simply adjusting to the fact that his son has married a white woman.'

'Yes, I do believe you're right,' responds Auntie who now turns to Shirley. 'What about you, young lady? Do you have a maid of honor?'

'My mother has agreed to fly down for the wedding, so I plan to have her give me away, but I don't know if anyone else is coming.'

'What about your father? Isn't he coming to give you away?'

'That's a painful subject, Auntie. He doesn't recognize our marriage.'

Shirley tears up at the mention of her father. 'I'd rather not talk about him. Can we discuss the bridesmaids?'

Violet gives Shirley a look of disappointment, then turns to a more approachable issue. 'You know James has two sisters. Maybe the eldest could be the maid of honor and the younger one a bridesmaid.'

'I like the idea of my sisters being part of the wedding. I owe them so much for their support of me.'

Shirley is hoping one of her friends would fly down with her mother.

'I'm not sure yet, but a close friend of mine might be able to come. Let me call her before we ask James' sisters.'

Despite all the excitement of the impending wedding, Aunt Violet has some concerns that need to be addressed. She turns to her nephew.

'James, one thing you need to do is talk to your father. He has some reservations about this marriage.'

'I was afraid of that, honey,' reacts Shirley. 'Do you think we can win him over?'

'Papa is a cautious man, but he's also fair. It might take some time for him to really accept us, but I'm convinced we can do it.'

'You should be aware, nephew, you not only need the support of your father, there's others requiring persuasion as well.'

'I want my whole family to accept us as a couple, and, for that matter, the whole black community of Stillmore.'

Violet gives James a quizzical look, and thinks to herself, *Nephew, get real. You live in Georgia. It's going to take some doing before a black and white couple will be accepted in Stillmore by anybody including your family*

'Let's talk about a subject that's easier to deal with, wedding pictures and flowers. I have a friend from church, who would be willing to be your photographer. His work is very professional.'

'That sounds great, Auntie. I think we'll need to trust your judgment on that matter. We don't know any local photographers.'

'As for the flowers, I'd like to take Shirley to the flower mart downtown to select the ones she likes best.'

'I'd love to do that, Auntie. When shall we go?'

'Let's head down there tomorrow before the others start coming in from out of town and try to tell us what to do.'

Shirley turns to James and proclaims, 'I like this lady, honey.'

CHAPTER 59

'Hello, ma'am, my name is James Walker. I served with Tom Stirling in Vietnam. Is he there?'

James found the phone number for a Stirling residence in Cordele by calling Georgia Bell information. He doesn't know if Tom is still being treated at Brooke Army Hospital or whether he finally made it home.'

'What did you say your name was?' the lady on the phone asks.

'Walker. James Walker.'

'Hold on.'

A minute later a familiar voice comes on the line.

'Walker, you black dog, is that really you?'

'Yes, it is, you rebel bigot. Hey Stirling, how are you doing? Did they stitch up that stomach of yours real pretty for Nancy?'

'My tummy may not be as beautiful as the rest of me, but Nancy will just have to get used to that. Hey, nice to hear from you, but what prompted you to call?'

'I got a favor to ask.'

'Hey buddy, anything you want. I owe you big time.'

'Would you come to my wedding?'

Stirling is floored by this request.

'Are you serious? With all those black folks sitting in that church staring at the one white guy, you want me to be there.'

'Yes, will you do it?'

Tom was glad to hear from Walker. But, asking a white guy to attend a negro wedding, that was too much.

'Walker, what made you want me to come to your wedding?'

'We became buddies in Vietnam. Remember? That's what friends do, share big moments together. And, you won't be the only honky in the church. Shirley will be there too. Plus, your Nancy is invited.'

'So, you went against my advice and got that white woman from California to marry you. And, now you drag her down to the Deep South to get hitched. You're crazier than I thought.'

'Okay, so I'm demented, are you coming?'

Tom is more than a little hesitant about this request. He's concerned how his friends and family would view his attending such a controversial event involving coloreds.

'I would feel like a hypocrite because you know I don't' approve of mixed marriages.'

'C'mon, Reb, I thought we got beyond all that petty crap in Vietnam.'

'Yuh, but we're not in Vietnam, we're in freakin' Georgia.'

'Look, if I can risk marrying a white woman in this state, you can take a chance by coming to the wedding of a negro friend.'

Stirling ponders that rebuff for a minute, then concedes.

'Okay, I'll show up.'

James hosts a dinner for the wedding party in Savannah two days before the big day. Because Stirling is in town, he decides to include him. Walker reserves a room in a local black restaurant. James has convinced his old high school friend, David Washington to be his best man. Shirley is thrilled that her black friend, Melissa has agreed to come and act as her maid of honor. Her mother attends the dinner along with the groom's parents, two sisters, Aunt Violet, and Reverend Jones. Tom busts into the room as the minister begins the blessing.

'Excuse me for being late,' he apologizes with red faced embarrassment. Stirling quickly takes an empty seat. The minister pauses while all eyes turn toward Tom. The minister restarts grace with an amused expression on his face.

Plates of fried chicken, collard greens, black-eyed peas and mashed potatoes are rolled in on carts and served to the guests by black waiters in white attire. Tom is introduced to each member of the party by James, receiving welcoming looks from some and somber faced stares from others. When the dinner dishes are cleared away and plates of strawberry shortcake are set in front of the guests, Stirling rises to make a toast.

'I know my appearance at this dinner seems out of place. I'm not related to anyone here, and only one person here knew me before I crashed this party tonight.'

Tom smiles and holds his hands up expecting a laugh for his opening remark. He receives only quizzical looks. Undaunted, he continues.

'James and I have a special relationship dating back to our time together in Vietnam. I suffered a severe blast injury from a Viet Cong attack on our base. Without hesitation, he picked me up in his arms and rushed to the base hospital within minutes from the time I was wounded. If it wasn't for James, I would have bled to death.'

'After surgery, I was depressed and feeling sorry for myself. He wouldn't let me wallow in self-pity. Every day, he would visit and force me to exercise or go outside for dreaded marches on the muddy roads outside our barracks.

'At the time, I hated him for it. But, after I recovered, I realized I would have been a sorry mess without him. He is one helluva friend.

'And, so tonight, I want to wish nothing but a long, happy and healthy life for James and his lovely bride, Shirley. To the happy couple.'

Stirling raises his glass. Marge, Auntie, and Reverend Jones follow suit. The Walker family barely lift their glasses from the table remaining seated and expressionless. Tom sits down with a quizzical look on his face disappointed by the reaction.

David Washington follows Stirling with an eloquent toast applauded by the entire party.

As the evening continues, Reverend Jones observes the interaction between members of the wedding party. A sober reserve describes James' immediate family. They act politely but exhibit no spontaneity and only talk among themselves.

CHAPTER 60

August 24th, 1968. The guests arrive filling the pews closest to the altar.
The church is alive with conversation. Organ music drifts down from the
loft, and the scent of Double Delight roses perfumes the air.

James stands near the front pew, acknowledging guests as they enter.
Auntie has invited several of his old friends from high school and a few
from college including Tyus, Jerome and Herschel. Tom turns up right
before the ceremony is scheduled to begin taking a place in the rearmost
row on the groom's side. Believing he is one of only two Caucasians
attending the service, he plans to make a quick exit after the service and
head back to Cordele.

The ushers escort the parents down to the front pew. Strangely, Marge
Stone is beaming, while the Walkers appear grim and stone-faced.

In a small room in the rear of the building, Shirley fidgets with her gown.
Melissa helps her calm down.

'Relax, girlfriend, you're already married. It's too late for him to back out
on you now.'

The bride primps her hair in the mirror while Melissa assists with the veil.
Shirley whispers in her friend's ear so James' sisters can't hear.

'I'm nervous about James' family. I don't think they like me.'

Then, she states out loud, 'I still feel heartbroken about my father.'

Melissa whispers back. 'Remember what you told me. It may take a while, but eventually you'll fit in.'

'I said that to you?' Shirley says out loud.

'Yes, you did.'

There's a knock on the door. 'We're ready for the bridesmaids, maid of honor, and the bride,' a man's voice calls from outside in the antechamber.

The two sisters exit first each wearing a pale, yellow dress and holding a bouquet of pink roses. Melissa smooths down the long white train at the back of Shirley's full-length white dress with lace bodice and bare shoulders, before leaving.

Finally, the bride-to-be takes a deep breath and exits the room. She looks for her mother to escort her down the aisle but has a shocking surprise. There before her, dressed handsomely in a black tuxedo, stands her father. Her face turns as white as her dress. For a moment, she is in shocked disbelief. Her heart had been aching since leaving Sacramento for what she feared was a permanent rift from Brent.

'Am I dreaming or is that my dad waiting to take his daughter down the aisle?'

'It's really me. I've been doing some soul searching over the past couple of weeks. I decided I want to keep my little princess in my life even if she ended up marrying the devil himself.'

'I want to hug you, Dad, but it'll mess up my makeup. C'mon let's go before I start crying.'

The music stops. Everyone turns and looks to the rear of the church. The organist begins again with a resounding rendition of 'Here's Comes the Bride'. Shirley flashes a broad smile and tugs her father's arm to begin the walk down that fateful ribbon of carpet. As they near the altar, her mother beams at the two of them with obvious pride in her demeanor. Shirley turns to look at her new in-laws in the opposite pew and confronts looks of indifference. James takes her hand and together they step up to the altar. The music stops and the voluminous space of the church holds a hushed silence broken only by the whirring of overhead fans.

Reverend Jones begins the service with a message to the congregation.

'This is a historic day. A day that brings us a new understanding of the relationship between the black community and the white. Let me caution all of you, the joining together of this man and this woman at this moment in time won't be easy for either white or black citizens to accept. It shakes tradition and expected behavior to the core. Shirley and James will leave here today as equal partners in their marriage. They are letting their love for one another blaze a path for equality among the races. Their brave decision will be tested in days and years to come. And, though they are both strong of character, they will need the unyielding support of you, their family and friends to help pave the way for a happy and fruitful future. And for that, we will all be better people.'

Reverend Jones looks out over his audience. By their rapt attention, he senses they have heard his message. He only hopes they will take it to heart.

The pastor goes on to conduct a traditional marriage ceremony. After the bride and groom exchange their vows, he completes the ritual with the expected final statement.

'You may now kiss the bride.'

The congregation claps and cheers as the couple returns down the center aisle into the vestibule to receive their guests. They line up near the front entrance; bridesmaids and groomsmen, parents of the bride, parents of the groom, and finally, groom and bride.

'Ah don't think Ah know my brotha anymore,' responds the older sister when asked if James seems like the same person. 'Ah think his time in Vietnayam made him a little mental.'

Marge confidently shakes hands and greets every guest with, 'Delighted to meet you. Hope you enjoyed the ceremony.'

Brent, noticeably uncomfortable, summons a forced smile and sweaty handshake to each guest.

Mr. and Mrs. Walker enthusiastically interact with each attendee inquiring about their personal lives but avoid talking about the wedding.

Tom falls in line as one of the last guests. The two sisters barely acknowledge him, but one of the groomsmen is curious.

'You must be from Boston or someplace up north.'

'No, I'm from Cordele, Georgia, about 80 miles west of here.'

'Really, I'd like to hear the story how you and James became friends. Maybe at the reception.'

'Maybe,' Stirling responds.

Tom feels better for receiving an affable greeting from at least one of Walker's friends. He moves on to the Stones, who greet him like some long lost relative.

'Did you get mixed up and come to the wrong church?' chides Brent chuckling.

After kicking him in the ankle, Marge enlightens her husband. 'No, Brent, this is Tom, James' friend from Vietnam. So glad you could make it. I'd like to hear more about your adventures together.'

Estes and Hattie are next. He receives deferential nods from both of them but no words. He then shakes hands with David Washington.

'James tells me you're a criminal lawyer in Atlanta. Walker once told me it was a guy like you that saved his bacon. Good luck with your work.'

Melissa receives him next.

'So, here's James' white friend. We have something in common. I'm Shirley's one black pal from Sacramento.'

'We do have things in common, I'd like to talk to you more about that,' he says.

Next, Tom greets the bride. 'You look beautiful today, young lady. And, just how did this guy get you to fall in love with him?'

'I think it was the uniform,' she coyly replies. Tom gives her a quizzical look.

'That never worked for me,' he answers with a smirk.

Finally, Stirling steps in front of his friend.

'You're a lucky dude, Walker. I pray the world is ready for you two.'

'I've been through a few battles before, so I believe we can handle things.'

Tom hears the black lady behind him in line meeting the new Mrs. Walker. She doesn't know what to say, but the bride puts her at ease by initiating the conversation.

'I'm Shirley. And you are?....So nice to meet you. I hope to get to know you better at the reception. Thank you for coming. It means so much to both James and myself.'

Tom intrigued, decides not to go home. 'I'm comin' to the party,' he tells Walker.

CHAPTER 61

At the reception, Auntie has several of her church friends pitch in, preparing food and arranging tables in her back yard. The weather is hot and muggy. As the sun shifts lower in the sky, the temperature cools providing some relief. The line for ice cold lemonade is longest. Several of the men, however, opt for rum and coke offered on the back porch. The band begins setting up their instruments in a corner of the yard under a canopy. Electrical cable connections for the keyboard, amplifiers and microphone snake along the grass into the house.

Auntie steps up to the microphone in front of the bandstand to make announcements. Her helpers shush the guests and direct attention toward Violet.

'Thank you all for coming today to celebrate the marriage of James and Shirley. We want each one of you to eat, drink and dance until you're delirious with joy. Cold drinks and snacks are available for you now. We'll start dinner around six p.m., and afterwards you can boogie along with our great musicians until the rooster crows next door.'

The celebration unfolds smoothly with guests intermingling amicably. When the wedding party returns from their photo shoot at the church, cheers erupt as the new bride and groom enter the yard. Shortly thereafter, the smell of fried chicken and barbecued ribs wafts over the gathering. All fixins' are set on two buffet tables, and Violet steps up to make a second announcement.

'The line forms to the right, wedding party first. I know our mouths must be watering, so let's eat.'

Dinner is consumed with expressions of delight interspersed with the clinking of glasses prompting smooching of the bridal couple after impromptu toasts.

As the tables are cleared, the dancing begins. The newlyweds step lively to a Sly and the Family Stone number, 'Dance to the Music'. Brent and Marge follow afterward, then the elder Walkers take center stage on the grassy area cordoned off in front of the band. Estes claims he is too tired to dance with either Shirley or Marge. Hattie begins a dance with her son, but she stops soon after they start complaining of an upset stomach. Estes and Hattie use her condition as an excuse to leave the party a few minutes later.

'Youah mother has a bad stomach ache, son. We gonna go back to the hotel.'

'Papa, why doesn't she lie down for a while inside Auntie's house?'

'No son, we has enough essitement fo' one day.'

James ushers Shirley over to say goodbye.

'I'm so sorry you're not feeling well Mother Walker. Take care of yourself. We'll come visit you real soon.'

The parents look down at the ground for a few seconds, then turn to leave.

'We be goin' now,' says Estes.

The newlyweds' faces reflect their disappointment.

Shirley whispers to James. 'I think your parents are unhappy with your choice of a wife. I wish I could change that.'

'We haven't spent enough time with them yet for Mama and Papa to feel comfortable with us.'

Her dad then approaches and taps her on the shoulder.

'May I have the next dance with my daughter?'

'Of course, Dad. I didn't know if we would ever be close again after our little disagreement back home. I can't thank you enough for coming. It means the world to me.'

He leads her out to the dance area.

'Your mother finally convinced me that family is more important than my sometimes unpopular views. And, James does seem like a fine person.'

On the other side of the yard, Tom is approached by the young groomsman who had spoken to him in the reception line.

'Hey whitey, I wanted to ask you how you and James met.'

'We spent a lot of time together in Vietnam and became drinking buddies there.'

'You both should have gone to Canada. Uncle Sam has drafted way too many of my black brothers that ended up getting killed for that lame excuse for a war.'

'It has gotten worse over there and here, too', replies Stirling.

'You don't support that fiasco, do you?'

'I was proud to serve our country.'

'You weren't serving our country. You were serving a bunch of greedy politicians and war mongering generals in Washington.'

'We went there to protect and defend a sovereign nation and prevent those damn commies from taking over.'

'Boy, did you swallow a pile of shit.'

'I don't appreciate your disrespectful attitude, boy.'

'What did you call me?'

'Boy. 'Cause you're obviously no man.'

Stirling and the negro start pushing each other. The young black throws a punch striking Tom on his injured chest. He staggers backwards and falls to the ground gasping for air.

'Go screw yourself, whitey.'

The photographer, who had been taking photos of couples in the dance area, turns and captures the ugly scene ending with the groomsman standing over Tom.

James rushes over along with a few other guests and helps Tom to his feet. The buzz of the crowd stops, and all focus turns to the fracas.

'I'm okay, just had the wind knocked out of me.'

The groom addresses his old buddy who threw the punch.

'I want you to apologize to my friend.'

'Sorry James, I ain't apologizing to no honky wedding guest, especially one who insulted me.

'All right then, you can leave.'

The groomsman gives Walker a dirty look then walks out of the yard. Reaching the gate, he turns and yells.

'Walker, you ain't nothing but an Uncle Tom.'

Auntie, becoming fearful the atmosphere of celebration is turning into one of confrontation, circulates among the guests slowly regenerating a party atmosphere.

'Okay, I want everyone to begin dancin'. Start moving those feet out there with the band. We'll be cutting the wedding cake in about 15 minutes.'

She orders the band to play an up-tempo number.

Stirling realizes his presence has struck a nerve.

I probably should leave now, but there's one thing more to do.

He goes over to the bandleader and requests, 'Sittin' on the Dock of the Bay' by Otis Redding.

'Mrs. Walker, may I have this dance,' he propositions Shirley.

'If you promise to be a gentleman,' counters the bride.

'For you, of course.' They begin to move slowly to the music. 'From what I've seen today, you've got an exciting future ahead of you,' he suggests.

'The part with James I'm excited about. But, I'm not too sure about the rest. Don't think I was the most popular girl ever to get married in that church today.'

'Probably not, but stay strong. I have a feeling you'll do fine. You married a pretty special guy.'

As the song ends, he bids adieu. On his way out, he corners Melissa.

'It was great for Shirley that you could be here for her. I'd love to stay and ask you to dance, but given the circumstances, that's probably a bad idea.'

'I completely understand,' she knowingly replies. Tom quietly leaves.

By nine o'clock, James and Shirley have finished the cake cutting, the bouquet toss and garter removal. Changed into their street clothes, they bid goodbye to the remaining guests. A rental car is parked in front of the house ready to be driven to Atlanta for their honeymoon. Before leaving, the new groom has a heartfelt thank you for his Auntie.

'You've made this a wonderful occasion for both of us. Shirley's dream has come true with her father walking her down the aisle in a big church wedding. And, offering your home for the reception, that was much more than we could have expected. We'll remember this day fondly for the rest of our lives.'

Auntie looks into their smiling young faces of hope and knows that difficult challenges will soon face them in this country made even more polarized by the tragic assassination of leaders and the continuation of a divisive war.

CHAPTER 62

Driving back to Cordele, Tom has a feeling of emptiness. Walker has found his partner for life while Stirling is experiencing confusion about his future. Sure, Nancy is there waiting for him after all these years. But, at this moment, he senses a gulf has developed between the two of them.

He recalls her words when she refused to go to Walker's wedding. *A negro is marrying a white girl, and you expect me to go with you? Ah think you need to see a psychologist, Tom. There's something wrong with your brain.* Tom argued with her, but she couldn't understand how he could have changed so much. During their college days, they would agree on most everything, but now it seems the two can't see eye-to-eye on anything.

He pulls into his parent's driveway past midnight this evening. The porch light is lit. A light glows through the living room window. He opens the front door.

'Hi Mama, you're waitin' up for me like back in high school, aren't you?'

'Well, it's not every day my son goes off to a negra weddin'. Ah wanted to make shooah you came home safe.'

'These are nice people, Mama. Despite my lifelong conviction about black men and white women, I believe they're going to be happy together.'

'Ah still think it's wrong and dangerous too.'

'They do need to be careful. There's still a lot of hateful people out there that would as soon put a bullet in their heads as one in a twelve-point buck.'

"We can talk more in the morning, son. Let's go to bed. You've had a long day.'

After church the next day, Tom drives down to Doerun. He's still perturbed at his fiancée for refusing to attend James and Shirley's wedding. Oblivious to his concerns, she has put that little tiff out of her mind and is devoting full concentration on their own upcoming wedding.

'Hello darlin', let's go sit in the parlor and discuss some decisions about owah weddin',' she suggests.

'Don't you want to hear about the one you and I were both invited to yesterday,' he remarks sarcastically.

'That negra weddin'. Ah'm shooah there was wild music and dancin' at the reception, but Ah want our marriage to be classy and the biggest social event of the yeeah. So no, Ah don't want to hear about it.'

'You've got the wrong impression. That wedding was actually very civilized. I don't need to tell you how disappointed I was that you refused to go with me. You need to be more accepting of blacks. The South is changing.'

'Are you the same person Ah became engaged to four yeeahs ago? Ah swayah you've turned into a nigga lovah.'

Tom can feel the anger welling up inside, so he waits until his emotions settle down. There is no way he can make Nancy feel regretful about refusing to go to that wedding.

'Enough about the blacks. What have you got in mind for our big day?'

'Well, Ah want the service to be in the big Sherwood Baptist Church in Albany. They can hold up to 300 people thayah.'

'That sounds fine. We need to give them a date.'

'Ah already did. June 14th of next yeeah. Ah always wanted to be a June brahd.'

'You didn't discuss it with me before you picked the date. What the hell were you thinking?'

'Don't you swayah at me. Guys aren't interested in that stuff. Besides, you should thank me for makin' that arrangement. Reservin' a good church in June is very competitive.'

'Nancy, dammit, this is my wedding too. I expect to have a voice in big decisions like that. Do I make myself clear?'

She is taken back by the forcefulness of his reaction and realizes she needs to be more deferential toward him.

'Ah'm sorry, sweetie. If you want, we can try to change the church and the date."

'No, no, that should be fine. But, I want to be involved with the guest invitations list, choosing a reception location, and members of the wedding party. For all that other stuff, you can pick what you want.'

'C'mon honey, help me choose the invitations.'

'I see you have several catalogues of sample invitations there. Why don't you pick the one you want?'

He gets up and walks out of the room.

CHAPTER 63

Tom Senior is concerned about the future of his plantation. Physically, he can't put in the long days he did in his younger years. His sore back limits his ability to do work that requires bending over or lifting heavy bags of fertilizer. During the years TJ was gone, Abner had passed away from a heart attack and DeWayne had slowed down considerably. He has become heavily dependent on Rastus to keep the business going strong. Father and son are sitting in the living room late one afternoon waiting for Myrna to call them to dinner.

'Sorry to hear about Abner, Daddy. I know how you counted on him to get the crops planted and harvested.'

'Abner was a good loyal colored man, son. But, I must admit Rastus has really developed into a dependable field hand too.'

'I'm surprised. He sure was a troublemaker when I was in high school. Goes to show, you never can tell how kids are going to turn out.'

'Rastus is married now with two small kids of his own. His mama lives with him too. He's serious about being head of the family.'

'Sounds like he's not the 'hot head' he used to be.'

'I never see that side of him. In fact, I count on him more than anyone else.'

'So Daddy, have you made any decisions about selling the plantation and retiring.? You're not getting any younger.'

'We talked about this before, TJ. The fact is I haven't found any farmers interested in the place, and I sure don't want to sell to a big business corporation. Your mother and I don't want to move either. We want to stay in our home as long as we can.'

Tom recalls one of his college classes where they were called on to resolve business problems similar to his dad's. He starts analyzing the situation out loud.

'If Rastus is able to run the farm, why not sell it to him. I know he doesn't have the money in the bank, but he could guarantee payments to you from crop sales, and, over the years, pay off the farm. That way you would get a regular income to pay for expenses and do anything else you wanted. You could structure the deal so the house and land surrounding it stayed as your property.'

'Are you suggesting I break the generations old tradition of Stirling plantation ownership by selling the land to a negro? Son, you disappoint me coming up with a foolish idea like that.'

Tom pauses for a few seconds to bolster his argument.

'Answer this, Daddy. Does Rastus work with sales?'

'He gives me input, and I go over the contract with him to make sure we've got ourselves fully covered.'

'So, he's involved with the business side.'

'Yes.'

'Does he understand how to negotiate a deal?'

'Well, he's never done that. I always do the selling.'

'Maybe if he goes through the whole bargaining process with you a few times, you can find out if he can handle the whole operation or not.'

'Son, you're not understanding my position. My hope is to find a young, white farmer, who has the desire and ability to successfully take over the farm.'

'Papa, you've been looking for someone like that ever since I graduated from college. And, have you found anyone? No. That's why you need to consider this option.'

'Do you have any idea how the local community will react when they find out I've sold my plantation to a colored?'

'Times are changing about these kinds of things. People around here know what kind of man you are. You are very respected now, and you would still be respected after making a deal like that. There would just be a little adjustment period.'

'Adjustment period! They'll want to run me out of town.'

'True friends won't feel that way. They'll support you no matter what decision you make.'

'Dinner's ready,' calls Myrna from the kitchen. The irresistible smell of fried chicken filters into the room.

'Enough said, son. Let's go get some of your mama's dee-licious cookin'.'

CHAPTER 64

He swings. A loud crack of the bat echoes through the stadium. As the ball soars over the left field fence, the crowd stands and roars. Hank Aaron rounds third base waving to the crowd after delivering his 505th career home run.

James nudges Shirley witnessing the game from the grandstand seats at Fulton County Stadium. 'Hank's a hero down here, honey. Makes me proud to be a black man.'

Atlanta in 1968 is the most integrated city in the South. Restaurants have been largely desegregated and opportunities for work in previously all white companies have become available to increasing numbers of blacks. And, even after the recent death of Martin Luther King, the city remains a hotbed for civil rights activities as well.

While on their honeymoon, James decides to visit the offices of the Southern Christian Leadership Conference. As they enter the lobby of the building, a young female receptionist listens on the phone with concern written on her face. The couple waits until she finishes the call, then he asks for information.

'Good morning, Miss, my name is James Walker and this is my bride, Shirley. I'm a graduate of Morehouse, and we're interested in getting more information about the SCLC.'

She takes out a handkerchief and dabs the tears on her cheeks.'

'You must excuse me. I was on the phone with Reverend Abernathy. He's still up in Washington after the 'Poor People's March'. There was great hope that the march would reenergize the President's War on Poverty. And, Congress would take action to improve housing and create jobs for poor people. The minister just informed me the whole effort was a big, expensive disappointment.

'Sorry to hear that,' says James with empathy in his voice. 'Is the Reverend planning any more demonstrations?'

'I believe I heard him talking about Charleston.'

'I might be interested in helping with that effort. When we get settled, I'll give you my contact information.'

As they leave, Shirley confronts him.

'Honey, I know we've only been married a couple of days now, but I want you to know I have not agreed to live in Atlanta or Georgia.'

'Did I say we were going to settle in Georgia? No.'

'You didn't say it. You implied it by volunteering to help Reverend Abernathy.'

'Darling, what I meant was if we do end up living in Atlanta or somewhere around here, I would want to actively support the SCLC. I couldn't give any contact information because we haven't made that decision yet.'

'You're darn right, we haven't.'

The next day, the new groom gives his bride a guided tour of his beloved Morehouse campus. Afterwards, while sitting in the waiting area at the Pittypat's Porch restaurant, she overhears a white man whispering to his companion.

'Won't be long before those two get blown away.'

Shirley waits until they are seated at a table before she responds to James.

'Did you hear what that white guy said about us in the waiting room?'

'I did. Look, you're going to find that kind of talk anywhere you go, even in California. I've listened to stuff like that all my life, so for me it's like water off a duck's back.'

Shirley is frightened and starts trembling.

'That wasn't a disapproving comment. That was a chilling prophecy.'

James can see his bride is shaken. He needs to reassure her.

'I hear what you're saying, dear, but I think you're getting a wrong impression. This town is a bastion of hope for race relations. It's like nowhere else in the South. Yes, bigotry still exists here, but it occurs in Sacramento, California too.'

'Back home we would get looks and talk about how we shouldn't be together, but nothing about killing us. Sacrament never had a lynching.'

'Honey, nobody is getting lynched in Atlanta. And, we're not the only mixed couple in town. Look to the right, about three tables over, another couple just like us. Please give this city a chance.'

'I know this place is special to you, but I don't want to feel like some alien who really belongs somewhere else. Plus, I have a great job in Sacramento. What prospects do I have here?'

'That's an important question. You know I want you to be happy. We can do some job hunting tomorrow. I've got a couple of old leads myself to follow up on, and maybe we can look for a similar position to what you have in California.'

'I guess we should check the possibilities. I'm not optimistic though.'

The following day, James finds himself sitting in the owner's office of Evergreen Waste Management Company. Shirley stays in the waiting room reading magazines.

'Well, well, well. James Walker, back from his stint in the Air force,' recalls Hiram Dawkins reaching over his desk to shake hands with Walker. 'So, you're looking for a job befitting a man with your background.'

'Nice to see you again, Mr. Dawkins. Yes, my new bride and I are considering settling down in Atlanta. So, naturally, we want to see if the job market has any challenging and rewarding positions.'

'It so happens we have a marketing position open. Does that kind of work match your qualifications?'

'I believe it does, sir. And, my Morehouse degree will likely open some doors to grow your business.'

'I like that attitude, Walker.'

The two men discuss details over the next several minutes, and before James leaves the office, he's given a tempting offer.

'I'll certainly give your proposal consideration, sir, and get back to you within a couple of days.'

'Don't you keep me hanging, young man! I've got several other applicants for this position.'

Shirley is excited for her husband as they leave the building. But, possibilities for her own employment have yet to be discovered. She fears she is going to be compelled to living in a place where she has no friends, no family, and no job.

'Okay, Evergreen sounds great for you. But, I can tell you right now, I'm not going to be happy here being the little homemaker wife waiting all day for her husband to come home from work.'

'Let's go down to City Hall and see if we can get you an interview.'

They approach the imposing 14 story structure on Mitchell Street and enter through the varnished wooden entry doors. At the information desk, they inquire about vacant positions and are directed to the employment office on the second floor.

Shirley approaches the window with the 'Job Applications' sign overhead.

'Good afternoon, my name is Shirley Walker, and I'm interested in applying for a public relations position. I have experience working in the office of Assemblyman Badham in California. If you have any openings that could use my background, I'd be interested in filling out an application for an interview.'

'I'm sorry, Mrs. Walker, there are only secretarial positions available at this time.'

'Well, since I'm here, I'd like to fill out an application in case an executive assistant position does becomes available.'

James sits on a bench in the wide space of the open room while Shirley stands at a counter filling out paperwork. Unexpectedly, the clerk at the window calls her name.

'Mrs. Walker, there's a gentleman here who would like to talk to you. I'll buzz you through the door next to my window.'

Shirley enters and is instructed to meet with Edward Orr inside the adjacent office. She walks in and comes face to face with a 30ish black man sitting behind his desk.

'Mrs. Walker, please have a seat. I was standing next to the jobs applications clerk and overheard you have experience working with a state assemblyman back in California. What kind of work did you do there?'

'I did some office work for him, but my main responsibility was accompanying Mr. Badham on trips visiting his district. I would arrange meetings, hotel reservations, and speech appearances. Is that background something of interest to you?'

Orr smiles. 'You may be in luck. Vice Mayor Maynard Jackson is looking for an event planner. Would you be interested?'

CHAPTER 65

'Honey, Ah know you want to find a job in Atlanta and live somewayah near the city, but why don't you take a temporary one roun' here until we get married?'

Tom and Nancy are sitting around the dining room table in Doerun making plans for their future together. He has been home now for several months. Recovery from his surgeries is complete, and he's getting restless.

'You're right, sweetie. I'll go nuts just hanging around until the wedding. Here's an ad in the paper for a bank job in Albany. Maybe I should try to get an interview?'

'Good idea. You could call from heah.'

He picks up the phone and dials the number. After being transferred to the personnel director, he requests a meeting and waits for a response.

'Uh huh, uh huh. Yes sir, Tuesday morning at 10:00 a.m. Works fine for me. Look forward to meeting you in person.'

He hangs up the phone and gives Nancy the thumbs up sign.

'That's great, Tom. Ah know you're gonna get that job.'

Nancy continues to obsess on all the details of their wedding, depending on her mother to have her confirmation on all her decisions.

'Mama, Ah believe the brahdsmaids should wear a pastel color dress so they don't get more attention than the brahd. How do you feel about pale pink?'

'That's an excellent choice, dear.'

'There are so many decisions Ah have to make. Flowahs, the photographer, reception menu, favahs for the guests, but do you know what? Ah love it.'

'What about Tom, dear? Is he helpin' you?'

'Kinda, but he doesn't seem as excited as Ah am. In fact, he seems different since he's come back from that Vietnayam.'

'He's been through a lot, sweetie. What with recoverin' from those war wounds and all. Give him some tahm.'

'Ah remember back when we were in college together, he was so good to me. Ah believed he would do anything for me. And now, when we're together, he seems miles away.'

'Ah've heard war can do that to a mayan. You need to get him talkin' about his experiences over thayah. Show him how much you cayah for him.'

'Tom's always been the one who cared for me, especially when Ah wasn't feeling so good. Ah don't really know how to care for him. He's always been the strong one.'

'Try dear. You've got a long future together. There will be tahms when you need to be understandin' and supportin' him.'

'Ah know your right, Mama. Ah just don't know how good Ah am at that. And, he does some strange things now that aren't like the boy I know befowah. Imagine goin' to a colored weddin' and askin' me to go with him. That's plum crazy.'

'Let's get back to the weddin'. What kinda flowahs are you fixin' to have?'

CHAPTER 66

Three months later, June 14th. The wedding day.

'How do Ah look, Mama? Is mah hair all right? What about mah drayess? Is it fittin' like it should? And, mah makeup. Do Ah need more color in mah cheeks?'

Mother and daughter are together in a side room of the Sherwood Baptist Church waiting for that knock on the door to begin the wedding service. The bridesmaids are looking through a crack in the double doors gossiping about the clothes the wedding guests are wearing. Nancy is looking in the mirror fearful of a myriad of details that could go wrong including how she looks on the biggest day of her life.

'Calm down, dear,' reassures her mother. 'You look beautiful. Don't change a thing. Ah don't think Ah have ever seen a prettier brahd.'

'Thank you, Mama. But, Ah am nervous. Hope Ah'm doin' the right thing.'

'Every girl feels that way before the weddin'. Ah shooah did, and yooah father and Ah are still happily married. Yooah gonna be just fine. And, Ah know Tom will be a good husband to you.'

Sister Elaine is one of the bridesmaids. She comes over to give a little encouragement.

'Yooah the lucky one, Sis. Marryin' the mayan you've loved all these yeeahs. Startin' out right. Not like me gettin' knocked up at 19 and forced to get hitched to an ignorant cracker with a big dick.'

'Go away Elaine. Yooah not makin' be feel any better. And, don't you talk to me about yooah idiot husband. That only gets me depressed about the whole idea of marriage.'

'Youah getting yooahself all worked up over nothin', dear,' advises Mrs. Gunn.

'Youah right, Mama. I need to relax. Maybe a glass of the white wine over there will help. Would you pour me some?'

Mrs. Gunn narrows her eyes into a scolding look yet concedes to her daughter's wishes.

'Thank you, Mama. Youah the only one who understands me.' She gulps down the glass of wine.

There's a knock on the door.

'We're ready for you ladies.'

'Mama, can you get me anotha glass of wine?'

'You really shouldn't have alcohol. Remember your Crohn's Disease.'

'Mama, Ah need another drink!'

Tom stands next to the altar with his best man, fraternity brother John beside him. He wears a black tuxedo, black bow tie, black cummerbund and pale pink handkerchief tucked neatly into his breast pocket.

He surveys the church and is awed by the large number of guests who have filled the pews even into the balcony, all dressed formally for the occasion. In the rearmost pew, he spots James and wife, Shirley sitting next to the center aisle. They nod and smile to each other.

The organist is playing music by Bach as a prelude to the ceremony. Tom has resigned himself to this day and a life with Nancy. He also harbors a sense of regret for loves lost over the past years. Stirling experiences little joy at his moment. An aura of entrapment hangs over him like a heavy, wet blanket.

The music stops, and the doors at the rear of the church open. The organ again bellows out with the sounds of 'Jesu, Joy of Man's Desiring'. The bridesmaids and groomsmen file in and take their places on the dais. During a silent pause, anticipation fills the chamber. At the entry to the chapel stands Mr. Gunn arm-in-arm with his daughter. Her $3,000 gown is a voluminous white sheathing with puffy full-length sleeves dwarfing her petite body further exaggerated by an eight-foot train extending behind.

Nancy shifts her countenance into a practiced smile as she begins down the aisle to the strains of "Canon in D" by Pachelbel. Her expression abruptly transforms into a frown when she turns her head and observes the presence of the Walkers in the rear pew. Passing the mixed couple, she instantaneously regains her grin the remainder of the path to the altar soaking in the affirming expressions on the faces of guests on both sides of the aisle.

Tom nods and gives her a comforting smile as he leads her to the dais. The pastor begins the service by directing Elaine to read a passage from second Corinthians at the podium. The minister follows with a short sermon on the sanctity of marriage. Then, he begins the vows.

'Thomas, repeat after me. I, state your name.'

'I, Thomas Stirling,'

'Take thee, Nancy Gunn,'

'Take thee, Nancy Gunn,'

'To be my lawful wedded wife. To have and to hold from this day forward,'

'To be my (cough) awful wedded wife. To have and to hold from this day forward,'

'For better or worse, for richer or poorer, in sickness and in health, to love and to cherish 'til death do us part.'

For better or worse, for richer or poorer, in sickness and in health, to love and to cherish 'til death do us part.'

According to God's holy ordinance, and thereto I plight thee my troth.'

'According to God's holy ordinance, and thereto I plight thee my troth.'

'Now you, Nancy. Repeat after me. I, state your name.

'Ah, Nancy Gunn,'

'Take thee, Thomas Stirling,'

'Take thee, Towmas Stirlin,'

'To be my lawful wedded husband. To have and to hold from this day forward,'

'To be mah lawful wedded wife, Ah mean husband. To hold onto this day forever,'

The pastor stalls for a second to consider whether to have the flustered bride repeat that last part of the vow. He decides to continue despite whispering in the audience.

'For better or worse, richer or poorer, in sickness and in health, to love and to cherish 'til death do us part.'

'For bettah or worse, richer or poorer, in sickly health, to love and harass 'til death happens.'

Louder snickering erupts from the guests. Nancy realizes she is not repeating the minister's exact words and begins to sweat. The veil begins sticking to her face. She tries repeatedly to discreetly blow it away unsuccessfully. Tom is becoming increasingly aware of his bride's poor performance and worries that she will lose control and faint.

'According to God's holy ordinance, the thereto I plight thee my troth.'

She responds to the final statement of her vows barely above a whisper to avoid further embarrassment.

'Accordin' to God's holy ordinary, and therebah Ah pledge to tell the truth.'

The pastor appears relieved to have the couple finally complete their vows. He makes his final pronouncement.

'By the powers vested in me by the State of Georgia, I now pronounce you man and wife. You may kiss the bride.'

The organist cranks out Mendelsohn's "Wedding March", while the audience stands smiling and cheering as the couple retreats from the church.

A white Cadillac limousine waits outside the church to whisk the newlyweds to their reception at Doublegate Country Club outside of town. After assisting his new bride into the back seat and settling beside her, Nancy pointedly expresses her displeasure with him.

'Ah have worked so hard to make this day the happiest day for both of us. But you had to invite that negro friend of yours and his trashy white wife. That ruins everything. The only thang my friends will be talkin' about will be that vile intrusion into our weddin'.'

'Frankly dear, I believe they're more likely to talk about the gaffs we made with our vows.'

'You don't understand, do you? Havin' those two at our weddin' is like havin' a big ole turd floatin' in a punch bowl. It spoils the whole thang!'

'Listen to me. James has been the best friend to me that a fellah can be. He saved my life in more ways than one. And, if I can't invite my good friend to my own wedding, that's a pretty sad statement. And, as far as his wife goes, I admire her courage for agreeing to live with him in the South.'

'Oh, don't give me that holier than thou attitude. If they understood our situation, they would have stayed home and just sent us a gift.'

Tom mutters to himself. *Is this what life is going to be like living with this woman?'* The remaining 10- minute drive to the country club is in tight-lipped silence looking out opposite windows.

The reception unfolds in a traditional way, precisely as Nancy planned. Twenty-five tables are set with place cards indicating seat assignments for 10 guests at each table. Dinner is held inside the large ballroom at the club to avoid any storms that might have ruined an outdoor event. A portable wooden dance floor has been laid down at the front of the room with an emcee and four-piece band stationed to one side.

The Walkers had decided not to challenge the 'whites only' rules of Doublegate and returned to Atlanta after the wedding ceremony much to Nancy's relief. The only coloreds at the reception are the servers and parking attendants.

Tom endures his required participation for greeting guests, posing for photos, as well as dancing with his wife and wedding party females. His mother takes particular joy taking to the floor for a fast number with her son. Reuniting with old friends from high school and college gives him a few moments of pleasure, but the time he spends interacting with his new wife is staged with a noticeable lack of spontaneous affection.

Nancy feigns unabated happiness at each carefully scripted event; the toasts, the dances, the individual greetings to guests at each table, the bouquet toss and finally the departure for their honeymoon in Bermuda.

As the day draws to a close, Mr. Gunn remarks to his wife with a sigh.

'I'm sure glad Elaine got married by a justice of the peace. Nancy cost me over $15,000 for this one-day affair. I could have bought two new Cadillacs and a truck for that amount of money.'

CHAPTER 67

'Congratulations on yooah marriage, Mr. Stirlin', greets Lily, a young female teller at the Bank of Lee County.

Tom has just returned from his honeymoon in Bermuda.

'Please, call me Tom. You make me feel like an old man being so formal.'

'Sorry, only being polite. I believe you've got several good years left.'

'Well, thank you, Lily. I'm encouraged by your uplifting prediction for my future.'

Despite being newly married, Stirling finds himself attracted to this vivacious girl. After five years of waiting, he has discovered sex with his new wife less than satisfying. She was so nervous that first night, she found his advances brutish despite his calming assurances during every phase of their lovemaking. By the end of their week in Bermuda, she had accepted the expectations of sexual union better. For Tom, the act had been mechanical and lacking spontaneity. He thought of previous lovers and longed for their unbridled passion.

'So, what's it like being married?' Lily asks.

'Well, it's so new to me, I don't know if I can really tell. I must say it's a big responsibility having the welfare of another person to care for especially since my wife has a chronic disease.'

'Oh, I know what you mean. I live with my father. He's still depressed after my mother passed three years ago. He needs me to be there for him every day. It can be exhausting.'

'If you'd like to talk, we could go to lunch sometime.'

'I'd like that,' she replies.

CHAPTER 68

The Walkers have been invited to dinner by Maynard Jackson, Shirley's new boss at City Hall. They meet in the foyer of a black owned restaurant downtown. Mrs. Walker introduces her husband.

'James, this is Vice Mayor Jackson. He's also a Morehouse graduate.'

'Always a pleasure to meet a fellow Morehouse man,' says Jackson. They shake hands as James smiles and nods.

'You should be very proud of your wife, James. She has been indispensable for organizing our public relations events.'

'I've never doubted how lucky I am to be married to this woman.' He gives Shirley a squeeze around the shoulders.

The hostess shows them to their table in a darkly lit room brightened by a votive candle inside a decorative metal holder set on a black tablecloth. Chairs are upholstered in dark leather. After they are seated, Jackson leads the conversation.

'So, what business are you in, James?'

'Sales and marketing for Evergreen Waste Management. It's a black owned refuse collection company.'

'That's great. In fact, I'm very interested in developing more city contracts for local black businesses.'

'That's really good to know.'

'Do you have any business cards?' Jackson inquires. Walker quickly pulls out his wallet and retrieves two Evergreen cards with his name and title, James Walker, Director of Marketing.

The Vice Mayor is curious about Walker. How did he end up marrying a beautiful white woman when he was brought up in the Deep South? He is well aware any attention paid by a black man to a white woman in the past often lead to tragic consequences. He recalls the case of Emmitt Till.

'Tell me, James. How did you and Shirley meet?'

Walker recounts his days in Sacramento with stories of the Miss Sacramento contest, his involvement with the black runners from San Jose State, and his court martial trial. Jackson is riveted.

'Mrs. Walker was very instrumental in supporting you back there. A strong woman can be a powerful ally for a man. I know because my wife, Bunnie is an indispensable advisor for me.'

Jackson changes the subject.

'James, you've been quite active with black issues in the past. Do you plan on continuing that work with any civil rights activities?'

'I would like to. I did give my personal information to the SCLC office hoping to become involved with them. To date, I haven't heard back.'

'I'm good friends with Andy Young over there. Let me see if I can arrange a meeting with him for you.'

'Mr. Young will see you now,' indicates the secretary. 'You may enter his office down the end of the corridor.'

James opens the oak door with a brass plate inscribed with the name and position of the person inside; Andrew Young, Executive Director, Southern Christian Leadership Conference.

'Good morning, Mr. Walker. Have a seat.'

The dapper man in a Brooks Brothers double-breasted suit stands to greet him from behind his large, polished oak desk. James shakes his hand and sits.

'I see from your resume you've had some interesting encounters with white authority.'

'Yes sir. Since my high school days, I've been involved in actions to better conditions for our people.'

'So you worked with Tommie Smith before the Mexico City Olympics. Fascinating. Tell me about it.'

Walker details his travails dealing with Harry Edwards, the San Jose State sprinters and the United States Air Force.

'Tommie Smith became a good friend of mine. His group was talking about boycotting events back then. But, I was shocked when they made that black power salute at the Olympics.'

'Black America owes a debt of gratitude to those two men for having the courage to stand up for our rights at a huge international event,' comments Young. 'And, we also need people like yourself to involve themselves in civil rights activities. The SCLC is going to begin a campaign in Charleston soon. Would you be interested in participating?'

'I live with my wife here in Atlanta, and there is also the matter of my full-time job.'

'I see. Would your wife support you working with us during the evening or on weekends?'

'I believe she would. What kind of assistance do you need?'

'We need help in a couple of areas; fund raising and non-violence training for our volunteers. Can you help us out?'

I'd be willing to help with both. My job requires me to be here in Atlanta during the week, but I can help with the money raising end of things in my spare time. As for weekends, maybe going to Charleston once a month might be possible depending on my wife's plans. I do like being where the action is.'

'That's what I love to hear. You'll be contacted either by me or one of my associates in the next few days regarding possible assignments. It's been a pleasure.'

James walks out of the office building feeling reconnected to a cause close to his heart.

CHAPTER 69

As the summer days of 1969 shorten, Tom feels more and more confined in his new life. He regards the people at work as the embodiment of the rural Georgia life he knew as a young boy. His Air Force experiences have changed his life expectations. He wants more than some regurgitated replay of his past.

Marriage to Nancy is especially troubling. Her hopes for the future have shriveled to a stereotypical southern belle routine; the country club charade including afternoon teas, fashion shows and a little charity work, enough to feign compassion for the lesser beings of Colquitt County. In contrast, Tom is itching to move somewhere near Atlanta where he can work in a city rife with activity that shakes up the status quo.

He lies in bed with his new wife, and begins caressing her face, neck and shoulders.

'Not tonight, deeah. Ah've got an awful headache.' Tom looks up at the ceiling and sighs.

Life at home has become a stagnant pond. With some financial help from both sets of parents, they have bought a small two-bedroom house on the outskirts of Moultrie. Nancy loves decorating and fixing up the place. He lets her make those decisions without much input.

After three months of marriage, their sex life is a disappointment for both of them. She didn't know what to expect but finds lovemaking crude and messy. He expects much more and regularly fantasizes about his former lovers.

'Honey, we haven't made love for over a week now,' comments Tom.

'Maybe, if you helped me more around the house, I could feel a little more romantic.'

He pushes the covers aside, climbs out of bed, and ambles into the bathroom to take a shower. As he stands relaxing in the warm water, he thinks about Lily at work and gets an erection. He begins to masturbate climaxing with a loud gutteral yelp, 'Ooo ooo ooo yahhh.' After finishing, he dries himself with a towel and returns to bed.

'That was an awfully long showah, Tom. And, what were those funny noises Ah heard you makin?'

'Oh….I remembered about a meeting I had forgotten about tomorrow with someone at the bank. By the way, I might be a little late getting home.'

'Good mownin' Mr. Stirlin'. How are you today?' Standing face-to-face with him, Lily gives Tom a big smile.

Her form fitting dress flatters her slim, taut body. Tom takes full notice as his eyes briefly glance downward from her face. He reengages her eyes and responds.

'I'm a little tired. Had trouble sleeping last night. Say, about that lunch we were suggesting, I have another luncheon engagement today, but how about dinner tonight. I need to talk to a woman about woman issues.'

'So happens, Ah'm free this evening. Ah'd be happy to meet with you, Mr. Stirlin'. That would be real nice.'

'Please call me Tom.'

CHAPTER 70

Nancy has become suspicious of Tom for the last month. He has been coming home late from work two or three nights a week. When confronted, he told her about projects at the bank requiring overtime to complete for his boss. One evening, he returns after nine o'clock. While he retrieves leftovers from the refrigerator to heat up, she rummages through his coat in the hall closet and finds a receipt from the Acme Motel.

'Explain this, you two timin' sneak,' yells a red-faced, teary-eyed wife. 'How dayah you cheat on me.'

He feels cornered sitting at the kitchen table with a plate of reheated fish and rice. What could be a believable excuse? He tries to make up a convincing story.

'What are you talking about?'

'Theeis!' She spreads open the receipt and shoves it in his face.

'That's not mine,' he replies with confidence. 'But, I bet I know how it got there. I went to lunch today with Frank from accounting. We wear the same London Fog raincoat and hung them up side-by-side on a rack. I'm sure that's his coat. In fact, he confided in me that he's having an affair with one of our employees.'

'Do you expect me to believe that story?'

'It's the God's honest truth, dear.'

'Why don't Ah believe you?'

'I can see how that piece of paper looks bad, but you have to believe me.'

'I can't accept your story 'til you start coming home on time and payin' moah attention to me.'

'Fair enough. I'll tell my boss my wife is gonna leave me if I don't spend more time with her.'

Nancy calms down some, but that story about the switched coats still sounds implausible. He walks behind her and begins massaging her neck.

'There, doesn't that feel better? Those muscles have gotten real tight. You've got to stop getting so upset about nothing.'

For the next four weeks, Stirling arrives home promptly after work. Nancy continues to be wary of his possible escapades with another woman and continually badgers him.

'You been flirtin' with those girls at the bank today?'

'You're the only girl for me, sweetie pie."

'Oh, don't you sweetie pie me. Ah see you all googly eyes and smilin' at that grocery store cashier every tahm we go shoppin'.'

'I'm only being friendly.'

'Yes, and Ah bet you'd be even friendlier if you could get into her panties.'

'You're driving me crazy with all your accusations. Can you try to be a little more positive toward our relationship?'

Tom stops by the local florist once or twice a week bringing home fresh cut blooms of the season. He helps with the housework; vacuuming, doing the dishes after dinner, scrubbing the bathtub. He mows the lawn and trims the hedges every weekend and even helps with the cooking, frequently barbecuing in the back yard. Nancy begrudgingly credits him with making these efforts, but always with a criticism for something he hasn't done.

'Did you change the light bulb in the entryway?'

'No, not yet.'

'Did you wash my car?'

'You didn't ask me.'

'Do Ah have to tell you everythang?'

Living with her is becoming more and more tortuous. But, the ultimate frustration for him is their sex life. She has consented to have relations with him only twice during the past month. Both times she just laid there on her back in bed and let him be the lone participant. On the second occasion, she was so dry, he had to stop and go into the bathroom cabinet for a lubricant to finish.

He doesn't know what to do about Nancy. Lily approaches him one day at work

'You look sad, Tom. Is something wrong?'

He had been avoiding her to help himself stay faithful to his wife. But, at this point, his home life had become too unbearable to continue.

'Would you go out to lunch with me today? I really need to talk to you.'

'Oh mah gosh, yes. Ah've missed seein' you.'

Where have you been? And, why didn't you call me?'

'I was working late at the office, and I guess I lost track of time.'

Nancy notices a long stand of dark hair on the back of his shirt collar.

'Ah don't believe you. Where did this hair on yooah shirt come from?' She reaches over and extracts the filament from his collar. 'And, that's not after shave Ah smell, it's some tramp's cheap perfume.'

Tom is tired of playing games. More than that, he can't stand living in the same house with Nancy anymore. He makes up his mind, it's over.

'I don't think you understand. The last four months we've been married have been hell for me. Our life together has been all about you, and for me, it's been a sham. So yes, I found someone who cares about me. It's time to call it quits, Nancy. This marriage has become a joke.'

'Huh. How dare you say that about me! You obviously don't appreciate everything Ah've done for you. So, as far as Ah'm concerned, you can take youah stuff and get the hell outta heah!'

Nancy is livid with rage. She stomps off to their bedroom and slams the door shut. A wave of relief comes over Tom. He feels a huge weight has been taken off his shoulders. A call to a friend from work gives him a couch to sleep on for the night.

CHAPTER 71

Black activism in Charleston, South Carolina emanates from the Morris Brown AME Church. Inside its walls, polished oak pews stretch back 17 rows from the altar surrounded above on three sides by balustraded balconies. At this moment, more than two hundred volunteers fill all available seating awaiting direction from their leaders. The parish preacher ascends the pulpit and speaks.

'In our city today, both negro hospital workers and domestic help are paid far less than they deserve. While the 'fat cat' executives and well healed home owners reap all their unjust rewards, our people, the hardworking backbone of this community, receive little more than scraps to eke out a meager day-to-day living.'

'That is going to change, starting today!' The crowd hoots and hollers in agreement. 'Amen, brother.'

'We plan to lobby for fair wages and the establishment of a hospital workers union. And, to achieve these goals, we are going to demonstrate. Now the key to our success is how we demonstrate. Non-violence is our credo. Beside me here today is Mr. James Walker from the Southern Christian Leadership Conference in Atlanta. He is going to lead you all in a training session for the do's and don'ts of a peaceful march. Mr. Walker, the floor is yours.'

Although James is well versed in the methods of non-violence, he has never spoken to such a large group before. He is understandably nervous but determined by the righteousness of their cause. He pauses for a moment staring out at the many faces like his own, who are looking back at him. He glances down at wife Shirley in the front pew. She smiles at him. With that encouragement, he begins.

'Good morning. We greatly appreciate your willingness to work for the cause of justice and equality. Before we undertake our mission for the rights of Charleston's negro workers, every participant here needs to understand and implement the full meaning of non-violent demonstration. First, let me describe our method.'

He explains the roots of the non-violent movement beginning with Mahatma Ghandi in India and later its practice during the civil rights marches in Montgomery, Birmingham and Selma. Walker then details the implementation of these tactics for their upcoming march.

'Today, we ask your cooperation to follow that same path. You must understand to suffer the indignations of harassment during peaceful demonstration will test your internal strength. It is not weakness to 'turn the other cheek'. The force of will is absolutely essential to suppress anger and the impulse to strike back when attacked.'

'You must be willing to endure the forces arrayed against you and continue the fight through faith in the ultimate goal of this crusade. This morning we will practice responses to conflicts that you are likely to encounter. Listen carefully to your teachers and react as instructed to their requests.'

'All right everyone, get ready to march,' Reverend Abernathy shouts through a megaphone. 'And, remember, keep your cool no matter what happens.'

Protesters have formed by the hundreds in front of the Morris Brown church. Anticipation fills the air, like runners at the start line before an Olympic race. With an arm gesture from their leader, the dark- skinned mass begins to move. Pent up emotions erupt into cheers. They walk several blocks toward the Medical College Hospital in high spirits waving banners. 'We Shall Overcome' and 'Fight the Power', are chanted repeatedly. White onlookers hurl insults, 'Go back to Africa where you belong'. Others throw stones. Several marchers are struck. Some are hurt and cared for by others. But the mass of believers moves inexorably forward.

As they approach the hospital, local policemen, state troopers and national guardsmen confront them with a cordon of interlocked arms blocking the entry to the hospital. The lead law enforcement officer steps forward.

'You are ordered to disperse immediately or face arrest for unlawful assembly,' shouts Police Chief Conroy through his bullhorn.

The demonstrators respond by dropping to their knees in prayer immediately in front of their adversary.

None of the marchers move. They remain praying palms together looking at the law enforcement individual directly in front of them. James kneels in the front row with Shirley to his right.

'You are all in violation of City of Charleston code 671(b) prohibiting unlawful assembly. Officers arrest these people.'

The lawmen wade into the first row hoisting the leaders to their feet, and dragging them off to the nearby paddy wagons. Some are struck with Billy Clubs. James feels two hands grasp the back of his jacket collar and jerk him to his feet. He feels the urge to pull away but instead relaxes like a rag doll. He reaches out for Shirley's hand, but she has been taken in a different direction.

'Get movin', boy, yells the officer. James barely keeps his feet under him as he is dragged to a vehicle parked one hundred feet away.

'I pray that you treat women with respect,' he barks out. A sudden blow strikes his head. James feels a sharp pain before his world goes blank.

When consciousness returns, James finds himself in a city cell with three other demonstrators and a throbbing headache. As he looks into their worried faces, he thinks to himself. *Where's Shirley? My God, I hope she's unharmed. And, Ralph and Andy better know how to get us out of here. My boss expects me at my desk Monday morning at eight.*

Walker stands in front of his boss' desk. With an angry glare, Dawkins dresses down his young executive.

'First, you twist my arm into contributing $5,000 to the SCLC. Then, you pay me back by getting thrown in the hoosegow for a week and a half down in Charleston. How do you think I can run a successful business with a loose cannon like you going off like that? Huh?'

'Sir, I only went down to Charleston for the weekend to do some training. Andy Young shamed me into marching with the demonstrators. I apologize. It won't happen again.'

'I'm letting you off with a warning this time only because your wife has apparently cajoled Maynard Jackson down at City Hall into getting us another contract. But, it better not happen again, or your butt will be on the street looking for another job.'

'I promise to make it up to you, Mr. Dawkins.'

Walker goes back to his desk and calls his wife.

'Honey, the boss is very angry with me for missing work. He gave me a verbal warning. I can't lose this job. I'll be black listed if I try to find another job in this city with a history of being fired.'

'James, I can't say I like being shoved around and penned in a jail cell for 10 days either. I'll always be willing to support your SCLC work, but let's give this demonstration thing a rest for a while,' she suggests.

'You're probably right at least for now. I'll give Andy a call and let him know about our decision.'

The Walkers are home preparing dinner that evening, when there's a knock on the door. James unlocks the deadbolt and opens.

'I'm shocked. Stirling, c'mon in. What brings you here?'

'I had an interview with Coca Cola today, and they offered me a job. So, I thought I'd drop by and see how you're doing.'

'Congratulations Tom, stay for dinner,' offers Shirley. 'We've got plenty to eat and there's so much to catch up on.'

Stirling reveals the news about Nancy, and his determination to start over in Atlanta.

'Where are you staying tonight?' asks James.

'I'm driving to Albany.'

'Nonsense, we've got a sofa bed in the living room. It's going to be great having you up here in Atlanta. And, you've got a place to stay until you find an apartment.'

CHAPTER 72

Tom begins his new position as Area Sales Manager for Coca Cola. He rents an apartment downtown near Five Points, where he has easy access to Atlanta's cultural events. Settling down in his new living room after his first day at work, he ponders his new life.

This job is what I've been hoping for since my first year at UGA. Am I happy? Yes….and no. It seems crazy, but I still have feelings for Nancy. I can see now, the two of us as a couple was probably never going to work, but I do care for her. Am I sad? About Nancy, yes. About my new job, hell no. I am determined to be the best damn sales manager they ever had.

For several weeks, Stirling keeps himself busy from the time he rises in the morning until he goes to bed at night. The sour taste of his marital split motivates him to keep active to avoid becoming depressed. He makes new friends and frequently socializes with the Walkers.

As he returns home late from work one night in May, the phone is ringing. His mother's voice is on the other end.

'Son, Ah have some bad news. Yooah father had a heart attack today.'

'What, no! That's terrible, Mama.'

'Please come home, son. Ah know it will boost his spirits, and Ah need you too. He's in the cardiac unit at Crisp Memorial.'

'Stay strong, Mama, and tell Papa I'm on my way. I love you both.'

He jumps into his yellow Chevy and speeds down Highway 41 toward Cordele, arriving at the hospital after 11:00 p.m. Tom Senior is asleep with Myrna dozing in a chair beside his bed. Monitor screens glow above his head displaying an array of vital signs. Tom wakes his mother.

'How's he doing?' he whispers.

'The doctor says his condition is stabilizin', but he's had a serious heart attack.'

'Don't wake Papa. I'm going to find the doctor on duty and talk to him.'

Tom's conversations with the doctors indicate Senior's future will need to eliminate any strenuous activity. Two days later, TJ sits down in the hospital room next to his father comfortably reclined in a stuffed chair with a blanket over his lap. They talk about life after the heart attack.

'Papa, everyone's relieved you're recovering okay. How do you feel?'

'Well, I've been better, but this thing has made me realize I can't push myself like I used to.'

'That's exactly what the doctors are saying. Also, you need to stop smoking and cut back on eating red meat.'

'They told me that already. I think I can quit the smoking, but cutting back on your mother's good cooking? That will be tough.'

'You know we want you around for a lot more years, so please, do what the doctors tell you.'

'I never thought I'd see the day when my son would be lecturing me.'

'Papa, we're only interested in your health right now. Knowing you, I'm well aware how often you push yourself too hard working the farm.'

'I know you're right, son. I'm just not ready to give it up.'

On the day of his father's release from the hospital, Tom takes time off from work to accompany his parents back home. They sit down in the living room and discuss changes that need to be made.

'You've got all the medications the doctor prescribed,' TJ notes. 'Mama, make sure he takes those pills every day.'

'Ah will, dear.'

'And, his meals need to be healthy. Salads, chicken and fish. All the stuff that's good for the heart. And, ease up on the boiled peanuts, they have a lot of fat.'

'Ah hayave the paper the dietitian gave us. Ah'll follow it like our lives depend on it,' reassures Myrna.

'Good, Mama.'

'Aren't you two being a little too strict? A man's gotta have a steak every once in a while.'

TJ and Myrna give him stern looks. 'What?' says Papa Stirling.

Three weeks later, Tom is back at the family home in Cordele. TJ looks at his dad sitting in the living room stuffed chair. His color is grayish and his face looks puffy.

'Are you feeling all right, Daddy. You look a little peaked.'

'Well, I've been trying to do everything the doctor said, but I've had to deal with some issues with the farm, and I was surprised how tired I got. Still think I'm going to get stronger, but right now I can't run the plantation like it needs to be done.'

TJ stops and reflects. *I think it's time to have a son to father talk.'*

'Papa, suppose it's too strenuous for you to keep running the farm. What will you do?'

'I guess I thought the day would never come. Fact is I've been giving some serious thought about that over the past week or two. Your mother and I talked it over. We believe our best option is to sell the farm to Rastus.'

'Wow, Daddy I know that must have been a hard decision for you.

The phone rings. Myrna walks into the foyer and answers.

'He's right here, Miles. I'll have him come to the phone.'

'It's Miles, TJ. He wants to talk to you.'

Tom's face scrunches into a quizzical look. *I wasn't aware Miles was in town.*

He picks up the receiver. 'Hey Miles, you finally made it back to Cordele. Howya doin'?'

'Stirling, good to hear your 'candy ass' voice. Hey, I was hoping we could get together for a couple of drinks and talk about old times. Are you up for that?'

'Sure Miles. I'm working up in Atlanta, but I've been coming down here on weekends to help my parents. Just name the time and place.'

'How about next Saturday, two o'clock at Riley's Bar downtown?'

'Let's do it. We've got a lot to catch up on.'

Tom hangs up the phone and scratches his head. He hasn't seen Trousdale for about a year and a half when he visited him at Long Binh Jail. He wonders about Miles' mental health. TJ returns to the living room where his father has something else to say.

'I've gotten hold of George O'Malley, the lawyer. He's coming to the house next week to draw up papers for selling the farm to Rastus.'

'Aren't you still worried what the neighbors will say?'

Big Tom shakes his head side-to-side as if to say, *the most important thing is the future of our family.*

CHAPTER 73

Riley's Bar is run down. The atmosphere inside is dark, partly due to a couple of stained glass light fixtures that shorted out. The accumulation of grime on the wood plank floor adds to the bleakness.   Stirling and Trousdale take a booth near a window. One of the seats has a strip of duct tape hiding a long tear in the red vinyl covering. Miles sits on that side.

A heavy-set waitress sashays over to their table loudly snapping a wad of gum.

'What'll ya hayave , boys.'

'I'll take a beer,' responds Tom. What do you have on tap?'

'We got Bud, Michelob and Gordon Biersch Doppelbayack.'

'I'll take a Biersch.'

'What sahze, 12 ounces or 18?'

'12.'

'How about you, Trousdale?'

'The usual. Jim Beam, double, straight up.' As she waddles away with her oversize buttocks flouncing her uniform side-to-side, he adds. 'And, bring us a bowl of peanuts.'

Stirling can see Trousdale has been going through tough times. His flannel shirt is dirty and has a button missing over his protruding belly. He hasn't shaved in a few days; his hair looks like a rat's nest. As added insult to the senses, he emits a foul odor combining a mixed scent of smelly armpits, stale tobacco, and 100 proof booze. Miles starts the conversation.

'Hey Stirling, do you remember the time I brought that skank to the fraternity party and she exposed her beaver on the stairwell?'

'How could I forget? I was hot for that Kappa chick I was dating and never saw her again.'

'Oh ya, sorry about that. But shit, we had some fun back then, didn't we?'

'Yuh, there definitely were some good times at Lambda Chi. But, tell me, what's going on with you these days.'

Trousdale's smile disappears.

'After they discharged me, some Marine doc said I needed to see a shrink at the VA hospital in Valdosta to control my violent tendencies. Hell, you know me, Stirling. I keep pretty good control of my temper, don't I?'

'From what I remember, you're okay most of the time, but I've seen you lose it on occasion.'

'Those Army psychologists, what the hell do they know about fighting a war. They sit in their posh little offices with a bunch of books on the shelf trying to make you think they know more about you than you do about yourself. They listen to a guy spill his guts about combat horror stories and end up telling him he shouldn't drink so much.'

'Is that what they told you?'

'Yuh! You know I've never really gotten help from anybody. The commanding officers I had in the Marines were control freaks. You couldn't tell them anything. Then, when I got shot, the doctors gave me shit for getting my wound infected. They throw me in the brig for a little altercation during a softball game. Then, when I finally get home, the people treat me like I'm some kind of criminal when I've been fighting for their freakin' freedom.'

'That part really stinks. I've been getting some of that same crap from people too. So, what are you doing with yourself now? Are you working?'

Miles ignores Tom's question and begins rambling on about his Vietnam exploits.

'I remember one time we were on a mission to take out an NVA weapons cache in the Highlands. The lieutenant made me the point, since I had done coon huntin' back home. We're quietly makin' our way through the jungle when I spot a sniper up a tree. I get the whole group to hit the ground while I take out that gook who was lying in wait for us.

'Then, all hell breaks loose. A whole brigade of NVA soldiers surround us and start shooting. I take out four or five of them, but two of our guys get hit. The lieutenant calls for a retreat, but before we can get out of there, a couple of their troops get right on us. I shoot one and engage the other in hand-to-hand combat. I wrestle away a knife he's holding and slit his throat. Finally, we're able to backtrack to an LZ where we got picked up by a Huey.'

'Jesus Miles, you're a freakin' hero.'

'You would think I would get a little credit for what I did, but that lieutenant raked me over the coals for shooting that first gook. He said that led to the death of two Marines.'

'You're shittin' me.'

'No, I'm not. But, lucky for me, when the Major debriefed everyone after that fire fight, he saw things different, and I was awarded a Bronze Star for bravery.'

'You should be proud of that, Miles. I bet you saved the lives of everyone in that unit that survived. My story isn't that heroic, but it sure took a long time to get better.'

Stirling goes on to tell about his recovery from mortar shell wounds.'

'So, tell me, how's your family?' Tom asks.

'Things aren't good at home. Mama left several months ago to live with her sister. She claimed Daddy beat her several times after he got drunk. He's not doing well either. Lost his job at the insurance agency because he didn't show up for days on end, and nobody knew where he was. He drinks pretty heavy still. I'm sure that's why he got fired. Now, he mostly stays home with his right hand curled around a bottle. Occasionally, he goes out on night raids with his KKK buddies. How are things with you?'

Stirling gives him details about his breakup with Nancy.

'I could have told you that was going to be a disaster. You're a guy who needs a little excitement in his life. I knew that prude wasn't going to give it to you. What about your folks?'

Tom tells about his dad's heart attack, that being the reason he was visiting so often from Atlanta.

'In fact, Daddy is in such poor health, he has to give up farming the plantation. He's in the process of selling it right now.'

'Really, anyone I know?'

Tom hesitates for a second and thinks, *Well, Trousdale's going to find out sooner or later anyway.*

'Rastus Jackson.'

'What! Your daddy is selling his plantation to a nigger. And, not just any nigger. The nigger that turned in my daddy to the Crisp County Police. Why the hell didn't you stop him?'

Miles stands reaching back to throw a fist at Stirling. Tom rises and moves away.

'Stop Miles. You're getting out of control over something that's none of your business.'

Trousdale unclenches his fist, approaches Stirling and gives him a violent shove slamming him into the wall behind. Tom winces as a sharp pain shoots down his spine.   The bartender rushes out from behind the counter and restrains Miles by clutching both arms.

'You're both leaving this establishment….right now!'

He ushers them both out the door.   Stirling leaves first keeping his distance from Trousdale, walking backwards toward his car.   He yells out.

'Move out of that house, Miles.   Your father's a bad influence.'

Trousdale snarls extending the middle finger of each hand.

CHAPTER 74

'Mr. Walker, you wished to see me?'

James is seated in Andrew Young's office. He is there to make a proposal. Since his request boils down to asking for money to resurrect the Stillmore Baptist Church, he attempts to soft pedal his plea with a more broad-based appeal.

'Yes sir. Thank you for giving me your time. I know how busy you are.'

'All right Walker, get to the point. I have a tight schedule this morning.'

'Well, sir. I'm sure you're aware how many black churches have been burned on bombed in cities and towns across the South.'

'All too aware, Walker. What's that got to do with this meeting?'

'I believe it would be in the best interests of the SCLC to allocate funds for rebuilding these churches. That assistance would increase solidarity among our black brethren.'

'Do you have a particular church in mind?'

James can sense Young is suspicious of his motives.

'I do have a close friend, Reverend Jeremiah Jones from Stillmore, Georgia, who had his church burned down five years ago because of me.'

'How so?'

Walker explains how the preacher helped him escape the clutches of the KKK after a Sunday service, and the building was burned down the next day.

'They have held services under a tent in the church parking lot since then because they lack the funds to rebuild. The tent roof leaks and some of the parishioners have to keep their umbrellas open inside when it rains. I believe it would be money well spent to have the SCLC donate enough money to allow them to build a new Stillmore Baptist Church.'

'Walker, you know our efforts in Charleston cost a lot of money. And, we're still in debt from the Poor Peoples March in Washington. There's just no money for a cause like this. It's a noble idea though. I will take this suggestion to our Board of Directors. We'll have it as an agenda item for the upcoming year's budget. Write up your proposal and give it to me before next month's meeting.'

James leaves the office confused. He can understand Young's position, but delaying another year is too long a wait. He also senses Young may be patronizing him for an idea that would possibly be pigeon holed.

On his way home, an idea strikes him. He calls his minister.

'Reverend Jones, I think I might be able to help you raise money for your new church, but I must know how much you need.'

'That's very thoughtful, James, but you don't need to go out of your way. You've got a busy life up there in Atlanta. Plus, our congregation has been contributing to a rebuilding fund for the past several years.'

Walker is determined to help.

'Reverend, please let me help you. It would do my conscience good. How much do you need?'

'Our bank has $20,000 in a savings account, but we need another $20,000 for the contractor to complete the construction.'

'Keep your fingers crossed, Reverend. I might be able to get that for you.'

Hanging up the phone, he talks to himself. *I'm the primary SCLC member soliciting donations in Atlanta. I'll ask our supporters for a little extra to help Reverend Jones.*

On the next Monday, James approaches his boss.

'Mr. Dawkins, I hear we snagged a new city contract for Evergreen.'

'Yes, we did. Thanks to Maynard Jackson and possibly your wife.'

'Vice Mayor Jackson is a big supporter of the SCLC. To show thanks, I think you should write a check for your annual contribution to them.'

Dawkins has his back to the wall. He knows he probably wouldn't have gotten this new deal with the city without the help of Walker's wife.

'Okay, Walker, you win. I suppose you want me to give the same amount as before.

'Yes sir, the same $5,000. But, there's another worthy organization I believe you would benefit by writing a check for them.'

'May I ask what charitable group is that and how much are you asking for?'

'The Stillmore Baptist Church needs funds to rebuild after their building was burned down by the Klan. Another $5,000 would be great.'

'Are you blackmailing me? Are you saying the city will void my contract if I don't make this contribution?'

'No sir. I have nothing to do with the city's decisions. I will make sure the media is aware how generous you have been in supporting worthy philanthropic causes like rebuilding destroyed churches. You'll be a hero in the eyes of Atlanta residents.'

Dawkins groans and pulls a checkbook out of a locked drawer in his desk.

James approaches all the companies on his SCLC donor list and adds a few new ones. Over half the organizations agree to write him an additional check for the church. In less than a month, he has raised more than the $20,000 needed. Early on a Saturday morning, he drives down to Stillmore to hand the money over to Reverend Jones. He knocks on the parsonage door. A few seconds later the preacher opens up.

'James, what brings you all the way down here on a weekend morning?'

The smell of coffee percolating and bacon sizzling wafts through from inside. The preacher motions for James to enter, and they withdraw to the kitchen.

'Reverend, I believe you can start building your church.'

'What are you talking about? You know we don't have enough money.'

'You do now. Look.'

He opens his satchel on the kitchen table and pulls out over two dozen checks written out to Stillmore Baptist Church.'

'There's checks in here ranging from $100 to $5,000 totaling $21,300.

'I don't know what to say. It's a miracle.'

'You don't know how guilty I've been feeling these past few years knowing I was the reason you didn't have a proper church for your congregation.'

'Nonsense, son, you are one of the main reasons I'm in this preaching business. Don't you realize, it's individuals like yourself that give our people hope?'

'I don't know anything about that. What I do know is that I wouldn't be where I am today without your guidance. But, I do have one request.

'What's that, son?'

'Please don't let anyone know I had anything to do with this money. The Klan would burn the new place down if they knew.'

'My lips are sealed, James. Thank you so much for this generous gift. Now, go sit down. I'm going to make the best darn breakfast either of us has ever tasted.'

'You wanted to see me, Andy?'

James has been called into Andrew Young's office for a meeting.

'Have a seat, Walker. You're in big trouble.'

James now suspects why he was called in. *Oh oh, I know why Andy's pissed. Maybe if I emphasize the large amount of donations I raised for the SCLC, he'll go easy on me.*

'Sir, I guess you asked me to meet with you because I raised so much money for the SCLC.'

'You are dead wrong. I know why you were being so diligent with the fund raising, and it wasn't to benefit our organization. You were trying to solicit money for your little house of worship down in Stillmore.'

'Andy, what I did was to benefit the SCLC and the church.'

'I don't see it that way. My take is you risked alienating our donors by being pushy for something not even associated with the SCLC. Plus, you went ahead on your own to do something I promised would be on the docket for next year.'

James realizes he can't win this argument. *'I need to show remorse.'* He engages Young with a sober faced look of repentance.

'I'm very sorry. I admit what I did was out of line. It won't happen again.'

'Walker, how do you think I found out about your actions.'

'I have no idea.'

'One of our donors complained to me how insistent you were demanding money for that church.'

'Oh no, I will call and apologize to him.'

'I don't ever want you to try a stunt like that again.'

'You have my word, Andy.'

CHAPTER 75

'James, I want you to come with me. Today is going to be a historical day for black people'

Stirling is telephoning Walker from his apartment in Atlanta.

'Whattya talking about?'

'My white father, Thomas Stirling, Senior, is selling his peanut plantation to his negro field hand, Rastus Jackson. They're signing papers today.'

'That is great news. Before I say yes, let me check with Shirley. She's eight months pregnant now and has some days when she doesn't feel so well. Hold on.'

A minute later he's back on the phone.

'She says I should go.'

'Great, I'll pick you up at one o'clock.'

Arriving in Cordele, Tom rings the front door bell and walks in behind James. Papa comes up to meet them, slowly shuffling along the parquet wood floor in his fleece lined slippers. He's bent over now, moving stiffly as if injections of molasses were inside his joints.

'Hello, Mr. Stirling, congratulations on your brave decision.'

'Mr. Walker, I see my son has brought you to witness my stepping aside as a farm owner.'

'Yes, I hope you don't mind. By the way, how are you doing? You look well.'

'I'm feeling okay,' Tom Senior replies downplaying his physical discomfort. 'C'mon in, both of you. Rastus is sitting at the dining room table along with my lawyer, George O'Malley.'

Two copies of a contract have been prepared by the attorney. He is sitting next to Rastus explaining the terms.

'I want you to understand, Mr. Jackson, although for business purposes you will be considered to own the plantation, the deed to the property won't become yours until the full amount owed for the farm is paid according to the schedule laid out in Appendix A.'

He turns to the back of the contract, and they pore over the payment plan for several minutes.

'Mistuh Stirlin', they is somethin' Ah needs to ask ya.'

'What's that, Rastus?'

'You know yooahselt some years de crops ain't so good 'cause of de weather or some pest we didn't kill. Ah won't be makin' enough money to pay you and all my otha expenses includin' mah family.'

Papa scratches his head. He knows Rastus is right.

'You could give me copies of your receipts for both crop sales and expenses. If they're bad enough, I'd consider a delayed payment.'

'Thank you, sir. Can we add that in writin' to dis heah contract?'

Papa Stirling looks at his son who nods his head. Then, he turns to O'Malley. His lawyer holds his arms to the side, palms up as if to indicate, 'Your call, big fella.'

'Okay, George, please add a statement to that effect into the papers.'

'Tom, I recommend this clause stipulate that partial payment to be made to Mr. Stirling in instances when revenues from crop sales do not allow for full payment of the amount owed after necessary expenses for farm operation and essential home expenses are deducted. The amount not paid shall be added debt, due at the end of the contract term.'

They all nod in agreement.

'I believe we now have a contract acceptable to both parties with changes made at this meeting,' notes O'Malley.

Rastus breaks out a big smile revealing a missing tooth among his lower incisors.

'Congratulations, brother,' remarks James as he slaps him on the back.

'This calls for a drink,' suggests Mr. Stirling. He leaves the room and returns with an unopened bottle of Hennessey XO cognac. From the corner hutch, five brandy glasses are taken from a shelf and placed side-by-side on the table. The master of the house cracks the seal and fills each tumbler halfway with the amber colored liquid. The scent of leather mixed with Myrna's Christmas fruitcake rises in their nostrils as each prepares to taste.

'Here's to health, happiness, prosperity and a bumper peanut crop for the next twenty years,' offers Big Tom.

'Ah second thayat,' confirms Rastus.

They each let out a cheerful shout as they down their drinks. Then, TJ leads them into the living room where they nibble on hors d'oeuvres Myrna had quietly left out while they were negotiating.

'Is Rastus the first black man to own a farm in Crisp County?' Walker asks.

'I believe he is,' answers O'Malley. 'And, Mr. Stirling here should be recognized for making such a magnanimous gesture in a town where many people are dead-set against an arrangement like this.'

'Proud of you, Papa,' compliments TJ. 'You've always been my hero. But, what you've done today makes you even greater in my eyes.'

'Thank you, son. And, Rastus, anytime you have a problem, don't hesitate to call on me.'

'Ah shooah will, Mistah Tom. 'Ah swayah, dis be the happiest day of mah life. In fact, Ah would like each one of y'all to come ovah to mah house to have a celebration drink on me.'

'I'd be happy to do that,' agrees TJ.

'Then, you can count me in too,' echoes Walker.

'I'm sorry, Rastus,' apologizes Papa Stirling. 'I'm just not up to it, but y'all go ahead.'

'I've got some other business to attend to so I'll be leaving,' says O'Malley. 'But thanks for the offer. The corrected copies of your agreement will be in your hands for signatures within a week.'

'Papa, we'll be back in an hour or so,' informs TJ.

Rastus leads the way down the dirt road toward the small tin roofed bungalow he inherited from his father, Abner. He's driving his 1955 black Ford pickup followed by Tom and James in the yellow Chevy. By the time they arrive, it's about five thirty in the afternoon, and Mrs. Jackson has started fixing dinner in the kitchen.

'This is the first time I've been back inside this place since high school, Rastus. You've got it fixed up pretty nice.'

'Yessiree, little by little, we done addin' some thangs to make it nahser. Ah made that maple rockin' chair ovah there in the corner and de oak dinin' table too.'

Tom looks around the room some more and spots a shotgun next to the front door.

'That shootin' iron looks familiar.'

'Oh, yooah father gave it to me a couple of yeeahs back. Ah believe it belonged to yooah grandfatha. Ah keep it there in case we get raccoons or some other varmints roamin' roun' the house.'

'Did a lot of hunting with that ole side-by-side gun when I was a youngun,' Tom remembers.

'I see you've got a number of books over there on those shelves,' James notices. 'You like to read, Rastus?'

'Oh, Ah glance at 'em a little, but mah kids are really into readin'.'

'That's great,' notes Walker. 'Keep those kids in school as long as you can.'

Rastus is too excited about becoming a farm owner to get involved in a discussion about his children. He wants to celebrate.

''Never you mind 'bout those books right now, Ah wants to have a good tahm. Let me go get some o' mah best liquor.'

He goes into the kitchen where his wife is boiling greens and tells her the good news. She screams with excitement giving him a big kiss. A minute later, he returns to the living room with three glasses and a bottle of whiskey.

'Southern Comfort, huh,' says Stirling. 'I bet you didn't know that's my favorite, Rastus.'

'Mine too, Masta Tom.

'Please, you're a farm owner now, just call me Tom.'

'How 'bout you, Mr. Walker? You like Southern Comfort?'

'Oh yes. In fact, Tom here introduced me to it back in Vietnam.'

The host fills the three glasses on the oak table and hands one to each of his guests. He then voices a few words of appreciation.

"Today's a day that be changin' mah life. And, Ah be happy to share it with you fellahs. Okay, down the hatch.'

The three men raise their glasses and empty them with one swallow.

'Whooeee! That's some good liquor,' cries Rastus.

The others laugh and pat him on the back.

'Errrrrrrh!'

A loud skidding sound from outside interrupts the conversation.

'Who the heck is thayat?' shouts Rastus.

A pickup truck has abruptly pulled up in front of the house spewing a cloud of dust as it braked to a halt. The vehicle door creaks open then slams shut. The sound of boots clomping on the concrete entry path follow.

'Rastus, step out here right now and show your face!' an angry voice calls out.

The host motions for Walker to open the door as he is closest to the entrance. James pushes open the door and comes face-to-face with a scruffy, mean looking white man about 10 paces away shouldering a rifle aimed directly at him. He dives to the floor of the porch as a shot rings out.

'Ah! Ah! Ahhhh! He got me,' screams James writhing in pain on the wooden deck.

Hearing Walker has been shot, Tom snatches the gun by the door and rushes out. Without stopping he cocks the trigger, aims and fires at the intruder hitting him in the chest and knocking him backwards to the ground.

The rush of adrenaline coursing through Stirling's body quickly dissipates. He transforms into a frozen state of shock. His face pales, and the hairs on his body stand on end.

Seconds later, Stirling drops the weapon and runs to the fallen shooter.

'Oh my God, it's Miles!' cries Tom.

He crouches down next to his old friend and examines his wound. A crimson ooze is spreading through the flannel shirt covering his chest, and a thin strand of blood starts to crawl out the left corner of his mouth.

'Miles, why did you come here?' Tom shouts. 'I can't believe this.'

With labored effort, Trousdale turns his head toward Stirling. The strong smell of alcohol emanates from his breath as he utters his final words.

'Remember Tom, the only good nigger is a dead nigger.' A frozen glaze then forms over Miles' face.

Miles is dead.

CHAPTER 76

Stirling snaps out of his daze, realizing his living friend, Walker needs him. He scrambles to the porch.

'James, how bad are you hit?'

Walker is holding his left shoulder, rocking back and forth in agony.

'Rastus, bring me that booze and a couple of clean long strips of cloth.'

'Ah do anything you want, Tom. Just say the word.'

He soaks one cloth in the alcohol and wraps it around the sleeve of the deformed upper arm. With a second cloth, he fashions a sling for the shoulder forming the material around the forearm and tying it in a knot behind James' neck.

'I think he can use another shot of that good whiskey, Rastus.'

'Comin' right up.'

'Hold on, James. We'll be there in a few minutes.'

Driving from the scene of the shootings, Stirling experiences flashbacks of the last time he rode to Crisp County Hospital with a gunshot victim.

Poor Onzell. He was such an innocent little fellah.

His mind shifts back to the present. He's racked with guilt for shooting his old friend, but, at the same time, blaming Miles for doing something so hateful. A thought strikes him.

Trousdale could have shot me. He was a freakin' war hero sharpshooter. Instead, I shot him. How could that happen?

They arrive at the hospital emergency room. Stirling assists Walker out of the car and into the building.

'We need help here. This man has been shot.'

The woman at the front desk calls back on the intercom for assistance. Within a minute, two interns arrive with a gurney to transport Walker back while Stirling stays behind to fill out paper work.

'I'll stay until I know my friend is stable and admitted to the hospital,' Stirling tells the receptionist. 'Then, I need to go back to where the shooting took place and make a statement to the police. There's a dead man there, and I killed him.'

The evening is beginning to seem unending for Tom. He waits until James is given a room on the orthopedic floor and discusses his care with the physician. He finds a pay phone in the waiting room and calls Shirley.

'Hello.'

'Shirley, this is Tom.'

'Why are you calling me? Something's wrong, isn't it?'

'James is okay, but there's been an incident.'

'Oh my God. What happened?'

Stirling explains the events and reassures Shirley that James is going to be all right.

Driving back to Rastus' home, Tom finds a Crisp County police car and a black sedan out front. A circle of people surrounds Trousdale's body. Two uniformed policemen and a coroner stand across from Rastus and his wife. The black man is attempting to describe the tragic incident, but one of the officers repeatedly interrupts him in a loud, accusatory voice.

'You're in big trouble, boy. Come out and admit it. You killed this here white man, didn't you?'

Stirling rushes down from his car and yells to the policeman.

'Officers, you're accusing the wrong man. I killed Trousdale.'

The lawmen turn around facing Tom with confused looks.

'Who are you, and where did you come from?' demands one officer.

'I'm Tom Stirling. I just returned from the hospital where I drove James Walker, the man who was shot by the dead man here. I'm the person you need to talk to. Jackson here didn't shoot anybody.'

Tom keeps talking until they finally accept his story. One officer continues to take testimony from Rastus, then excuses him.

'Stirling, you're coming down to the station with us. There's formal charges that need to be filed.' Tom is accompanied to the police car, but before entering the vehicle, Rastus shouts a parting comment.

'Tom, you saved me and my family a lot of misery today. Ah hope they let you go. We'll say prayahs for you and James.'

'Thanks. Good luck with the farm.'

The coroner remains to deal with Trousdale's lifeless body according to local protocol. He produces a camera and begins taking photos.

As the police car heads toward the station, Stirling's mind races with fears for his future.

Am I going to jail? Don't I get a lawyer? Maybe I can call Mr. O'Malley, but he's not the right kind of lawyer. Oh God, I'm going to lose my job. My life is ruined.

Reaching the station, Tom recognizes the night duty officer, Milt Jaeger, a deacon at his parent's church in Cordele.

'Milt, I mean Officer Jaeger. I'm glad to see someone here I know.'

'These are serious charges against you, young Tom. These officers say they have a case against you for second degree murder. You need to make a plea before a judge. Do you have a lawyer?'

'No.'

Jaeger arranges for a local attorney to come in for the arraignment. Arriving 30 minutes later, he sits down with James in a small office at the back of the police station. After preliminary discussions, the lawyer acting as court representative reads the charges against Tom.

'Thomas L. Stirling, Junior, you are charged with the involuntary manslaughter of Miles Trousdale on January 3rd, 1970. How do you plead?'

Stirling, feeling a strong sense of remorse, sees no alternative but to state the truth.

'Guilty, your honor."

Jaeger enters the room and whispers in the lawyer's ear. In response, he nods his head.

Tom has resigned himself to spend the night in the local jail.

'Mr. Stirling, you are released of your own recognizance. You should hire competent legal counsel to defend you in a court of law making yourself available at our request. Do you understand the circumstances?'

'Yes sir,' quickly replies Tom with a sigh of relief.

Tom is driven back to the scene of the tragedy to retrieve his car. It is now 12:00 a.m. He steers his Chevy slowly along the dirt road back to his family home.

What's Daddy going to say about this? He'll be so disappointed in me.

As he turns in the driveway, the porch light is lit. He quietly enters.

Sleepy-eyed, Tom Senior and Myrna approach TJ in the hallway.

'We were worried about you, son,' states Papa. 'Why were you out so late? And, where's James?'

Stirling describes the events since he left the house earlier in the afternoon. The parents sit on the sofa in the living room riveted by their son's story and concerned for his welfare.

'Son, I feel sad for the pathetic death of Miles. But, it was hate in his heart that brought him to this end. You, on the other hand, did a heroic thing protecting the life of another human being, black or white.'

'Ah'm just glad you're all right, Tommy,' says a relieved Myrna. 'Ah was getting so worried when you didn't come home. Can Ah fix you something?'

'No, Mama. Thank you both for everything you've done. I'm so tired right now, I don't know if I can keep my eyes open any longer. If you'll excuse me, I'm going to bed.'

He walks to his childhood room, drops his clothing on the floor, and crawls between the sheets.

Recurring images of Rastus, James and Miles play over and over in his head. He thrashes under the covers trying to imagine how the day's disastrous events could have been avoided.

I could have shot Miles in the right shoulder. I should have recognized Miles and yelled at him to drop the gun. Why didn't I go to the door first? Why didn't he shoot me? Why, why, why?

Utter exhaustion finally overcomes him and a short, fitful night of sleep follows.

CHAPTER 77

After two days at Crisp County Hospital, Walker is transferred by ambulance to Emory Memorial Medical Center in Atlanta. He is scheduled for surgery to reconstruct his shattered left humerus. James rests in his ward room on the day before, visiting with Shirley.

'How do I look?' he asks lying in bed, dressed in his hospital gown.

She smirks, 'If I said a little pale, would you believe me?'

'If I said you look a little pregnant, would you believe me?'

They both laugh.

'The doctor says I won't be able to help you with housework for a couple of months until this arm fully heals.'

'He did not. And, there's nothing wrong with that right arm of yours.'

Walker smiles.

Shirley leaves for home after a short while as her back begins to bother her. An hour later, a familiar figure enters the room.

'Well, look who's here. I've been worried about you. Thought they might have you locked up in jail,' surmises Walker.

'I do feel fortunate to be walking around free,' concurs Stirling.

'I only heard they might let you go home, but you had to keep in daily contact with the authorities down there in Cordele.'

'It's an amazing story for which I will be forever grateful.'

'Okay, you got me. What happened?

The morning after the shooting, I had gotten up around ten o'clock. There was a knock on my parent's front door. Who do you think was there?'

'Rastus, Mr. O'Malley? I don't know.

'No, Miles' father.

'You're shittin' me. He must have been ready to shoot you.'

'That was my first reaction when I heard who was there.'

'Well, obviously he didn't kill you 'cause you're standing in front of me.'

'Papa let him in and they went into the living room. After a few minutes, Daddy came and got me. "Son, you need to come and talk with Mr. Trousdale," he said.

'I was ready for him to call me vile names and threaten my life.'

'Is that what he did?'

'No, in fact, the opposite happened.'

'You're kidding.'

'He said Miles believed he had nothing left to live for. He was going to kill Rastus, then end his own life. Miles had loaded up his pickup truck with his Remington 700 rifle, put a Colt .45 pistol in the glove compartment and a bottle of Wild Turkey on the front seat. Mr. Trousdale was on the couch when Miles told him all this, too drunk to stop him. Oh, and Miles told him one last thing. *Tell Tom he's the best friend I ever had.*

'Do you mean he forgave you for killing his son?'

'Not only did he thank me for looking out for Miles, he went down to the Crisp County Police Station and had them drop the charges against me by changing to report to self-defense.'

'Who would have thought a KKK guy would do something like that,' comments a bewildered Walker.

'I felt like I'd sunk into hell and a racist bigot helped me escape.' Tom can feel himself getting emotional, so he changes the subject. 'But hey, what about you? Ready to get that shoulder fixed up tomorrow?

'I don't like the idea of being cut on, but it should be better than getting shot.,' assesses James with a pained look on his face.

'Good luck, buddy. I'll check in on you later.'

James is rolled into a surgical suite the following morning. Hours after the procedure, the surgeon enters his room after Walker had awaken from the anesthesia.

'The operation went fine. We had to put in four screws to stabilize the bone. And, I have a little souvenir for you.'

He holds out his hand, revealing the flattened slug from the rifle shot in his palm.

'You can put this in your trophy case.'

'Very funny, doc.'

Walker falls asleep. When he wakes, he looks outside his window and sees the sun going down. He wonders why his wife isn't there and calls for the nurse.

'Did my wife come by while I was asleep?'

The RN answers with a wry smile. 'She did call and say she wasn't feeling well.'

James feels deserted. He eats a small portion of his evening meal, takes his pills and goes back to sleep.

The next morning, Walker gets a big surprise. Stirling comes to visit.

'I know the first thing you wanted to see after your surgery wouldn't be my handsome puss, so I brought a friend.'

In walks Shirley, holding their new baby.

'Are you kidding me? When did you have that thing?'

'Thing! That thing you call a thing is our new son.

'Did I miss something? Last time I saw you, you were pregnant.'

'While you were getting that tiny little pellet out of your arm, I was delivering a nine pound, five ounce baby out of my belly.'

'Come over here. I want to hug you both.'

Tears come into both their eyes as they embrace.

'Look, he's black like me. And, good looking too, like his daddy.'

Tom disagrees, 'If he has any good looks, he gets them from his mother.'

'What are we going to name him?' asks James.

'I know exactly what his name is going to be,' announces Shirley. He's going to be called 'Billy' after his uncle.'

'Perfect,' agrees Walker.

CHAPTER 78

'Honey, Reverend Jones is on the line. He wants to tell you something.'

James realizes he hasn't heard from the preacher in several months. Something must have happened. He picks up the phone.

'Reverend, is anything wrong?'

'No, James, I have good news. They just put a final coat of paint on our new church. We can take down the tent.'

'That's great. I'm very happy for you.' Shirley taps him on the shoulder. 'Please excuse me for a second, the wife is trying to tell me something.'

She whispers in her husband's ear. He nods his head.

'The missus has an idea. Our son is now two months old. If you will agree, we would like to have him christened in your new church.

'I would be honored to do that for you. Let me know when.'

The organ plays a soft lullaby as friends and family file into the new Stillmore Baptist Church. The wood framed building stands on the footprint of the destroyed structure like a phoenix rising from the ashes. Oaken pews stained and varnished shine brightly in the light from the dropped overhead fixtures. The choir loft is placed to the right of the altar while the church organ sits to the left. A polished maple pulpit faces the congregation adorned by a white altar cloth emblazoned with a gold cross.

Reverend Jones stands in front of this podium wearing his black robe and starched white collar. Next to him on one side are James' parents, Estes and Hattie. On his opposite flank are James, Shirley holding baby Billy and Tom Stirling as the Godfather.

In the pews, those attending include Aunt Violet wearing a stylish wide brimmed hat embellished with bright colored silk flowers, James' two sisters, and several other family and church members.

The Reverend raises his hand. The organ music stops, and a hush settles over the congregation. He steps forward to address the gathering.

'This is a special day in the history of the Stillmore Baptist Church. Almost 20 years ago, I stood at the pulpit of our old church in nearly the exact spot where I stand today, presiding over the funeral of one of our valiant fighters for the rights of black people, Mr. Billy Walker.

The Reverend pauses.

He had been taken from us by a vicious act of hate. Why you ask? Because he stood up against the tyranny of racism. After his death, some here did not cower in fear or accept the humiliation and subjugation of our people. No. Those who followed in Billy's path are able to stand proudly today with the knowledge that our lot in life has made wonderful progress since that bleak day so many years ago. Those advances have been attained because of black brothers and black sisters who fought the good fight and risked their lives. One of those brave souls is standing before you today. James Walker, a fellow champion for our freedom, graces us with his presence in this beautiful new House of God to christen his infant son.'

The preacher approaches Shirley and gently takes the child.

'The baby that appears before you today, has been named Billy Walker in tribute to his martyred uncle. As I sprinkle holy water on his head welcoming him to the community of Christians, I pray that he grows up healthy and strong. I pray he lives his life devoted to Christ. And I pray he becomes committed to carry on the black man's struggle for justice and equality until on that glorious day, it shall come to pass. I ask this in Jesus name. Amen.

The parsonage is a small two-story home adjacent to the church. The downstairs layout includes a galley kitchen, dining room, powder room and spacious living room with a fireplace built against the center of the outside wall.

Reverend Jones has invited the entire gathering from the christening to his home for a reception after the service. Ladies from the women's society have prepared a large cut glass bowl of fruit punch and small water cress sandwiches for the occasion, set out on the dining room table with paper plates, cups and napkins.

A blaze crackles in the hearth of the fireplace, giving added warmth to the room on a chilly, windy March day. Several guests stand conversing in the living room including Shirley and Tom.

'I know you would be a good father, Tom. Have you and Nancy talked about getting back together?'

'No, our divorce lawyers are in the process of working out final papers. We've been separated now for six months, and both of us need to move on.'

'Sorry to hear that, but from what James tells me, it's probably for the best.'

'I would love to have what you and James have. Guess I just haven't found the right woman.'

'You will, Tom. You're too good a man to be out there without an equally good lady.'

Across the room, Reverend Jones converses with James.

'I can't thank you enough for your generous help for rebuilding our church. I'm thrilled to have my House of God back.'

'Reverend, I owe you my life. Without your strength behind me over the years, I wouldn't be half the man I am today. I appreciate that from the bottom of my heart.'

Aunt Violet comes over to join them.

'Bottom! Did I hear the word bottom? As in my black bottom pie? I just brought one in from my car made special for this wonderful occasion. Do try some before it's all gone.'

'Auntie, the pie can wait. The Reverend and I are talking about the journey I've been on since Billy departed. He has been an unwavering supporter for me, and so have you. Those high school years in Savannah turned my life around.'

'Truth be told, nephew, I was a lonely woman back then in a big old house with only me living there. You brightened up my home, son. It was a joy to have you.'

James hears a little voice crying. He sees Shirley holding little Billy and talking with his parents.

'Excuse me, I think I might be needed for parental duty over there.'

He steps over next to his wife.

'Papa, Mama, what do you think of your new grandson?'

'Why, we be learnin' all 'bout de little fellah from Shirley heah.' Hattie exclaims. 'You have a strappin' young boy, James. And, I heah Shirley's parents done sent de chrissenin' outfit he be wearin'. Wasn't that nice? Too bad dey couldn't make de ceremony.'

'Yes, Mama, Billy can be a handful, but we love him. Papa how did you like the Reverend's words at the church?

'He shooah does know how to get de people all fired up, don't he?'

'Yes, he does. But about what he was saying. Did you agree with him?'

'Well, son, Ah believe you be a lucky chile your whole life followin' de word of Reverend Jones. Takin' chances like ya did. Ah thought you would end up like Billy, an' here you are with a good job and a nice family. Ah'm happy fo' you.

Shirley looks at James and beams.

'I'll be back in a minute. I need to talk to Tom before he leaves for Atlanta.'

Stirling had gotten his coat and was heading for the door.

'Wait up, Tom,' says James raising his voice.

He catches up with him at the front door.

'I don't know if I thanked you for saving my life back at Rastus' house.'

'Just did what anyone else would have done.'

'That's not true. You did a very brave thing. But, I've got to ask you. How did you know that shotgun was loaded?'

'I didn't, but there wasn't any time to check. The thought that plagues me is why didn't Miles shoot me? He had time to gun me down before I cocked that old shootin' iron and fired at him.'

Walker pauses for a second.

'I believe we found out a lot about friendship that night,' concludes James.

'Yes, indeed we did,' agrees Tom.

Tom extends his right hand. James reaches out with his. They briefly shake hands. Then, impulse overcomes both men. Simultaneously, emotions compel them to wrap arms around one another then exhale with a deep sigh. The tension held by generations before them is softened.

About the Author

H. Dwight Kelsey, MA is a graduate of Stanford University. His stories of the Deep South portray characters drawn from his experience living there and are described with incidents of gross injustice met with intrepid resolve. These events contrast sharply with moments of wry humor and define relationships of cultural opposites. His new novel is due for release in late 2017.